KJ BURRAGE

PRINCE
OF
SCALES

BOOK 2
THE DRAGON'S HEIR

ISBN Paperback: 978-0-6454001-5-1

ISBN Hardcover: 978-0-6454001-6-8

ISBN Ebook: 978-0-6454001-7-5

Cover Design done by MiblArt

Themes in Prince of Scales

This title was written with upper YA readers in mind. While Prince of Scales is not essentially gory or "spicey", it does include some themes and incidents that are (hopefully) heartbreaking. These themes include: discussions including the consumption of alcohol, anxiety and depression, PTSD like symptoms, blood and corpses, death including executions, grief, mentions of past poisoning, physical abuse, kidnapping, violence and torture and mentions of slavery.

For Peej Caskey, a woman who has lived her life valiantly, no matter the
circumstances.
Nothing fazes this woman. *Absolutely* nothing!
Who else would drop *everything*, drive twelves plus hours and spend over
a month with a shocked, grieving widow? She was the hands and feet of
Jesus in my darkest hour.
Who else would kick my rear end when I said I "can't write", tell me I
speaking rubbish and encourage me to take up my keyboard? You guessed
it, Peej is partly responsible for this journey! (A huge chunk if I am honest).
Now it's my turn to have your back, I'm always here. I'm not going
anywhere. I love you dearly.
Thank you, my friend of great valour.
PS. I think our friendship has one hell of a story!

Contents

SILK PALACE
SION
SION
ARAH
THE STRONGHOLD
TORRYN
HABRON
PALLARYN
SILVERDYNE
ADAVAN FIELDS
ANDROSSAH
HALBETH
AVIAH VALLEY
PARU MOUNTAINS
KUDAH
HAVEN BAY
THRANGUL
PARUHULISE
KORKALIE
TORQUI
ADDRYN SEA
RAMA

SILK PALACE
SION
STONETHAW RANGE
TORRYN
ARIMAC
HABRON
PALLARYN
TANNRYN
LAKE OF MIRROR
SILVERDYNE
ANDROSSAH'
PALDERA RIVER
HALBETH
AVIAH VALLEY
PARU MOUNTAINS
HAVEN BAY THRANGUL
PALDERA RIVER
KUDAH
PARUHULISE
KORKALIE
TORQUI

CHAPTER ONE

Jodathyn

The Isle of Torqui

Tornyth, Winter's Dragon, was finally free of his prison of human flesh. While Jodathyn slumbered, he enjoyed the pure, unadulterated pleasure of flight.

From his snout to the tip of his tail, his scaled body shivered with excitement. The wind swept around him, caressing the supple membranes of his wings. A low rumbling sound of contentment reverberated in his chest. Hearing the Wind Song's sweet refrain of hope, his dragon heart burst with joy.

Along with freedom came peace. He and his human heart were intertwined; with his manifestation, Jodathyn could finally be whole. No longer was he battered and bruised in the bowels of the prison ship. Mandros, the dragon of Flame and Fury, had plucked his drowning human from the depths of the ocean.

Dipping lower, Tornyth watched schools of fish skimming under the surface. He flared his nostrils at the tantalising scent of prey. His talons sliced through the water, and he watched in fascination the silver streaks of the scattering fish. The cool salt spray of the ocean was pleasant on Tornyth's scaled belly.

As he flew onwards, Tornyth caught sight of a fleet of ships. His scales were warmed by the flames as they burned. He could hear the screams of perishing enemies; their voices raised, cursing the name of Arturyn. The ships bobbed and sunk below orange waves, and Tornyth climbed the air currents, leaving his foes to their watery graves.

It was among the dampness of white clouds that Tornyth found himself surrounded by a myriad of dragons. Every hue that he could imagine was represented in the scales of the circling reptiles. On his right-hand side, an ancient one with golden horns approached him. Azure scales gleamed in the sunlight as wise eyes observed him with an eerie interest. Scaly lips parted, revealing long, sharp fangs. The blue dragon stretched out his neck to give Tornyth a playful nip.

Tornyth's yelp sounded more like a pampered hunting dog than that of a mighty beast. Swaying his head to the side, the blue dragon rumbled with laughter. A large amber eye winked at him.

It was hunger pains in his belly that woke Tornyth from his pleasant dreams. Yawning wide, he was pleased to find himself still within his scaled body. He stretched, feeling the inhuman strength of his limbs. Hopeful that a meal was nearby, he ran his tongue along his teeth.

Mandros was sitting by the cave's entrance, quiet and still. His giant wings were unfurled to catch the cool breath of wind. Tornyth's instincts told him the emerald dragon was communing with the Wind Song.

"You look well rested, *elt mynrell*. Soon we will hunt." Mandros tucked his wings against his sides, swaying his head to pierce Tornyth with an assessing gaze.

Mynrell? Tornyth echoed in his mind, savouring the sound of the unusual dragon word. A thrill of excitement snaked its way up his spine. *Heir. The green dragon has claimed me as his own.*

"Do you know when your last meal was? A dragon doesn't need to eat or drink as often as a *vehyl*."

"My human…" The word seemed wrong on the tip of his tongue, and Tornyth corrected himself. "*Elt vehyl* didn't know how long we were on the ship."

Curling his tail about his body, Tornyth relished the way the tip wiggled in front of his snout. It served to provide him with some amusement and distraction. It was unpleasant to dwell on the feeling of helplessness he had felt while trapped in Jodathyn's flesh.

Mandros growled. "I wouldn't wish the prison ships upon anyone."

"I'm hungry," Tornyth murmured.

Mandros' lips peeled back into a grin. "I'll teach you to fly first, impatient one. Then we'll fish."

Snorting in protest, Tornyth stood. "*Teach* me to fly? I already—"

"You will find flying in the waking world different to your dreams and visions," Mandros replied.

Tornyth imagined himself plummeting to the ground in a tangle of wings and scales. His belly lowered to the ground. "Is it difficult, *Rshon Aluel*?"

Tornyth glanced up at Mandros. Even though the emerald dragon had rescued him and been the one to help him manifest, it felt clumsy calling him dragon-father. His natural born father, King Hadryn, had insisted Jodathyn call him *Your Majesty*. When he had dared to call the late king *father*, he had been punished. Sometimes when he lay awake at night, he could still see Lord Frayn jeering at him from behind his father's back. Although he had been very young at the time, Jodathyn had endured Frayn's teasing in grudging silence. He hated that he was jealous of Frayn and that his father had made it no secret he had loved Frayn more than him, his own natural born son. He had grown to loathe Frayn and all he stood for.

"I wouldn't ask you to fly, white scales, if you were not ready to hear the Wind Song."

Tornyth shifted, dismissing his thoughts about his *vehyl* father and sidling his hind quarters closer to the cave wall.

"I taught my three children born of my human heart to fly. Teaching you will be no hardship. Now come, let's sit in the warmth of the morning star and listen to the Wind Song."

Slinking towards the mouth of the cave, Tornyth joined Mandros. The emerald dragon nudged him into the sun, and then he upturned his snout to the sky. His amber eyes closed as he rumbled in pleasure. He stretched out his massive wings and basked in the warm glow of the sun.

"Spread your wings, *elt mynrell*. Hear the song of the wind and feel the strength of the morning star."

Feeling foolish, Tornyth obeyed Mandros's command. He shuffled over to find his own patch of sun and unfurled his wings. The blood in his veins sung as it flowed through his body. He felt light-headed; the sky was calling to him. His claws raked the ground beneath him. The waiting was driving him mad.

Meanwhile, Mandros seemed content to observe his frustration. Tornyth had the distinct feeling the green dragon was waiting for a sign.

"I'm worried about Nym, my friend," Tornyth said. "And Carvelle, my nephew. There're evil men, *rokun*, hunting him. My brother's throne is in jeopardy. I must go to them."

"Hush, Tornyth," Mandros rumbled. "You need time to regain your strength. Listen to the Wind Song."

Tornyth tried to mimic the stillness of Mandros until he couldn't take it any longer. "I am curious," he said, shifting his weight. He glanced up towards the puffy white clouds, wishing he was among them instead of being grounded and listening for the elusive Wind Song. "Before I manifested, my scales were iridescent with blues and greens. I seem duller now."

"You are no longer trapped in dreams. You are here in the world. A true dragon." Mandros exhaled, tilting his head skywards. "Now hush. How can you hear the Wind Song if you are talking?"

"I don't hear anything," Tornyth grumbled.

"Relax—you're tense," Mandros replied. "Instincts will come when you allow them to."

"I am relaxed," Tornyth muttered. He cracked his eyes open to see Mandros observing him with an unblinking gaze. "I dreamt I was flying over the sea. There were other dragons of many coloured scales ... It felt real."

"You and I are connected, *mynrell*. We are kin."

"They were your memories?"

"Yes. My memories of war and peace."

"There was a blue dragon with golden talons and horns."

"Yes," Mandros said. He nodded his head slowly. His face was devoid of all emotion. "I dream of him often."

"Who was he?"

"*Elt Aluel*."

"Your father? He was magnificent. He was watching me."

"Indeed."

"Where is he now?"

"Dragons are long lived, not immortal." Mandros raised his eyes once more to the clear blue skies. "Our wait is nearly over."

"What are we waiting for?"

Mandros remained silent. His body was taut as he continued to stare ahead. Tornyth studied the green dragon, deciding it was best to leave him alone to his thoughts. Mandros had previously indicated that he, too, had the Sight, so Tornyth reasoned he may be having a vision.

"*Aluel*!"

A shout from the heavens broke Tornyth's reverie.

"*Aluel*. Everyone has been looking for you!"

Searching the skies, Tornyth couldn't find the owner of the rumbling voice. He turned concerned silver slits towards Mandros and shuffled to close the gap between them. Mandros looked down at him, a contented smile creasing his scaly face.

"Sidrah, are you still barging around?" There was a hint of admonishment and amusement mixed in Mandros' tone. "Your *sudunyn* is impatient and hungry."

The muscles in Tornyth's forelegs bunched together, tensing in case he needed to fight or flee.

Mandros, however, nudged him forwards, unconcerned about the presence of another dragon. "Your *sudunah*, Sidrah, has arrived. Go greet her, little white scales."

Curious, Tornyth lifted his snout and sniffed the air. The words Mandros had used this time were known to him. Thanks to his study of the ancient tongue, he had been able to decipher the meaning quickly. The use of the words brother and sister held his interest. It seemed that there were other dragons in Mandros' family.

When Tornyth spotted a great dark shadow on the horizon, he bit his tongue to stifle his cry of alarm. His instincts screamed that the incoming dragon was a potential threat. If she decided to attack, he knew he would not stand a chance.

Mandros retreated to allow the impressive black dragon to land, and Tornyth shied away. Blinking, he lowered his belly while the female dragon tilted her head with a low growl. Dragon instinct interpreted her sound of one used for greetings and soothing frazzled nerves. He glanced at Mandros, who was still at ease. The black dragon was no danger to him.

"Sidrah, you have a new *sudunyn*. May I present Tornyth, Winter's Dragon."

The black dragon moved confidently across the outcrop, and Tornyth noticed small silver specks amongst the darkness of her black scales.

Ignoring Mandros, she extended her long neck; her nostrils flared as she sniffed the air.

Overwhelmed, Tornyth stepped back, crushing his own tail in his attempts to retreat. He yelped as the black dragon continued her slow advance. Although Tornyth wouldn't describe Sidrah as delicate, she moved gracefully. While slender, she was of similar size to Mandros and easily dwarfed Tornyth.

Mandros stretched one wing, then the other, and yawned. "Tornyth, this is your *sudunah*, Sidrah, the Noble and Honourable, the Great General of Rama."

"Greetings, Sidrah most Noble," Tornyth mumbled.

"So, you have found Winter's Dragon," Sidrah said, turning towards Mandros. "He is a little—"

"Don't say *petite*," Tornyth growled. Stretching out his neck, he went to nip Sidrah's snout for her rudeness. Stunned at his own outrageous, aggressive behaviour, he staggered backwards.

Far from being enraged, Sidrah glanced up at Mandros and smirked. She returned her amber gaze back onto Tornyth and nudged him playfully with her snout. Tornyth stumbled, and Sidrah rumbled with laughter.

"Very well ... We'll settle for a feisty dragon of *modest* stature." The black dragon continued to circle him, and the muscles in her forelegs rippled. "You look tired, *Aluel*."

Tornyth eyed Mandros, feeling a stab of guilt that he didn't observe the exhausted stance of the green dragon earlier.

"I fear Tornyth's *vehyl* was in a bad way when I found him. It was a difficult night. From what I have felt, Tornyth's poor little human has been given the suppression herbs from birth. I was able to call the dragon out of his drugged *vehyl* last night."

"Drugged from birth? His dragon should have died in his infancy." Sidrah halted her perusal. "No dragon has been able to manifest from a human while drugged. The effects need to wear off first."

"I was impatient. Tornyth persistent," Mandros said.

"You called for him while his human was drugged and he *manifested*?"

"He has some strength in him."

"A blessed miracle. Stretch out your wings, Winter's Dragon," Sidrah commanded, turning her attention back to Tornyth.

Tornyth unfurled his wings. He didn't like sitting in such an open position. He was vulnerable to attack.

"Do you suppose he will grow over time?"

"No," Mandros said, his voice lowering. "I fear the tonics have done their damage. Tornyth will not grow."

Sidrah frowned at this revelation. "Has he flown?"

"You interrupted, *mynrell*."

Sidrah and Mandros eyed Tornyth with their large, luminous eyes. Sighing, Tornyth studied the edge of the outcrop. What he wouldn't give to leap into the sky and soar among the updrafts.

"Come, Tornyth," Sidrah said. She stepped aside to let Tornyth pass. "Spread those wings and fly. I won't let you fall."

Tornyth opened his mouth to protest that he didn't know what she was expecting of him, but the black dragon was quicker. With her powerful side, she pushed him. Tornyth growled in surprise. She was stronger and was able to easily nudge him to the edge.

"Sidrah," Mandros said, a hint of warning in his deep rumble.

"He'll be fine, *Aluel*. It's a natural process," Sidrah replied. Tornyth sprung forward and nipped her nose. She shook her snout, looking almost bemused by his efforts. "Don't be so reluctant. Off you go."

One moment Tornyth's claws were firmly in the rocky ground, and the next he was over the edge. His wings snapped open in panic as he heard Sidrah's booming laugh above him. For a dizzying moment, Tornyth thought he might plummet to the earth below. But he wobbled and found that he was hovering in mid-air. Sidrah was beside him, steadying him with her foreleg.

"You pushed me off the cliff!"

"All young dragons will instinctively fly," Sidrah said. "No need to get upset."

Mandros peered over the cliff face, his claws crumbling the rock beneath his weight. Tornyth watched the chunks fall until his dragon eyesight could no longer see them.

To stay in the air, he was forced to pump his wings up and down. Infuriatingly, Sidrah seemed to have no difficulty keeping her place. For her, it was effortless.

"I'm more than capable of flying and feeding a *petite* male dragon, *Aluel*," Sidrah said. She met Mandros' gaze. The green dragon seemed tense. "Forcing a dragon to manifest through the fog of the suppression herbs ... You rest. I'll look after Tornyth."

"Very well," Mandros replied with a dip of his great head. He turned upon the outcrop, and Tornyth could hear him lumbering away. "Look after white scales."

Sidrah nipped Tornyth's hind leg. "Follow."

Tornyth was left with very little choice but to obey and imitate Sidrah's movements. Compared to the black dragon, he felt slow and clumsy. Sidrah, however, did not seem at all concerned with Tornyth's lack of grace.

"It will take time, *sudunyn*," Sidrah said as she wheeled around to check on his progress. "You have a new body. With use and experience, this will become second nature."

"I'm hungry," Tornyth complained.

"Soon," Sidrah cried. "Keep up."

Tornyth heard Sidrah's playful growl, then there was a sharp sting on his tail. Surprised, he yelped as the black dragon flew past.

Startled by the sudden bite, which only stung momentarily, Tornyth watched, astounded at the agility of the black dragon. With a bellow of delight, he copied her. Sidrah was relentless as she demanded that he keep pace with her. She growled and snapped orders. She was as bossy as Kieryn.

When Sidrah banked to the side, Tornyth attempted to copy. He turned swiftly and raked his belly on the treetops as he skimmed above them. Exhausted and embarrassed, he landed on the soft sand in a heap. He watched the waves of the ocean as they came crashing to the shore.

Sidrah landed beside him, fanning out her large wings to provide shade, and nudged him. "Your endurance will improve with each flight."

Tornyth looked up at her doubtfully. "I'm hungry."

"Typical male dragon. It's play or food."

Tornyth lolled his head to the side. "Is there water nearby? Or should I drink the sea water?"

"*Sea water*?" Sidrah looked amused. "Best to find fresh water, white scales. The first dragon flight can be taxing. I shouldn't have pushed you so hard. I'll hunt. Stay here."

Tornyth curled up on the hot sand and watched Sidrah take flight. The burn of the sand and the heat of the sun melted away his tension and worry. His eyes closed as the glorious warmth of the day lulled him to sleep. It was hard to believe there was a time that he didn't want to be a dragon.

Mandros was right. He was finally free. He would like to see Kieryn try and keep him behind the palace walls now. Rumbling, he slipped further into a pleasant sleep where he could fly with the birds, see his first glimpse of snowy mountains and the raging emerald seas ...

Somewhere in a place between sleeping and waking, Tornyth realised he was human once more. He stood in the middle of a field. A gentle wind tousled his hair. The whisper of blood and vengeance was on the wind.

Leaves of red and white cascaded from the sky, sprinkling the ground. He lifted his eyes ... ominous grey shadows streaked across the sky. There was smoke and fire.

Desperate, he turned around to catch sight of Nym. Her silver hair was streaked with sweat, her skin waxen. A grimace twisted her sharp features as she crossed swords with a King's Guardsman. Behind them fluttered the High King's banner.

Jodathyn screamed out a warning, his feet moving swiftly across the ground. Will Hartcurt, a young lord in his brother's court, grabbed his sleeve. The shadows around them blurred his handsome features.

"Solan isn't the only danger. Hurry, we must go, Your Majesty."

"Will! What's happening?"

Will's lips trembled; his face was ashen.

"Will, why are you afraid?"

Behind Will's shoulder was his childhood friend, Illeanah. Her cheeks were streaked with tears. Her lips were parted as if whispering a soft prayer. She knelt upon her knees, her torn and tattered trousers soaking up blood. Trembling, she sighed. "Oh, Jod, forgive me ..."

Jodathyn stretched out his hand to touch her. He could see she was afraid, and he wanted to comfort her. She needed him, and he ached to be at her side. But her image shattered at his touch.

Jodathyn's chest heaved with pain as he collapsed on his knees. A terrified scream ripped from his lips. An answering battle cry turned Jodathyn's focus to an armed man running towards him. Even with his face twisted in fury and his black beard spattered with blood, Jodathyn recognised his brother. The sword in Kieryn's hand was slick with blood. Kieryn howled, and the sword came swinging down.

Jodathyn's world was of blood and fire ... Above him, he could hear Galgothmeg's roar of triumph. Pallaryn was going to fall.

A heavyset thud shook the ground and woke Jodathyn. Before he opened his eyes, the sand grit in his teeth and eyelashes told him he had returned to his human form. Groaning, he rolled over onto his back. He peered up at Sidrah.

Sidrah bent down and urged him to his feet with a clawed hand. Stumbling, Jodathyn obeyed the silent command and allowed the black dragon to usher him further up the beach.

"The great morning star isn't too kind to *vehyl* folk," Sidrah rumbled. "Silly bag of bones. You should have found somewhere more suitable to doze."

"I didn't intend on falling asleep," Jodathyn said. He yawned and flopped himself into the shade. He pressed his palm into the sand, fascinated by the foreign texture. Grabbing a fistful, he let it trickle between his fingers. It was finer than the dirt he had played with as a reckless child. "I hadn't expected to wake up human again."

"It happens when exhaustion takes over," Sidrah assured him.

Licking his lips, Jodathyn looked up to Sidrah, who was observing him with open curiosity. "I always wanted to see the coast," Jodathyn confessed. "I wanted to be a part of the Summer Festival and see the coloured boats out on the water. My brother never allowed it."

"You are young yet," Sidrah replied. "There's plenty of time to experience the world."

Jodathyn sighed, dropping another fistful of sand. "There is no guarantee of tomorrow. Who knows what future I have now." He glanced at the deer hanging from Sidrah's claws and felt his belly cramp. "Please, I have not had water or food for days."

"Forgive me, *sudunyn*. I'll take you to water, and then you can rest."

Despite her great, bulking size, Sidrah was remarkably gentle as she grasped Jodathyn around his middle. She brought him close to her snout, studying his ruined trousers. Her slitted eyes flashed with anger as she surveyed the runes marring Jodathyn's tanned skin. A furious growl rumbled low in her belly, and her hackles rose.

"Who dares mark one of dragonkind? Shall I tear them to shreds? And those scars down your back ... Who dares?"

"Mandros dealt with them," Jodathyn said. Wasn't it bad enough that he had an overprotective big brother? Now he had an easily angered dragon for a sister. "Please, I don't wish to discuss it."

"The scars upon your back are old. Tell me who ..."

"I'm told he died many years ago. It's in the past."

Sidrah seemed to come back to herself. She stared at him, blinking her amber eyes slowly. "I suppose you aren't *elt mynrell* for me to fuss over." Moments later, Jodathyn was settled on her back. He was thankful when the black dragon didn't make any further remarks about his disfigurements.

Sidrah lifted them into the air and after a short flight, she landed next to a stream. Not waiting for his dragon sister to lower herself, Jodathyn slipped from her back and stumbled to the water. He fell to his knees and cupped his hands to drink. When he was sated, he turned to Sidrah, who was observing him.

"What is your *vehyl* name?"

"Jodathyn."

There was a glint of amusement in the black dragon's answering smile. "A good name, *sudunyn*."

"I have a distinct impression that you are laughing at me."

Sidrah smirked. "Forgive me. Perhaps you were named after a Jodathyn I knew well."

Staring pointedly to the deer still held in Sidrah's claws, Jodathyn shrugged his shoulders. "Can I eat now?" He didn't mean for his question to sound so plaintive.

Sidrah brought the deer up to her snout to breathe on it. Within seconds, the venison was well cooked. Jodathyn wasn't at all worried about the blackened edges. Grateful to have something to fill his belly, he scooted closer and scarfed down the food.

"My personal guard always complained that I was tiny and noisy." Jodathyn swallowed a mouthful of deer. Sidrah cocked her head to the side before lowering herself to the ground nearby. "He believed I was named after Arturyn the Unifier's son, Jodathyn the Small and Mighty. I was born small, so perhaps there is some truth to that."

"The name suits you well, *vehyl*."

Jodathyn took the time to lap up the hot fat running down his fingers. "There was another with me on the prison ship. Nym Torkelle, born of Korkalie. Mandros left her upon the beach … You haven't seen her? She's pale, gaunt but sinewy, has strange grey hair, hazel eyes that pierce your soul, and a wicked tongue."

"That wasn't a particularly flattering description of a *vehyl* female."

Jodathyn snorted. "She's not one to cross, I can tell you. No doubt she's got an equally unflattering description of me."

Sidrah huffed. "I wasn't looking for a human female. *Aluel* wouldn't have left her if he had foreseen danger for her. And he is *Rshon Aluel* to you."

Ignoring the last comment, Jodathyn shifted. He felt a twinge of guilt that he hadn't given poor Nym much of a thought. Wondering if she had food and drink, he went back to his meal.

"There are some things that are only for dragons," Sidrah told him. "Your first hours with *Aluel* as a dragon were sacred. I dare say that is why he hid himself so well."

"I was asleep for most of the time," Jodathyn pointed out.

"Still. They were sacred hours."

Rubbing at his slave tattoos, Jodathyn finally voiced his worries. "What will happen to me now?"

"What do you mean, *sudunyn*?"

"I can't go home marked and defiled like this, and the dragon ... I can't go home."

"I could live in Malara Gorge," Tornyth whispered inside his head. *"There was plenty of room for a dragon there, and maybe the farmer friend might be near for company."*

Cocking her head to the side, Sidrah looked down on him quizzically. "You are *Aluel's mynrell* ... the word itself is dragon tongue and has many meanings: son, daughter, heir, offspring, chosen one, fosterling ... all equal."

Jodathyn shook his head. "You're saying I'm equal to you, the dragon of Nobility and Honour? Doesn't that make you angry?"

"Anger would be a petty response to the family's newest addition. It wouldn't be noble or honourable behaviour at all. Come now, I'll take you to the dragon home. I'm sure *Aluel* is anxious to have you returned to his side."

Chapter Two

Jodathyn

The Isle of Torqui

Mandros was waiting for them when they returned to the dragon cave. The emerald dragon sat with his nose raised to the sky. His posture was stiff, while his tail swished back and forth. Something was wrong.

"What do you sense, *Aluel*?" Sidrah lowered herself to the ground. She ignored Jodathyn as he slipped from her back and stood by her foreleg.

"Inside quickly, Jodathyn," Mandros rumbled. He jerked his head towards the cave, then returned his eyes to the sky to continue his search.

Jodathyn's first instinct was to appease Mandros. But there was something in the emerald dragon's face that caused him to pause. "I don't sense danger."

"Inside, *vehyl*," Mandros growled. His nostrils flared, and his lip curled so that Jodathyn caught a glimpse of his fangs. It was strange. A day or two ago, Jodathyn would have been afraid of an agitated dragon. The sight of an infuriated Mandros was not frightening, merely disconcerting.

"Mandros ..."

"*Rshon Aluel ...*" the green dragon corrected; his gaze flicked back to the sky. "Obey. Enemies are close."

"This isn't the time to test him," Tornyth whispered.

Jodathyn agreed, but his tentative steps faltered as he became level with Mandros. The emerald dragon's lips twitched, concealing a snarl. Then he growled a low warning so that the ground quaked. Jodathyn hurried into the cave.

Standing at the cave's entrance, Jodathyn turned, expecting the dragons to follow him. Sidrah's attention briefly left Mandros' face and flicked towards him. He felt a spike of annoyance. From his limited experience, he knew that dragons could speak to each other's minds. He had done so when he had reached out to Mandros on the ship. Now, however, he felt them blocking him from being included in the conversation.

"Wise is the dragon who doesn't put his snout where it's not wanted," Sidrah said. She frowned at him and spread her wings. Jodathyn squirmed and averted his eyes as the large black dragon leapt into the air. Mandros' gaze never left the horizon.

Not wanting Mandros to think he was intruding upon a private matter, Jodathyn padded around the cave to study each of the paintings in detail. The bright orb of the dragon's lantern still burned bright so that the tiny details of each painting were visible.

"Something is wrong," Jodathyn said, keeping his back turned as Mandros lumbered into the cave.

"I am your *Rshon Aluel.* You must learn to obey."

"I apologise." Reaching up to touch the painting that kept most of his attention, Jodathyn sighed.

"You've learned to placate others with empty words, white scales."

"A consequence of living in the palace, I fear. One does what one must to survive the anger of the powerful." Jodathyn's brow furrowed. "Are we in danger?"

"Enemies are close by. Your *sudunah* will scout the island."

"What about Nym?"

"Sidrah will find her."

"We should attack."

Mandros rumbled and shifted. He looked long and hard at Jodathyn. "Normally, I would. Today we lie low. Sidrah will keep your Nym safe."

"I'm sure Nym will have a lot to say about being abandoned. She has an abrasive tongue," Jodathyn said.

"We're ancient dragons with thick hides. We can handle one sharp-tongued, two-legged *vehyl*."

Snorting in disbelief, Jodathyn let his eyes once again travel up the painting before him. From on high, Vadroil leered at him. "Why paint Vadroil?"

"Our histories are made up of many stories. Some stories are full of joy, victory and bounty. Others are full of pain, obstacles and heartbreak. What good are our histories if we don't honour both moments of greatness and despair?"

"I don't understand."

"What Vadroil did has forever left its mark in Rama. I never want to forget the hard lessons I learned in my youth," Mandros replied. "I attribute my greatness from the victory I had over *rokun* and *rshon* evil."

"*Rokun* is the word for evil human, yes? Is there a word for evil dragon instead of *rshon* for all?"

Mandros pointedly looked to the runes on Jodathyn's arm. "It's tattooed on your skin, Prince of Scales. Those words will not pass through my lips."

Jodathyn rubbed at the skin of his arm. "I can't help but think upon my similarities to Vadroil. I have his Sight."

Mandros sighed as he studied the painted Vadroil. "You've been misinformed."

"How so? My mother—"

"Was a foolish *rokun*. Vadroil's primary power wasn't the Sight, as you call it," Mandros said. From the swish of Mandros' tail, Jodathyn hazarded he was testing the green dragon's patience. "Vadroil's ability to manipulate the will of others was legendary. His Sight was a secondary gifting and not one he had mastered."

"*Manipulation of will* ... that sounds a dreadful power." Jodathyn shifted. His eyes darted to Mandros. He wondered if he also had the ability to manipulate people's actions.

"Indeed. It is a gift that should be used sparingly," Mandros replied. "Can you guess where enslaved dragons originated from?"

"Vadroil?"

"Yes," Mandros said. "In his greed, he turned on his own people and perfected a method in which he could enslave the vulnerable. The Grey Shadows were born of Vadroil's strife."

"Grey Shadows?"

"Enslaved dragons with no mind of their own, used by Vadroil and his dread generals."

"What about my Sight?"

"Your gifting of Sight is significant. If it was not so, your dragon would have been murdered many years ago." Mandros' nostrils flared.

"*Murdered*?"

"The act of suppressing a dragon to stop them from manifesting is murder, *mynrell*," Mandros snarled. "Any that sanctioned the use of those tonics are guilty. Under dragon law, it is punishable by death."

Jodathyn sucked in a breath. His first thought flew to Kieryn. Surely his brother hadn't known the severity of his actions ... or had he?

"You won't mete down punishment, will you?"

"What could you say that would justify the use of the herbs? Why should I not rain dragon fire down upon *rokun* foolishness?"

Jodathyn squared his shoulders and stepped up to the green dragon. He placed his hand firmly against the scales of Mandros' foreleg. "Please, *Rshon*

Aluel, don't. My own father, the High King, brought me as a babe to his council for judgement. They would have found me guilty of harbouring a dragon and ended my life. My brother, only a child himself, spoke for me. If he had not intervened, I may not have survived my father's wrath. Kieryn ... Kieryn doesn't deserve to die. He protected me the only way he knew how."

"Your father, O Prince of Rama. Does he still sit high upon the throne?"

"I'm not a prince."

Mandros chuckled. "Does your father sit upon the throne?"

"No. Kieryn is the High King, and I am loyal to him. There's nothing you can do that will change my mind."

"Ah," Mandros rumbled. "Does your king deserve such a bold and loyal dragon who thinks he can manipulate the King of the Skies?"

Jodathyn blinked. "The King of the Skies?"

Mandros laughed, and some of the tension in his body seemed to dissolve. He didn't seem angry, Jodathyn mused. Indeed, he looked rather pleased as he lay down, his head resting along the cave floor. "I am king, little white scales. More reason you should learn obedience."

"My brother ..."

"Even if he hadn't shown you mercy and earned my respect, the house Pallarus will never suffer dragon fire."

"Why not?"

"'Tis sad that even a prince of the house Pallarus doesn't know of his great ancestry."

"I know of Arturyn the Unifier ..."

"I wonder how well you know his story?" There was a smirk on Mandros' face. "You weren't blessed with a dragon through your mother."

Jodathyn cocked his head to the side. "What do you mean? She was descended from Vadroil."

"How do you suppose Vadroil was killed?"

"The first king of Rama, Arturyn the Unifier, killed him in battle."

"Indeed, that is true," Mandros said. "How did Arturyn kill him?"

"The stories don't say."

"They don't say so that you don't understand your own heritage," Mandros snapped, and a ripple of irritation graced his scaly face.

"Great dragon, are you saying Arturyn had dragons of his own?"

"No. Your guess is getting closer, *mynrell*."

Understanding hit Jodathyn like a thunderclap. How had he not seen it before? "Arturyn was a dragon!"

"Indeed, I am," Mandros rumbled.

Jodathyn's grey eyes widened. "You're Arturyn? But Arturyn had three sons."

"*Vehyl* history is wrong. My daughter, Arturah, took the throne after me, and my sons were Kyran and Jodathyn."

Jodathyn blinked rapidly. Dizzy, he slumped against the wall of the cave. "So how did you kill Vadroil?"

"I took a hold of Vadroil's throat in my jaws, and I held him down until all the breath in his body had fled."

"Suffocation ..." Jodathyn shuddered at the memory of his illicit excursion from the palace. He remembered the bite of the rope as it was tightened around his throat and his desperation for air. If it hadn't been for Will, he would have never made it back home.

There was a steel glint in Mandros' wise amber eyes. "I'm a battle dragon. Battle fire runs in my blood. I feel no guilt over the death of Vadroil or any who helped him."

Jodathyn winced. "I didn't mean to imply you should."

Mandros stretched his wings lazily. "You do not have the battle fire within you."

"Then why choose me?"

"Your heart and your strength called to me," Mandros said. "I knew from the moment I laid eyes upon you that you were *elt mynrell*. I would not allow another dragon to take you from me. You—"

Jodathyn surged to his feet as a shriek echoed through the sky. The sound was so great that his ears rang. Pressing his body against the side of the cave, he sent a concerned glance to Mandros.

"Sidrah!" Mandros called. His great head swayed side to side. For a brief moment, his eyes became unfocussed. Jodathyn could only watch helplessly as he heard a low noise rumbling from Mandros' throat. Instinct told him that the green dragon was ready to fly into a fight.

"That shriek wasn't Sidrah!" Jodathyn didn't like the way his voice wavered.

Mandros roared, sweeping his head around to pierce Jodathyn with amber eyes that burned like fire. "Stay!"

There was no question of disobedience. Jodathyn nodded his head, forcing his body not to quail under the weight of Mandros' anger.

Satisfied with Jodathyn's response, Mandros burst out of the cave and was airborne.

Waiting for a few heartbeats, Jodathyn slithered towards the cave's entrance. He was careful to remain in the shadows. Soon he could hear the outraged roars of many dragons rip through the air. Poor Nym was out there!

There wasn't much he could do but stay in the cave and wait for Mandros to come back. He felt like a coward.

Jodathyn didn't know how long he stayed hidden in the shadows. While he listened to what he could only assume was a dragon fight, he noticed dark shadows in the sky. There were three of them. Gaunt, grey dragons with torn wings. Their scales were dulled, and their jaws hung slack. Saliva dripped from their fangs, and they moved like puppets upon a string. Jodathyn studied them in horror, realising for the first time how terrible the fate of an enslaved dragon was.

"Jodathyn! Catch, I have something that belongs to you!"

Sidrah flew low over the outcrop, and he had only moments to dart forward to catch what she had dropped. A screaming, heavy body collided with him. He toppled over with an oath. Rough hands pushed him away.

"Nym!" Jodathyn couldn't help it. He burst into nervous laughter.

"Insane wrath-lizard!" Growling, Nym rolled off him, grasped his shoulder, and then ran for the cave. Jodathyn took a moment to assure himself she was uninjured and then let himself be dragged to safety.

Nym threw Jodathyn into the cave, pushing him so that he was belly down.

"You're safe," he said.

"Hush! What if they can hear us?"

Jodathyn took a moment to study Nym. She was wet through and covered in mud. He sniggered.

"Jodathyn, you unholy dragon fodder, be quiet!"

Jodathyn laughed all the harder at the streaks of mud running down her flushed cheeks. Nym narrowed her eyes at him, gritting her teeth until they cracked. Punching his arm, she snarled, "That's for worrying me to death, you cretin! To hear the black glorified lizard talk, you have been having the time of your life with your new pets."

"Don't you let them hear you say that," Jodathyn warned, biting his tongue.

Nym huffed. "That black dragon swooped down from the sky without warning ... so I stuck her with my dagger. She dropped me in a lake."

"That'll explain the—"

"Down!"

A Grey Shadow landed in front of the cave entrance. Beside Jodathyn, Nym whimpered, brandishing the short dagger that she had stolen from the prison ship's crew. Jodathyn glanced down at the flashing blade, wondering what Nym thought she could do against a dragon.

The grey dragon looked about with large, dull eyes. There was no discernible life in them. Then, slowly, it turned its attention towards the cave.

"Jod ... It's coming this way." Nym's voice wavered.

"Get behind me," Jodathyn hissed in her ear.

"What's the plan?"

"Bite, scratch, and claw."

"Jod ..."

Jodathyn didn't waste any more time. He rose from where he was crouched, hidden. The dragon swung his head around to pin Jodathyn with a terrible lifeless gaze. Stepping past Nym, he closed his eyes and manifested into Tornyth. His sharp dragon hearing caught the surprised intake of breath from Nym. He ignored her in favour of sheltering her with his body. If the Grey Shadow wanted Nym, it had to get through him first.

"Rshon ... kairn ..." The words that came from the Grey Shadow's mouth sounded twisted, as if the act of speaking caused the creature pain.

Bristling at the insult, Tornyth tried to let the words wash over him. Words would only wound his feelings, but the grey dragon's teeth, claws, or talons could kill him. Now wasn't the time to allow his emotions to distract him.

"Brigyn rshon ... kairn ..."

"What's he saying?" Nym moaned.

"Winter dragon bastard," Tornyth translated. "Or mongrel." He eyed the entrance of the cave, but the grey dragon was blocking it. To escape, he would need to move the attacking dragon.

Inhaling, Tornyth hoped fire breathing was instinctive. He let the heat build within his belly until it churned within. He opened his mouth, and flames burst forth. In response, the grey dragon dodged out of the way, his unnatural, jerky movements faster than Tornyth had predicted. Fire blackened the entrance of the cave, tarnishing the ancient paintings.

Dead eyes glared back as the Grey Shadow rumbled, a warning sign that he was also preparing to spew fire. Frantic, Tornyth glanced around the cave. They were cornered.

"Mandros!" Tornyth bellowed.

Lowering his horns, Tornyth charged the grey dragon. With all his might, he rammed into the Grey Shadow. He was surprised how slow the grey dragon responded to his charge.

He stumbled from the cave, the Grey Shadow biting onto his tail. He could feel the teeth clamp down and the pain blossoming.

"Argh! Get off, you lumbering death troll!" Nym ran between them, stabbing the Grey Shadow through his nostril.

"*Rshon mahthyt*!" Tornyth swore, escaping as the Grey Shadow released his tail to turn his attention to Nym.

"Nym, run and hide!" Tornyth cried, growling as he grasped Nym around her middle and tossed her towards the scraggly bushes at the edge of the outcrop. Nym leapt to her feet and disappeared from view.

Tornyth turned and snarled at the Grey Shadow, "*Elt vehyl*!"

Bellowing, the Grey Shadow thundered towards him. Not wishing to leave Nym vulnerable to attack, Tornyth stood his ground. The grey dragon shouldered him, forcing Tornyth to retreat. He was relentless. He bit down on Tornyth's shoulder and whipped his head around.

The piercing pain of the grey dragon's fangs in his scales wasn't enough to incapacitate Tornyth. Wrenching his body around, he ripped himself free from the Grey Shadow. He rolled to his back, using his claws to rake the Grey Shadow's neck. Tornyth's sharp talons punctured the underbelly of his adversary.

Thick, black blood oozed from the wound, but the Grey Shadow gave no sign that he felt the injury. Rounding onto the grey dragon, Tornyth snapped at his neck. The grey was quicker and grabbed on to Tornyth's forearm.

Tornyth roared in pain and thrashed in the Grey Shadow's grip. The grey dragon continued to close his fangs around Tornyth's front leg.

With a resounding thump, the grey dragon wrestled Tornyth to the ground, holding on to the white dragon's limb. Tornyth scratched at the Grey Shadow's face. One of his claws lodged into its eyes. Blood ran down his scales. Gritting his teeth, Tornyth ripped the eye out. Infuriated, the Grey Shadow snarled but gave no other outward sign that the injury bothered him. Tornyth's forearm snapped like a twig as the grey dragon tightened his grip.

Bellowing, Tornyth turned his head towards the sky. "Mandros!"

"*Terini kairn*," the grey dragon murmured.

The Grey Shadow released his grip. Tornyth attempted to roll over to take advantage. But the grey dragon readjusted and pressed him into the ground with his forelegs. Struggling under the Grey Shadow's weight, Tornyth managed to catch the underside of its chin with his own horns.

"Mandros!"

"Not my hatchling!"

There was a blur of green and a deafening screech. The Grey Shadow was lifted from Tornyth's back, its claws ripping at his scales. The heavy weight was lifted, and he could stand once more. Dizzy with confusion and adrenaline, Tornyth swayed his head side to side. Of Mandros and the Grey Shadow there was no sign.

"Mandros?"

From the cover of the shrubs, Nym crept out of her hiding place. She lifted a hand, which trembled as she plucked twigs and leaves from her hair. "You're hurt, dragon!"

"Mandros! *Aluel*! Please! Where are you?"

The slow drip of blood down his scaled neck wasn't what concerned Tornyth. He lifted his snout to sniff at the air. The sounds of the dragon battle had died away. He and Nym were alone.

Chapter Three

Orion

The Road Halbeth

They were dancing on the edge of a blade. One wrong step, and they could all lose their lives. No doubt the grumblings of rebellion in Yanyima would spread, leaving Orion in a difficult position. Jodathyn had foolishly tasked him with protecting Prince Carvelle. So now, if the young prince lost his life, it would all be his fault.

They had fled from Yanyima with their tails between their legs. For the first few miles, they had all mounted the stallion to get as far as possible from the village. Once Orion was satisfied, he had them all dismount to give the horse a break. This had displeased Theo. The thief had glared and kicked at the loose stones on the road. He kept up his theatrics until the prince gave him a telling off. Orion was careful not to show his amusement.

Orion's tolerance of the thief's attitude had diminished since Jodathyn and Nym had been taken. Theo acted like Orion's leadership was a burden for him to bear. The thief had no empathy for how he was feeling, alone responsible for the Crown Prince's protection.

"We have to stop," Theo said.

Stomping forward, Orion ignored him, his eyes trained on the darkening shadows among the trees. The little travelled road between Yanyima and Halbeth wound through dense forests. It seemed to Orion the trees were pressing down on them. He longed to get out of their oppressive gloom.

Theo grabbed on to Orion's elbow, yanking him off balance. Orion wrenched his arm away, snarling in frustration. "I didn't ask for this!"

"Neither did I. Neither did the prince. Yet here we are." Theo dropped Orion's elbow and shoved him. Hard. "Horse boy, the sun will be setting soon. We can't go on. I thought you were military trained."

"Fine," Orion gritted out, stopping by the grey stallion to help Prince Carvelle dismount.

Prince Carvelle slipped out of the saddle and into Orion's waiting arms. Reaching out, the prince patted Orion's shoulder. "We're all frightened, Orion. You'll keep us safe. I know you will."

Shoulders slumping, Orion murmured an apology. He glanced at the thief through his fringe, his cheeks burning with shame. Theo shook his head at him, grabbed his lute, and found a soft patch of grass. Orion felt another spike of anger. The thief had ignored his apology and was leaving him to set up camp alone. Served him right, hoping that the other boy might share the burden.

Orion bent, grabbing a fistful of grass to help brush down the stallion's coat. The familiar rhythm of the chore lulled him into a sense of peace. Once the animal was watered, he continued to set up camp and prepare dinner. Orion grumbled as Theo's eyes never left him as he rummaged through the packs to find the bread and cheese the thief had stolen.

Prince Carvelle was a bundle of energy. As any child of six summers, the prince was attempting to make himself useful. When Orion tripped over him for the third time, he took his hand and sat him by Theo. He understood, he truly did. He remembered being young and inquisitive, getting in the way of the older warriors.

"You've been a marvellous help, Little Highness. Please sit and eat."

"It's bread and cheese. *Again*." Large eyes full of misery peered up at Orion. With an impatient sigh, Orion returned to his chores.

Orion served Theo, who didn't even look at his dinner. Instead, the thief nodded at the grass beside him, as if Orion was there to serve him. Huffing, Orion placed the thief's rations down. Theo strummed his fingers along the lute strings, not making any move to take up his food. Orion would have loved to lob the piece of stale bread at the thief, but he refrained. His mother taught him better than that.

"Was stealing a lute necessary?" Orion drawled, unimpressed.

"Unlike your warrior spirit, I'm not happy unless I'm creating. If I'm going to leave this world, I'm going to have this moment of happiness," Theo said, his fingers resting upon the strings. "I wouldn't expect someone like you to understand."

"What do you mean, *someone like me*?" Orion looked outraged. "If you mean someone who isn't so selfish and self-absorbed—"

"You're a self-righteous prat, Orion Maysden. My life doesn't revolve around barking orders and shooting people!"

"Stop it!" Carvelle snapped, looking up from his dinner. "I like you both plenty. Stop fighting. It's not helping."

"Apologies, Prince," Orion replied. He glared at Theo, who smirked at him, and then he returned to the company of the horses. Sometimes beasts were more understanding than people. He stood by the stallion's head, patting the long, velvety nose and feeling helplessly alone.

"Do you know any songs?" Carvelle asked, turning his curious gaze to Theo. "I caught Uncle Jod trying to translate a tavern song. He made me promise not to tell Papa. It was about a lady and a dragon man. The words were a bit grown-up."

Theo chuckled and shook his head. "I can't say I know that one. I have been working on a tune in my head from one of the stories you have told us, Prince Carvelle."

"Really? I shall like to hear it." Carvelle bounced up and down. He glanced up at Orion with his wide brown eyes. "Come eat with us, Orion. You were famished in Yanyima ... I heard your belly. You haven't eaten all day."

"Very well," Orion conceded. He grabbed some food and sat himself cross-legged beside the prince. Having finished his own dinner, Carvelle climbed into Orion's lap and glanced up at him adoringly.

"Keep in mind I was a stonemason and not a musician," Theo said, stuffing food into his mouth. "It's not very good."

"Let us be the judge of that," Orion quipped.

Worn out from their flight from the village, Prince Carvelle yawned as he settled himself further into Orion's lap. Theo smirked as he began to sing.

> *Friends, have you heard the story,*
> *The story of the Apple Tree Prince?*
>
> *There was a house of Aviah Vale,*
> *A place of woe and despair.*
> *A drunkard was the knight,*
> *Who once ruled there.*
>
> *The king is dead, the king is dead.*
> *Our dear prince was sent away,*
> *To live in that wretched hall,*
> *One cold and dreary day.*
>
> *Friends, have you heard the story,*
> *The story of the Apple Tree Prince?*

Pure of heart, our prince found friends,
O' friends of lowly birth.
There was a great apple tree,
Proud it grew from earth.

Together they made a vow,
The oath of unending loyalty.
That's how a simple man,
Came friends with royalty.

... and that's where I got up to."

"If you continue Uncle Jod's story, you should be careful mentioning the dog whip," Carvelle said seriously. "It's a part of the Apple Tree Prince's history ... but Papa says it hurts him still."

"Our past makes us who we are. The good and the bad." Theo sat back, crossing his feet over his ankles as he continued to strum on the lute.

"You have a decent voice," Orion murmured, his eyes fixed on Carvelle. "Jodathyn's story should have a happy ending."

Theo saluted.

"Uncle Jod's story isn't over yet," Carvelle pointed out. "He's not dead. I know it!"

The next morning, Orion and Theo worked together to clear out their campsite. For the first time since Galgothmeg had taken Jodathyn and Nym, there was a peace between them. Both were content to work side by side in silence. Lifting his head up, Orion exchanged a look with Theo.

The thief was biting his lips, his thoughts clearly on the fate of his sister. They could only hope Nym and Jodathyn were alive.

As Orion swung into the saddle, Theo reached up to grasp his boot. "I'll scout ahead today to look for any trouble."

Surprised by Theo's offer, Orion nodded. In uncertain times, it was always best to have someone in your travelling party actively looking for potential threats. "It's a good idea."

"I'm sorry. I have made myself an extra burden." Theo shifted from one foot to the other, his gaze averted.

"I'm sorry too. My father would be ashamed of how I treated you," Orion replied.

"One whistle, *all is well*, two in quick succession, *danger ahead*." Theo bent with a crooked smile and lifted Prince Carvelle into the saddle. "I'll check on you every now and then."

Snaking his arms around Carvelle's slim waist, Orion watched Theo melt into the tree line. For a long moment, he stayed in the clearing. Then, as Carvelle began to wriggle against him, he clicked his tongue and nudged the stallion into a steady walk.

Wide-awake and full of enthusiasm, Prince Carvelle seemed content to chatter. Orion could hear the longing in the prince's voice as the youngster spoke of unimportant details of his life. He spoke of hiding among the fine silks of his mother's gowns in her closet. Of sitting at his father's feet, playing with his toy soldiers during the long hours the king spent hearing noble's complaints. Out of all the highborns in the palace, he loved Uncle Jodathyn the most. Orion let him chatter; there was no harm in the prince keeping his mind occupied with thoughts of home.

Even though Theo frequently trilled a whistle signalling all was well, Orion couldn't relax. He continued to scan the road ahead, watching the surrounding vegetation for any signs of danger. It was nearly time for the mid-day meal, but the forest stood dark and foreboding around them. Cursing his decision to take this road, Orion tugged the prince closer to his chest. Prince Carvelle leaned against him, staring unblinking at the wall of trees. Orion couldn't imagine what might happen to him if he failed to protect Carvelle.

"Do you think Theo is well?" Prince Carvelle whispered. "Are there bandits in these parts?"

"I dunno," Orion murmured. He shifted in the saddle, regretting that he hadn't considered more carefully their chosen path. "I'm sure—"

Two quick whistles pierced the air.

"Danger," the prince gasped.

The grey stallion pranced sideways as Orion reined him in. Snorting, the horse pulled his ears back. Orion felt the creature's unease as if it were his own. He ran his hand over the animal's neck and let it feel the soft touch of his gifting. *"Peace, friend. Be still."*

"Orion?"

"All is well, Your Highness," Orion said. His fingers were itching for his bow. "We'll wait for Theo here."

"There's something odd about you," Carvelle murmured, nestling closer. "I feel the power flowing through you."

Flinching as if he had been struck, Orion looked down at the prince. "You mustn't speak of power."

"I don't see why not," Carvelle replied. The prince twisted around to stare up at him. "Uncle has power. His dragon never hurt me. And never will."

Orion hummed in response. Straining, he leaned forward and listened for any sign of the thief. A few tense moments passed before Theo emerged from the thick undergrowth like a wraith. Theo waited until he was standing beside Orion to speak. "There's been a fight; scattered bodies up ahead."

"Survivors?"

"I don't know," Theo muttered. He bit his lip and looked away. "Sorry. I didn't stay to look."

Frowning, Orion considered their position. A skirmish which left dead men behind was concerning. In continuing, they might find themselves trapped. However, he didn't want to head back to Yanyima. If Theo had been able to gather more intelligence about the armed men, he could make a better decision. Orion shook his head. It was unfair to expect Theo to know what to do when facing a potential armed threat.

Orion sighed and dismounted the horse. "We'll want to avoid meeting any armed men. Let's see if we can work out which way they went. Carvelle, stay behind me."

Confident that he was the best choice to take the lead, Orion helped Prince Carvelle dismount and nudged the small boy behind him. He notched an arrow, glancing over his shoulder. Theo was holding his sword before him like he was warding off monsters. Orion inhaled and resisted the urge to give the thief a quick lesson in swordsmanship. He was sure with danger this close, Theo would see his instruction as judgemental. The last thing he wanted to do was to break their tentative truce. Or worse, make his companion more anxious than he already was.

The three boys crept forward until Orion could hear the gruff murmur of voices. Theo pointed to their right. "The bodies are close," the thief mouthed.

Orion ushered Carvelle into a small thicket. "Stay hidden, Your Highness. Theo and I will check if it is safe."

"I could help," Carvelle replied, looking up at Orion.

"Carvelle, sometimes helping includes listening to other's commands. I need you to stay out of sight. Do you understand?"

Pouting, Carvelle nodded and took a hold of the reins of the grey stallion. "I'll stay with, Zoryn."

Orion shifted.

"It's the name I gave the horse," Carvelle explained. "I like *Z* names."

With Theo by his side, Orion inched closer until he glimpsed two men sprawled on the ground. Dark pools of blood stained the foliage around them. If they weren't dead already, they would be soon. Cringing, Orion studied the scene. He counted at least another half a dozen bodies strewn on the forest floor. From the looks of the fallen, they had been set upon without warning.

Orion turned his gaze to a few uninjured men wandering through the dead. They ignored the possessions left behind in favour of removing any significant items that might identify for whom these men worked. Orion wished he could get closer to get a better look. His initial thought that this had been a robbery gone wrong was incorrect. This had been a calculated attack. Curiosity got the better of him. He put his hand on Theo's arm to warn the thief to stay put, then inched forward.

Orion sucked in a deep breath. From his new position, he saw the insignia of a golden horse on a red background being removed from the dead. It was Lord Solan's family crest. Who in their right minds would attack him? Did the slaughter of Lord Solan's men have anything to do with their misfortunes? And if so, how?

Orion had suspected that Solan was behind Prince Carvelle's kidnapping. It had been no secret in the palace that Jodathyn was wary of Lord Solan. From his observations of Jodathyn, Orion knew his master had good instincts about people. Besides, only a fool would trust a man like Solan.

The men walking among the dead wore no identifying symbols. It was a smart tactic. If any of Solan's men survived and escaped, they wouldn't be able to say who had attacked them. Remaining where he was huddled amongst the bushes, Orion watched in morbid fascination as the murderers left the scene.

When the sound of their chatter died away, one of the bodies groaned and moved.

Orion jumped. He had thought all the men were dead. Before he could contemplate the complications of the corpses being still alive, Theo pushed past him.

"Theo!"

The thief did not heed his warning. Instead, he ran out into the open to stand over the injured man.

"Theo!" Orion hissed.

Ignoring him, Theo knelt at the groaning man's side and turned him over. His long fingers prodded at a nasty gash on the man's forehead. The ghastly grey pallor of his skin and his eyes rolling into the back of his skull spoke of his impending demise.

Theo flapped his hand about helplessly. Orion rolled his eyes. From his vantage point, he knew there wasn't anything he could do for the dying man. The best they could do was check what had been left behind. Any weapons, coin, or provisions could be of use to them. The dead did not need worldly possessions.

Stepping out of his hiding place, Orion stalked over to another corpse that had a quiver strapped to his hip.

"What are you doing?" Theo turned, watching Orion with an incredulous stare. "You're going to *steal* from a dead man?"

"They're Solan's men," Orion replied. He bent to pick up the dead man's bow. "Lord Solan is Jodathyn's enemy. Make no mistake, if they caught us with Carvelle, they would show us no mercy. It's best to be prepared."

"But stealing from *the dead* ..."

"Solan would have profited if you had been sold to the prison ships. He is the one behind the prince's kidnapping and attempting to kill Jodathyn. I know it!"

"At least say a prayer."

"Fine. You pray. I'll gather."

Theo huffed, studying the man at his feet. While they had argued, he had passed into the Otherworld. "What burial ritual do you think would be appropriate?"

"Whatever you are comfortable with," Orion muttered. "They're hardly going to complain."

Running his hands along the curve of the bow, Orion pulled the string back and let it go with a promising *thwack*. It was a good weapon to inherit. As he bent down to pick up the quiver and check the arrows, he heard Theo's startled yelp.

A horseman in the colours of Solan thundered into the clearing, his sword held high above his head. Orion could see the steel glint in the man's eyes, assessing them. He opened his mouth to yell at Theo to run. The thief had already turned upon his heel but was too slow; the warrior was already upon him. The sword swung down but instead of cutting Theo down where he stood, he was cracked over the head with the hilt of the blade. Orion winced at the sound of the sword connecting with Theo's skull.

It only took a few heartbeats for the warrior to take out Theo. But in that time, Orion notched an arrow. The warrior wheeled his horse around, and Orion aimed for his face. His father had taught him well.

Seeing himself at the end of an arrow, the unnamed warrior hesitated. Orion didn't expect one of Solan's men to baulk at killing him.

Not willing to show any sign of weakness, Orion fired a warning shot. The arrow hit the ground between the horse's forelegs. His steed snorted and took a few swift steps backwards. The frown on the warrior's face deepened.

"Who are you, boy? Why are you rummaging around my fallen brothers?"

Orion had another arrow notched. He lifted his chin to show the horseman that he was unafraid and took a step to where Theo had fallen. Confidence was key.

"Stay back," Orion warned. "I'm an excellent shot."

"That doesn't answer my question."

Orion let loose another arrow. It flew over the big man's shoulder and hit the trunk of a tree behind him. The warrior growled as he fought to maintain control over his mount.

"I said stay back," Orion repeated.

"It is you who is stealing from my brotherhood."

Orion shifted. While in Silverdyne, burial rites for wrongdoers were ignored, but stealing from the dead, friend or foe, was considered a crime. He had been caught breaking an important warrior's code.

"You're in trouble, boy? You've not told me your name."

"Nor have you told me yours," Orion replied. He took another step towards Theo. "I can see you work for Lord Solan. He is no friend of mine."

"Don't be a little fool. I have the upper hand, boy," the warrior said. "Now, if you please, what is your business here?"

Orion shook his head, at a loss of what to say. He knew if the warrior wished to attack him, Orion would die. The stranger was well over six feet tall, with bronze skin of one who has worked his whole life outdoors. His hazel eyes shone with shrewd intelligence. He wasn't a man to underestimate.

The warrior sighed and shifted in the saddle. "Shall I give you my name, thief? Will that loosen your tongue?"

Orion didn't answer, but his eyes slid back to the path where the prince was hiding. If he died, Prince Carvelle would surely perish too.

The warrior noticed, but in the next instant, he said something that caught Orion's interest. "Voran Axtin, born of Astyan."

"*Axtin*? And you work for *Solan*?" Orion berated himself. He should have seen it earlier.

Voran's eyes flashed. "You've come across an Axtin before, boy?"

Orion found himself staring agog. "I worked with Valt Axtin."

"My *cousin*?" Voran sheathed his sword, rubbing his hand through his auburn beard. "You work for the palace then? For Jodathyn?"

Orion's mouth was dry, and his palms were slick with sweat. He could see Voran putting the pieces of the puzzle together.

"Jodathyn and the prince are missing, and I find a servant out here. Are you for or against Jodathyn?" Voran barked, his lip curling. He proffered his blade in Orion's direction.

Tilting his chin up, Orion stared back at Voran. He couldn't show any fear. "Perhaps I should ask you the same thing. But I'm going to hazard you are against Jodathyn."

Voran laughed at Orion's cheek. Orion did not relax.

"Why would Jodathyn have a foreigner for a manservant? Eh, you're one of those Sionian traders posing as a horseman. Can see it plain as day."

Orion frowned and shook his head. "My father was a horseman of Silverdyne who married a Sionian woman. I am a Ramian horseman who has earned his horseman's lock. I'm not a foreigner. I'm guessing you are an uneducated oaf from the eastern coast ... plain as the red in your beard, good sir."

Their tense standoff was broken by horse hooves and Carvelle crashing into the clearing. The little boy gave a great yell and threw a rock at the warrior. The rock landed with a wet thump three feet from where Voran was standing.

Orion twisted around where he stood. "Carvelle!" The prince's name burst from his lips. A part of him was curious how the small prince had hurled himself into the saddle. The other part of him was horrified that he had exposed his presence in front of the big warrior.

Voran Axtin smirked, mischief lighting up his hazel eyes. "You're escorting the young Crown Prince back to the palace, I take it?"

Orion turned, poised to shoot the warrior if necessary. "It's what Jodathyn wanted."

"Just because I have worked for Solan doesn't mean I'm for the man." Voran held up his hands, dropping his sword. He reached up and tore Solan's insignia from his uniform. He dropped it to the ground, grinding it into the soft dirt with his boot. For good measure, he spat on it. "There. Now you know I'm not going to harm you. You can put your bow down."

"Tearing one's insignia off is considered desertion." Orion watched the warrior for a few more heartbeats, then slowly dropped the bow and the quiver to the forest floor. Prince Carvelle dismounted and picked up another rock. Orion stayed him with a sharp gesture.

"Tell me, how does my cousin fare?"

"Valt was killed whilst trying to protect Jodathyn." Sometimes it was best to be blunt.

Voran considered this information with a small frown. "It's as I feared."

"Uncle Jodathyn was fond of Valt," Carvelle said. Orion shushed the prince with a wave of his hand. "Papa said when uncle was scared as a boy, he would sneak into his personal guard's bed."

Voran crossed his arms against his chest and grunted. He looked unimpressed.

"Are you deserting Lord Solan?" Orion inquired, nodding at the scrap of Voran's insignia.

"Jodathyn is the only Pallarus I will tolerate."

"Why?" Carvelle asked. He cocked his head to the side.

"Jodathyn is afraid of house Solan," Orion added, "yet you work for him."

"Why do you think I worked for the old weasel? If I can't be close to Jodathyn to protect him, then I'll watch his enemies." Voran sighed and turned to his fallen comrades. "There's not much we can do here. How about I help you take your friend to a local tavern? We can patch him up and we can talk, Sionian, over a mug of beer."

"I don't drink beer," Carvelle said.

"I'm Ramian," Orion said between gritted teeth.

CHAPTER FOUR

Jodathyn

The Isle of Torqui

Tucking his mangled foreleg close to his body, Tornyth stumbled towards the cave. Thick, black dragon blood burned as it trickled down his scales, sending a shiver of uneasiness up his spine.

True to her tenacious self, Nym had overcome her fear and had joined him back in the open. Tornyth sat down on his haunches as she reached up with a pale, trembling hand.

"Are you in there, Jodathyn?"

"It's me," Tornyth confirmed. "In my dragon form, I am Tornyth, Winter's Dragon."

Nym's eyes travelled up into the blue sky, and she bit her lower lip. "Can you make it to the cave? We shouldn't stay out here in the open."

Tornyth nodded. In his current condition, he wouldn't be able to fight off any dragons. It was painful and awkward, but he staggered to the cave on his three good legs.

"Did I hurt you when I picked you up?" Tornyth asked as he collapsed in the entry of the cave. He didn't feel he could move further.

"You were gentle for a hulking, pale-moon lizard. It's not polite to throw a lady," Nym replied. "Are you going to change back to Jodathyn anytime soon?"

"I didn't think you counted as a lady." Tornyth huffed with a smirk despite the pain. "And I'm not entirely sure what will happen to my broken leg if I manifest back."

Wincing, Nym eyed the injury.

Tornyth yawned. He noticed that Nym's lips were tinged blue, and she was shivering. "Lie down at my side; my scales will warm you."

Grumbling, Nym padded over to his side and let her body go limp. He felt her burrow her bony shoulders against his ribs but did not protest. Instead, he closed his eyes.

"You're like a heated pillow."

"Don't get used to it."

"We need to look at your injuries."

"Do you have any hidden healer powers that I'm not aware of?"

Nym snorted, then ran her hand down Tornyth's side. "No. I wish I could do something to help you."

"Have you eaten? Dragons seem to forget how often *vehyl* need to—"

"Tornyth!"

"It's the black dragon," Nym cried.

"Her name is Sidrah."

Nym sent Tornyth a derisive look and then scrambled to her feet. With one silver eye open, he watched her. His ashen-haired companion was unafraid of dragons.

"He's hurt!" Nym cried out, waving her hands about. "He's in the cave!"

Tornyth closed his eyes again. He could feel the slight stirring of the ground as the obsidian dragon made her way into the cave.

"*Aluel* is not far away." Sidrah's long snout touched his side, and Tornyth stirred.

"Is he hurt?"

"A foolish question," Sidrah replied. "He's fine."

Tornyth huffed.

"Hold out your leg."

"It hurts!"

Sidrah rolled her eyes, studying his folded form with an unconcerned gaze. "Male dragons are always so dramatic. Now give me your leg."

"It's broken," Tornyth replied, obediently straightening his leg. He shifted as a sharp pain tore through his body. "That creature snapped it in its jaw."

"Evil wrath-lizard." Nym ran a comforting hand down the scales of his cheek. The touch of her fingers was pleasantly cool.

"You need to be more careful around Grey Shadows. They fear nothing. They feel nothing. All they know is their master's orders. The only way to stop a Grey Shadow is to kill them."

The black dragon stretched out her long, elegant neck and breathed healing onto Tornyth's foreleg. He watched in rapture as the bones fused and the torn scales knitted together as they healed. Sidrah breathed again on the slash at his neck. His scales and muscles pressed in tightly until there was no sign of the wound.

"Thank you."

Nym glanced up at Sidrah. Her eyes narrowed. "This doesn't mean I forgive you!"

Sidrah snorted. "I don't need forgiveness from the likes of you."

"Why you ... scaled brained—"

"Enough! Both of you!" Mandros had returned. Tornyth had been so fascinated by his healing that he had not heard the green dragon landing. He lifted his head as Mandros' piercing eyes swept over him. "I told you to stay in the cave!"

"Begging your pardon, dragon. But that horrible piece of dragon dung was in the cave and would have burned us to a cinder."

Tornyth had to give it to Nym. When faced with the steel gaze of Mandros, her voice didn't as much as quiver.

"I spewed fire!" Tornyth cried, feeling elated and proud of himself.

"You're a dragon. Of course you did, you dim-witted goat hoarder."

Mandros flicked his gaze over Nym and then to the blackened state of the cave wall, his face impassive.

"I'm sorry, *Aluel*," Tornyth mumbled. "I know they were important ancient—"

"Preserving history and tradition should never come at the cost of the future." Mandros harrumphed in the back of his throat. "Thank goodness you're safe and for Sidrah's healing power."

"My healing power doesn't give you leave to take unreasonable risks."

"Define *unreasonable risk*," Nym quipped. She sent a sidelong glance to Tornyth, who manifested back into Jodathyn in front of her eyes. "Would taking on Galgothmeg, the dragon of Death and Destruction, count as an unreasonable risk?"

"Death and Despair," Jodathyn corrected. He rubbed his forearms, hardly believing that only a minute ago, one had been badly broken.

"Who has told you about Galgothmeg, *mynrell*? I thought you uneducated in the matters of dragons."

"We had a run-in with Galgothmeg near the village of Corlyn," Jodathyn answered. A moment later, he winced at the look of rage that flittered across Mandros' face. The steely glint in Mandros' eyes spoke of ancient hurts that had festered over time.

"Galgothmeg in Rama?" Sidrah said with an exhale. Her voice was low. "*Aluel*, we cannot allow this."

"And yet, *elt mynrell*, you survived." Mandros' words were quiet as he glanced down at Jodathyn and Nym.

The green dragon's demeanour abruptly changed. His lips curled back into a terrible snarl; his eyes burned with the promise of violence. Opening his maw, he roared in fury, swishing his tail about his body in a deadly arc. Terrified at the larger dragon's display of fierce displeasure, Jodathyn flattened himself against the wall. The green dragon had morphed from a wise and noble being into a beast of war within seconds. His heart thudded in his chest.

"I need to fly. To burn something," Mandros grumbled, stalking toward the mouth of the cave.

"Dragon blood runs hot," Tornyth said. *"I want to go burn something too."*

"Otherworlds, be quiet, dragon," Jodathyn whispered. Every muscle in his body was taut as Mandros glared back at him speculatively. The green dragon dipped his horned head and then without another word, he was gone.

Sidrah shook her head. *"Aluel* will return when his blood has cooled. You two stay here, and I'll hunt and bring you something good to eat."

Wandering about the cave, Nym told Jodathyn of her own adventure. Mandros had left her in a place that was close to water and wild fruit. She surmised that the green dragon, despite abandoning her, had left her where she had water, food, and shelter.

As she studied the painting of the burning ship, she brushed her fingers along the snarling green dragon. Jodathyn looked up at the likeness of his new *aluel*. He had some trouble accepting that the same dragon who had rescued him was also a fierce warrior. Ancient texts always did say dragons were creatures of war. Was it possible that one day, he, too, would become a bloodthirsty creature?

"I'm afraid to say, the temptation of food and sleep was too much," Nym said. She moved along to the next painting. "I did not set out to rescue you straight away."

"I didn't need rescuing." Jodathyn sighed.

"I know," Nym said with a smile. "What is it like, being a dragon?"

"For the first time in my life, I feel like myself. I feel strong. Unstoppable." Jodathyn paused with a soft smile as he remembered his first flight. "I wonder if there are more like me in Rama."

"Possibly," Nym said, kicking at the stones. "The use of suppression herbs to dampen anything unusual has become a common practice. You're lucky you aren't a lowborn."

"I know," Jodathyn murmured. He glanced toward the entrance of the cave. He felt a twist of guilt. "And I'm grateful."

"I'm sure your scaly kin will return soon."

"I think you would make a wonderful dragon."

"Listening to Wind Song? Noooo, thank you." Nym ground a few pebbles underneath her boot. "I have decided I loathe flying. Otherworlds, it makes me sick to think about it."

A heavy landing announced Mandros' return. Jumping from his spot, Jodathyn went to meet him at the entrance. In the green dragon's claws, he held a stag. He seemed serene, as if he hadn't stormed from the cave in an awful temper.

"Are you well, *vehyl*?"

"I'm well, *Aluel*."

Mandros nodded his crowned head and shuffled into the cave. He set down the stag and lowered his snout and cooked it with one blast of dragon breath. "Tonight, we feast."

"I've brought dessert!" Sidrah had returned. In her front claws, she carried dozens of a strange fruit Jodathyn had never seen before. They were the size of his fist, orange and covered in soft, hairy spines. "These are a nutritious, sweet treat when cooked over a flame."

Mandros nudged the deer over to Jodathyn. "Eat."

Nym didn't hesitate. She jumped over Jodathyn's outstretched legs and hacked a piece off for her and Jodathyn with her knife.

Nodding his head, Jodathyn bit into the cooked meat. After his dreadful experiences aboard the prison ship, he felt he was eating like a king. He wondered if Nym was feeling the same way.

"The Grey Shadows ... are they enslaved? Is that what they were going to do with me?"

Mandros exhaled. "Enslaved and trapped within their own minds. Who they once were in their human existence has been expunged."

Jodathyn shivered at the thought of becoming like the grey creature. It was a cruel fate.

"Have there been other dragons sold to Artroth?"

"We patrol Rama's borders and look for ways to rob Vadroil's allies of any unmanifested dragon. There hasn't been a healthy dragon in centuries," Sidrah told him. "You are different, *sudunyn*."

"Different? How?"

"For all others we have intercepted, it's been too late for their dragons. The use of suppression herbs and the distress of the prison ships makes their dragons weak, prone to bloodlust, and unstable. Many are unable to manifest without coercion, which destroys the dragon within."

"Then ..."

"We do what we can for the *vehyl*," Sidrah murmured. "We settle them on their own little island. The elders and the ones that have healed look after the vulnerable among them."

"Jodathyn, from what I can tell, is not completely mad," Nym said. She tore into the venison with her teeth.

"No," Mandros rumbled, looking smug. "He's stronger."

"In Rama, we call that Pallarus stubbornness," Nym said.

Knowing that Nym did not yet know the human identities of the dragons, Jodathyn sent Mandros and Sidrah an amused look.

"The ships were terrible." Nym stretched out her legs. "I'm never going to sea again."

"Don't be so sure, Lady Nym," Mandros said. "I foresee another adventure upon the sea for you."

"I'm never boarding a prison ship again."

"I didn't say anything about a prison ship."

Nym turned back to the green dragon. "So you can see things. What's in Jodathyn's future?"

"I'm not some cheap fortune teller." Mandros seemed affronted. But Nym stared at him with an unblinking gaze until he answered her. "Three daughters. A leader, a builder and a redeemer."

Nym looked amused and playfully nudged Jodathyn. "Three girls, Jod! Another ill omen for you! Unlucky you!"

"Doesn't sound unlucky to me," Jodathyn muttered as he shifted away.

"Everyone knows about your three bad omens."

Mandros' eyes opened again, and he lifted his great head. "What omens would these be, *vehyl*?"

"I was born on the first day of high winter. It also coincided with the first snowfall of the season. My birth killed my mother."

Sidrah rumbled with laughter. "Humans have twisted things around quite considerably. Lady Nym, do you know how dragons get their coloured scales?"

Nym looked up, mystified. "I thought it had no significance."

"Our colouring honours the birth of our *vehyl* heart. I was born at midnight ... if you look carefully, you can see the silver stars in my hide to show the constellations on the night of my birth. Not many dragons are born during the winter seasons."

"Why would that be?"

"Dragons are creatures of warmth. Winter is cold," Sidrah said as if it explained everything. "Tornyth is the only known dragon that was born on the most auspicious day of high winter. The feast day."

"So his birth has nothing to do with Vadroil?"

"Argh, you humans are so stuck on Vadroil. *Vehyl* babies have a habit of being born when they are ready. I should know. My human heart had five children!"

CHAPTER FIVE

Kieryn

The Village of Habron

Kieryn stared in wonder at the smooth dome in front of him. He had assumed that a monument created by a dragon's claws and breath would be ugly. But what the flames left behind was a beautiful tomb. The twisted black rock would forever stand a testament of the life of a simple apothecary who had meant so much to his brother.

Donatein's death had been his failure. It was only right that he should honour the old servant who gave so much to house Pallarus.

Fiddling with the loose petals in his gloved hands, Kieryn looked down at his meagre offering. The Shredding of the Flowers ceremony for Donatein Manideep seemed an appropriate funeral rite, as he had spent many years in Pallaryn serving. Under the watchful gaze of Tiernan, Kieryn had plucked the yellow petals off whatever wildflowers he could find on the hills of Habron.

Kieryn lifted his eyes to see the villagers of Habron approaching. He felt no fear of them; his guardsmen would keep them at bay until he was ready.

Kieryn set one foot in front of the other, his lips murmuring a prayer known by the people of Habron. As he circled the dragon-made tomb, he sprinkled the petals, letting them fall as was the custom in Pallaryn. He circled the grave three times, turned about face, and repeated the action. When he finished, he bowed deeply to Donatein's final resting place. Reaching out, he broke with Habron tradition and spoke to the dead man.

"Be at peace," he whispered. The words caught in his throat. "I'm sorry that you paid the cost of my failure. May blessings follow you to the Otherworld. One day I will bring Jod to you so he can say his final goodbyes as a good son ought."

Captain Tiernan shifted uneasily, studying the villagers with his keen blue eyes.

"Twelve years of service, Captain," Kieryn murmured. "And now he's gone ..."

"Donatein Manideep was a good man, Sire," Tiernan agreed. "He will be difficult to replace."

"I think I shan't try," Kieryn replied. "I've done what I can here. I will go and speak with the folk of Habron."

"As Your Majesty commands."

Closing his eyes, Kieryn whispered another apology to the dead man under his breath. The wind upon the hill was strong, buffeting his cloak and cooling his warm skin. Jodathyn had been here. Did that mean Carvelle was also nearby? Did the villagers have news for him? Is that why they shifted so uneasily?

Turning his back upon the dragon monument, Kieryn knew that in this life he couldn't atone for his role in the death of an innocent man. When it was time for him to step through the veil separating the mortal realm from the Otherworld, he would face Donatein once more. The thought sent a shiver of dread up his spine.

He had taken the road west to Habron to pay his respects and atone for his part in Donatein's death. Although the Northerner's March had wide, well-maintained roads, Tiernan was nervous of that route. Those roads were famous for dense forests, which were perfect for ambushes. It also happened to be Solan's territory. Keen to avoid Solan's influence, they had elected to take the western road from the citadel. They still had quite a distance to go to reach Kudah. Kieryn hoped he could leave Habron immediately. He did not wish to stop. Ammerie's journal had promised he would find Jodathyn in Kudah. Surely wherever Jodathyn went, Carvelle would also be.

Raising his gloved hand, Kieryn indicated to his King's Guard that he was willing and ready to meet with the people. They parted for him to walk through their ranks.

"We had not thought that Habron would grace us with a visit from our High King, Your Majesty."

Kieryn's eyebrow rose at the village magistrate who regarded him with awe. The man wanted an audience, that was clear. Kieryn swallowed past his own impatience to leave Habron now that his duty of honouring the dead was complete. He was king; it was his duty to hear the living.

"You wish to have a word with me, magistrate?"

"Indeed, I do, Sire." The magistrate seemed to remember himself and knelt. Even with his head downturned, Kieryn could see how stiffly the man held himself.

"Then rise and speak."

Stumbling to his feet, the magistrate didn't dare look Kieryn directly in the face. His eyes shifted to the side, eyeing the silent King's Guardsmen.

"I fear I have ill tidings," the magistrate said, licking his dry lips.

"My days are filled with ill tidings. Speak, man!"

"A day or two ago, a dead messenger was found under awful circumstances. We fear he may have come from the palace."

"What makes you think he was my messenger?"

"He had been attacked."

"An attack doesn't mean the messenger was from the palace." Kieryn fought to keep the hard frown off his face. The magistrate must have heard the challenge in his tone, as his eyes flicked to the ground.

"He died alone," the magistrate stammered. "His attackers left him upon the road."

Breathing in through his nose, Kieryn made an effort to soften his voice. "Pray continue."

"He wrote in the dirt," the magistrate said. "'King's letter Sion stolen.'"

"That would certainly indicate he was from the palace," Guardsman Carew said, earning himself a sharp elbow to his ribs, courtesy of Jael. Carew rubbed his ribs, sending the dark-skinned healer an injured look.

Ignoring Carew's gaff, Kieryn felt lightheaded. At the Autumn Festival, he had asked Lord Whitoak to use his network to send a letter to Sion in secret. It felt like another lifetime when he had returned to Pallaryn without his son. Odelle had been distraught when she had come to his rooms. Once his queen was blissfully unconscious, Kieryn had written the letter to the king of Sion, begging for help. He had sent for Whitoak as soon as his wax seal had cooled. He knew even then that Jodathyn's life was in grave danger. Whitoak had known of his worry, had promised him he would assist ... Why had it taken Whitoak's messenger so long to reach Habron, and how did someone know to track him down? His favourite had a huge network of spies working for him. It should have been safe to send correspondence into Sion.

"I wish to see the unfortunate man," Kieryn said. He glanced at Tiernan, whose deep frown told him his captain was troubled by the news. "Indeed, he was on a mission for the crown. I should honour him as is appropriate. Lead on."

It had not been an easy death. Kieryn looked down upon the messenger's face. The healer of Habron had done his best to clean the poor man's body ready for burial, but the signs of his struggle were still apparent.

The messenger's bruised chin held the hint of facial hair. He was not much more than a boy. With his eyes closed and his soft, dark curls, he looked so tragically young. Whitoak had sent one of his younger riders.

An old woman busied herself around the stone chamber, pottering away and murmuring to herself.

"Old Ninah was once our healer," the magistrate whispered at his elbow. "She seems to be mostly trapped in her own little world now. Please forgive any trespass on her account."

"Old Ninah has good hearing," the old woman snapped. She squinted in Kieryn's direction like one who had failing eyesight. "Speaking of trespass. Who is this in my domain?"

"Kyan, born of Arah." Kieryn spoke before the magistrate could sputter in outrage on his behalf. "Please, mistress, what can you tell me about the messenger?"

"Waste of a precious life," Ninah muttered. She gathered jars of ointments and hobbled her way over. "He can't have been past his twenty-third summer ... The lawman said he had nothing on him to identify himself."

"So young ..."

The old woman thrust the jars into Kieryn's hands. "Here. If you are going to barge around my domain, you can at least help me, *Kyan of Arah.*"

"It would be an honour, Mistress Ninah."

"Oh, Otherworld Dragons, not much of an honour. Follow me. Keep up."

Kieryn followed Ninah obediently as she tottered from the cold stone chamber and into a small room lined with sick beds. Patients shuffled, staring with wide eyes. He couldn't blame them. Who would have thought that the High King of Rama, along with his famous King's Guardsmen, would visit their small town and assist the once-healer?

"That poor boy you were interested in," Ninah said, "it took him at least three days to die … all alone."

Kieryn felt his heart sink. Lowering his head, he mumbled a quick prayer. "I would like him properly honoured. He served Lord Whitoak of Androssah. I will pay the healers to see it is done correctly."

"Androssah, you say? The people surrounding the Lake of Mirrors bless their dead with water."

"It is as you say, Mistress Ninah. One of my men will go and fetch some fresh water that would be suitable for his funeral rites."

"Majesty," Carew murmured at Kieryn's elbow. "I'll fetch the water, and then I shall go to Sion to deliver your message."

Catching Tiernan's straightening shoulders and jaw clenching, Kieryn shook his head. "Fetch the water, but don't go to Sion. I fear the roads are watched, and you'll be vulnerable."

Carew dipped his head, clicked his heels together, and left the sick room. Tiernan watched him go with a frown.

"Found this little orphan a week or two back." Ninah had kept walking among the sick. She stopped by a trembling child, who looked up at him with fearful eyes. "She won't speak and tell us her name. She's afraid, poor thing. Won't you give it a try, Kyan of Arah?"

Looking down at the mousy little girl before him, Kieryn felt his heart shatter. She could only be a few seasons younger than Carvelle. Her large brown eyes were full of the same fear he had seen in Jodathyn as a child.

"Don't be afraid, little one," Kieryn murmured. He stepped past Ninah and sat upon the child's bed. Glancing up at the old healer, Kieryn felt her gaze looking down at him.

"They're so vulnerable when they are this small. What must the poor wee one be feeling?" Ninah said. "Can you imagine what it must feel like for the parents of a lost child?"

Kieryn wanted to scream. He did know. He felt his son's loss every waking moment. He was tormented by the thoughts of what might have happened. And here was another child. Lost and nameless.

"I know the pain, woman," Kieryn replied. His voice gruff. The magistrate stood patiently to the side, out of hearing.

"They think I'm half mad," Ninah said, tapping her nose.

Kieryn glanced down at the small girl child. "Why don't you tell me from where you came?"

The child shook her head, and her long dark mane whipped about her face.

"Come little one, how about you speak your name," Kieryn pressed. He lowered his head to the child's level. "You can whisper in my ear if you wish."

The girl considered him for a long moment, then slowly crept a little closer. Wrapping her small hands around his neck, she lifted herself onto his lap to speak into his ear.

"Larelle."

"That's a pretty name," Kieryn whispered back. "Can you tell me where you were born of?"

"A lake."

"Do you know which lake?"

Larelle shook her head. "It was a pretty lake."

Kieryn smiled in order to hide the frown he felt tugging on his lips. Rama had several regions with lakes, and all of them were beautiful in their own way. The slip of the girl crawled further into his lap and ran her fingers curiously through his beard.

"I like your beard."

Kieryn pressed her small hand against his cheek. "Can you tell me about your Mamma or Papa?"

"I was found by the lake." Larelle sighed and shifted. As she did so, she revealed a marking on her porcelain skin. Kieryn gently grasped her arm to take a better look.

"This child has a tattoo ..." Kieryn could only stare in open-mouthed horror at the ugly mark of an eye and spear.

"The bad men," Larelle said. Kieryn could feel her trembling. "They took me from the lake; they gave the innkeeper coins."

Dumbfounded, Kieryn looked up into Ninah's impassive face. He felt a thrill of horror snake up his spine. Introducing him to Larelle hadn't been made on a whim, he realised. The old woman had to have known about the tattoo. She wanted him to see it.

"It's the mark of a criminal, my king," Ninah murmured. "And her being so young and innocent ..."

"Protect her," Kieryn ground out. Standing swiftly, he turned to pierce the magistrate of Habron with his most imperious stare. His teeth ached with the rage he was feeling.

His own thoughts of his failure tormented him. When Jodathyn was born, he had vowed to protect him, and he had failed. Now he feared it was too late for both Carvelle and Jodathyn. His power had been inadequate to protect them. Glancing back at the large brown eyes full of fear and abandonment, he made a snap decision. It wasn't too late for Larelle.

"It's not safe for me to take her with me now, but I'll be back. I swear by all that is good and honourable in this world, I'll find her safety."

"As you command, Sire."

Kieryn bent to brush the girl's hair back. "I'll come back for you, Larelle, lake maiden, and I will find you a place you can be safe from the bad men."

Larelle looked up at him, her brown eyes glistening. Kieryn stroked his finger along the girl's cheek, then turned his back.

"Larelle is my ward now. If any come to harm her, magistrate ... kill them."

Kieryn could hear his footsteps match his racing heart as he left the sick room. It was one thing to have knowledge of how other Ramians suffered. It was completely different to experience it for oneself. He came to the throne an underaged boy. Because there was no heir and Jodathyn had been deemed unsuitable, Kieryn had been cloistered away.

In the days of his great-grandfather, the High King walked among his people. It was not something he had been allowed to indulge in. Times were changing. The assurances of his council, even Whitoak, had him blinded to the truth.

"Majesty, the child ..." Tiernan's eyebrows drew together. His captain was concerned.

"I believe an escaped slave. If we can't find her unfortunate parents, I fully intend to raise her, yes," Kieryn murmured without turning to look at Tiernan. "Putting a halt to the prison ships doesn't seem to have made much of a difference. It was a deficient gesture."

"Forgive me for being blunt, my king, but taking the child as your ward is a risky move. The council will not support it."

"I am a grown man," Kieryn replied. His fist clenched at his side. Had his council controlled him from the day his father died? "I have made the decision to take the child into my family as the head of house Pallarus. The fact I am High King is irrelevant. Therefore, the council's opinion holds no weight. To bring her to Pallaryn without expressing my full intent to take her as my ward could potentially put her in harm's way."

Tiernan snorted. "Not that I don't enjoy seeing some of those pompous nitwits put in their place ... You're playing a dangerous game, Majesty."

"A game I'll win, Captain."

"And the child's parents?"

"Nothing in this world can compare to losing a child. If we find them, I'll take Larelle to them myself." Even as Kieryn spoke, he knew that it was unlikely they would find her parents. He would search for them, praying he might be able to find them for Larelle. But he feared she was already an orphan at such a tender age. It was something else that likened her to Jodathyn.

Kieryn rounded the stables; it was time to leave. The hope he might find his son in Kudah beckoned him. He was met with the sight of Carew struggling with a large blond man who was at least a foot taller than him. Jael had his hands on a young woman dressed in simple leathers. Long black curls, plaited into a simple braid, framed her pleasant, deep copper face. She watched, smirking as her counterpart snarled and fought Carew. They struck Kieryn as an odd pair.

"My king, these two have been tracking us," Carew said, giving the blond man's arms a twist.

Carew's prisoner roared in rage. "We came voluntarily, dragon dung."

"I would not say your actions were voluntary, young man," Jael said. There was a flicker of amusement in his brown eyes as his lips puckered into a smile. "The woman has complied with our request, Your Majesty. The man would not disarm or give us his name."

"Their horses are obviously stolen—"

"I told you they were a gift!" The blond man struggled in Carew's grip.

"A likely story."

"It's hardly my fault Jodathyn has a taste for the finer things in life. Prince Carvelle calls her Zarine."

Every fibre of Kieryn's being went taut at those words. "Release him."

Carew frowned at the order, but he dropped the tall blond man onto the ground. Kieryn only had eyes for the stranger, who brushed off his knees and was glaring heatedly at Carew.

It was the woman who spoke. "Your Majesty, my name is Fydellah Nahilya, and we have news of Jodathyn and Prince Carvelle. Hear my words and know the truth."

Kieryn felt a pressure against his mind. For a brief moment, he felt numb, unable to move or think. Then a wave of reassurance washed over him, and he knew the woman's words were true. He wished he had Will at his side. His clever spy would have been able to tell him without any doubt if a power had been used on him. Stepping forward, Kieryn observed the calm expression on Fydellah's face. A part of him was afraid that if he moved too quickly, he would find this moment a dream.

"Fy ... You are the slave Will rescued?"

"I am her." Fydellah shifted. Her eyes slid to the guardsmen as if she expected to be placed under arrest.

Kieryn searched his mind for what Will had said about her. *Dangerous to cheats and liars.*

"Will went to the safe house, looking for you and my brother. You were not there."

"The prince's kidnappers came, Your Majesty, and we were forced to flee. Jodathyn and I stole the horses and escaped."

"And Carvelle, what of my son?"

"Hail, hearty and cheeky last I saw of them," the blond man grumbled. "I've proof, my king. Jodathyn left his festival cloak with me."

"How is it *you* crossed paths with my brother, stranger?"

The blond man cringed. "My name, my king, is Ruevyn Kelvie ... or you may have heard me referred to as *Whisperer*. Prince Carvelle ran to my farmhouse in Sant Burgundy screaming that someone was killing his uncle. Naturally, I went to investigate to find Jodathyn was fending off five men. I chased the brutes off but not before Jodathyn was stabbed."

Kieryn hissed. "My brother ..."

The farmer, Ruevyn, laughed. "They had him trapped. But your brother, bless his soul, charged them. I don't think they realised how brutal Jodathyn can be when cornered."

A self-satisfied smile lit up Tiernan's face. "Jodathyn *brutal*?"

"Aye. He slashed open a man's face with a knife he had stashed in his boots."

"Perhaps you should switch to knife work instead of fists, Captain," Jael chortled, shaking his head. "He might enjoy that more."

"One of you gents should teach him not to headbutt. He nearly gave himself a concussion."

Kieryn could hear the sound of soft chuckles ripple through the ranks of his guardsmen.

"I stitched him up. The stoic fool that he is, he marched out the next morning into Malara Gorge. It was my hope they could get through to the intersecting roads. Belrah is close by."

"Smart." Captain Tiernan leaned forward and touched Kieryn's shoulder. "If Jodathyn was worried about being pursued, it makes sense he hasn't turned back to the capital."

"Whitoak never told me his spy *Whisperer* was so young," Kieryn said, peering down at Ruevyn. "You would have been a child yourself."

Ruevyn bowed his head. "I was quite friendly with your brother, my king."

"Aviah Valley? You were a child at Aviah Valley?" Kieryn felt a twisting knot in his stomach. He tasted acid as he contemplated the weight of Whitoak's actions. His spy was not only a child but a former resident of Aviah Valley. "Whitoak said there were no other children at Aviah Valley."

Ruevyn nodded. "I am two summers older than Jodathyn. I played with him as a child, Your Majesty. We weren't the only children that lived in Solan's summer house."

"Why did he lie?" Closing his eyes, Kieryn swallowed bile. He breathed in and out, but it did little to calm the storm of his mind. Whitoak had betrayed him. He had counted on his favourite as the closest thing he had to a friend. Whitoak had promised to always speak the truth to him, no matter how unsavoury. The breach of trust stung. "Why didn't Whitoak bring you straight to me?"

"I worked for Lord Whitoak for many years," Ruevyn said with a shrug. "I never thought to question him."

"You did his bidding," Kieryn murmured. "This doesn't make him much better than Solan ..."

"I was never beaten or starved."

"You were a child," Kieryn replied, shaking his head. "You should have been brought to Pallaryn."

"I am a farmer now, Your Majesty," Ruevyn offered. "At the time, Pallaryn was not safe."

"Still isn't," Fydellah murmured, flicking her dark curls over her shoulder.

"Are you safe from your past, Ruevyn Kelvie?"

"No, Your Majesty."

"A child was the first downfall of Lord Solan?" Kieryn's face split into a smile, but it didn't reach his eyes. The stories of the spy Whitoak had called Whisperer had been the cornerstone of how Solan had been disgraced. Without the tales of Aviah Valley, Solan might have greater sway within the council. Once again, Kieryn lamented that he was unable to cut off the old dragon's head. "Very well, Ruevyn, bring me my brother's cloak as proof."

Chapter Six

Jodathyn

The Isle of Torqui

Yawning, Jodathyn rolled over and bumped into a soft body. At his side, Nym muttered a curse in her sleep and nestled closer. Her hair tickled his nostrils as she pressed her face into his chest. Opening one eye, Jodathyn shivered and yawned once more. His muscles protested as he stretched his stiff limbs.

"She's warm," Tornyth rumbled. *"I want to fly. I want to hunt."*

A quick cursory glance around the cave told him that both of the dragons were absent and their modest fire had dwindled. The cloud cover was low, and the cave was full of dewy mist. He grimaced. Outside he could hear the soft pattering of rain.

"It's first light. Go back to sleep." Nym's voice was groggy. She squinted at him; her hazel eyes were glassy with sleep. "You'd think that a person would get used to the cold."

"I'm hungry," Jodathyn replied instead.

Nym reached up, grabbing Jodathyn's arm and tugging. "I'm cold. Lie down. Your body is warm."

"I could relight the fire," Jodathyn replied.

Nym blinked and then pushed him roughly from her. "Go light me a fire, dragon breath."

Chuckling, Jodathyn rolled to his feet and once he was clear of Nym, he manifested into Tornyth. He plodded towards the mouth of the cave; more kindling had been collected and left for them. He snapped the larger pieces in his grip and fed the fire. Now that he had spewed dragon fire, reigniting their fire was a simple task. One powerful exhale and tongues of flames licked the kindling.

"Looks like you've made yourself useful after all, palace brat." Nym sat up to watch him as he returned himself back into his human form. There was little point staying within his dragon body if there was no need.

"Meat or fruit for breakfast?"

"You choose." Nym made a disgusted sound in the back of her throat. She flung out her hand and waggled her fingers. The dark circles around her eyes gave her a haunted look. Jodathyn wondered if his face also bore the signs of their misadventure.

After grabbing two pieces of the strange roasted fruit, Jodathyn handed Nym the food and sat down beside her.

"We have to get to the mainland," Nym whispered, turning the fruit over in her hands. Her silver hair swept forwards, hiding her facial expressions from Jodathyn's gaze. He knew she was thinking about her brother, Theo. He heard the longing in her voice.

"I miss our little prince," Tornyth moaned. *"Can't you give me some meat for breakfast?"*

Jodathyn wished he could say something to comfort her. Instead, he sunk his teeth into his breakfast and let the tangy juice slide over his tongue. He finished his meal in a few quick bites, ignoring his dragon's complaints.

"I plan to talk to Mandros today," he said, licking the sticky juice from his fingers. He eyed the meat and wondered if it was a good idea to give into his dragon. "I forgot to ask, are you in pain? We should ask Sidrah to heal you."

"She already healed me," Nym admitted, finally biting into her fruit.

"Was that before or after you attempted to stab her?"

Jodathyn laughed as Nym only grunted in response. She punched his arm, a smirk upon her lips.

"Here they are," Jodathyn murmured, hearing the twin thuds of two massive dragons landing. Moments later, Mandros appeared, followed by Sidrah. They were both laden with deer and fruit. Nym grimaced at the puddles of rainwater in the dragons' wake.

"What's all this?" Jodathyn asked, cocking his head to the side.

"Provisions," Sidrah answered, "for while we are away."

"Where are you going?" Jodathyn asked sharply. Nym sent him a withering glare.

"The news of Galgothmeg is not something that we can ignore, white scales. Rama is vulnerable. I will convene a dragon council and return with more battle dragons. The journey will be swift."

"But—"

"You will stay here, *mynrell*. You'll be safe in the cave. We have brought you food, and we're collecting water for you outside."

Jodathyn shook his head in disbelief. "My nephew, the Crown Prince … I must go to him. He's in danger. I need to return to the mainland."

"All in good time," Sidrah rumbled. "The skies of Rama aren't safe for you to fly alone."

"Then take me back!" Jodathyn snapped. "I can't stay—"

"A few days won't hurt," Nym said.

Shocked by Nym's quiet words, Jodathyn rounded on her. "Even now, they might be hurt or—"

"Jod," Nym soothed. She held up her hand to forestall whatever he was going to say. Her brow creased as she lowered her voice as her shoulders slumped. "We've been gone for days."

"If you leave this island, the Grey Shadows will hunt you down." Mandros speared Jodathyn with a hard amber stare. "You're not ready to face them alone. Even experienced battle dragons work in teams."

Frowning mutinously, Jodathyn crossed his arms against his chest and glared back. As Jodathyn's frown deepened, the green dragon plucked him off the ground, ignoring his yelp of surprise.

Mandros brought Jodathyn close to his snout. "You must obey me in this. As your *aluel,* I only want to help you."

"I'll look after him," Nym said, coming to stand next to Mandros. She reached out to touch his scaly foreleg. "Your dim-witted fool will be safe."

"Someone has to look after him. Male hatchlings can be most precocious," Sidrah commented. "I'll be back soon, *sudunyn.* May the sun kiss your scales, the stars bless and guide you."

Jodathyn watched with ill humour as the black dragon unfurled her vast wings. In one mighty leap that left the ground trembling, Sidrah was airborne. Moments later, she disappeared from view.

"I am *not* a hatchling!" Jodathyn muttered.

"You need to develop a thicker hide, *mynrell,*" Mandros rumbled. "Compared to Sidrah's long years, you are very young. And it's only natural that a dragon points out their superiority."

Jodathyn huffed.

"My daughter was a general and mother. She was one of the greatest women to ever walk Rama." Mandros considered Jodathyn's glum expression. "I will return, my son of Flame and Fury. You don't need to save Rama alone."

Jodathyn swallowed as Mandros gently placed his feet back on the ground. "I'll await your return."

Mandros' growl was almost a purr. "May the rainstorm help you grow and the moon give you her light in your darkest hour."

Jodathyn nodded, his eyes still downcast. Mandros pressed his snout into Jodathyn's hands before he leapt into the sky and disappeared.

Jodathyn remained at the mouth of the cave, staring fixated to where he had last seen Mandros. He stood motionless and silent.

"Do you think it's harder for them to fly in the rain?" Jodathyn lifted his chin to regard the heavy rainclouds. He pursed his lips.

"Men." Nym sighed as she turned back to the cave. "When you lot get hungry, you become grumpy."

Huffing in defeat, Jodathyn returned to the cave. He sat close to the fire and rubbed his bare arms.

"Hopefully one of the dragons brings you back a shirt," Nym said. "So you can cover up."

Jodathyn's startled grey eyes glared up at Nym. He shifted his weight and scowled into the flames.

"Not that you are ugly ... As far as the male species is concerned, you're quite nice to look at."

"You don't have to lie to me," Jodathyn mumbled. "I've heard it all before."

"I'm not lying. You're quite easy on the eyes. I won't have a complaint if you want to walk around with no shirt. You can even leave your pants off if you wish." Nym waggled her eyebrows.

Jodathyn's face twisted into something that was between bemused and brooding. "I hate being left vulnerable like this."

"Some women think battle scars are dashing."

"Do you?" Jodathyn snarled. Nym was being liberal with the truth. "These are marks of slavery, not battle."

"Prance around the palace with no shirt, palace brat, and see how many ladies swoon at your feet. I'd keep your pants on for that experiment."

Jodathyn snorted, staring at his hands folded in his lap.

"Curse this ill-begotten weather. I'm thirsty."

A smile curled on Jodathyn's lips. "It's raining. I'll go see how the dragons collected the water."

"Jod—"

"You're already cold. Besides, I can manifest into a warm beast at will." Jodathyn was already striding toward the entrance. He stepped out of the protection of the cave and felt the cold beads of rain falling on his naked skin. At the far side of the outcrop, the dragons had created stone basins. From where he stood dumbfounded, he knew they had made them from dragon fire. Just as the cave had been created.

He stepped through the rain, barely noticing the cold seeping into his bones. When he bent to test the weight of the basin, his eyes drifted to where he knew the mainland of Rama was. Mandros did not understand. He needed to go home. Carvelle needed him.

Making up his mind, he stooped down, using his knees to lift the basin. It was heavy, but he was able to stagger towards the cave. By the time he reached Nym, he was huffing and puffing from the exertion.

"My hero," Nym quipped as Jodathyn almost dropped the basin on the cave floor. She bent to drink deeply. Jodathyn's eyes returned to the mainland.

"Jodathyn?"

"We'll wait until the rain has cleared. Then we'll go," Jodathyn announced.

"Mandros told you to stay here."

"I never took you as a rule follower."

"He's going to be furious."

"Probably."

"He's claimed you, scaly dragon dung. Don't you think annoying the giant flying lizard is a remarkably unintelligent way to get into trouble?"

Jodathyn raised his eyebrows and crossed his arms against his chest. "So now I'm unintelligent?"

Nym snarled back at him. "Listen, Jodathyn, little white scales ... I know enough from Theo's incessant prattling that dragons have their own culture. Mandros has claimed you. You *belong* to him."

"I belong to no one. No man and certainly no dragon." Jodathyn shrugged his shoulders. "Carvelle needs me. I have a way off this island."

Nym paused, looking doubtful. "Wait. You're going to fly off this island?"

"Well, unless you have a better idea. I'm not much of a swimmer."

Jodathyn sat perched on the very edge of the outcrop. He let his legs dangle over the side before angling his head back to smirk at Nym. She scowled back at him, looking like she very much wanted to run over and pull him to safety. Delighted, he leaned forward and heard her terrified gasp.

"Stop it, Jod! Stop it! You'll fall ..."

"I won't," Jodathyn assured her with a toothy grin. He called Tornyth forward and before he knew it, he was back in his dragon skin.

"Theo will not be pleased that I have flown with three different dragons before he has had a chance," Nym murmured, taking a step closer to Tornyth.

Looking at Nym through his dragon eyes, he marvelled at how much detail he could see. He could mark every one of Nym's freckles on her face, and he could see the different tones of silver that made each strand of hair on her head. At one time, she had been a brunette. He wondered what had happened to her hair.

His sense of smell heightened too. Sea salt and grime from the slave ship clung to her skin. Is this what he smelled like to Mandros and Sidrah? Otherworlds, he hoped not! "When we land, you need a bath."

Nym scowled at him indignantly.

He lowered himself to the ground so that Nym could climb onto his back. She clung to his spines, and he felt her heart pounding.

"Do not drop me, dragon."

Tornyth rumbled in pleasure. "I'll try not to."

Before Nym could open her mouth to say something sassy, Tornyth leapt into the sky. Clinging to Tornyth's back, Nym screamed. She flattened her body along his back so that he could feel her trembling along his spine.

"I think my ascent may have been a little fast."

"Ill-conceived snow lizard," Nym swore under her breath as Tornyth soared on the updraft. He enjoyed watching the island of Torqui grow to a small green dot. He did a lazy loop, taking in the ocean below. *Mandros hasn't taken me to learn how to fish yet*, he thought, feeling a pang of regret.

With a beat of his wings, he looked to the horizon and spotted the Ramian mainland. Using his tail as a rudder, he turned his body around and headed for home. He was careful to ensure that he flew higher as he neared the coastline to decrease the chances of any ships spotting him.

He flew along the land, searching out a few settlements that might be suitable. It seemed wise to look for a place where he could land in private. No point alerting nosy *vehyl*. His human was easily identifiable. Nym was right. He needed a shirt to cover up his distinctive markings.

He flew until he found a small forest area, which was close to a village. Nym would be able to walk to the village and get him a shirt, while he would be able to hide from curious human eyes. He also spotted a stream of running water where they could wash off the last few days of horror.

With a grace that belied his great size, Tornyth landed by the stream. Nym, he noticed with some amusement, slid from his back looking a little dazed. She patted his side absently and wandered over to the bush to vomit. Tornyth chortled as she wiped the sick from her face with her sleeve.

"Otherworlds, I'm not so good at heights as I assumed."

Tornyth grinned and ambled to the running water. Dipping his snout into the stream, he lapped up the delicious coolness to quench his thirst. Once he was sated, he blew his dragon breath over the water.

"Sidrah told me that dragons can heat bodies of water to bathe in," Tornyth said. "That was how she seduced her *vehyl* husband."

Nym raised an eyebrow. She walked over to where the water was bubbling. Dipping her hand into the water, she sighed in pleasure. "Are you seducing me, snow dragon?"

"No," Tornyth replied serenely. "You are too prickly for my human. And you stink."

Pretending to be outraged, she raised her hand, splashing Tornyth.

"*Vehyl* heart can have a bath when you go in search for a shirt to hide certain disfigurements." Tornyth turned away to find a place to curl up for a nap while he waited.

"Don't peek!" Nym cried after him.

"Wouldn't dream of it!"

Tornyth hadn't thought that Nym would have been the type of *vehyl* female that liked to bathe frequently. He was surprised how the shadows had lengthened upon her return.

For a moment, she sat beside him and patted his side, brushing her wet hair behind her ears.

Tornyth rumbled. "You smell better."

Nym ignored the jibe. "I'll head to the village and find you a shirt. It's not a long walk."

"Thank you."

Nym stood and stretched. She looked back at Tornyth, biting her lips. For a long moment, Tornyth didn't think she would speak. But she sucked in a deep breath and blurted, "Your scars aren't hideous."

"My human doesn't like to be reminded. His heart is still scarred."

Nym stroked the side of Tornyth's snout. "Sometimes a broken heart takes a long time to heal, scaled water-heater," she said with one last pat before striding off towards the village. Tornyth watched her go. He feared Nym might be going soft on him.

Once she was out of eyesight, Tornyth transformed back into Jodathyn, who made his way back to the stream. He stopped by the water's edge, testing it with his hand. Warm water bubbled around his fingertips. He was astonished that it was still a perfect temperature.

With the assurance he was completely alone, Jodathyn stripped before slipping into the water.

Now that his battered body was fully emerged, he understood why Nym had taken so long. As the water lapped around his sore muscles, he found himself relaxing. All the aches and pains from the last few days seemed to melt away into the water.

He closed his eyes and drifted away in a pleasant haze. Allowing himself to float on top of the water, he lost all track of time.

"Look at you, Mashikah the Damned, standing so blindly beside your mate, Mandros the Arrogant." The angry snarl of a yellow dragon jolted Jodathyn back into awareness.

Knowing that he was once more in the midst of a vision, he glanced around. He stood beside Mandros, who gave no indication that he was aware of his presence. Sidrah stood alongside another female dragon. Milky white eyes speared him where he stood. She swayed her head to the side, running her long pink tongue along her fangs.

"Mashikah the Damned is not so helpless that she can't teach you a lesson, little fool."

"You plan to take him for yourself, Mandros," the yellow dragon snarled, ignoring the disdainful, empty glare of Mashikah. "You may be pallu, *but you had no right to do so without consulting the dragon council."*

"I am sovereign, as you have said," Mandros replied. "Tornyth was mine to claim."

"So greedy," the yellow snapped. "Did you inform Roane? He's as adept as you in the mental arts, yet he's still heirless since the battle of Haven Bay."

An olive-green dragon with a crown of bronze stepped through the gathering crowd of dragons. Deep scars ran down his scaly face. "Indeed, Mandros hasn't spoken to me of Winter's Dragon. But he is a loyal friend and has my trust."

"Dragons born in the depths of winter are said to be more powerful. Are you sure this isn't another grasp for power from Mandros' clan?"

"The vehyl *is Pallarus," Sidrah rumbled. "Our blessed bloodline. He is for Pallarus to claim."*

The blind female dragon, Mashikah, snorted.

"And Mashikah, what say you to your mate's gall to take a dragon born of winter for himself?" The yellow dragon turned bright amber eyes towards Mandros' mate. He was baiting them, Tornyth realised. The yellow dragon was wanting a fight.

"Winter's Dragon within my family certainly isn't pleasing," Mashikah replied. "But that isn't the discussion we are having."

"Galgothmeg in Rama is a clear sign that we're on the precipice of war." A large male of molten gold scales stepped forward to stand beside Mandros.

"And here is Zapyr the Splendid, come in from the sea breeze to grace us with his presence." The yellow dragon stretched out his neck and snapped at the newcomer.

"Or was he keeping Deovyn away from our proceedings?" An orange dragon laughed to the side. "Lord Mandros should keep his own mynrell *in check before he takes on another."*

Zapyr's lip curled as he flashed his long white fangs.

"Peace, Zapyr," Mandros rumbled. "My mynrell *are already preparing to fly to war. And Deovyn hasn't been a hatchling for many long years. He does twice the service to our kind than yourself."*

Jodathyn had so many questions. He wanted to turn his face to Mandros and ask them. But before Jodathyn's eyes, Mandros' form melted away as if the green dragon had never been there. He was standing outside of an unfamiliar dragon home, high in a rocky mountain. The land about had many spires of rock and was barren.

"You hope this Tornyth will win us notoriety." The gold dragon stood before him.

"I don't want another bloodline claiming him for their own ... his power will ensure our continued survival and consolidates the power of our family," came Mandros deep rumbling voice from behind.

"No!" Jodathyn cried. "My fate isn't something for you to toy with. I'm not your weapon."

Mandros lifted his head, sniffing the air. "Are you here?"

Frightened by what Mandros might have planned for him, Jodathyn wrenched himself from the vision. Anger curled in his belly. He wouldn't be Mandros' pet to obey his every whim.

CHAPTER SEVEN

Jodathyn

The Village of Kudah

"What are you doing in my bathing spot?"

Shocked by the sudden intrusion, Jodathyn's eyes snapped opened. He floundered, dunking his head under the water. He sucked in a mouthful of water before he staggered to his feet, gasping for breath. He emerged coughing and splattering, shaking the water from his hair.

"I must say, you are making quite a spectacle of yourself."

"One would think a stranger might have more manners than to spy on a vulnerable man," Jodathyn wheezed, bringing a hand to his chest. Even the short trip under the water brought back the memories of his near drowning. He blinked in an attempt to ward off the feeling of dizziness and glared up at the one who dared interrupt his moment of peace.

The intruder was a young woman, whose thin pink lips were pressed together to contain her laughter. Cheeks burning, Jodathyn bent his knees and sunk further into the water. It was a terrible attempt to protect his modesty. Pathetic, really.

"She's impressed with us." Within him, Jodathyn could feel the dragon moving. Tornyth was pleased by the woman's attention.

"You're the one, sir, who is naked in a public bathing space."

"Yes, well, I usually bathe naked."

Jodathyn's eyes left the woman's lips and studied her attire. The bodice of her pale blue work dress was embroidered with bold colours. He could see a red scarf tucked into the pocket of her apron. Although the hem of her skirts was well worn, it was finer than the dresses he had seen the laundry maids in the palace wear. Her long black hair was braided into a crown upon her head. He concluded that she was middle-class.

"Pardon, miss. I wasn't aware I was trespassing." He lowered his eyes. The tattoo on his wrist itched. There was more to be concerned about than his modesty. "If you don't mind turning around ..."

"I'm not the fool who didn't keep my pants on." The woman glanced down at the pile of Jodathyn's clothes. Her lips curled in disgust, and her brown eyes pierced him with clear suspicion. "You don't have a shirt."

"I do not," Jodathyn agreed, willing his voice to remain steady. "Please, miss, I needed a place to rest and happened upon this stream."

"Ethirah."

"Excuse me?"

"My name is Ethirah."

"Look, Miss Ethirah, let me get out and I'll move on. I'm not wanting trouble."

"I'm not stopping you from getting out, dearie," Ethirah replied.

"Step out to her ..." Tornyth said. Jodathyn's dragon didn't seem to be bothered about being put on show.

"Someone's coming." Ethirah's head shot up, her head tilting to the side as she listened.

"That would be my companion," Jodathyn murmured. It would be best to assure Ethirah that Nym was not a threat. She didn't look like she could cause any problems, but Jodathyn had learned not to underestimate people.

"Jod! We're near Kudah. There are fighting bouts starting tomorrow. I thought I might enter to earn us some coin."

Nym came crashing towards them. To Jodathyn's mortification, she kept coming forwards until she was in view. She studied Ethirah curiously, and a sly, teasing smile lit her face.

"Seducing maidens. Really, Jod ... Remember our lessons: 'gentle, soft and sweet.'"

Jodathyn's embarrassment was complete. He cursed Nym and eyed the man's shirt she held within her grip.

"Don't look so coy," Nym said, laughing at Jodathyn's dilemma. She turned her attention to Ethirah. There was something predatory in her expression. Jodathyn shivered. He didn't like to think about what Nym might do if the intruder proved to be a danger. "I'm Nym Torkelle, born of Korkalie, and you are ..."

"Ethirah, barmaid of Kudah. I work for Curran Norrys, a Ramian." Much to Ethirah's credit, she lifted her chin. Her gaze didn't waver from Nym's hard glare. "I stumbled upon your handsome companion, who has yet to properly introduce himself. This is a public spot used for bathing."

"You heard the lady," Nym snapped, rounding her hard hazel eyes on to him. "Out. It's her turn."

"Turn around," Jodathyn said, gritting his teeth.

"Aren't you a prudish little highborn?" Nym teased. "Didn't you swim with other children when you were young?"

"No!" Jodathyn replied. His words came out more forceful than he intended. "Of course not!"

Nym scoffed. "Timid lizard."

"They are laughing at us." Tornyth stirred under Jodathyn's skin in agitation. *"Show them we aren't afraid."*

Trying to ignore his dragonlike thoughts, Jodathyn turned his head away. *"If they want to see, let them see. We are a strong son of the skies ... We shall not be shamed."*

Deep within his flesh, Tornyth stretched. His dragon instincts were nudging him to throw caution to the wind and step out from the water. Not knowing what was coming over him, Jodathyn stood and strode out of the stream.

Standing before Nym, naked as the day he was born, he held out his hand for the shirt. "I believe that is for me."

Nym was unable to make a sound in reply. She stared back open-mouthed at Jodathyn's boldness.

"You have the confidence of a Sionian man," Ethirah said.

"Confidence can be faked," Jodathyn replied with a toothy smile. He sauntered his way over to his discarded clothes to give them a view of his other side. Nym, he noticed, was refusing to look in his direction. Served her right. "I'm pretending you are ugly *male* servants. Enjoy your bath, Miss Ethirah."

Jodathyn kept his pace even as he strode through the wooded area. He would give the women some peace to get to know one another and enjoy gossiping about him. He trusted that Nym would alert him if Ethirah proved to be a threat.

Jodathyn's first instinct was to find a warm boulder to dry himself in the sun. Not wanting to be caught for the second time that day in such a scandalous and vulnerable position, he buried that instinct and dressed in his rags.

He felt burning shame as he recalled Ethirah's clear distaste. The young woman had thought him no more than a vagrant. Sighing, he conceded to the fact that perhaps he was closer to a vagrant than a royalborn prince.

"She knows."

Jodathyn shrugged his shoulders and huffed in defeat. "Knows who I am or knows we're escaped prisoners?"

Nym's lips puckered into a frown, making her seem more severe than she usually did. "Both," she said.

"My scars ..." Jodathyn grunted.

Nym's silence answered Jodathyn's lingering question.

"How did you explain the hot water?"

"Magic," Nym replied. "She's Sionian born. Apparently, magic is common."

"Sionian ..." Jodathyn murmured. He recalled the feast Kieryn had called to honour the visiting Sionian king. Their visitors had brought their own magicians, which had upset the majority of the great lords. He had loved every moment of their visit. By the time the Sionians left, he had interviewed every member of their delegation, including the Sionian king and his elderly uncle. "Of course Sionians are unafraid of magic."

"She might be asking you how you have Sionian magic," Nym warned. "I thought I would leave that one to you."

"It's not Sionian magic," Tornyth whispered. *"It's Ramian."*

Uncomfortable, Jodathyn rubbed at his forearms. The tattoo upon his skin itched. Nym's gaze followed his movements.

"The shirt is too big," she said.

"Rolling the sleeves would only reveal the tattoos. What's the story? You're some unsuspecting travelling fighting woman who has taken pity on a bumbling, smelly beggar?" Jodathyn held out his arms from his body. The sleeves hung limply over his hands.

"Nonsense. You'll come with me. I work for the innkeeper who owns the large establishment on the outskirts of Kudah. We shan't meet anyone upon the road."

Cringing, Jodathyn turned, finding he had forgotten about Ethirah's presence. She was standing only a few lengths away, watching him with her disconcerting gaze. He noted the famous Sionian red scarf weaved into her hair.

Jodathyn was a fool. Her deep copper complexion, high cheekbones, and colourful embellishments on her bodice were clear indications she was Sionian. He also noted with some amusement that her eyes were level with his chest, and he was by no means a tall man. There was a steel glint in her eyes, however, that clearly said she took no nonsense from anybody.

"That is very kind of you. But not ..."

"I can get more suitable clothing," Ethirah continued. "And I'm sure if you agree to work for your keep, a comfortable bed for the night."

Biting her lip, Nym eyed Jodathyn. "If I can enter the fighting bouts and win the coin, it will help us."

Jodathyn nodded, raising his chin. If he had to work for a good night's rest in a real human bed, then he would work like he had never done before. "I am unafraid of work."

Nym shrugged and indicated for Ethirah to show them the way.

The tavern was not far. The two girls walked ahead, Nym questioning Ethirah of the best roads to take in and out of Sion. Ethirah revealed that she was originally a silk merchant and was quite knowledgeable of the safest and quickest roads in Rama.

"You'll want to stay away from mountains and their villages," Ethirah said.

"Why?" The mountains had always intrigued Jodathyn. He had seen illustrations in books and heard tales how some of the peaks of mountains disappeared into the clouds. He had always desired to see them for himself.

Nym glanced over her shoulder at him. "Mountain people can be less welcoming."

Ethirah nodded her head. "Bad things happen in the mountains. Ramian mountains are cursed."

Jodathyn considered Ethirah's strange words. Was this a Sionian belief he hadn't stumbled upon? He glanced around the wooded road. From his studies, Jodathyn knew Kudah was famous for its mines. The lack of mountains perplexed him. "Where are the mines?"

"The mining road can be accessed from the far edge of town. Not here," Ethirah said. "Here's the tavern: The Guardsman's Rest."

The tavern was much larger than the one he had visited in Pallaryn. Forests surrounded the long, rectangular building. Around the back, he spied the stables for out-of-town visitors. To the far left was a place locals could tether their horses. A pleasant garden, with twisting paths and benches, completed the homely look of the tavern.

"It's quiet here, so we attract discerning travellers who are looking for a hot meal."

Looking down at his dishevelled state, Jodathyn sighed.

"I'm sure some of my brother's clothing will suit you well enough." Ethirah eyed Nym. "The weather will turn in a few short weeks. Soon you'll freeze. We've warmer cloaks and blankets."

"This is all very kind of you," Jodathyn muttered.

"You might not be thanking me come morning." Ethirah grinned up at him. "Curran!"

Striding forward, Ethirah pushed the door open with a flourish. Worried, Jodathyn glanced around the tavern as he stepped over the threshold. There wasn't a patron in sight.

A muscled man with a ready smile on his bearded face greeted them. Jodathyn studied him, feeling nerves ravage his gut. The stranger's piercing eyes slid over Nym's defensive stance to him. The warm smile slipped from his face; his brow furrowed. "Ettie, what have you brought home, girl?"

"These travellers require safety and anonymity," Ethirah said. "We've helped those in need before. This is Nym Torkelle, born of Korkalie and—"

"Jodathyn Pallarus, born of Pallaryn ... the Son of the Crown. High King Hadryn's second born."

Alarmed at being quickly identified, Jodathyn took a step back. He considered the merits of turning tail and running. He swallowed past the lump in his throat and clenched his fists to stop his trembling.

"He doesn't mean any harm," Tornyth whispered. *"I sense no malice in him."*

"Yes," Ethirah murmured. "I brought home a real Ramian prince."

"I'm not ..."

"A prince," Nym finished. "We know."

"I didn't think you would want me to leave him out there to fend for himself," Ethirah continued.

"Do not be afraid." Curran lifted a giant hand, reaching out to grasp Jodathyn's shoulder. He dragged Jodathyn, unresisting, into the light. "Dragons bless the Otherworld. You favour your father and grandsire."

Jodathyn stared up at Curran, his jaw slack. He had been compared to his father many times before, but never his grandfather.

"Once upon a time, I was a guardsman. Only a season before your birth, an injury forced me to leave your father's service. I came home to a traveller's inn."

Jodathyn fiddled with the fraying ends of his shirt. "My nephew, the Crown Prince. Have you heard any rumours of his whereabouts? He was snatched by kidnappers, and we've been running for our lives since."

Curran shook his head. "Lad, if I knew where the princeling was, I would be bringing him to safety. What's happened? Rumours are circulating that you have kidnapped the boy."

Jodathyn shook his head. "The kidnappers were meant to kill him and frame me for his murder. I managed to free Carvelle but at Corlyn, we ..."

"We were separated and taken to the prison ships," Nym said.

"We escaped," Jodathyn continued, feeling a spasm of horror in his muscles as his body remembered the daily beatings. He scratched at his bronzed skin with his nails.

Curran grasped Jodathyn's forearm, stopping his frantic movements. Pulling back Jodathyn's sleeve, he inspected the tattoo and the raw skin around it in silence.

Jodathyn snatched his arm back, attempting to retreat. His eyes were wide. In the back of his mind, he panicked that this man could send him back to the prison ships.

"Scratching isn't going to remove the tattoo." Curran held up his hand. "In Kudah and coastal towns, keep your tattoos hidden at all times. Do not trust anyone."

Jodathyn could only stare up at the ex-guardsman. He felt a longing to rip at his skin but refrained.

"Those tattoos are an advertisement that you are a runaway criminal. This could get you sent straight to the docks." Curran's face wrinkled, and then he cleared his throat. "Don't fear me. I will not betray you."

"He understands," Nym interrupted.

Curran's eyes narrowed. His gazed flicked to Nym before he returned his attention back to Jodathyn. "Do you need a medic?"

Jodathyn shook his head. "I am well, sir."

"Ettie, take him upstairs and get him some of your brother's clothes. Jodathyn, nothing in this world is free. I expect your help in the tavern tonight. When serving, you'll go by the name of Locke, born of Belrah. Not too many in these parts would have seen the late king."

"As you wish, sir." Jodathyn nodded as Ethirah gestured he should follow her. Their footsteps sounded heavy as they ascended the stairs and walked along the landing. She guided Jodathyn to the first room.

"You can sleep here tonight. This is where my brother slept."

Swinging the door wide, Ethirah let Jodathyn step through the doorway. She followed him and immediately opened a chest at the end of a sturdy looking bed. In silence, Jodathyn watched as she pulled out some clean trousers, shirts and a jerkin. "I'll take some to Nym downstairs," Ethirah said, handing Jodathyn a pile of clothes.

"Thank you," Jodathyn whispered. He smiled and nodded, unsure why such a simple act had touched him so. He ran his fingers along the material. It was Sionian made, he decided, clean and almost new.

"Sleep. Tonight, the tavern will be full because of the fighting bouts." Ethirah smiled at him. Her eyes held a glossy sheen. "Wouldn't want the High King to lose his brother, now would we?"

"Ethirah ... wait." Jodathyn fumbled with the bundle of clothes. He dipped his head, feeling like a fool, but he didn't know why. He felt his cheeks redden. "The name you gave us is Ramian. Do you have a Sionian name?"

Ethirah paused by the door and stared back with a smile. "My friends call me Ettie ... In Sionian, my name is Et-hir."

"Et-hir ... *honeybee* ... It's a beautiful name. Is this what you prefer?"

Et-hir blinked at him. "Not many Ramians have asked me this."

"I'm highborn, forgive me, but the importance of names has been instilled in me from a young age," Jodathyn murmured.

"Then call me Et-hir," she said, returning Jodathyn's smile. "Ettie, if you're my friend."

The door clicked behind her.

Later that evening, Jodathyn stood at the bottom of the stairs, staring in astonishment how full the out-of-the-way tavern was. Wondering what Curran was expecting him to do, he stood at the bottom, gazing out at the patrons.

Travellers from all over Rama were congregated under one roof. There were some blond heads from the north and those with gleaming eyes and rich sepia skin from the western regions. A couple of Sionian traders sat together, whispering and drinking, their long flowing hair and deep red scarves marking them as foreigners. In the corner, he caught sight of a minstrel that was strumming on a lute. Everyone was in good cheer.

"Evening, Locke," Et-hir said, coming to stand by his elbow. She pushed a tray of food into his hands. "Follow my lead."

Grasping the tray so that his knuckles turned white at the pressure, Jodathyn followed Et-hir to the table of Sionian traders. His skin prickled.

Jodathyn had never appreciated the anonymity of servers. Even as Et-hir greeted the guests in their native tongue, they didn't look up to acknowledge him. He placed the plates down, nodded his head politely, and followed Et-hir back to the kitchens.

"I didn't think Sionians travelled much further south than Silverdyne," Jodathyn said.

"You're misinformed," Et-hir replied briskly, pushing another tray in Jodathyn's direction. "I came to Kudah with a troop of Sionian silk merchants, and I never left."

"Don't you miss home?"

Et-hir laughed. "I have travelled far and wide and explored many places. Home is where I rest my head. Who knows where I will travel next?"

Jodathyn smiled at the thought. It must be wonderful to have such freedom, to see the world and have no constraints. "What about your brother?"

Curran decided to come barging through the kitchens. He took one look at Et-hir's crestfallen face and Jodathyn's befuddled expression. "The guests won't feed themselves," he barked.

Apologising profusely, Jodathyn resisted the urge to roll up his sleeves. In his haste to leave the kitchens, he stumbled over his own feet. He froze as the patrons near the kitchen turned to stare at him. Then, slowly, he straightened his posture and moved towards a table with two older men.

"Settle down lad." A man with a balding head laughed as Jodathyn settled the plate before him.

"Any chance of Curran's famous ale, boy?" his companion on his other side asked. He tucked straight into the stew, mopping it up with his bread as he ate with gusto.

"Careful with these two." Jodathyn's inner dragon's hackles rose.

Realising he was serving two local lawmen, Jodathyn flinched at the question; dread curled in his belly. He eyed them, imagining they could see the tattoo on his wrist denouncing him as a criminal. The muscles in his body stiffened. He opened his mouth to speak but to his horror, he could not form any words.

"This is Locke, born of Belrah. He fell ill on his travels and has taken rest at our inn," Et-hir said, rescuing him. She came to the table with a mug of ale for each of the lawmen.

"Belrah," the elder of the lawman mumbled. "Heard they lost some criminals in the forests. What do you make of it, Locke?"

"I don't rightly know what to think," Jodathyn muttered. "How does a group of well-trained men lose a ragged band of thieves?"

"Ha! He's a clever one, he is, Floyde," the younger lawman said, lifting his cup in his friend's direction. "A quick thinker is always trouble."

"Never you mind, Lawman Ripley. Did you hear about the dead men in Sant Burgundy?" Lawman Floyde asked. Even in the dim light of the tavern, Jodathyn could see the older man was waiting to see his reaction.

"I think that is enough of that talk," Et-hir told them with her hands upon her hips.

"Yes, of course," Lawman Floyde replied. "A more pleasant conversation ... You didn't give us a family name, Locke of Belrah."

"Manideep." A deep longing tore through Jodathyn's chest as he spoke his manservant's name. Averting his gaze, he buried the fierce pain that had lodged itself within his chest. Oh, how he wished that he had been born a Manideep and not Pallarus. "Locke Manideep."

"Such a finicky lot, you Ramians. Your fascination with names and hometowns is singularly most odd," Et-hir said, sending Jodathyn a warning look.

The lawmen nodded and returned to their meals, no longer interested in the young stranger serving them. The conversation was over. Jodathyn sighed in relief and stepped away from their table.

As he returned to the kitchen to grab more food to serve, a minstrel started a bawdy song. Over the bard's singing and the crowd's cries of glee, there wasn't opportunity to start a conversation. This suited Jodathyn fine. He didn't want to keep telling tall tales to keep his identity secret.

Halfway through the night, Curran offered him a bowl of steaming stew and told him to find a place to sit and enjoy his meal. Thankful, Jodathyn meandered over to a small, quiet corner to watch everyone with rapt attention.

"A prisoner ship went down off the coast," a man's voice grumbled behind him. Jodathyn leaned back. A quick glance over his shoulder confirmed it was a table of locals.

"So I heard. The lawmen are looking into the captain. Seems like he had boarded two extra prisoners that weren't on the manifest ..."

There was a grunt and the sound of a chair scraping along the floor. "The captain paid a lot of gold to have those unfortunates. The magistrate of Thrangul is awfully tight-lipped."

"They were no ordinary prisoners."

"What do you think? Were they being silenced? Wonder what great lord they threatened."

"Well, we'll never know. They'll be resting in watery graves now."

Shuddering, Jodathyn hunched his shoulders and refused to look in their direction. His worried expression must have got Curran's attention, for in the next moment, the innkeeper was sliding in a chair beside him.

"Are you well, Locke?"

Jodathyn shifted and nodded his head in the direction of the table behind him. The men were still debating who the mysterious prisoners might be. Curran brought his finger to his lips to signal Jodathyn to remain quiet about the matter.

"Drink up, lad," Curran said, handing him a mug of ale. "You're not a bad worker."

"Were you expecting worse?" Jodathyn queried, staring down at the meaty stew and the lumps of vegetables.

"Perhaps," Curran said with a smile. "Eat up. You need your strength to recover."

"What's happened to Nym?"

"She's headed to town to enter tomorrow's fighting bouts. It's good coin if she can win."

Jodathyn's eyes wandered over to the minstrel who seemed to be teasing a couple with a cheeky song. Around the couple, everyone was laughing and clapping. Curran leaned in closer.

"Tell your brother you must have a medic see you."

Jodathyn shook his head. "I don't require a healer."

"Locke, I have seen hardened men crumble under the pressure of what you have been through," Curran muttered under his breath as he rubbed his brow in agitation.

"What do you mean?" Jodathyn asked. "Have you seen escaped—"

"Hush," Curran growled in warning.

Jodathyn shook his head, mopping up the remainder of his stew with a hunk of bread. "I'm not keen to talk about my situation."

"That's the reason why you need a medic. Trust a man that has seen too much in his lifetime." Curran stood, clapping him on the back. "Back to work with you when you're done here. The night is young."

Jodathyn finished his meal and went straight to the kitchen to help with the piling up of dishes. It was early morning when he crept upstairs to seek his bed. With how hard he had worked, he expected that sleep would come easily. But when his head hit his pillow, he found himself staring at the ceiling. Sleep eluded him.

The talk with Curran had churned up some uneasy memories of the prison ship. Jodathyn tried to forget the sound of the cane whooshing through the air to strike him. Every time he thought his body might finally relax, he felt the flaring pain of the beatings he endured. Then came the memory of insatiable hunger and sea sickness. Anytime he closed his eyes, he could see the red of the first mate's blood spattered over the cell. He could smell and feel the blood coating his face and eyelashes. The tang of the man's blood was in his mouth.

An incoherent cry caught in Jodathyn's throat as he sat upright in bed. Knowing he would not find any rest, he threw off the covers and padded his way downstairs. The wood flooring of the tavern was cold on his bare feet, but he resisted the urge to return to his rooms. Like a wraith, he stepped through the front door and wandered to the dusty road.

Jodathyn stood in the moonlight, staring in the direction of where he thought Pallaryn was. "Please leave me alone," he whispered in the dark. He knew it was his imagination, he did, but he could see the apparition of the first mate. The dead man stumbled towards him, throat cut open in an ugly red arc. The moment he had handed Nym the dagger, he had felt the heavy press of responsibility for the man's murder. Jodathyn could feel the cold hands of panic gripping him as dead eyes pierced his soul.

Behind the first mate stumbled the kidnapper from the woods. Around his neck, he still wore Jodathyn's leather belt. His fingers clawed around his neck as his eyes bulged. He collapsed upon the road, writhing in the dirt.

"Go away!"

A warm hand grasped his shoulder. Jodathyn shuddered as he sagged, and hands propped him up as his legs gave way underneath him. He sucked in shallow breaths as if he had been drowning.

"Hush, lad, it's over now. You're safe."

"I'm sorry."

Jodathyn was wrapped in a fierce hug. His cheek was pressed against the abrasive material of a man's jerkin.

"Whatever you are seeing, it's not there."

Jodathyn shook his head, pushing his way out of Curran's embrace. The barkeep looked down upon him, his eyes glinting with an emotion that Jodathyn couldn't place.

"Why did you come out to me?" Jodathyn whispered.

"Nym told me a little about the ships," Curran replied. "It'll take some time to heal."

"I can't go home like this," Jodathyn mumbled. His misery was complete. The defilement of the tattoos was bad enough. If the great lords ever found out that his mind was broken …

"Of course you can."

"Not like this." Jodathyn rubbed his forearm. He knew the rubbing would not erase the ink, but he couldn't help himself. "I will only bring shame and dishonour."

"The dishonour to house Pallarus is not of your doing." Curran reached out to still Jodathyn's hands. The barman's fingers were warm and calloused. Jodathyn tried to pull away, but Curran held him firm.

"Kieryn can't accept this …"

"He will …"

"I killed a man. Two men … I can still taste his blood." Jodathyn's eyes flicked up, expecting to see revulsion in Curran's face. What he saw was pity. Wrenching his hands from Curran's grip, Jodathyn stared down the darkened road. All he could see was his victims standing before him and raising accusing fingers.

"Sometimes death is necessary if you want to live."

Jodathyn trembled at the thought.

"You need to see a medic."

"Otherworlds, hang your medic," Jodathyn cried. "Kieryn can never know about this. You must promise …"

Curran lifted an eyebrow. "Must I?"

"I demand—"

"Jodathyn, it's best that you tell your brother everything before he finds out through another source. These things have a way of eventually finding you out."

Jodathyn shook his head. "He'll be angry."

"A king's anger is a terrible thing to behold," Curran replied. "But you need to allow your brother an opportunity to help you."

"You don't understand," Jodathyn gasped. "You have never seen the look in his eyes every time he thinks about … my disfigurement. It's unbearable. This–this will be worse!"

"Shall I write to the trained medics in the palace then? I still have contacts among the guardsmen."

"The King's Guard are loyal only to the king. If you write to them, they will inform my brother."

"I'm very well aware of the loyalties of the King's Guard," Curran said. He wrapped his arm around Jodathyn's shoulder. "You'll need help and guidance. There's no shame in that. Come now, it's cold out here."

Jodathyn looked down at his bare feet and wriggled his toes. They felt numb. In a strange way, he liked the feeling. "I am fine. Nym is fine."

"You can't compare yourself with Nym. She's dealing with her circumstances in her own way."

"I'm in the position where I can't afford to be affected. I cannot allow myself to feel or hurt, lest I injure my family more."

Curran tugged on Jodathyn's arm. "If you want my opinion, that is a whole load of dragon dung. I watched your father fall prey to his demons. Don't make the same mistake he did."

CHAPTER EIGHT

Illeanah

The Citadel of Pallaryn

Illeanah skimmed her fingers along Jodathyn's elegant handwriting, then closed her book with a definite thump. The memory of Jodathyn gifting her the rare book on Sionian sciences still left a warm glow in her chest. She could still see his excited grin as she opened the book for the first time to read the dedication. He had always been kind and thoughtful.

When she had questioned how he was able to gift her the book, Jodathyn had toasted to her good health. As he had no coin of his own, she could only conclude that he had convinced the king to allow him to purchase such a generous gift.

Illeanah's thoughts returned to the High Autumn Festival. Jodathyn's behaviour at the festival had been irrational. It wasn't like him. And when she had called him names … he had allowed it, remaining silent, his expression broken. If only she could turn back time, she wouldn't have left him in a fit of anger. She should have swallowed her fury and demanded answers from him.

Her childhood friend was somewhere out in the wilds. And here she was in the citadel, alone with bitter regrets. Tears filled her eyes as she grasped at the gold chain her father's spy, Ruevyn, had in his possession. She had been surprised to see him, considering he was involved in a murder and had run from her father's service. But she had shrugged it off. Perhaps he had thought to crawl back on his belly to earn more coin from her father's coffers.

Initially, she meant to do exactly what she had told Ruevyn. Return the chain to Jodathyn's rooms. But she found herself reluctant to do so. It stayed around her neck, waiting for its owner to come home.

Her fingers tightened around the chain as tears threatened to spill over her cheeks. It was futile, but she wished Jodathyn was sitting opposite her, sharing wine and witty conversation. When she heard that Lord Solan had commanded that Jodathyn be killed on the spot, it had taken all of her strength not to react strongly. The thought that she may never hear his voice again pierced her heart like a dagger.

Oh, she loved Jodathyn Pallarus, Illeanah realised. But not in the way she had always anticipated. From childhood, Jodathyn had been a loyal companion. She had always thought that she would grow to love him more and they would possibly one day marry. Jodathyn Pallarus would only ever be a cherished brother. Nothing more.

"Tears are not for a Whitoak."

Illeanah let her fingertips linger on the beautiful leather binding of her book, trying not to let her vision blur with yet more tears. Her father continued to watch her wordlessly, a deep frown on his face.

"I can't imagine why he was so determined to destroy our friendship," Illeanah replied. She lifted her chin and met her father's challenging gaze.

Regally she stood and poured wine for them both. The frown on her father's face deepened as she passed the goblet to him and he noticed which book she had left on her chair. She reflected that he looked more like a grim shadow with each passing hour.

"You need not worry, Father," Illeanah said. She couldn't prevent a note of bitterness entering her tone. "I do not love Jodathyn the way you fear."

Lord Whitoak snorted, lifting the goblet to his lips.

"He's a good man, Father. The thought of losing him is unbearable ... He's my kindred spirit. He's the brother I love dearly, though we don't share parents."

"Jodathyn is fond of you."

Illeanah didn't like the way her father said the word *fond*. "Jodathyn is in love with the idea of me. Few people have ever shown him kindness ... He deserves a woman who can love him deeply."

"And the dragon?" Her father didn't look convinced.

"Perhaps we should have faith in Jodathyn," Illeanah answered. "There has to be a way to keep him safe from the dragon."

"The herbal tonics were designed to keep us safe from *him*. When King Hadryn spared Jodathyn's life, Kieryn promised the tonics would be faithfully administered so that any gifting in that boy would be smothered. Now we are on the edge of a great divide."

"That's hardly Jodathyn's fault. He is the kindest soul in Pallaryn. He's a good man."

"Kindness and goodness don't provide protection."

In dismay, Illeanah watched as her father drank slowly from his goblet. She knew he wasn't savouring the tart wine. It was a tactic he used with the lesser nobles, and the use of it now infuriated her. Silence, he had taught her, could be used as a weapon. She had seen it happen before, men crumbling and revealing more to her father than they intended to. They panicked, and in their eagerness to fill the void with something other than silence, they betrayed their own confidence. Raising her chin, Illeanah stared back. Whitoaks didn't crumble.

Illeanah knew that her father claimed she was his greatest achievement. Unlike other fathers, he had encouraged her love of learning, relished it, used it to boast amongst his peers. If her father still thought of her as a silly child who could be manipulated, he was sadly mistaken. He had raised her to think for herself, to be as stubborn as her poor dead mother.

Gliding across the room, Illeanah stepped out of her father's line of sight. She moved towards the large window that looked down upon the castle gardens. Her fingers grazed the wilting leaves of a rose that sat in an expensive glass vase. Unbidden, her gifting warmed her fingertips and a leaf rejuvenated.

Gasping at her carelessness, Illeanah jerked her head around.

"What is it, daughter?" Thankfully, her father had not been paying attention. He had not seen what she had done. Hands shaking, she plucked the single lush leaf from the stalk and crushed it. "Illeanah?"

Illeanah knew that she needed to say something. She leaned over the windowsill, searching for the right words to say. Below in the courtyard, several lords had gathered. She peered down, trying to make out their faces. "There's a disturbance in the courtyard below."

A richly dressed stranger paraded around the gathering nobles. He was a tall man, with broad shoulders. From the way he moved, Illeanah judged him as a type of man who believed in his own superiority. While Solan looked suitably unimpressed, Kamoore was rubbing his hands and jittering on the spot. Although it was clear that the three lords knew each other, Illeanah did not recognise him. She had spent many seasons visiting Pallaryn and thought she knew the identity of every great lord. It paid to be aware of the names of those who may oppose you and your family.

"Father, Solan and Kamoore are in the courtyard greeting a stranger. Do you suppose you should seek him out also?"

With a groan, her father moved from his seat to join her at the window. His face fell and stilled as he looked out upon the lords in the garden. "Lord Frayn is nowhere to be seen. One would think he would be eager to curry favour with a new pompous simpleton."

Illeanah turned to her father. Lord Frayn, the youngest member of the king's council, was one of the most common victims of her father's barbed tongue. Since the upstart thought to ask for her hand in marriage, he had become her father's favourite target. An only child of an ancient and noble house, he had been quite spoiled. Her father's disdain for him ate away at his confidence like acid. And Illeanah felt the first stirrings of pity for the man. It seemed since the king's sudden departure from Pallaryn, Frayn had become a recluse.

Illeanah tilted her head to study her father's expression. He returned her gaze; his mask was one of unbothered neutrality. He could have been a statue except for the small throbbing vein in his neck.

"Thylyssa."

"You know this man?"

"He's a western lord who fell out of favour a few years back. The king banished him from Pallaryn on the pain of death. Frayn will want to stay away from him ..."

"If Thylyssa is here—"

The door to her father's study opened and shut with a clatter. Startled, Illeanah whipped around to see who had the audacity to enter without invitation. Not many would approach her father so boldly and risk his anger. Being the king's favourite certainly had advantages.

"Will Hartcurt, I hope you have an explanation."

Will leaned against the closed door as he faced them. His normally bright countenance had fallen; Illeanah could see that his hands were trembling as his expression darkened. Will closed his eyes, and Illeanah thought he might have been mumbling a prayer through his parted lips.

"What has gotten into you?" Illeanah asked, shooting her father a glare to say she would handle the imp Will Hartcurt. "I hope you aren't here to seduce me in front of my father."

Will's eyes snapped open, and he regarded her with open amusement. Whatever had shaken him, he swept it from his mind. Before Illeanah's eyes, he went from a quivering mess to a poised lord. She briefly wondered if Will's absent father had entrenched the use of societal masks in him as well.

"I wouldn't align myself with house Whitoak even if it was my only option." Will grinned, flashing his perfectly white teeth. With his deep sepia skin tone and his confident posture, he certainly inspired jealousy from other young noblemen.

"How dare you!"

"We don't have time to quibble," Will said. He stepped further into the room, looking her father in the eyes. "I'm helping you for the king's sake. I wouldn't be weeping tears of mourning if you are arrested."

"Arrested? What nonsense are you speaking?"

Will's expression remained grim. "Thylyssa is here. It can only mean that a coup is planned."

Illeanah's father snorted in disdain.

Will frowned. "Thylyssa is a brutal man, Lord Whitoak. Your time is up. You have to leave."

Illeanah turned to stare at her father, who seemed unaffected by the news.

Indeed, he crossed his arms against his chest. "I have nothing to hide from His Majesty."

The muscles around Will's jaw tightened. He seemed frustrated and eager to leave. Illeanah had to wonder why he stayed. "Lord Whitoak, they plan to arrest Illeanah for giving Jodathyn's servant your horse."

Illeanah gasped; she could feel the blood draining from her face. No one knew what she had done, not even her father. She had been sure of it. How had Will come by this information?

"Illeanah, you also spoke to a young man at the gates who had seen Jodathyn. You took the evidence and did not seek out Lord Solan."

"*Illeanah*!"

Tilting her chin up, Illeanah met her father's incredulous stare. She could see it in his dark eyes; it shocked him that she would ever contemplate doing something so reckless.

"It gets worse, Lord Whitoak," Will continued. He seemed to be eyeing the older lord as if debating the wisdom of his actions. "The council has accused the king of delaying Donatein Manideep's trial and allowing another of Jodathyn's servants to escape the citadel. The messenger you sent on His Majesty's behalf had been waylaid near Habron. Solan has produced a letter written in the king's own hand. A letter which asks for help to save Jodathyn's life. In it the king details his worries of Jodathyn's power and he asks, since the Sionians are unafraid of magic, if Jodathyn might find sanctuary in Sion. The payment the king offered the Sionian king for such a service is significant."

"Go on."

"The council plans on arresting the king on the grounds of treason and removing anyone who will support him. To complicate matters, one of the king's manservants found a half-written letter to the king of Sion and gave it to Solan."

"I sent that letter," her father interrupted, waving a dismissive hand. He started to turn away, but what Will said next caused him to pause.

"I interrupted the king writing a second letter after Donatein Manideep was executed. He was determined to get Jodathyn out of the country. I can only surmise he had forgotten about it with everything happening. We don't have much time; the queen is in grave danger, and she is not in any condition to be put in the dungeons."

"What would you know of the queen's condition?" Whitoak barked.

"You and I both know her unborn child is at risk," Will replied.

"The queen is *pregnant*?" Illeanah was a little surprised. Traditionally, house Pallarus announced a pregnancy immediately. That the queen was with child and the king hadn't said anything was unusual.

"Obviously," Will replied with a roll of his eyes.

"You're going to kidnap the queen," Whitoak snapped.

"No," Will said. Illeanah could see a vein in his temple thrumming. "With or without you, Lord Whitoak, I plan on escaping the citadel with a pregnant queen. I cannot stay if Thylyssa is here."

"Ran into trouble with Thylyssa, did you?" Illeanah did not like the cruel edge her father's tone had taken.

"You can say that," Will snapped. "I'm the reason he was banished. All this time arguing isn't helping. I have some King's Guardsmen that are going to assist ... I hate to leave them behind."

"The King's Guard?"

"It pays to be friendly to those with different skills," Will replied. "Now, do you have any weapons?"

"Whatever for?" Illeanah asked.

Will raised an eyebrow. "I guess we'll stop at my rooms on the way."

"We most certainly will not!"

"Of course, the incredibly chaste and noble daughter of the great Lord Hallidyn Whitoak wouldn't want to be seen with such as me."

Illeanah made a disgusted noise in the back of her throat. One thing was for sure. She didn't want to go anywhere with Will Hartcurt. Who knew what nefarious plans he had?

"I'm not planning anything but escaping Pallaryn before it falls."

Taken aback by Will's quick response, Illeanah drew herself to her full height. "What possible protection could a man like you offer us?"

Will turned away from them. "I am the king's spy, the one he hid from all others. If you paused to think for a moment, Lady Illeanah, you would have realised I know things that not even your esteemed father is privy to. You can either believe my reputation or you can roll the dice and take a chance I might be able to protect you."

"Go with him, daughter."

Illeanah turned towards her father, her mouth agape. "You want me to go with Will?"

"Yes. One last kiss goodbye, daughter, and go."

"Aren't you coming?"

"Go with Will and help the queen. She will need a woman with her. I'll go to find our king."

Illeanah was too shocked to move. She parted her lips to draw in a breath and found that she couldn't speak. She watched helplessly as her father took a step closer and pulled her to him. His hands ran down her long hair. "Tie your hair back, daughter. It wouldn't do for it to hinder you in a fight."

"Father, please ..."

"Goodbye, daughter. Flee to Androssah if you must. I'll see you again."

Illeanah had to wonder if it was the lighting in the room or her imagination, but she saw tears gathering in her father's eyes. The next moment his facial expression hardened as he looked up at Will. "Look after my daughter, or I'll feed you to my dogs."

Exhaling, Will dipped his head and left the room muttering, "If Jodathyn's pets were anything to go by, I don't have much to fear."

Illeanah found herself pressing her lips against her father's bearded cheek.

"No tears."

Illeanah turned and followed after Will. He was waiting for her just outside.

"This way."

Helpless, Illeanah stepped out into the corridors. She glanced about. Since the prince's disappearance, everything had been quiet. She remembered the days she would have loved the palace to be calm so that she might study in peace. Now the stillness left her anxious.

Will had the good grace not to say anything to her as he led her to his chambers. He walked three paces ahead, his head held high.

When he stopped by a door and opened it, he said, "You can either stay out here or come in … either way, it doesn't bother me."

Illeanah critically surveyed Will's bedchamber as she stepped over the threshold. It was small, cramped and sparsely furnished. She was expecting something a little more ostentatious.

"I'm not the king's favourite, Illeanah," Will said, barely hiding his amusement. "I'm frugal with my coin. Being smart with money was the one thing my father taught me."

"I'm not judging your decorating tastes," Illeanah protested.

Will glanced up at her, his shrewd eyes glinting as his lips twitched. He turned, gathering up an armful of cloaks, which he strode across the room with and dumped into Illeanah's arms. "I care very little about the judgement of others."

"You were uproariously drunk at the Autumn Festival. I saw you dumping a goblet of wine down Jodathyn!"

Will chuckled, shaking his head. "You're not as clever as you think you are, Lady Whitoak. Was I drunk, or was I doing the job His Majesty pays me to do?"

Illeanah harrumphed. "These are men's cloaks."

"Out on the road you'll be glad of the warmth, my lady," Will replied as he passed her. In his hands he held a sword and a dagger. He placed the dagger on top of the pile of cloaks with a self-satisfied smirk.

Illeanah wanted to scream in frustration. She wouldn't be taken in by Will's handsome features. She was smarter than the other women at court. Will was a flirt and a danger. He wasn't like Jodathyn.

Chapter Nine

Orion

The Village of Halbeth

Orion gathered his weapons as Voran did a quick search of the bodies. Prince Carvelle sidled closer, a puzzled expression on his face while he observed the red-haired giant.

"Careful with him!" Carvelle cried as Voran bent with a groan to pick up the still unconscious Theo. Dashing forward to help, Orion assisted their new companion to slump the thief's prone body into the saddle of his warhorse. Voran seemed intent on ignoring the prince's stare and heaved himself into the saddle behind Theo.

"My companions are Orion Maysden, born of Silverdyne, and Theo Torkelle, born of Korkalie. They've been looking after me," Prince Carvelle said.

Voran huffed.

"Your stallion is even bigger than Zoryn," Carvelle said as Orion helped him onto the back of the grey stallion, seeming unaware that Voran did not wish to converse with him. "What's his name?"

"He's a horse," Voran grunted. "He doesn't need a name."

"I'll call him Zyan," Carvelle replied with a nod.

Voran scoffed.

"His Highness is fond of *z* names," Orion said. He glanced over to Voran. His likeness to his cousin was uncanny, but that was where the likeness finished. Perhaps it was uncharitable, but Orion wished he was Valt accompanying him. He missed the company of Valt.

Unblinking, Carvelle continued to stare. "Zyan is the perfect name for your great big red stallion."

Voran sighed heavily.

"You served Uncle Jodathyn?" Carvelle's golden eyes lit up in admiration. Orion winced at the clear hero worship on the young boy's face. From the palace grumblings, Orion hadn't been able to glean too much information about Valt's predecessor. But what he had heard was that he wasn't a man to place one's trust in.

"You shouldn't ignore Prince Carvelle," Orion admonished.

Slowly Voran turned his head and curled his lip at Orion. His bushy eyebrows drew together in an irritated frown. Then his hard hazel eyes swivelled to Carvelle, who was looking up at him.

"I served your uncle, Jodathyn, and then I was dismissed," Voran muttered. He turned his dark gaze to Orion. "How long have you served Jodathyn?"

"Only a few seasons. You?"

"Six years of my life. One blasted mistake, and I was removed from my post ... My reputation was left in tatters. Worse, I wasn't allowed to say farewell or see for myself the boy would survive."

"*Survive?* What type of mistake did you make?"

"Didn't Donatein tell you?" There was bitterness and hurt in Voran's voice, and his hazel eyes were cold. "The old man thought he was the only one who loved Jodathyn."

"Well, Jodathyn and house Pallarus need your help now," Orion replied. With the whisper of rebellion on the wind, an extra sword would always be welcome. If Voran proved to be a nuisance, Orion could find a way to cut ties with him later.

Voran stared unseeing ahead, his jaw clenched as he rested his fists against his knees.

"What about Jod? I doubt you'll find him much changed," Orion insisted.

"You call him Jod?"

"You can't tell me you haven't ever used his moniker," Orion said with a nonchalant shrug. "I've heard plenty of guards call him Jod when no highborns are around to hear."

"Tell me, Orion, what are you doing out here with the Crown Prince?"

"He shot a man for me. Right between the eyes!" Carvelle cried from the front of the steed.

Orion tried to hush him as he answered Voran's question. "I do not know if that is within my capacity to answer."

Voran regarded Orion for a moment. "Then perhaps you can tell me where Jodathyn is."

Orion sighed and fiddled with the reins of the horse.

"Someone took Uncle Jod away. I miss him terribly."

Orion patted the prince's hair down and cringed. It had been difficult for the young boy. Now and then Orion had to remind himself that Carvelle was only six summers old. They were all under strain and afraid for their lives.

"By who?" There was a steely edge to Voran's voice. His words held the same flinty quality that Valt's had when Orion overheard him discussing Jodathyn's injuries after his tavern misadventure. Jodathyn was key to convincing Voran to join them. It seemed that his master had a habit of collecting older men who were protective of him. Considering the trouble Jodathyn got himself into, it wasn't a bad trait.

"Probably the same people who kidnapped and tried to kill me," Carvelle answered, with the blunt honesty only children possessed. "He's coming back for me."

Orion turned his gaze to the larger man and shook his head. "We don't know."

"How old are you, Maysden?"

Orion was not expecting a question like this one. "Sixteen," he murmured.

Voran sniffed in reply. "So young," he mumbled to himself.

Just like that, Voran indicated that the time for talk was over. He turned his face forward, his expression stony. No matter how hard he tried, Orion could not engage the man to talk.

Eventually, after what seemed like hours, they rode into the yard of a traveller's inn. Thankfully the inn itself seemed to be further away from any other dwellings. If Orion could keep Carvelle quiet, maybe word of their visit wouldn't spread to potential enemies.

"Barkeep, we need a medic and baths," Voran snapped as he flung the tavern door open. He dragged a semi-conscious Theo behind him. He fished into his leather belt and pulled out a thick gold coin, then flicked it at the owner. The barkeep caught the coin with a grin.

"That's generous of you," Orion muttered. He kept his eye on the curious prince, who was wandering about and gawking at everything from the rafters and fireplace to the minstrel's lute, which was left in a dark corner.

"Do your companions need a change of clothing, Sir Voran?"

"No, thank you," Orion started, shaking his head at Carvelle as little fingers went to pluck the strings of the lute.

Voran punched Orion's arm. "A change of clothes would be appreciated. This one here smells worse than my cousin's pig farm."

Voran flung the door to his room wide and hurled the unfortunate Theo through the opening.

Orion opened his mouth to protest, wincing at the way Theo's glazed eyes looked helplessly back at him.

"I'll look after this one," Voran grunted and slammed the door behind him.

Shocked but not entirely surprised, Orion stared at the door. He contemplated knocking on the door to force Voran to make alternative arrangements, but the amused look from the barkeep's serving boy made him reconsider.

"He's mighty cranky today," the server said. He eyed Orion up and down. "What did you do to upset him?"

Raising his eyebrow at the impertinence of the server, Orion stepped past him and to the other room they had been shown. Carvelle hurried after him, sending a quizzical look at Voran's shut door.

"It's not Orion," Carvelle said. "It's me. Sir Voran doesn't like what I remind him of."

"Oh, and what might—"

"It's been a hard, long day," Orion interrupted, shooting Carvelle a look that he hoped the prince might interpret as a command to be silent.

"Course," the server muttered. Orion didn't appreciate the way his nose scrunched up as he peered at their dirty clothes. "The medic won't be long. I'll get some water to fill the tub and you can wash up. Sir Voran asked for new clothes ... I'll get those as well."

Orion felt his body relax as the server turned and shut the door to the room behind him. He felt relief wash over him, realising that Voran did not want to have any charge over Carvelle. It felt uncomfortable and wrong to leave the prince in anyone else's care.

Orion shrugged off the pack of supplies and sat down to unlace his boots. He eyed the large tub in the middle of the room. "I suppose I should go help the poor fellow," he murmured, glancing down at his aching feet.

"Why?" Carvelle asked. "He's a servant."

"So am I, Your Highness."

"Not here in this tavern." Carvelle cocked his head to the side. "You're a soldier, Orion. That's what you're meant to be."

So Orion watched the coming and going of the servant as he filled the tub so they could bathe. Being waited on seemed strange. Living in Silverdyne, every member of the family had their own chores to do. He was used to doing things for himself. He wondered if his master felt the same stirring of helplessness he was feeling.

"I'll return with some garments," the server said with a bow as he finished.

Carvelle whooped with glee and was already ridding himself of his travel-stained clothes. Orion caught the look of mirth on the servant's face as the door closed behind him.

Without a moment's hesitation, the prince was in the tub. While Orion waited for the server to return with clothing, he lathered the hard bar of soap to help Carvelle to wash his hair.

"Do you think Uncle will be alright?" Carvelle asked.

Cupping some water in his palms, Orion rinsed the suds from the prince's hair. "He's out there somewhere."

"We'll find him much changed next time we see him," Carvelle said with a sage nod. He opened his mouth to continue speaking but Orion, who was listening, heard the footsteps of the server returning. He held his finger to his lips.

A knock sounded on their door. Voran entered, his arms laden with fresh clothing. For a long moment, the older man watched as Orion rubbed at a stubborn dirt smear on Carvelle's face.

"The Pallarus boys will have any man bending over backwards for them," Voran grunted.

"Orion has been looking after me since Uncle Jod was taken," Carvelle replied. "I shall tell Papa he has done a most excellent job thus far."

Orion felt his cheeks redden.

"The medic is with your friend," Voran said.

"His name is Theo, born of Korkalie," Carvelle saw fit to mention. Orion hid a smile behind his hand as the prince reminded the older man of his manners.

"The medic is with *Theo* now," Voran repeated. The stern lines around his lips twitched. Orion thought he looked like a man who seldom smiled. "You're surprisingly loyal to your master for one who hasn't served for very long. That should give me some comfort in the days that will follow."

"Does that mean you're going to help us?" Orion called out as Voran retreated from the room. "How do I know I can trust you?"

"Voran Axtin is a very strange man, indeed," Carvelle said, standing out of the bath. "Your turn, horse boy!"

Keen to see how Theo was doing, Orion bounded down the stairs the next morning. He found the thief sitting at a table, cradling his head and glaring at Voran.

"Do you mind telling me why this oaf who conked me over the head is joining us on our ridiculous quest?" Theo asked upon spying Orion and

Carvelle. The prince scurried to Theo's side and tucked himself under the thief's left arm.

"Before you ask, I feel wretched." Lolling his head to the side, Theo looked down at the prince. He picked up a bread roll and handed it to the younger boy, who took it with a wide grin.

"The healer said he's fine," Voran grunted.

Theo glared up at Voran. Carvelle patted the thief's hand.

"We're going to need every sword we can get," Orion replied, taking his seat opposite Theo. "Voran is Jodathyn's ex-personal guard."

"Don't look so pleased," Theo hissed. "We hear rumours even in the muddy backwater of Korkalie. The story is the ex-guard was disgraced."

"Theo's concerns are understandable. Why don't you tell us why you were dismissed? How can I be sure I can trust you?"

Voran regarded Orion from under his bushy red eyebrows. "What is the fall of any great man?"

Orion blinked and looked over to Theo. Theo shrugged and lay his head on the table.

"A woman."

As far as Orion was concerned, Voran still wasn't making much sense. Theo, however, raised his head. The expression on his face was smug as he smirked and waggled his eyebrows.

"Otherworlds, guarding Jodathyn Pallarus could be boring. That boy can study a tome for hours. I figured not much harm comes from reading, so one day I left my post to have alone time with my woman. That was the last time I saw him. When I came back, he was gone. The boy had scampered off to climb a tree with his book."

Theo made a sound in the back of his throat. "Sounds like he hasn't changed much."

"Reading never killed anyone," Orion said.

Voran grumbled, staring into his cup. "Someone had poisoned him. Overcome, he fell from the tree and broke his arm. He lay in that quiet courtyard for at least an hour."

"An hour. How could you leave him alone for that long?" Orion cried.

"I don't understand," Theo said. "You didn't poison your master. So why did you lose your position?"

"He left his post," Orion hissed between clenched teeth. "A dreadful sin for any guardsman. You should have been put to death."

"That seems a bit extreme," Theo muttered.

"Not for a guardsman who is responsible for someone of a royal bloodline," Voran admitted. He picked up his empty cup and stared down at it glumly. In disgust, he banged it back down on the table. "I left my post. Jodathyn wasn't able to summon help. If he was left there much longer ... he would have died."

"The king would have been furious."

"He was away," Voran said flatly. "A King's Guardsman came to me. He wouldn't say what condition Jodathyn was in, just commanded me to leave Pallaryn. I punched him in the face."

"You seem to have a knack of hitting people," Theo grumbled.

"How long are you going to hold a grudge over a little bump on your head?" Orion snickered, taking in Theo's thunderous expression.

"It wasn't a *little* bump!" Theo snarled. "I was unconscious."

"Dare say your state of unconsciousness was an improvement for your companions." Voran glanced away. The mischievous glint and the smirk on his lips told Orion that the big man was enjoying teasing Theo.

Theo ground his teeth.

"I do apologise for the misunderstanding and the injury to your noggin."

Theo glared viciously up at the large man. "*Misunderstanding*?"

"Well, I did take you to somewhere safe, and I paid for a medic, new clothes, and food and lodging. I think we're even."

Theo shuffled, returning to his simple breakfast of bread and cheese. He tore an extra hunk off for Prince Carvelle, who was eyeing his plate. The little prince could certainly eat. "I suppose when you say it like that, I guess you're forgiven."

"Oh, most magnanimous of you," Orion said dryly.

Theo didn't respond to the teasing; he smirked.

Orion mulled over Voran's story. His mistake nearly cost the life of the one he was sworn to protect. It was unforgivable. But he was also the best shot they had. "What do you suggest we do?"

"We need to get our hands on any weapons or provisions we can. It's going to be a long, hard road to Pallaryn," Voran said.

"I really do want to go home." Carvelle sighed.

"I maintain we need to get to ground and then make a move," Theo murmured.

"I can tell you as one of Lord Solan's men that his old summer house in Aviah Valley is abandoned. But not for so long that we can't reasonably expect to find provisions," Voran said, brushing his hand down his beard. "I might be able to get some help from the outlining farmhouses. Solan is not liked in Aviah Valley."

"In a house like that, we would have somewhere to hide ... to barricade ourselves in, if need be," Orion said.

"Exactly," Voran replied.

"Honestly, I don't know why I stay with you lot. The likelihood of Jodathyn and Nym returning becomes slimmer by the day ... I'm going to end up with either cold steel of a sword in my guts or a rope necklace with a long drop," Theo said.

"Eat your breakfast," Carvelle said. "That's not going to be your fate, Theo Torkelle."

CHAPTER TEN

Jodathyn

The Village of Kudah

"Our Nym isn't here."

Jodathyn continued to clear up the breakfast dishes as his dragon whinged and whined about Nym's absence. His stomach cramped as he thought of all the ways they could be discovered. When he finished clearing the dishes, he returned to the tables to scrub them clean. As he worked, he felt his muscles tensing and his eyes drifting towards the door of the tavern. By mid-morning, he dropped his rag and glared at the door as if it had committed a great wrong.

"She should be helping us."

Rubbing his right arm, Jodathyn picked up a broom to sweep the floors.

"Come. I will walk you into town." Et-hir came up behind him, taking the broom and leaning it against the wall. "There's no reason to fret. The entertainment fighters often spend the night before bouts hazing each other."

"Nym can look after herself," Jodathyn answered tightly. "I'm not worried."

Et-hir retrieved a basket from behind the counter and took Jodathyn's arm as she sauntered past. "I, for one, find your concern sweet."

"I'm not concerned," Jodathyn protested, shaking his head. He took Et-hir's basket, which was full of jars of dried fruits.

"Maybe I should rescue more handsome rouges. I wouldn't have to carry my wares to market myself," Et-hir said, quirking an eyebrow.

Jodathyn chuckled and swept into a bow. "Glad to be of service."

As they walked into the village of Kudah, Jodathyn couldn't contain his curiosity. "Have you been to many places?"

Et-hir lifted her hand to her lips and laughed. "More than you can count, prince. I was born and raised a silk trader."

"Do you miss Sion?"

"Rama is very beautiful."

Jodathyn felt his lips twitch at the misdirection. "Can I find a way to repay your brother for the clothes?"

Et-hir glanced over at him, and her large golden eyes filled with tears. She seemed to be struggling to breathe as she twisted her small hands in her apron. "He went to work in the mines and never returned. I stay in hope—"

"Truly, I'm sorry." Jodathyn felt his stomach drop. He stepped closer, reaching out his hand, thinking he should do something to comfort her. "Is this common?"

Tornyth raised his head. *"You've upset her."*

"Mines are dangerous. Tyr knew the risks." Wiping at her eyes with her apron, Et-hir faced Jodathyn. She smiled through her tears, and he couldn't help but think that even in her sorrow, she had a beautiful smile. "My brother would have been glad to help. One day I'll return to Sion."

"I would love to visit Sion one day." Jodathyn replied. A long-suffering sigh escaped his lips. "The Sionian king extended an invitation, but Kieryn declined on my behalf."

"That's outrageous!" Et-hir cried. "A grave insult to Sion. Your king spat on my king. Does your brother not trust in the honour of my people?"

"I think my brother doesn't trust the honour of his lords," Jodathyn replied. "Kieryn spoke at length with your king in private about the matter. I was angry at the time, but your king pat me on the head and told me to obey my brother, grow strong, and that the Silk Palace would be still standing when I was ready to visit."

"My king wasn't angry?"

"No," Jodathyn confirmed. "Kieryn and he had a wonderful time at the departure feast, and he left me with a leather ledger."

"A simple gift. Any Sionian trader could have given you one of those. Did he not leave you with Sionian silk?"

"The ledger was fascinating. I'm afraid to write in it lest I ruin it," Jodathyn said. "Your king left me with half a dozen silk shirts. And Queen Odelle was gifted a lovely dress of blue silk."

Et-hir's gaze had a wistful, far-off look.

"Tell her she's pretty ..."

"Perhaps one day you'll have a gown of Sionian silk in a lovely deep red," Jodathyn said. "Just like your queen."

Et-hir swatted his chest. "You're a tease. I was a seller of silk, not a princess!"

"You could have matching ribbons in your hair—"

"Stop." Et-hir swatted him again.

"Held into your braids with little gold honeybees. I can see a horde of angelic little girls dancing at your feet, ready to worship the ground on which you tread."

"Golden clasps? Now I know you are jesting!"

The conversation brought them outside a small bakery. Jodathyn wandered over and peered through the window at the sugary treats. His mouth watered as he thought of all the fine food he was missing back at the palace.

"The baker buys my dried fruit for some of her sweet things," Et-hir said, joining him at the window. She looked around at the other shop fronts, biting her lip. "Let's not linger here."

Jodathyn thought her caution was peculiar, but he dismissed the niggling feeling of worry as he followed her into the bakery. He trusted that she wouldn't lead him into danger.

The door shut behind them, and Jodathyn inhaled the smell of freshly baked bread. His stomach grumbled appreciatively.

"Men!" Et-hir laughed. She gestured to a spare space on the counter. "I fed you this morning!"

"It's almost time for the mid-day meal," Tornyth grumbled.

Grinning sheepishly, Jodathyn placed the basket of dried fruits on the counter. Et-hir leaned over and rearranged the jars to her liking. She grasped on to Jodathyn's forearm. "Don't talk too much. Keep your story simple, and remember, you are Locke."

Jodathyn nodded. If he was being truthful, he wanted to sidle closer to Et-hir. He wasn't sure what was wrong with him, but there was something about her that drew him in. Silently, he berated himself for his feelings. She had been kind to him, that was all. Surely, she wouldn't appreciate his attention. He stole an anxious glance sideways, only to find her staring back at him. To avoid her scrutiny, Jodathyn turned upon his heel and inspected the sweet goods behind him.

"Ettie! Darling, what have you brought for me today?" Jodathyn felt Et-hir's attention move from him and to the woman he assumed was the baker. He took the opportunity to study the tall, middle-aged woman. Her silver curls were swept into a bun on the top of her head. Her work dress and apron were dusted in a fine coat of flour. Turning his back, he listened to Et-hir and the baker haggle over the price. When he heard the sound of coins changing hands, he returned to Et-hir's side.

"Who might this tasty morsel be?" the baker asked. Although the woman was attempting to tease him, something wasn't quite right with the way her hands twisted in her apron.

"This is Locke," Et-hir replied before Jodathyn could answer for himself. Together they watched as the baker walked over to the window of her shop. "He's visiting Kudah."

"Vehyl, something is not right."

Puzzled, Jodathyn followed the baker's stare. Outside, across the market square, he spotted a well-dressed man. He was short, with a head of blond hair and a pointed beard. His skin was terribly pale.

"He's looking for you," the baker whispered. "Quickly, out the back. Both of you!"

Et-hir grabbed Jodathyn's sleeve and dragged him through the baker's shop. Confused by the change of atmosphere, Jodathyn allowed her to drag him.

"What's happening?" Jodathyn could feel a sharp stab of anxiety pricking his skin. He rubbed at his tattoo. "Who is that man?"

"The magistrate of this town—he hates anyone not of Kudah. He's made the last year living here as a foreigner a misery," Et-hir whispered. She pushed Jodathyn to the far corner of the room, which he realised was the baker's kitchen. "Quiet, please."

Hearing the front door to the baker's shop open and close, Et-hir gripped on to Jodathyn's arm. He could feel her trembling against him. Why was Et-hir so afraid of the magistrate?

"Baker, you would tell me if you have seen that Sionian wretch."

"Who is he to call our Ettie a wretch?" Tornyth rumbled in irritation. *"I'll roast him."*

Jodathyn closed his fingers around Et-hir's hand. It was the only thing he could think to do to comfort her. His actions felt silly and clumsy, but at the same time, the warmth of her skin felt soothing. Et-hir grasped at his hand, squeezing it for all her might.

He didn't like how this well-dressed man had the normally confident Et-hir scared. It did not sit well with him that she felt it necessary to hide.

"Can't say I have seen her," the baker replied.

"Heard talk of others in town," the magistrate barked.

"Nor have I heard that, Magistrate Swyft," the baker said. "I have been baking all morning. Would you like a cake?"

The magistrate grunted. Jodathyn could hear the sounds of his boots across the floor. The door opened.

"If you see her, tell that Sionian woman she has an account to settle."

"You already took her brother Tyr ..."

"Careful, woman. You are speaking insurrection." The front door slammed shut.

Et-hir didn't move.

"I don't understand," Jodathyn murmured. "What was that about?"

"About a year ago, the Sionian traders I was travelling with were charged triple the fee for selling in Kudah," Et-hir whispered. "Orders of your king ..."

Jodathyn shook his head. "I have heard of no such rumour. Who's the lord who presides over Kudah?"

"Lord Kamoore." The baker had returned and was standing at the door.

"Kamoore is weak, but I never thought he would deliberately do something so stupid in Kieryn's name. Kieryn wouldn't do something like this ... I would have heard about it." Jodathyn shook his head in disbelief. Kamoore was playing a dangerous game.

"*Kieryn?*" The baker's shrewd eyes narrowed in suspicion. She looked Jodathyn up and down slowly.

"That is your king's name, isn't it?" Et-hir asked. She stepped in front of Jodathyn to take the baker's attention off him. It didn't work.

"We don't call our king by his first name. It's disrespectful." Crossing her arms over her chest, the baker glared at Jodathyn. "Who are you?"

The moment he uttered Kieryn's name, Jodathyn felt uneasy. Much to his detriment, his fatigue from his sleepless night had loosened his tongue. His mind was awhirl, trying to concoct a plausible explanation for his gaffe. The baker's eyes narrowed in suspicion.

Jodathyn opened his mouth to speak, but no words spilled forth.

"I think you know," Et-hir whispered. "You must keep it secret."

"If you were to ask my advice, Locke," the baker said, "avoid the mines. Do not seek work or shelter there. There have been too many accidents and disappearances in those mountains."

"The mountains are cursed," Et-hir replied.

The baker rolled her eyes. "It's not the mountains that are cursed, Ettie."

Hands on her hips, Et-hir studied the baker with her chin held high. "After we paid your magistrate, his men caused a fight in our settlement. They took and arrested Tyr … Your Ramian mountains swallowed him up. They're cursed."

"The account the magistrate speaks of?"

The expression on the baker's face soured. "He wants Ettie to work in the mines in place of her brother."

"You can't!" Jodathyn cried.

"They can force me," Et-hir said.

"Have you committed a crime?"

"No."

"Then they have no right to force you to do anything," Jodathyn said. "Trust me, this is considered 'illegal apprehension' under Ramian law. We need to find you a magistrate that will defend your rights."

"Are there any good magistrates in Rama?" the baker grumbled. "They're getting worse."

"I know someone that can help us," Jodathyn replied, his mouth twisted into a sly smile. "Your magistrate won't stand a chance against him."

The baker's frown deepened. "They're sending another lot of prisoners to the mountains tomorrow morning. It's too late for them."

"What type of crimes did they commit?"

"Failure to pay taxes." Et-hir sighed.

The baker wiped her hands on her apron as she ushered them from her shop. "Stay out of his way."

"Are we going to rebel tonight?" Et-hir asked Jodathyn as they stepped out of the baker's shop. She intertwined her arm with his and pressed herself close to his side. Jodathyn looked down into her large brown eyes. He never understood why Kieryn had trouble disagreeing with Odelle. He thought maybe he had an inkling of what the queen's special powers over the king might be.

"We need a plan." Jodathyn found himself answering before he reasonably thought over the wisdom of his intention to free the prisoners.

The slow, shy smile on Et-hir's face was worth it. "The fighting bouts will have everyone squeezing into the meeting hall tonight. We have the cover of darkness to hide us."

A thrill of excitement wove its way up Jodathyn's spine. Too long had he been condemned to keep his silence. Strange that as the Son of the Crown he had less power than when he was on the run from the great lords. This could be another way he could hurt Solan and Kamoore.

Under his skin, Tornyth rippled in pleasure. *"If you do this, you'll impress the* vehyl *female. She might find us worthy."*

Later that night, Jodathyn entered the meeting hall alongside Curran. Et-hir had declined to go, as the magistrate was on the lookout for her. She would meet him by the jailhouse when the time was right.

Jodathyn stepped over the threshold and took in the sight of the crowd, which was a raucous jumble of sweat, shouting and ale. It looked like every villager had crammed into the meeting house to watch the fighting bouts.

Nym still hadn't returned to the tavern, so Et-hir had slipped away to find her to inform her of their daring plan. Jodathyn was glad he wasn't the one telling Nym. He could almost imagine the fury twisting her gaunt face.

"I want a quick word with Nym," Jodathyn shouted.

Curran turned to regard him with a frown. "Stay away from the drunks and keep your shirt on."

Confusion wrinkled Jodathyn's brow. "Why in Otherworld would I take my shirt off?"

Curran raised an eyebrow. "Stay sober tonight and keep your wits about you."

Jodathyn nodded and stalked towards the raised stage where the combatants were watching the milling crowd. As he walked, he could feel Curran's gaze on his back. He hoped the barman was feeling overprotective because of his stint as a guardsman. It would be a disaster if Curran suspected he was plotting something.

Jostling through the crowd, Jodathyn fought his way through the press of people until he reached Nym. She glared down at him, her eyes giving nothing away. She flicked her gaze towards her five large competitors and rolled her eyes at their bolstering.

"Are you sure about this?" Nym asked as she knelt. Her lips barely moved as she spoke.

Jodathyn nodded.

"Be careful, dragon dung," Nym cautioned. There was no sting to her tone. "I won't be there to watch your back."

"I can do this," Jodathyn said.

"You're doing this for the girl," Nym replied. She glanced around at the crowd. "I don't see her."

"I want to cause damage," Jodathyn growled.

Nym frowned. "I'm serious, Jod. You're not made for a life of crime. Be careful."

"I'm made to cause trouble," Jodathyn replied. He could feel Tornyth's impatience crawling under his skin.

Nym hissed, bringing her face closer. "Keep your scaly fiend under control."

"What—"

"Your eyes …"

Another contestant came over to join them, effectively cutting their frantic conversation short. By the pointed look Nym was giving him, Jodathyn could safely assume that she had seen Tornyth lurking behind his eyes. It hadn't been the first time someone had mentioned it. "Who's this? Your beau? He's a bit pretty for you, don't you think, girl?"

Hearing the remark, the other four contestants laughed at the jibe. Taken aback by the insult, Jodathyn frowned. Nym looked over her shoulder and smirked. "He's my brother," she said. "Anyone who messes with him, messes with me."

The men laughed and clapped each other's backs.

"Erm …" Jodathyn said, stepping away. "Good luck … *sister*? See you in the morning. No doubt with a fresh black eye."

Instead of flushing with anger as Jodathyn hoped, Nym nodded and looked pleased. "You see, gents, he made a fine travelling companion."

At a loss for words, Jodathyn stepped away and went in search of Curran. Et-hir had gone to great lengths to tell him to stay near the barkeep. She said Curran would keep the magistrate and lawmen away if needed. They had a healthy respect for Curran. They wouldn't argue with him unless they felt it necessary.

Jodathyn dithered, searching for Curran. A drunk farmer shoved him to the side, pushing him into an older woman. He inhaled the cloying scent of ale and cheap perfume. The woman grabbed his shoulders with a triumphant cry as she pressed her lips to his. Jodathyn tried to pull away, but the woman grasped on to his ears with her nails. "A fine prize I have caught."

The crowd about him cheered with glee. Jodathyn's eyes could only widen, and he slapped the woman's offending hands. "I'm not interested."

The woman held on, digging her nails in.

"Release me!" Jodathyn demanded. He pulled back and stepped into the path of Lawman Floyde. The beer the lawman was carrying sloshed down his shirt and over his boots.

The balding lawman growled at his empty cup. He pinned the woman with a hard stare. "Move along, woman. You owe me a beer."

Looking disappointed, the woman wisely retreated into the crowd. Lawman Floyde grasped Jodathyn's shoulder as he grabbed a rag from a server and attempted to dry his boots. Jodathyn noticed they were well made; he wondered how much coin lawmen made.

"Waste of Curran's beer," Lawman Floyde grumbled.

"Floydie!"

Lawman Floyde rolled his eyes at the grinning face of Lawman Ripley. "Spilling your beer this early in the night. Such a disgrace!"

Lawman Floyde scowled. "Get me another one, Rip."

His companion's foul mood didn't wipe the smile off Lawman Ripley's face. "At once, sir." Jodathyn could plainly see that Lawman Ripley had already been deep in his cups. But when the lawman turned to regard him, he seemed to sober up a little. "Still in Kudah, Locke? Might want to consider moving on soon. Magistrate Swyft isn't so keen on out-of-towners."

Jodathyn nodded his thanks and made his way over to Curran, who had been watching the whole scene play out.

"All well, Locke?"

"I think I may have been kissed by a whore." Jodathyn blinked.

"Haven't you kissed a woman before?"

"I've most certainly kissed a woman." Jodathyn didn't appreciate the teasing tone of Curran's voice. Never mind that his first kiss was a drunken Nym giving him a lesson. "Thrice, counting the whore."

Curran scoffed back a good-natured laugh and patted Jodathyn's back. "Relax. Stay by me and don't go anywhere with a whore. You're in for quite an experience tonight."

Jodathyn opened his mouth, tempted to tell Curran of his illicit plans later. A feeling of guilt and dread curled in his stomach. Curiosity and suspicion lit the barman's eyes as he paused to study him. All traces of amusement were gone. "Do you wish to confess something, Locke?"

"No," Jodathyn said.

"On your grandsire's grave, I'll keep you safe," Curran murmured.

Jodathyn felt his lips parting. He wanted to ask Curran how he had known his grandsire. It seemed an odd thing to say. But he clenched his jaw shut. No good would come of it if he talked too boldly in a crowd like this. The baker was already aware of his identity.

"How old are you, Curran?" Jodathyn asked instead.

"Fifty-six summers," Curran replied with a sidelong glance. He handed Jodathyn a mug of ale as the fighters were being introduced. "This ought to be good."

From what Curran had told Jodathyn, he had left his position in Pallaryn just before his birth. His father's reign had been a relatively short ten years. With some quick calculations, he decided it was entirely possible the barkeep served his grandfather as well as his father.

"He looks well for an old vehyl," Tornyth commented.

Jodathyn choked on his ale and averted his eyes at Curran's suspicious gaze. One day his dragon was going to get him into trouble.

Careful to sip at his ale, Jodathyn watched as Nym goaded a burly man to fight her. She twirled her borrowed sword; her attention focused upon the crowd as her opponent returned her insults. Against the confidence of Nym, his attempts were overcompensating for his lack of skill. His face flushed crimson, and his jowls wobbled in response to her lack of concern. Jodathyn smiled into his mug and chortled. There was nothing Nym's opponent could do to intimidate her.

"I told you she was good for our team." The dragon inside him stirred. The warmth of the alcohol seemed to please the beast. *"We should watch her fight—then cause trouble."*

Jodathyn agreed with his dragon side in silence. He would watch Nym, show his support, make sure he was seen, and then he would make his way towards the cell with the prisoners.

With a tremendous roar, Nym's opponent rushed at her. Nym yawned and sidestepped him. She lifted her sword out of the way as he thundered past. All around her, the crowd hollered and clapped. Her blade flashed as she twirled it lazily.

"She's enjoying this," Curran muttered at his elbow.

"It's easy to enjoy things one excels at," Jodathyn replied. "I'm glad to have such a fierce companion at my side."

Curran's gaze slid over to Jodathyn. "Indeed."

It seemed that Nym's opponent had not learned from his mistake. Bellowing, he stamped forward, his sword slicing through the air. Nym stepped up to meet him and their blades clashed. Seconds later she was spinning away from him. He dove after her, and Nym ducked under his blade. She swiped at his knee, and he yelled as he lost his footing. Jodathyn winced as the big man crashed down on the stage. Never one to show undue mercy, Nym stood over him, her foot poised on his lower back. With one simple kick, her opponent landed face first onto his nose.

The crowd hooted with laughter.

"What is it that you excel at, Locke?"

Jodathyn shrugged, keeping his eyes averted. "I suspect not much. I'm simply not like Nym."

Curran sniffed. "Nym told me she didn't deserve such a loyal and courageous friend."

Lifting his mug to take a gulp, Jodathyn refused to answer. Under the surface, Tornyth was pleased. *"Ghost hair likes us. We have a friend."*

"You have much to offer Rama. I pray one day you will see that for yourself."

"All I have ever wanted was to prove myself worthy," Jodathyn said. "I'm beginning to think I was not born for greatness."

"All are born for greatness. It's up to us to find it within ourselves," Curran replied.

"That's why we're freeing prisoners ... because of us, some unfortunates will be set free."

Jodathyn shifted. His dragon's thoughts were right. To achieve greatness, he needed to reach out and take it. The great lords may have robbed him his place within the palace, but here in the villages he could still do something of worth. He could only hope that when he crossed the bridge to the Otherworld, his father might greet him and be proud.

The drinking continued, and Jodathyn lingered to watch the following bouts. The fights became fiercer. The noise around the meeting hall was deafening. Jodathyn noticed that Curran had not drunk beyond his one ale. The barman rested his hand upon Jodathyn's shoulder, and his clear eyes scanned the room.

When the competitors were whittled down to three, a small interlude was called. The final bout would be an all-in fight. Nym pranced around the stage, encouraging the cheering and shouting from her supporters. Some young men stripped off their shirts and beat their chests. Stunned by the display, Jodathyn turned to Curran, who raised his empty mug. "As I said, keep your shirt on."

"Can't imagine anyone would enjoy the sight of my body," Jodathyn replied.

Curran's dark eyes twinkled. "I can think of someone who has enjoyed the sight."

Flushing, Jodathyn shook Curran's hand from his shoulder. "I need some air and to relieve myself."

"Be careful," Curran replied. "No dallying. The magistrate has his men watching."

Jodathyn ignored Curran's pointed stare and slipped away among the crowd. As he turned his gaze towards the stage, he saw Nym pause and watch him. He lifted his hand and waved. Her lips parted; he could see his name forming on the tip of her tongue. Frantically, she shook her head. Her hard hazel gaze told him she thought he was being a fool. Worried that Nym intended to thwart his plan, Jodathyn pushed through the crowd towards the door.

Stepping from the meeting hall, Jodathyn looked around the dark village, observing as each of his breaths formed a small puff of cloud. He blew into his hands and rubbed them together. He stamped his feet, looking around to see if anyone was watching him.

"We're alone. The final bout is ready to begin; we won't have much time."

Jodathyn turned neatly upon his heel and jogged through the dark village, careful to follow Et-hir's instructions. The cells were behind the magistrate's house, which was the second largest building in the town. It was also the only building to have steps.

Nearing the building, Jodathyn spotted Et-hir waiting in the bushes. When she heard him, she lifted her chin to greet him. "I've seen no sign of anyone."

"They're at the bouts," Jodathyn replied. "Just like you said."

Brown eyes ablaze with mischief, Et-hir shifted to stand. Her shaking hands smoothed her apron as she bit her lip. Tilting her head to the side, she regarded Jodathyn with a curious expression. She stepped close to him so that she was only a hand width away.

Looking down on her, Jodathyn hadn't realised how tiny Et-hir was. Under the moonlight, she looked ethereal. He longed to reach out and brush a stray lock of silky black hair back. He immediately buried those feelings, scolding himself for even imagining reaching out to touch her.

"Can I call you Ettie?" Jodathyn asked. "Are we friends yet?"

"I daresay we are." Et-hir pushed herself up on her tippy-toes and brushed her soft lips against Jodathyn's cheek. He forced his hands to remain at his sides, even as his mind cried out for him to reach out and bring her trembling body closer to his own. "In Sionian stories, the hero always wins a kiss from the heroine."

Jodathyn's own body tingled with adrenaline. Never before had he felt so brave or reckless. He wondered what his brother might have to say about this newest misadventure and then dismissed the thought. Kieryn wasn't here to punish him. Et-hir was pleased with him, and his dragon blood was singing in delight.

"Maybe..." Jodathyn replied, his eyes darting to the side. The husky sound that had escaped his lips didn't sound like him at all. "Maybe I shall endeavour to be a hero more often if the reward is so sweet."

Chapter Eleven

Jodathyn

The Village of Kudah

As Et-hir grabbed Jodathyn's hand to lead him through the dark, he tried to shake the temptation to take her into his arms. The memory of her soft lips pressing against his cheek left him feeling pleasantly warm inside. He followed after her, stumbling in a delightful haze of disbelief and confusion.

When Et-hir's fingers intertwined with Jodathyn's, Tornyth raised his head.

"Kiss her again," his dragon whispered. Jodathyn could sense his keen interest.

"This is an impossible dream," Jodathyn replied sternly to his dragon.

How could he tell her the dragon that lived inside his brain desired to kiss her? Nothing would come of their feelings for each other. She was a barmaid. He was a son of a king, a criminal, and had a dragon living inside him.

Et-hir seemed to be unaware of his internal struggle as they crept along in the dark. She was careful to keep them within the shadows. Jodathyn saw the small brick structure before Et-hir tugged on his hand and pointed through the dark. Where the magistrate's home was constructed of large bricks and looked inviting, the jailhouse looked dismal.

Jodathyn could only describe the cell as a pile of haphazard bricks with narrow, open slots. In the dark, he thought he could see faces pressed against the bars of a strong steel gate that left the building open to the cold night air. He couldn't imagine being locked up with only the body warmth of others to provide comfort.

Fortunately, only one guard was watching the jailhouse. He stood at the gate, out of the arm reach of the prisoners. On his belt, Jodathyn spied the silver glint of keys.

"We need to move quickly," Jodathyn said. "I don't know how long the last bout will take."

"Not long," Et-hir replied. She squeezed Jodathyn's hand. "Are you still going to do this with me?"

"Yes," Jodathyn answered. He studied the guard with some uncertainty. It would be up to him to subdue the man. He let go of her hand and started to stride towards the stone building.

Upon seeing Jodathyn's form coming towards them, the prisoners started to chatter and call out. Jodathyn knew that he didn't look like he posed much of a threat, so he wasn't surprised when the guard turned to watch his approach. He kept his stride unhurried and plastered a pleasant smile on his face.

"Good evening," Jodathyn said.

"What ya doing out here?" the guard grumbled.

Jodathyn grinned and blinked innocently. "I'm afraid I'm here to cause you a wee bit of trouble."

The guard responded with a snigger. "Is that so?"

"He's laughing at us. Hit him!" Tornyth roared.

Still grinning, Jodathyn pulled back his arm and punched the guard as hard as he could. His fist landed with a crack in the middle of his nose. The hapless guard stumbled, fell and hit his head against the iron bars of the door.

Jodathyn could only stare dumbfounded at his fist as Et-hir approached gleefully from behind. He expected that he would have to throw a few punches, but one well-placed fist rendered the guard useless. Gingerly, he toed the man's boot and laughed. The guard didn't respond.

"He'll have a sore head come morning," Et-hir said. She bent and wrenched the key from the guard's belt.

Letting Et-hir take charge, Jodathyn watched as she unlocked the barred gate. It opened slowly, creaking in the dark. Jodathyn glanced about them, expecting to see half a dozen guards converging on them. But the night was still and silent, except for the delighted cries of the prisoners as they filed out.

"Head to the woods," Jodathyn said to them. "Don't go to your homes. Head to the woods and get away from here."

An old man with silver hair hobbled past. He grasped Jodathyn with his wrinkled, weathered hands. They shook as he held on to Jodathyn. The old man would not have survived the work of the mines for long.

"Bless you." The old man reached up and cupped his cheeks.

"Go, please," Jodathyn begged.

Once the old man had hobbled away, Et-hir and Jodathyn were left alone by the cell. They glanced at one another and laughed.

"What have we done?" Et-hir asked with a giggle.

"That's what I would like to know."

Jodathyn spun around on his heels, like a boy who had been caught stealing pies from the kitchen. He stomped down the immediate sense of guilt and schooled his features to look politely confused. It would be suspicious to be found outside of the empty cell.

"I told you to come straight back."

It was only Curran.

Jodathyn sighed in relief; the barkeep wouldn't hand them over to the lawmen.

"I went for a walk," Jodathyn replied sweetly.

Curran's brow furrowed, and his lips pursed until Jodathyn fancied he could see white pressure lines on his skin. He strode forward and grasped Jodathyn's elbow and started to drag him forward. "I can very well see what you have done. You're in enough danger as it is …"

"No one is out here."

"Your father was a fool too," Curran snarled. He gave Jodathyn's elbow a tug.

Jodathyn was forced to jog to keep up with him. "I wouldn't know."

"Curran, it wasn't all his idea." Et-hir hitched up her skirts to dart after them.

"I am well aware of your part," Curran replied.

"Release me," Jodathyn demanded as Curran's fingertips pressed into his skin.

Growling, Curran thrust Jodathyn ahead of him. "Get moving, boy. Of all the foolish enterprises … Now I'll have to smuggle you two out of Kudah."

"Smuggle?"

"Not another word," Curran warned, giving Jodathyn a small shove in the middle of his back.

Unsure what to do with Curran's displeasure, Jodathyn decided the wise thing to do was to obey. He walked forward into the dark and had to wonder why the barkeep was so infuriated. From what he had gleaned, he concluded Curran was no stranger to helping the less fortunate. Perhaps it was just his previous calling. Jodathyn knew some guardsmen took their oath of loyalty seriously. Curran had spoken of both his father and grandfather enough to pique his interest. What type of guard had Curran been?

"Jodathyn!"

Jodathyn's foot paused midstride. The stern voice was reverberating around in his mind. Since leaving Torqui, he had expected Mandros to contact him. He felt a small tingle of relief that the green dragon had returned for him. He smothered the feeling. The vision of the dragon council was still fresh in his mind, even though he had refused to think about it.

"Jodathyn, you better be on this isle … Come here now, you disobedient vehyl."

"What's wrong?" Et-hir asked. She took a few quick strides forward, taking the crook of Jodathyn's elbow. "Even in the dark, I can see your Ramian complexion paling further."

"Headache," Jodathyn replied, bringing his fingertips to his temple for added effect. This wasn't the time to explain about the green dragon that had claimed him as his own. "Sometimes I get a sudden pain …"

"We need a place to hide," Curran grumbled. "I should have sent for a healer last night. No time now."

"I can look after myself," Jodathyn protested.

"Jodathyn! Return to me at once."

"No!" Jodathyn projected before he could think of a more suitable reply.

"No?"

"No!" Jodathyn sent through the link. He let the dormant anger over his vision simmer, and now his rage and hurt were boiling over. *"I saw what happened at the dragon council … I am no longer interested."*

"Where are you?"

Jodathyn ignored the voice, wincing at Mandros roar of anger. He saw now why the green dragon was called Flame and Fury. Perhaps it was the wisest course of action to sever ties with him now.

"You really don't look well," Et-hir told him.

Jodathyn shook his head. "It's fleeting."

"Mynrell, tell me where you are at once."

"You're not my puppet master. I am not here for your glorification."

When Jodathyn stumbled over his own feet, Curran growled and steadied him. Worried by how angry the barkeep was, Jodathyn looked up at him through his lashes. For the first time, he noticed that Curran's attention wasn't solely on him. He had been focusing on what lay ahead, as if he was expecting something.

"Curran ... what's wrong? You seem agitated."

"Keep moving," Curran murmured. "We need a place to hide."

"Curran, you're scaring me."

"*Now* you're scared?" Curran hissed. "You might have thought about the consequences of your actions before freeing a cell's worth of prisoners. Do you know what will happen if you are arrested and your tattoos are unveiled? They'll flog you, mark my words," Curran continued, as if he hadn't heard Jodathyn's reply.

"I've been whipped before," Jodathyn said.

Curran's lips drew into a tight line. His eyes roamed over Jodathyn's face. "Yes," he admitted in a small voice. It was barely a whisper. "I would have spared you that if I could. The brewery is up ahead."

Jodathyn wondered why Curran was so insistent on reaching the brewery. Did he have someone there willing to help them? Was Nym waiting for them? He followed Curran in silence. With the mood both the barkeep and Mandros were in, he didn't particularly feel like a further telling off. All he needed now was for Kieryn to be informed. He almost missed his brother's lectures. Almost.

Like all of the shop fronts in the village, the brewery was dark. Curran opened the door and unceremoniously shoved Jodathyn inside. Et-hir stepped over the threshold of her own volition.

Curran led them through the quiet workshop and to another door, which he wrenched open. Now that the threat of being arrested was close, Jodathyn felt light-headed. Quivering, he looked at the back room as his eyes adjusted to the darkness. It was full of barrels.

Ignoring them, Curran stepped into the room. He inspected the barrels and finally he made his selection, wrenching the lids off two barrels. Neither were positioned right at the front. The barkeep turned around and stared at Jodathyn expectantly. "What are you waiting for? Hop in."

Jodathyn could only stare at the barrel in horror. He reeled back, not caring if his fright was obvious. "I can't!"

"Get into the barrel, boy."

"I can't!" Jodathyn repeated. He was frozen in place; a cold sweat ran down his face. He was vaguely aware that his hands were shaking. Clasping his fingers together, he refused to look in Curran's direction. The barkeep was staring at him with a stern yet curious gaze.

"Whatever your worry is, it's time to face it. As unpleasant as it is, it's a tight space or getting arrested."

Jodathyn resisted the urge to glance back at Et-hir. He knew she wouldn't be able to help him. When he seemed to be unable to move, she walked past him and jumped into the barrel. She turned back to him, her deep brown eyes pleading. "Please, Jod, do this for me."

Et-hir crouched down into her wooden prison so that Jodathyn could no longer see her. Shaking his head and cursing, Curran placed the lid on top of her barrel. When he was done, he turned pointedly to Jodathyn. The barkeep didn't look like he wanted to take the time to understand Jodathyn's predicament. "I don't care if small spaces make you frightened. Get in, or I'll put you in myself."

Taking a deep breath, Jodathyn did as he was told. He stepped forward and laid his hands on the edge of the barrel. The image of the night he was nearly drowned in a barrel resurfaced. It would have been a shame to die in a barrel full of beer with a rope about his neck. Attempting to rescue a slave without help had been very foolish thing to do.

Closing his eyes, Jodathyn ignored the rushing sound in his ears and leapt in. He settled himself into the cramped space of the barrel. His world was plunged into darkness when Curran replaced the lid.

"I'm sorry, lad, I really am."

Hugging his knees to his chest, Jodathyn practiced the deep breathing Donatein had so patiently taught him. He could feel his chest tightening in panic. Curran tapped on the barrel.

"I have to leave," Curran said. "Stay down until Nym or I come and fetch you."

"Yes, sir," Jodathyn replied. He longed to reach up and press his hands against the lid to free himself.

Above him he heard an exasperated sigh and Curran's boots against the hardwood floor as he left. A hush fell over Jodathyn. In his head, he counted to one hundred and thirty-four in the ancient tongue before he heard Et-hir's small voice.

"We forgot about Nym."

"Curran will keep her safe," Jodathyn replied.

"Why don't you like small spaces?"

Sighing, Jodathyn rested his forehead against the side of the barrel. He dragged a deep breath through his nose. Donatein had always been insistent that he face his fears, but the old man never knew what a coward he was. For the most part, he was able to keep his newfound fear of small spaces a secret.

"Jodathyn."

"I had a bad experience with a barrel." And that was all Jodathyn would say on the matter.

CHAPTER TWELVE

Illeanah

The Citadel of Pallaryn

Rough hands grabbed Illeanah around the waist and jerked her backwards. Incensed at Will's most undignified behaviour, she batted him away. Instead of letting her go and apologising for his appalling lack of manners, Will pressed her closer to his chest. He was stronger than he looked, Illeanah mused as he dragged her into an enclave. She opened her mouth to give him a piece of her mind, but he muffled her with his hands.

"Shhh ... unfriendly guards," Will hissed. He was too close. His chin was resting on the top of her head. Illeanah struggled. The only man who had ever held her like that was her father. Not even Jodathyn had dared embrace her. He was much too shy and gentlemanly for such displays.

Illeanah breathed in deeply, taking in the clean smell of lightly scented soap. Will Hartcurt was known to enjoy lavish amounts of soap when he bathed. That was, of course, according to palace rumour. The fact that she had overhead some of the younger King's Guardsmen teasing Will over his fascination with soap, and that he did indeed smell cleaner than any man ought, meant that the rumours must at least have some truth to them.

"Nothing wrong with smelling clean," Will muttered.

No wonder he was the king's spy. Somehow, he had read her body language and divined what she was thinking. She would have to be more careful with how she presented herself, lest Will learn more secrets from her. "Clean or not, this is not how you treat a lady. Didn't your mother teach you any manners?"

At the mention of his mother, Illeanah felt Will stiffen. She wondered at that. It was well known that Will's mother doted on Tomas, Will's elder brother. She assumed she spoiled Will as well.

"Please don't speak to me of my lady mother," Will gritted out.

"Why not?"

"Hush," Will hissed. "Here they come."

Sure enough, Illeanah could now hear the steps of approaching guardsmen. She was curious how Will had known they were coming. His hearing must be exceptional.

Slowly she twisted to study Will's face. He seemed drawn, and he looked much older than his twenty summers. His dark eyes drew her in; she could see deep loneliness and regret. Only a little older than she was, and Will had been without family for at least five years. The rift between Will and his father had been sensational news. She vaguely remembered Jodathyn trying to befriend the older boy. He had been rebuffed quite rudely.

Will's lips parted. For a brief moment, she could see his confident façade crumble and saw how afraid he was.

The footsteps drew closer, and Will stiffened. Illeanah stepped involuntarily backwards, and Will's arms tucked her in closer to his chest.

She could hear the steady thumping of his heart, which she was sure matched her own.

The owners of the footsteps marched past. From her hiding spot, Illeanah could make out the red and gold of Solan's men. She hated him. Her father said it was irrational to completely ignore the favour that Solan could offer them because of one mistake. It was the one thing she could not agree on with her father.

"Solan allowing the gross negligence and mistreatment of the king's brother wasn't one mistake," Will muttered from above her head. "Come."

Will took her hand and ushered her out into the corridor. Illeanah let herself be dragged along obediently. She felt adrift on a sea of uncertainty. All she knew was Will Hartcurt might be her only chance at freedom. She had never expected him to amount to too much.

They drew closer to the private chambers of the Pallarus household. As they passed the corridor that led to Jodathyn's rooms, Illeanah paused. It was still and abandoned.

"Otherworlds, I miss Jod," Illeanah said with a sigh.

Will looked at her, and his dark eyes softened. "He didn't want to break his friendship with you."

"He was afraid he would ruin me," Illeanah replied. "It hurt to see him pull away like that."

Will grunted. "I was rude to Jodathyn all those years ago out of respect of the king. My reputation would only hurt Jodathyn, so I kept my distance."

"Jodathyn is very kind," Illeanah remarked.

"It's his greatest weakness."

"'Tis not a bad weakness to have, truth be known."

Will tilted his head and nodded. "Let me do the talking with the King's Guard."

Illeanah shrugged and was happy for Will to take control. He eyed her critically, as if she was behaving in a way he had not anticipated. Then with a huff, he continued towards the royal couple's private quarters.

They were stopped by a pair of young King's Guardsmen, who couldn't be much older than they were. Illeanah peered around Will's shoulder, wondering what the lord was going to do.

"Is it true, Hartcurt?" one guardsman asked. He glanced to his companion, whose hands were resting on the hilt of his sword. "Thylyssa is here ... and Solan has granted him full pardon?"

"It's true."

The second guardsman glanced up at the staircase leading to the royal wing. "She's in danger, then?"

Will nodded.

"I hope you know what you are doing, Will," the first said. "We'll cover your tracks for as long as we can."

"You should leave Pallaryn, Allard."

Allard shifted; his eyes darted back towards the corridors. His teeth bit into his lip. "I'll not abandon my post."

Clapping him on the shoulder, Will looked Allard full in the face. "You have been a good friend to me. *Araae helpheliwyn. Terini gorthorawyn ...*"

"Live valiantly. Die honourably," Allard replied, using the ancient words the King's Guard was famous for. "Hopefully without the *die* part."

"If you get the chance, Lord Will," the second guardsman said, "can you let my family know I did my duty?"

"I'll do so personally, Tryst. Your uncle would be so proud."

Tryst swallowed; his fingers played with the clasp on his cloak. He unpinned it and let the black cape fall to the ground. Pressing the clasp into Will's hand, he said, "My wife is due to give birth any day ... I fear I will never see my child. It's all I have to give."

Will wrapped his arms around Tryst and pulled him into a fierce hug. "Is she in the citadel?"

Tryst shook his head. "Thank Otherworlds, no. Jael suggested that she would be more comfortable with her mother's family. She's in Habron."

"As soon as I am able, I'll find her," Will said.

Tryst gathered his will and stepped aside. "The way is clear. Get Queen Odelle to safety."

Illeanah thought she saw Will tear up as he stepped past, but he said nothing more. He led her with such confidence towards the royal chambers that she had to ponder where it came from. She was the daughter of the favoured lord, and yet she didn't know the way to the king or queen's rooms. Here was Will, a scandalous lord of ill repute, and he moved with such surety it didn't make sense.

"These are the queen's chambers," Will told her as he stopped by a door. "I may need a woman's touch to get her majesty to come with us."

Illeanah wanted to tell Will that if he wanted a woman's touch, he had the wrong lady. She wasn't known for being good with people, especially other women.

Hesitantly, Will raised his hand and rapped on the door. He was shaking. The door opened, and one of the queen's ladies frowned at them.

"Her Majesty is not seeing anyone."

"Tell her Willyrd Hartcurt demands an urgent audience."

"I know who you are, and she is not well."

As the lady pushed the door to close on their faces, Will held out his hand to stop it. "I insist on speaking with her majesty at once."

"Disgrace!"

"I am Willyrd Hartcurt."

"I know who you are."

"And I know for a fact that His Majesty has commanded that if ever Willyrd Hartcurt comes to the queen's door, I am to be admitted immediately."

The lady huffed and turned a heated glare at Illeanah. She seemed to reconsider her position as Will refused to budge. With a contemptuous look, she opened the door further and ushered them inside. The expression on her face was as if something unpleasant had been wafted under her nose. Will didn't seem bothered by her attitude at all. Illeanah wondered if he had become accustomed to people thinking so little of him that it no longer upset him.

Illeanah turned and shut the door. She guessed whatever Will had planned, he wouldn't want any unwanted intrusions.

"I'll let my mistress know you are here."

Will inclined his head as if he had been treated with civility. While they waited, Illeanah took a chance to study the queen's private quarters. The room was stunning. Large glass windows let in plenty of natural light. Vases of flowers were dotted about the room. In the corner, Illeanah spied an abandoned embroidery. The queen was embroidering yellow flowers.

Will followed Illeanah's line of sight. "She does that when she's upset ... the yellow flowers."

"How do you know all these things?"

"I'm the king's spy. I'm just as close to His Majesty as your father."

The queen entered, sans lady. Illeanah was surprised at how simply she was dressed. Her hair was braided in a simple style, and her dress and slippers were plain. She looked pale, tired and sad.

"Your Majesty." Will knelt, and Illeanah belatedly followed his example.

"Will, dear, always such a pleasure, and Miss Whitoak ..."

"Your Majesty, there's a plot afoot to harm the king."

Queen Odelle's face froze into visible confusion. Her hand darted towards her stomach. If Illeanah had any doubts she was pregnant, it had now been confirmed.

"Pray go on."

"A coup is coming. Your unborn child is at risk. Anyone of Pallarus bloodline—"

"A successful coup will need to rid Rama of all Pallarus claimants to the throne," Queen Odelle continued. Her posture seemed outwardly calm, but Illeanah could see the slight tremor of her lips.

"They're coming for you," Will warned in a low voice. "The unborn princess will not be safe. The move to arrest those loyal to you has already begun."

"They can't touch me," the queen protested. "I am the king's wife. I must stay here."

"Majesty, they plan on arresting the king. You cannot stay."

"I cannot fail Kieryn."

"Pallaryn is about to fall," Will said. "I have contacts in the citadel. We can hide and get you to safety ... for the babe and for the king."

"My ladies ..."

"Your Majesty, as heartless as it may seem, we need to go without warning anyone."

Queen Odelle looked crestfallen. Her large eyes clouded over. "Is there no other way?"

Will shook his head. "Your Majesty, you can't serve the realm if you're dead."

"The servant tunnels," the queen whispered. She clasped her hands in front of her, pulling off her golden rings. "The maids were gossiping that's how Jodathyn's manservant escaped."

"Find a purse to take the rings, Majesty," Will said as the queen turned to hide the rings. Illeanah and the queen looked up at him incredulously. "We might need to buy safety."

"You want to sell royal jewels?" Illeanah gasped.

"What is a jewel in comparison to life?" Will replied.

"Yes, you're right, Will. As usual." The queen glanced up at him with large, soft eyes. She spun on her heel and went to her dresser. Illeanah saw her pull out a velvet purse and two small vials with dark liquid. "Where is safe if they take my husband from me too?"

"I'll find a place," Will said fervently.

Illeanah almost believed he was speaking the truth. "Jodathyn told me there's a hole in the palace wall," she said. Never had she felt so useless.

Will could handle the queen on his own. He didn't have to smuggle her out of Pallaryn at all. "That's how he escaped the palace the night he got in trouble at the tavern."

Will's eyes glinted. "I was hoping you would be able to show me."

Illeanah started and turned towards Will. She knew he had said he was the king's spy, but how did he know so much? She hadn't breathed a word to a soul about Jodathyn's escape hole. Out of curiosity, she had looked for it to see if she could find it. Using Jodathyn's description, it had been remarkably easy to find. As far as she was aware, Captain Candyde and Jodathyn's dead guard, Valt, were the only ones who knew of its existence. She couldn't imagine Jodathyn sharing this information.

Dismissing the puzzle that was Will, Illeanah nodded her head sharply. "I can show you."

Illeanah was not pleased to be on her belly in the soft earth, crawling through a cramped space. She had allowed the queen through first. Will had insisted that she go second so that he might act as a lookout. Grunting, Illeanah pushed the bundle of cloaks and the dagger through the hole. It was a tight fit even for her. Jodathyn was lucky not to have gotten stuck.

She scraped her elbows on the brick on her way out. Biting back an unladylike curse, she heaved her way out of the hole. The queen was on her knees at the other side, delicately brushing off each of the cloaks.

"You should call me Della," the queen said. "My name is too recognisable."

Stumbling to her feet, Illeanah looked around as Will began to wriggle his way through. "I suppose Nia will do for me," she said.

"I'm too well-known in Pallaryn for an alias," Will admitted. The pained expression on his face indicated that he might be stuck. Without thinking, Illeanah bent. She grasped his hands and tugged. A moment later, the queen was at her side helping her. Together they wrestled Will from the castle wall.

"That settles it. You're a bigger man than Jod."

Chuckling, Will brushed himself off and wearily looked back at the palace wall.

The queen's attention was on the citadel's streets. She wrapped herself in a cloak and turned back to Will as if expecting him to tell her what to do next.

"When you say you are too well-known—"

"It's simple, Nia," Will interrupted. "I have used my charm and guile to build my own little network of common folk. Out here, I'm respected. No one, unless they work for my brother, will bother us or question what we are doing."

"We'll not be harassed?" The queen looked nervous. Illeanah couldn't blame her. She couldn't remember the last time she had stepped foot in the citadel and mingled with lowborns. Typical that Will would be so comfortable with the idea.

"As long as you are with me, Della, no one will harass you."

Illeanah grabbed a cloak and wrapped it around her shoulders. She was thankful she was wearing a modest emerald-green gown with minimal embellishments. Still, the cloak would hide her clearly superior garment. Even if it was a man's cloak.

"Your husband will not be angry," Will said. He took the queen's hands in a rather presumptive grasp. "He is excited for his unborn daughter; he would see her live. He would never say you have failed him in doing this. I know his mind."

A sudden understanding hit Illeanah. There was a reason Will seemed to be able to respond to her thoughts. A reason why he made such an excellent spy. It wasn't mere instinct. He was much too accurate for that. And the way the queen was now looking at him with relief ...

"You have power?" Illeanah croaked.

"I am unafraid of my gift," Will answered levelly. His fathomless eyes gave nothing away. Illeanah knew he had been waiting for her to come to this conclusion, like a spider in a web. "Unlike some, my power is known to those I help."

"Can you read my thoughts?" Illeanah demanded. "Have you been rummaging around in my head uninvited?"

"Yes, I know your thoughts," Will admitted. His shoulders drooped. "It isn't something I can cease doing because you dislike it. I can't stop your thoughts from entering my own head."

"If you are so powerful, why didn't you foresee Prince Carvelle's abduction?" Illeanah challenged. Thrusting her finger in Will's sternum, she accented each word with a harsh prod.

"Will needs to be in close proximity of the person to read them," the queen said.

Will shifted, his gaze turning to stare fixedly at something over Illeanah's head. "Believe me, Nia, I do not wish to read your thoughts ... but I can no more stop them than fly."

Illeanah sniffed and crossed her arms against her chest.

"We're about to enter the more ... colourful part of town," Will said. He lowered his voice. She thought he sounded nervous. "I am well-liked here. Wherever I lead us, we're safe."

"Of course you're liked here," Illeanah couldn't help mumbling.

"Nia, my dear, perhaps remember Will is doing the best he can," the queen admonished. Illeanah's hackles rose, even though the queen had used a calm, mollifying tone.

They continued to walk the cobblestone streets. Illeanah noticed more and more painted faces of whores. Much to her dismay, some even had the audacity to call out crude propositions. Illeanah was sure her face was burning crimson. She didn't know how such a gentle woman like the queen could be so unaffected by their crass behaviour.

Will took the lead and ignored Illeanah's revolted stare as he handed a thick silver coin to a pregnant whore. She shuddered as Will closed the woman's dirty fist around the silver, and he leaned in close to say something to her.

"No, it's not my child," Will said as they turned into the next street. "Sometimes a little kindness has a way of finding its way back to you."

Illeanah didn't reply.

"Pallaryn is my playground. This is where I work—help those who want an education or start small businesses. Those that want help, I find a way. And the guild ... to them, I'm a pain in the rear end."

Illeanah was about to open her mouth to ask Will who or what the guild was. But he stopped them by an old, decrepit building.

"A brothel?" the queen gasped upon reading the sign in the doorway. "My husband forbade you to ever return."

"This is a different brothel," Will replied. "It's the perfect place to hide, and Madam Nurlah is a wonderful host."

Will started climbing the steps up to the brothel. A buxom lady with a mountain of blonde curls met them at the front door. She returned Illeanah's look of horror at her sheer red gown with practiced indifference. Shrewd brown eyes, rimmed with thick, black kohl, gazed at Will and then the queen, who clearly didn't belong in a brothel.

"Madam Nurlah, I would hope to beg you for shelter for tonight. We'll be gone come morning."

"Don't speak such nonsense." Nurlah nodded sharply so that her curls bounced on her head. "A lovely hot meal, a bath and a rest is always available for Will and his friends."

Will bounded the last few steps to approach her. He gave her a quick hug and peck on the cheek and turned back to Illeanah and the queen. "This is Della and Nia. My cousins."

"Yes, I can see from their pasty complexions they are from the west country too!"

Will smirked up at the madam.

Madam Nurlah's dark-painted lips parted into a smile. "Now, tell me, have you heard any more from the last foundling you stowed away here? You were quite taken with feisty Fy, if memory serves correctly."

The madam laughed as Will flushed.

Illeanah decided that perhaps the madam wasn't so bad after all.

CHAPTER THIRTEEN

Kieryn

The Fields of Tannryn

Kieryn had always been aware that his presence was a burden to his men. They would never be allowed to relax while the High King was near. It was best that he remove himself from the camp. Tonight, he used the excuse that he needed time to reflect and retired to his tent early.

To be High King was to be alone. He ate his meal in isolation and then sat upon his pallet, waiting for sleep that would never come. Spreading Jodathyn's cloak of burnt orange over his lap, he wondered where his brother was spending his evening. Was Carvelle safe at his uncle's side?

He couldn't bring himself to lay his head down to rest. He watched as one by one the candles burned low, casting eerie shadows around his tent. The sounds of the guardsmen around the campfire quieted.

It was late. Most of his men had sought out their own beds for the night, and he was free to walk about the camp.

Leaving the solitude of his tent, Kieryn caught the eye of the sentry. At the man's polite stare, he turned his back and walked in the opposite direction. Kieryn had little desire to converse with his men tonight. His mind was full of its own worries.

As he entered the darkest part of the camp, however, Kieryn heard voices.

"Jod was notorious at Aviah Valley for his high pain threshold. I wouldn't worry so, Fy. An injury isn't going to slow him down."

"Ruevyn, those men are still out there!"

Kieryn paused, spotting the two strangers who had joined them in Habron. Fydellah was one who seemed to prefer quiet reflection and observation. His guardsmen had discovered that she was a fiercely independent woman and had given up offering her any help. She held herself with confidence; she was a woman who knew her value. Kieryn could see it in the way she moved: she was highborn.

On the other hand, when he calmed down, Ruevyn was a talkative character. He was charismatic and charming. The type of man most people would instantaneously like. He made friends easily among the guardsmen. With the exception of Carew, whom he seemed nervous of.

Hiding himself in the shadows, Kieryn approached the voices. He could see their dim outlines in the dark. That sat close together, continuing their hushed conversation, which they believed was private.

"The kidnappers are dead," Ruevyn muttered.

Fydellah made an outraged sound in the back of her throat and hit Ruevyn's arm with her fist. "Why didn't you tell me that?"

"Didn't seem important." Ruevyn shrugged.

"*Not important*! What happened to them?"

Again, Ruevyn shrugged. "They were burnt. Their campsite was mostly ash."

"Do you think ...?" Fydellah lowered her voice.

"Jodathyn's dragon came out to play? Yes ..." Ruevyn copied her tone of voice. "The ground shook with a roar the night those men were killed. I dare not say too much. Jodathyn isn't dangerous."

"The dragon killed people ..."

"Men intending to kill him who had *stabbed* him and threatened a little boy. Jodathyn took care of them. Not much different than me ramming a sword through their guts or the king having their heads removed from their shoulders."

"I can't imagine him as a dragon, all teeth and claws and talons..."

"I can," Ruevyn said. "He'd be a large beastie ... but I'm sure he would still be nimble. He'd be the type to fly through the storm just to have more fun."

Kieryn smiled ruefully at the image of Jodathyn spreading his wings and tumbling through the clouds. As a youngster, his brother had him in a constant state of worry that he might fall or hurt himself with the mischief he got into. Trees and the palace walls weren't the only things Jodathyn climbed.

The duo's laughter died down.

"I've seen him," Fydellah said. "The dragon in his eyes. He says his name is Tornyth."

"Jodathyn's dragon has always been there for anyone who had the wits to see him. He can be seen most often when he is angry or scared. But I have also seen the dragon when he's very happy. Strong emotions draw the beast out. It's strange how unaware Jodathyn is of its presence."

Kieryn clenched his fists to his side. He had thought he knew his brother well. Yet another knew of his dragon from his childhood. The farmer had been a witness to the dragon growing within Jodathyn, while he had been blissfully unaware how strong the beast truly was. And Fydellah, she knew the creature's name.

"Tornyth," Kieryn whispered, testing the name. He felt a shiver of dread. The name was a proclamation of a return to glory. For who or what, he did not know. Was Jodathyn already lost to him?

"The herbs didn't work." Fydellah shifted again, the shadows hiding the expression on her face.

Ruevyn scoffed. "Not the way they had hoped. I'm glad I never told Whitoak. I didn't trust the man not to hurt Jod."

"Would the king's favourite really hurt Jodathyn?" Fydellah asked.

"Yes," Ruevyn replied. "Whitoak would *remove* Jodathyn if he felt he was in the way."

In the back of his mind, Kieryn could see the outline of Whitoak's face asking him to do away with Jodathyn. While he had been furious at Whitoak for making such a ridiculous suggestion, he had concluded his favourite was only concerned for his throne and son. Were the lord's motives more selfish in nature?

When Whitoak had brought Jodathyn home, Kieryn had been grateful. Whitoak had also been a driving force in convincing the council that Odelle was a suitable bride. He hadn't hesitated to bring Whitoak into his close confidence. He had been too eager to have someone wise and strong to help secure his rule.

"That house, Aviah Valley, did they treat Jodathyn ..."

"Just like one of the household *servants*, yes. He ate the same food and slept upon the straw next to me. Whenever the king's messenger came to see Jodathyn, they would wash him in a great hurry and tell him what words to say. They threatened him if he dared to deviate from the proper responses. You've not seen real courage until you've seen a child steal from a knight. We used to take coins to try and feed the other children. It made him so happy to think he did something good." Ruevyn stopped and chuckled. There was no mirth in the farmer's laughter. "Jodathyn was a brave little fool. If only I had been able to stop him that day. They almost killed him with the dog whip ... That's when I ran away and found Lord Whitoak to tell him my story. I wanted to get Jodathyn help."

"It always seemed extraordinary to me that a child would go to such lengths to sacrifice himself for a pup."

"Extraordinary," Ruevyn repeated, but the tone of his voice didn't seem to match his words. "Jodathyn always had a soft heart."

"Is that how you became friends?"

Ruevyn nodded. "When my mother sold me, I was a frightened boy. The other servants didn't have patience for my tears. The newly orphaned Jodathyn, only three years old, would cuddle up to me at night and do his best to comfort me. He would tell me stories of how his great papa would come and save us. We only had to live in faith."

A soft smile spread across Kieryn's face. This sounded like Jodathyn as a child. It seemed that his brother had not grown out of his soft heart as Kieryn had hoped. A soft heart was easily crushed in a cruel world.

"What about you, Fy? What happened?"

Fydellah sighed, twisting a wayward curl around her finger. "Envious of my powers, my sister betrayed me. I was ambushed in the dark, my friends slain, and I was forced upon a ship in chains. Spent months locked up in a dirty cage. You would know the hunger, of course, and the tattooing. The name calling was horrid and the spitting disgusting. My captors thought to use my power to rat out other potential magic users. After all, they can't lie to me. I wouldn't ... I couldn't ..." Fydellah bit back a choked sob. "Even after the beatings ... I couldn't."

"You were very brave," Ruevyn murmured. He lifted his hand as if to reach out and comfort her, then thought better of it.

"Do you think so?" Fydellah whispered. She brushed her tears away with her hand.

"I know so." Ruevyn sighed. "I can't imagine the horror of being betrayed by a family member. But you are strong."

"I don't want to be strong," Fydellah confessed.

"I understand a little bit," Ruevyn murmured. "I was only a child so I can't say I understand what you are describing ..."

"Your mother sold you too," Fydellah replied.

"My mother cried with grief in the days leading up to selling me," Ruevyn said. "At least I knew in her heart she loved me, and she was in pain too. I can still hear her screams as they pried me away … My story is different than yours."

"Pain is pain."

For a long while, Ruevyn and Fydellah fell silent. Kieryn was about to turn from his place where he was eavesdropping with a heavy heart when Fydellah dragged in a deep breath.

"You said that you never killed a woman. I know that is true. But I also felt the unsaid truth. You've killed men."

Kieryn cursed his feet that were rooted to the ground. He didn't want to hear Ruevyn's reply to Fydellah's question. Upon reflection, it seemed wrong that he was skulking in the dark, eavesdropping on their every word. He wanted to call out a warning to alert Ruevyn to remain silent.

"Yes," Ruevyn groaned. "I've killed."

Kieryn wanted to scream. He was the High King of Rama; it was his traditional right and duty to uphold the law no matter who had broken it. To ignore crimes, whether petty or great, went against everything he vowed when he had become king.

Although, a voice whispered in his mind. *No one knows you heard this conversation … You've freed others with powers, protected Jodathyn, let servants escape … You've broken the law many times over. What good are traditional vows of kingship when the people of Rama suffer?*

He felt a pang of guilt at the thought. What good was his power if he failed to uphold the law? From the time he could walk, he had been taught it was his duty to be the most upright man in Rama. And he had failed, just as his father had predicted. Hanging his head in shame, Kieryn tried not to envisage the face of his father.

"Just because the crown has done something in the past doesn't make it right, fair, or just." Kieryn's lips moved as he mouthed the words silently to himself. They had been Jodathyn's words, spoken to chastise the great lords. He had been too merry with festival wine to take too much heed to his brother's wisdom.

Could it be the law had failed Rama? What good was the law if it failed to protect the people like Donatein, Jodathyn, Will and the two who were whispering before him? Tradition be damned. If good people suffered because of the law, the law needed to be challenged.

He leaned closer to catch the next words Ruevyn Kelvie spoke. As much as the pair's whispered conversation pained him, it gave him much to think about. Safe, well fed, and protected, he had never thought about life as a mistreated slave held against his will. Ruevyn's and Fydellah's experiences were so far removed from his own that it held a strange allure to listen and hear more.

"When I escaped Aviah Valley and told Lord Whitoak what had befallen Jodathyn to help overthrow Lord Solan, he took me to Androssah to work for him. No matter how much I begged, Whitoak would never let me see Jodathyn. Everything was fine until I became a man and started to question his benevolence. Lord Whitoak doesn't like to be questioned."

"Let me guess, Lord Whitoak wasn't exactly benevolent."

"I was safe as long as I brought value to his lordship. So I started to look elsewhere. One of the lawman's daughters in Androssah was a lovely lady with a pretty smile. I sought to woo her to get into her father's good graces. Along the way, I fell in love with her. Elyssa was one of the kindest souls you could ever hope to meet ... She was always running about Androssah with a basket of muffins and a streak of flour in her hair. So I asked her to marry me. Her father knew my secret past and was in favour of the match. We were to wed this coming high spring. I had even organised some extra embroidery for her wedding dress ... little apple blossoms."

"Apple blossoms?"

"I'm quite fond of apples." Ruevyn's voice broke. Kieryn could hear him swallowing as he built up the courage to continue his story.

"A slaver came to town. When they couldn't get to me—I came home to her lifeless body on the floor surrounded by flour and muffins. Elyssa's father told me to flee Androssah ... but I couldn't.

"I went to the inn, barged down the slaver's door, and strung him up from the rafters. Elyssa's father caught me. Slavers like the man I killed have protection, and he begged me to flee. Otherworlds forgive me, Elyssa's father took the fall. I fled to Sant Burgundy to start a new life, and the magistrate in Androssah had no choice but to hang an innocent man. Lord Whitoak demanded it. By the time I heard … it was too late. Elyssa's father had joined her in the Otherworld."

For a long moment, Kieryn stood silent in the dark, listening to Ruevyn's sniffles. It was his duty as High King to uphold justice, but listening to Ruevyn's grief, he resolved to forget he heard the conversation. One dead slaver never hurt anyone. Whitoak had some serious questions to answer as well. He wondered how he might confront his favourite without exposing Ruevyn's secret.

"I'm so sorry," Fydellah murmured. "I didn't mean to pry … Did Lord Whitoak know it was you?"

Ruevyn sniffed. "Judging by Lady Illeanah's reception of me in Pallaryn, yes, he knew … it means he knew Elyssa's father was not to blame either."

"Then why—"

"Tidying loose ends," Ruevyn murmured bitterly. "It's what some of the great lords do."

Kieryn closed his eyes. How had he been so foolish and blind? Ceasing the suffering of his people should have been his priority. He should have stopped his lords a long time ago. They were becoming a plague to the people of Rama.

Kieryn stepped out of the gloom and towards the whispering duo. He watched with amusement as their eyes widened at his presence. The muscles around Ruevyn's jaws clenched, his face quickly paling. "Tell me, Master Kelvie. I have always been told that illegal slavery in Rama is a minor, inconvenient, niggly problem. I take it you and Miss Nahilya would agree that I have been an ineffective High King?"

"With all due respect, my king, if you want to enact change, forget pretty words and act," Fydellah said, tilting her head up so that her eyes glistened.

"And what would you have me do, Miss Fydellah?"

"It is not my duty to tell you what to do," Fydellah murmured. "Perhaps you could begin by listening to those who are suffering. Hear our voices. From the highborns among us to the lowest criminal."

"Highborns have the *right* to be heard by our king." Ruevyn scowled. "A lowborn like me, a gutter urchin, I have to rely on the magistrates in the local towns. Many are controlled by the great lords and gold."

Hanging his head, Kieryn clenched his fists and squeezed them for all his might. The blossoming pain kept his fury at bay. "How could this happen?"

"My king, this is not a new problem that Rama is facing." Fydellah clasped her hands in front of her.

Kieryn looked up, perplexed.

"Please forgive me for what I am about to say," Fydellah said. "But your grandfather was not a great leader. In his reign, which was long and mediocre, the great lords whittled away his power. They only consolidated their power during your father's reign and you ..."

"I continued the pattern. I thought I was fighting for my people."

Ruevyn shrugged. "You weren't a man when you became king. You had to fight to get where you are today. But the fight for your people isn't over, Your Majesty."

"I see that now." Kieryn sighed. Deep in thought, he approached and sat down alongside Ruevyn. "Who can I trust? How do I tear their power from their grasps without civil war?"

"Strike hard and fast?" Ruevyn suggested.

"Dismantle the guild in Pallaryn," Fydellah added.

"Miss Fy." Kieryn sighed. "Are you able to detect wrongdoers with absolute certainty? And would you be willing to do so?"

Watching, Kieryn saw Fydellah swallow at the lump in her throat. "When I was locked in that horrible cage, I dreamed of doing this ..."

Kieryn looked into the dark night. "What if I gather the youngest slaves, keep them somewhere safe, guarded, educated while we attempt to find their families ..." He trailed off, glancing at Ruevyn, who was watching him intently. He shook his head and continued his monologue of thought. "Older ones we will need to look at case by case. Assess the damage and address the issues ... Will might come in handy here."

Ruevyn shifted. "It would indeed be a swift justice to see the great summer houses owned by particular lords used to house, educate and care for the child slaves. Could you imagine Solan's face if we used Aviah Valley for this purpose?"

"I don't intend for Solan to live long enough to see that day." Kieryn grinned, baring his teeth. "Lord Solan's property will be mine and will be funding this enterprise ... I can think of a few others that may need to volunteer their wealth. Might you consider advising me on some matters, Master Kelvie?"

"An honour, my king."

"I should have listened to Jodathyn. We had such a terrible argument over Miss Nahilya's fate ... I commanded him to be quiet, and now he is paying the price."

"My king, your brother will do everything in his power to return your son," Fydellah murmured. She approached, her movements smooth and graceful. "Prince Carvelle said they had climbed a tree to hide from the kidnappers. Jodathyn is more resourceful than we think."

"Jodathyn was always a prolific climber." Kieryn chuckled, despite the worry and fear warring in his stomach. "I saw a mark recently—a tattoo of an eye and spear. Can either of you tell me about it?"

The curling smile on Fydellah's face faded. "It's the mark of the guild."

"Guild?"

"Slavers," Ruevyn clarified, rolling up his sleeve to reveal the tattoo of the same mark. He nodded to Fydellah with a sharp gesture. "It's how they identify runaways like us. They call it Vadroil's Eye."

"You should get those marks covered over," Kieryn said, his voice softening.

"No one would be willing to cover the tattoo."

Kieryn turned upon his heel to head back to the privacy of his tent. "Perhaps Lord Solan might find himself funding the employment of a tattooist as well."

"Do you suppose he means to?" Kieryn heard Ruevyn whisper to Fydellah. Living in the palace in Pallaryn, a keen sense of hearing was a must.

"My power says he speaks absolute truth."

CHAPTER FOURTEEN

Jodathyn

The Village of Kudah

Jodathyn had sat in the barrel for so long that his legs were cramping. Finding it difficult to stay awake, he rested his forehead against his knees. He longed to jump out of the barrel, but he had disappointed Curran. And now because of his actions, Et-hir and Curran were in danger. He gritted his teeth and tried to bury his terror of confined places.

His mouth felt dry, and his skin was coated in a fine sheen of sweat. "I'm weak," he mumbled. "Stay still and silent ... you have to be brave."

Fatigue finally won, and Jodathyn found himself dozing so that he was in a half aware state.

Alone in the dark, Jodathyn could almost feel the rippling of scales as a dragon shifted around him. Even in his dazed condition, he realised another dragon was trying to commune with Tornyth. He wanted to jolt away, remembering that he was angry at Mandros for not telling him that he was a tool to be used. Mandros had not been honest with him ...

But it wasn't Mandros. The muscles about him constricted so that his breathing became laboured. Instead of the glistening emerald he had quickly become accustomed to, he saw a flash of red … and dark, endless black eyes.

Jodathyn pressed his hands to his mouth. Galgothmeg was looking for him. He must have realised he had not perished at the abandoned hut. The red dragon was infuriated and was determined to finish the job.

Jodathyn could have groaned at his foolishness. Because of his own stupidity, he was stuffed into a barrel, hiding from the lawmen, and a murderous, ancient evil was looking for him.

Against Galgothmeg, Curran could do nothing. And the red dragon was close.

Jodathyn fought the urge to claw his way out of the barrel. He clenched his fists and bit down on his lip to stop himself crying out. He was so caught in his haze of panic that he didn't notice the sound of men's voices. It was the sound of barrels being opened and tumbled to the ground that pulled him out of his initial terror. He was plunged into a deeper sense of horror.

He was trapped within the barrels; there was nowhere for him to go. In moments, he would be discovered and dragged out into who knows what mess. He had only one hope. Dragons.

Jodathyn was well aware of how angry Mandros was with him. Even now, he could feel a slight tingling rage that was not his own. He was unwilling to call the green dragon for help.

"*Call Sidrah if we cannot go to* Aluel!" Tornyth cried.

Shaking, Jodathyn closed his eyes and projected his thoughts with all his might. "*SIDRAH!*"

"They're here somewhere," came a muffled voice. "The magistrate's no-good spy saw them."

"Best to keep Curran out of this mess if we can," another voice said.

For a long moment, there was a terrible silence. Jodathyn panted, trying to regain control of his breathing. It was then that he heard the sound he had been dreading. A barrel was tipped over, and he heard the sound of Et-hir yelling. He could her the hitch in her breath as she started babbling and pleading in Sionian. As afraid as he was, Jodathyn knew he couldn't stay in the barrel.

"Sidrah, I need your help."

"Call for your aluel ..."

"Sidrah! Please!"

Silence.

"Fine. Goodbye, Sidrah."

Jodathyn steeled himself and with one last steadying breath, he pressed his palms against the lid of the barrel. With one push, it sprung free, and he stood. Leaving Et-hir to deal with the lawmen on her own was not an option.

"I believe you're looking for me."

Two lawmen, who he recognised immediately as Floyde and Ripley, turned to regard him. Et-hir was wedged between them, glaring.

Lawman Floyde approached, his hand outstretched, as if to pacify him. "Locke of Belrah, you are to be detained."

"You're arresting me?"

"'Fraid so, lad. Best to come with us without a struggle," Lawman Ripley grumbled. He heaved a resisting Et-hir to her feet. "We're just doing our jobs."

Jodathyn nodded. He held out his wrists, knowing he had a better chance of keeping his identity secret if he seemed to be compliant. "I know. Let Et-hir go. I persuaded her to join me on this madness. I didn't give her much choice. I forced her to help me."

Floyde shook his head. He stepped forward and bound Jodathyn's wrists with a thick rope. Jodathyn had to repress a flinch. "Don't be lying, boy. The Sionian woman is known for threatening to free prisoners. There's plenty of witnesses to testify to that."

"She's put you up to this no-good foolery," Ripley remarked, toeing Et-hir with his leather boot.

"Leave her alone!" Jodathyn snapped, wrenching against Floyde's grip.

"She's confounded you with her Sionian magic."

"I said leave her alone!" Jodathyn roared as Ripley went to kick her again.

"Now, now, Lockie … settle down. Let's get this unpleasantness over and done with. You been in trouble with the law before, boy?"

"No." Jodathyn swallowed past the lie as Lawman Floyde steered him out of the brewery and into the night.

"Well, you've made a right fool of the magistrate, so I expect you will be carted to the mines to work off your misdeeds. Now, a nice lad like you, cause no trouble and your sentence will be over quicker."

"Et-hir …"

"You're mightily taken with the pretty little Sionian lass, aren't you?"

"This is all my fault," Jodathyn muttered.

Lawman Floyde chuckled; there was very little humour in his laugh. "I've seen plenty of youngsters set up by those they hope to woo. Et-hir, as you call her, has been in trouble before."

Trying to turn himself around so that he could face the lawman to give him a piece of his mind, Jodathyn was shoved in the back. "Keep moving. You don't want to be seen resisting."

"If you want to get rid of your magistrate, take my word for it, petition the king and tell him what is happening in Kudah," Jodathyn said.

"I'm doing my job, boy."

"The king doesn't know about what is happening here, and if he finds out … your magistrate won't last long before him."

"Quite an imagination you have," Lawman Ripley interrupted. "Now, Curran Norrys, have you seen him this evening?"

Jodathyn swallowed. He knew he couldn't take his time in answering the question. It would be suspicious. But he had to be wise in answering. He had no idea how much the lawman actually knew of his movements that night.

"Locke?" Floyde's voice was a low growl.

"The barman? Yes, we had an ale or two together at the bouts."

"Your friend you came into town with, what of her?" Jodathyn didn't like the way Lawman Floyde's eyes narrowed in suspicion.

"Again, I saw her at the bouts. If you ask her competitors, I approached her to wish her luck and farewell."

"Farewell?"

"Yes. We had decided that we would part ways in Kudah. We met on the road and decided to travel together this far."

"I see."

As they approached the long, rectangular building that belonged to the magistrate, Jodathyn could see quite a crowd had formed. He couldn't help but startle. It was late and cold. What were so many people doing out of their beds at this hour?

"You've caused quite a stir," Floyde drawled. "Be a good boy and speak only when spoken to."

An old woman, who seemed to have trouble walking, hobbled over toward them. She grasped at Jodathyn's jerkin with wrinkled hands. She pressed her forehead against his chest, weeping. Dumbfounded, Jodathyn stopped so that he didn't step on her.

"That's enough of that," Lawman Floyde said gruffly.

"Thank you, thank you, thank you!" the woman was crying. "My husband wouldn't have survived the mines. Bless your dear little wayward heart."

"I said enough!"

"Evil slugs like the magistrate only win when good men do nothing," the old woman replied. She lifted her head from Jodathyn's chest and waggled her finger underneath Lawman Floyde's nose.

"I'm following orders."

"Bah, orders," the woman croaked. "You can take your orders and—"

"Kya, I would hate to arrest you."

"I'm dying anyway ..." The old woman reached up and tapped Jodathyn's cheek. "I remember when I was a young woman, a slip of a girl, and seeing your grandfather the first time. Oh, he was a handsome boy, just like you."

Jodathyn shuddered. It seemed like it was more than his scar that would give him away. He hung his head, hoping to keep curious eyes off him.

"Now, now, honey," the old woman crooned, brushing a stray lock from his face. "It'll all turn out fine."

"You know the family?" the lawman grunted.

"I'm a Sionian, and I recognised the family," Et-hir said from behind them.

The old woman withdrew her hand from Jodathyn's face and looked up at the lawmen, puzzled. Her wizened eyes crinkled as she turned away, chortling.

Snarling in frustration, Floyde pushed Jodathyn through the crowd of people. He clunked up the steps, keeping a firm hold on his prisoner. Thinking about the judgement that was about to be passed down on him, Jodathyn didn't even begin to hope for a fair trial. He felt nauseous and light-headed as he listened to Et-hir's frightened sobs behind him. He would have loved to comfort her, but the lawman kept him marching forwards.

Careful to remain silent and watchful while they were in the magistrate's domain, Jodathyn allowed himself to be escorted inside. They were swiftly taken to a reception hall, which was presided by Magistrate Swyft. Jodathyn was no fool; the man was neither fair nor just.

From his large, wooden, throne-like chair, the magistrate glowered, and Jodathyn was reminded of some of the more gluttonous lords at court. Set before the magistrate was a platter of delicacies. His hands were decorated with gold rings, and his servant was pouring him a goblet of wine. Despite the late hour, the long tables that ran along the perimeter of the hall were laden with food and drink. What Jodathyn wouldn't give for a goblet of wine to smother his nerves.

Jodathyn smoothed his face into an emotionless mask so that he wouldn't be tempted to curl his lip in disgust. The last thing he wanted was to insult Magistrate Swyft in his own home.

"So, the Sionian decides to grace us with her presence alongside a new felon."

Jodathyn's knees erupted with pain as he was thrust forward onto the floor. He yelped and stood himself back up. He knew it was foolish and prideful. But he would not bow to such a terrible magistrate.

"Down!" Lawman Floyde growled, pushing Jodathyn over. Jodathyn's palms hit the cold stone floor. He peered over to Et-hir, who was crouched beside him.

"What a handsome, bold lad. You will fetch a pretty piece of coin."

Jodathyn sensed an uneasy movement behind him. "Sir," Lawman Floyde shifted. He stared down at Jodathyn and then returned his gaze to the magistrate. Jodathyn had seen this posture before. It was of a man who was struggling to serve one that he had an intense dislike for. "He's not the type who gets himself in trouble with the law. Perhaps we can be merciful. Seems a shame to send a well brought up boy into slavery for a mistake. I know the types. He's a diligent worker—"

"What is a pity, lawman," the magistrate continued, "is that I have a number of escaped prisoners. He has been captured, and I will benefit."

"Please, no!" Jodathyn cried. "Mercy!"

"They always cry mercy," Magistrate Swyft said. He took a slather of meat and pushed it into his mouth. There was an uncomfortable pause as the magistrate chewed and smacked his lips.

"The king has commanded us to stop sending criminals to the prison ships." Lawman Floyde shared a glance with his companion. Neither of them looked comfortable with the direction the conversation was heading.

"The king is not here," Magistrate Swyft said, with a grand gesture of his arms.

Jodathyn could not allow himself to be dragged back to the docks and back into slavery. He swallowed his pride and reached out to his dragon sister. There had to be a way to let her know of his desperation.

"Sidrah! Please! I won't go back to the prison ships! Please!"

"Now up he goes," Magistrate Swyft continued. He skewed a piece of cheese with his knife and waved it imperiously about. "I want a good look at my merchandise."

"Up, boy," the lawman said. His voice was low and grave. Jodathyn's upper arms were grabbed, and he was forced to his feet. He didn't offer any resistance. His crime and identity had been carved onto his skin. There was only one thing he could do to escape.

"Get the tattooist in here to mark him ..."

Tornyth rippled beneath his skin, and Jodathyn tried to will the dragon to burst forth. Unfortunately, Lawman Floyde's gloved hands were still upon his arm. The man's eyes widened in disbelief, and Jodathyn knew he felt the dragon physically moving beneath his skin. In the next instant, his companion had a knife under Et-hir's throat.

"Rokun," Jodathyn croaked.

"You fight us, boy, we'll kill the girl." Floyde spoke quickly, his tone taking on an edge of urgency. "Keep that beast locked away!"

"A dragon?" Magistrate Swyft looked venomously delighted. "Do you know how much coin that will put in Kudah's coffers?"

Jodathyn roared in rage and felt a blade pressing into his back.

"Stay still," Floyde hissed in his ear. "I'm trying to save your life!"

Under his skin, Jodathyn could feel Tornyth twisting and writhing. The magistrate's hall was suddenly busy with more lawmen, all with swords drawn. "You might kill some of us, dragon," Magistrate Swyft said from the safety of his chair. "But you'll be dead before you leave this room."

"I don't want to kill anyone!" Jodathyn cried. He twisted in Lawman Floyde's grasp. "I want to live! That's all I have ever wanted."

When the magistrate was confident that Jodathyn had been restrained, he left his chair to stand just out of reach. "Hold him firm while I examine him."

"*Do not struggle,*" Tornyth whispered. "*There's a way out.*"

Before his eyes, Jodathyn saw a waking vision. Carvelle reached out to him. His tiny hands touched his snout. "Uncle, you are magnificent."

"This is what we fight for. We will be free once more."

Reaching out, the magistrate grabbed a fistful of Jodathyn's hair and wrenched his head back. "So you have a power as well, boy. That is good news for me. We'll get some medicine in you to stop those pesky powers and mark your lovely skin."

"*Rshon mahthyt!*" Jodathyn growled.

"Dragon Dung, am I?" Magistrate's Swyft's hand left his hair. A servant ran forward with a dagger, which the magistrate held up to Jodathyn's face. Leering, he cut away the arm of Jodathyn's shirt.

Moments later, Jodathyn was standing bare chested for everyone in the hall to see.

The magistrate barked out a laugh at the tattoo on Jodathyn's forearm. "A good boy, you say?"

Lawman Floyde grabbed Jodathyn's elbow, stretching out his arm. "It says Enslaved Dragon."

"Flying Lizard," Jodathyn corrected. "It's a hateful title meant to diminish and demean."

"Well, he'll soon have another marking," Magistrate Swyft said, rubbing his palms together.

"This is your last chance to let Et-hir go," Jodathyn told them seriously. "I survived and escaped a prison ship once ... and those who dared touch me died screaming among flame and fury."

"Who are you?"

"Pallarus ..." Lawman Floyde gasped. "The scarring on his back ... You're him."

Jodathyn raised his chin. "I might be worth a lot of coin. But if you take it, you won't be alive long to enjoy it."

Magistrate Swyft stepped back, and for one moment, Jodathyn hoped he had gotten through to them. Instead, another lawman approached with a cup filled with the herbal tonics.

"Drink or we will severely punish your woman."

Jodathyn's eyes flicked towards Et-hir, who was still slumped on the floor. She glanced up at him, and there was a sly quirk of her lips as she turned her hands. He spotted the silver glint of a blade. With all the confusion in the meeting hall, she had gathered her wits to steal the knife from somewhere. Doing his best not to show his surprise so he wouldn't bring attention to her, Jodathyn returned his stare to the magistrate.

"Let these beasts in human flesh do what they will ... they will be repaid in kind."

Tornyth show him the vision of Kudah from up above. He could smell his own blood drying on the cobblestone streets. Two dragon shadows, one larger, one small, flew overhead.

"We will endure," Tornyth promised. The cup was pushed to his lips.

Now that Tornyth was a manifested dragon, Jodathyn could feel the effects of the herbs acutely. He felt the very moment the dragon within him was quelled.

The magistrate jeered down at him.

"Celebration is a little premature," Jodathyn told him. "I am not defeated yet."

"Look at him!" Magistrate Swyft crowed. "He thinks that because he was sired by the loins of a king that he is superior. Well ... let's have some entertainment. Bring him."

At the magistrate's proclamation, Et-hir gave an all-mighty yell. She lunged towards a lawman with the dagger in hand. *"Unhand us you unholy, dirty Ramians!"* she screamed in her native tongue.

Sneering at her, the lawman grabbed her arm and twisted it. Et-hir gasped in pain as she released the knife. Using his weight against her, the lawman pushed Et-hir to the ground.

As he stepped up to strike her, Jodathyn cried out. "No! Lay her consequence on me!"

Et-hir's large eyes widened, making her look more innocent than she was. She shook her head, strands of her black hair falling out of her practical braid. Her lips parted as she whimpered.

The magistrate licked his lips. "Very well, we shall do as you ask. Take the girl to the cell. It's him I'm interested in. We'll make him bleed right and proper!"

"No!" Et-hir cried. She reached out to Jodathyn, trying to touch him.

Jodathyn was forced to his feet. He watched in mounting despair as Et-hir was dragged away. Lawman Floyde moved him towards the entryway, and at the top of the steps, he was paraded to the people of Kudah.

"Keep your peace as much as you can." Floyde pressed him close so he could whisper in his ear. "This won't be pleasant. I'll do what I can."

"I will fight." The words seemed to stick in Jodathyn's throat. "I will always fight."

Even though it was late, the crowd had only grown since Jodathyn had been inside.

"Good people of Kudah, I have brought before you Jodathyn Pallarus, the enemy of all free Ramians, to you for judgement."

At the magistrate's dramatics, Jodathyn raised his eyes. The crowd before him murmured and swayed. They seemed confused but unwilling to help him. He stared resolutely ahead. He could not show any fear in front of so many of his countrymen. The Pallarus bloodline must be strong at all times.

"He is guilty of setting loose evil-hearted men and women and defying the law and order of Kudah. He possesses magic and a dragon. He is a proud young fellow; now he will be humbled."

Jodathyn tilted his head up, ensuring that his line of sight was above the crowd. He couldn't bear to look into the sea of faces to see emotions of fear, hate, and pity. In vain, he tried not to think of Curran and Nym. Were they in trouble too? Had they got out of the village? Had Curran abandoned him to his fate?

"Strip him naked!"

At Magistrate Swyft's command, Lawman Floyde knelt and untied the laces of his boots. "Kindly step out of your boots." The lawman's voice held a note of resignation.

Jodathyn glared down at him. The cool wind was already tickling his back and belly. "Go drown yourself in a stinking cess pool." He lifted his foot and kicked the lawman in the face.

Falling backwards, Lawman Floyde clutched at his nose. Two of his companions ran to subdue Jodathyn as the magistrate laughed. Hands were all over him, and his clothing was quickly removed until he was bare and shivering. The crowd remained strangely silent.

Lawman Floyde approached again and took his arms. Jodathyn grinned at the blood on the man's face. "Don't make this worse," the lawman hissed.

Jodathyn was propelled down the stairs and through the milling crowd. He was escorted a little way to a market square. His feet were ushered up some rough stairs until he came face-to-face with a large wooden pole. His belly was pressed against the raw timber, and his hands were momentarily freed so that he could be chained. He was forced to strain and stand on the very tip of his toes as he hung limply from the pole.

"Imagine this, a baseborn Pallarus at our mercy." Magistrate Swyft had followed them. The cruelty in the man's eyes told Jodathyn that he was enjoying every moment of the "punishment."

"I'm a legitimate son of a king, moron," Jodathyn snarled.

"You were whelped between a consort's thighs. Your mother was a seductress." The magistrate leered at him. Swyft was prideful; he did not like to be called names. Jodathyn tucked that away for later. Anything to chip away at an enemy's armour.

The first lash of the whip came with a crack and a sharp sting as its cruel tendrils cut into the tender flesh of Jodathyn's bare back and buttocks. Spasming, Jodathyn screamed at the impact and again as it tore away from his spine. There was no point in trying to withhold his cries of agony. He poured all his rage at the world and its cruelty into the harsh sound of his voice.

Wrapped up in his own physical torment, Jodathyn did his best to recount his favourite myths and stories. At the breaking point, Jodathyn tried to reach out to Mandros. He knew it was unlikely the green dragon would want to hear from him now, but he had no one else to reach for.

Warm rivers of blood dripped from Jodathyn's wounds as he hung limply to the whipping pole.

When the whipping stopped, the crowd dispersed. They were still silent. Jodathyn was left to hang in his vulnerable position.

At least, Jodathyn thought he was alone.

Tottering up the steps, the old lady from earlier approached. "You don't look like a dragon, my dear."

"I don't feel like a dragon, truth be known." Jodathyn's voice was hoarse from his screaming. Exhausted, he was forced to lean on the pole to alleviate some of the pain.

"Sometimes you can't see what a person is capable of from the outward appearance, dear boy," the old woman said. She stepped into Jodathyn's view and lifted her shaking hands to dab at the tears at Jodathyn's eyes with a ragged, stained hanky. "They will pay for every stripe, for every bloodstain and every tear you cry in this place."

CHAPTER FIFTEEN

Jodathyn

The Village of Kudah

Jodathyn's world was consumed by fire. His dry, cracked lips opened to emit a terrible, inhuman groan. He lay naked, face down in the dirt. Knees curling towards his abdomen, he hoped that he might be able to escape the agony.

"Hush, now, I'll do what I can for you."

Jodathyn's eyes fluttered open, and he twisted his head, looking for the voice above him. Strong hands stopped him from rolling onto his back.

"You'll not want to do that, my lad." A cool cloth dabbed his back, which caused sparks of fire to split him open. A pair of hands helped him sit.

Jodathyn blinked past the pain and came face to face with Lawman Floyde. Feeling a stab of betrayal, he attempted to struggle.

"Peace." The lawman lifted his hand.

"Leave me alone, please!" Jodathyn rasped. He swallowed thickly; it felt like he had swallowed a hunting dagger.

"I only want to help you," Lawman Floyde said.

Ashamed that he was sitting in his own blood and grime, Jodathyn refused to look at him.

The lawman turned and patted a pile of material. "Here, I brought you some clothes. Let me help you dress."

"Et-hir …"

"You have bigger issues to worry about," the lawman told him. He scrubbed his hands over his face; his expression was pained. "I'm sorry … I never wanted … Bless the Otherworlds, if I had known, I would have stayed silent."

"I'm here," Et-hir whispered in the dark. "It's cold, Jod. Let the lawman help you."

Tilting his head to stare at Lawman Floyde, Jodathyn wasn't able to conceal his distrust. For his part, the lawman offered his hand. Et-hir was right. His body shivered uncontrollably and if he attempted to stand, he was sure he would fall on his face.

Seeing no other viable option, Jodathyn accepted the lawman's hand. The older man grasped his hand and then his elbow. He was silent as a grave as he aided Jodathyn into some clothing.

"There, Locke, my lad."

"Jodathyn."

The lawman looked up, and his mouth downturned into a deep frown.

"If I'm to be humiliated and punished, I would hear my own name. Lest I forget who I am."

"I'm so sorry." Lawman Floyde sighed. "I had no idea that the situation would escalate."

"Liar." Jodathyn harrumphed. "You betrayed my dragon."

"You gave me no choice."

"You could have let me fly free. You still could."

"He can't do that, Jodathyn," Et-hir said. "He has a family."

Jodathyn's face crumbled. He stumbled back and slumped to the floor. He pressed his knees up to his chest, ignoring the pull on his tight muscles. He rocked as he spoke. "And I … I am just the son of a highborn whore."

"Jodathyn …" Et-hir crawled over to his side.

Lawman Floyde shifted. His gaze flicked towards the bars of the cell. "It is my duty to inform you that tomorrow you will be escorted to the market square where your sentence will be carried out."

Jodathyn closed his grey eyes, waiting to hear the inevitable. "I thought I was to be sold."

"There is a rumour that your proven death has a higher reward," Lawman Floyde said. He rocked back and forth from his toes to his heels. Still, he refused to look down upon Jodathyn. "You're to die bathed in flames."

A smile touched Jodathyn's mouth, and he could feel the nausea churning his stomach at the thought. He raked shaking hands through his matted hair; a nervous laughed bubbled from his lips. "My world is already on fire."

"Jodathyn …" Et-hir reached out a small hand to grasp at his fingers.

"It's a less cruel fate for one so afflicted with a dragon." Jodathyn turned to assure Et-hir. "The prison ships would take my spirit and the Artrothian slavers will rip out and extinguish my soul. I would be facing centuries of torment. This way … it's better … By lunchtime tomorrow, I will be ashes on the wind."

Tears ran down Et-hir's face, and Jodathyn reached over to wipe them away from her cheeks.

"I'll be free. Please don't cry … My suffering will be over soon. Who knows, my dragon is the son of Flame and Fury. Perhaps the embrace of the flames will awaken him."

Embarrassed, Lawman Floyde turned to leave.

"When you see the shadow of two dragons tomorrow, it's time to get as many women and children to safety."

"What do you mean, boy?" Lawman Floyde glared down upon him.

"I'm a prince of scales. Ancient power runs in my blood," Jodathyn said. "*Elt Aluel* will no doubt see this as an act of war against dragonkind."

Without another word, the lawman stood and averted his gaze. He paused at the cell gate, and then he stepped out into the dark, making sure to lock the cell securely behind him. For a long moment, Jodathyn watched him striding along the grass towards the magistrate's house. The lawman didn't look back.

Jodathyn chortled until tears ran down his cheeks. He crawled to the locked bars, and even knowing it was useless, he yanked on them with all his might. "I am Pallarus! A son of Arturyn! A dragon of Rama. You can't ..."

"Jod, please, you're scaring me."

Jodathyn turned to Et-hir, and his expression softened. He dragged in a deep breath. He would be calm. For her. He was Pallarus. No matter what, a royalborn son was always strong. He rested his forehead against the bars and huffed in defeat.

"Are you really a dragon?" Et-hir huddled closer to him.

"Yes. Although he is bound by the herbs they have given me." Jodathyn pulled away from the cell door and slumped. "Have you seen Nym or Curran?"

Et-hir shook her head. "They haven't let anyone back here."

"We need an escape plan—"

Jodathyn's body may have been exhausted and in pain, but his mind was already plotting an escape. He didn't know how much he was able to communicate to Sidrah or even if his stubborn sister had passed his message along. He knew that two dragons would be seen over Kudah skies, but he couldn't rely on them making it before he was executed. No. His liberation was his own to orchestrate.

Since he was unable to manifest into Tornyth, he couldn't simply tear down the horrid stone building and fly away. An airborne dragon was a free dragon. Flying away would have been ideal …

Mandros had succeeded in calling Tornyth while drugged, but he was under the impression that it was nothing short of a miracle. He closed his eyes and rested his head against the stone wall.

"I wish you were here, Donatein," Jodathyn muttered. "You would know exactly what to say."

"Who's Donatein?" Et-hir picked up his hand in hers and laced their fingers together.

Jodathyn didn't answer. Heart hammering in his chest, he leaned over and pressed his lips against hers. He kept it gentle, sweet and swift, like Nym had taught him.

It was ironic. Nym had kissed him while they were in a prison cart being hurled away to safety. Now he was kissing Et-hir while a prisoner, waiting for his execution.

He pulled away, blinking, an apology already forming on his tongue.

"Tyr wouldn't believe it. Me, kissing a Ramian prince."

"I'm not a prince."

"In Sion, the king's bastards are treated well. You Ramians are a strange lot. I've heard rumours of how poorly the palace treats a trueborn son." Emboldened, Et-hir grabbed Jodathyn's borrowed shirt and tugged him closer. "Let me show you how a real Sionian woman kisses her man."

The kiss with Nym had been enjoyable. But Et-hir was like coming home. Where Nym had been all take and demand, Et-hir was warm and giving. He felt her shift closer to him. Without pulling away, she grasped his hands and placed them around her waist.

Jodathyn didn't want it to ever end. When Et-hir leaned back to stare at him with a soft smile, he followed her, their noses almost touching.

Et-hir giggled. "Have I awoken the dragon, Your Highness?"

Jodathyn hummed. "Just one more kiss …"

They came for him at dawn. Having been awake for the last few hours, Jodathyn had seen their approach. He peered back as two stone-faced lawmen stared at him through the bars. He had hoped that if he was going to die, then at least he would be given the tenuous comfort of a familiar face. The fact it wasn't Lawman Floyde taking him to his death was disappointing.

"It's time."

Nodding, Jodathyn nudged Et-hir awake. She had fallen asleep with her head resting on his shoulder. He had left her there, allowing her a few hours of peace. She stirred as the door creaked open, and her large eyes darted about and widened upon seeing the lawmen.

"No!" she cried, clutching on to Jodathyn's arm. "You can't have him!"

Jodathyn took a moment to compose himself. He pressed his sweaty palms against his thighs. "Please, one moment."

He didn't wait for the lawmen's permission. He took Et-hir's shaking hands in his own. "Thank you for all your kindness. I have lived a good life, one that I am proud of. All I hope for is that I leave his world with courage and made my brother proud."

Et-hir stared up at him, her brown eyes welling with tears. She clung to his hands and brought his dirty knuckles to her lips. Her tears were warm against his skin. "I think your brother should be very proud; I have never met a man like you." Et-hir lifted her head and pierced the lawmen with a ferocious snarl. "You are killing a good man for a bad man's profit."

"We do as we are told; our families stay safe."

"For how long?" Et-hir cried. "Is anyone truly safe in Kudah?"

Jodathyn stood. The ground beneath him felt like it was tilting. He lifted his chin and squared his shoulders. Donatein had told him that a confident posture was the first step in being unafraid.

"I release you of any responsibility of my death," Jodathyn said. He vaguely remembered the ceremonial words of forgiveness. He hoped he hadn't butchered them. "You have my forgiveness of my murder."

One of the lawmen's eyes softened. He bowed his head, mumbling a prayer under his breath. His companion, however, rolled his eyes. "This is an execution. This is Ramian law."

Jodathyn laughed, his voice having the beginnings of a hysterical twinge to it. "I have not seen my death warrant. It has not been presented to me with the king's signature as the law dictates. You know my bloodline, yet I was strung up and beaten, and now you will kill me without the proper observances of the law."

"We have no choice."

"Despite your protests to the contrary, there is always a choice." Jodathyn stepped forward, taking one last glance at Et-hir. "Under Ramian law, Magistrate Swyft is committing murder."

The lawmen's patience was spent. They grabbed Jodathyn's elbow and steered him into the sunlight. Jodathyn couldn't help but to blink and stare up into the morning sun. He felt the rays of warmth bathing his skin.

In the distance, he saw a plume of smoke. There was a forest fire somewhere. With a pang of regret, he breathed in the scent of woodsmoke. Deep down, he wanted to burn Kudah to the ground—but that was just a dream. Perhaps Mandros would forgive his impertinence and raze the magistrate's residence. It was a pretty thought.

He took a deep breath and then placed one foot in front of the other. It would not do for the people of Kudah to see how afraid he was.

Jodathyn was brought to the front of the magistrate's house. He couldn't help but gasp at the sight that met him. It wasn't the stack of wood that had been chopped for the occasion that gave him pause—but a strange bronze statue of a dragon head, which was placed over the kindling. To the side of the large head was a hinged door. To the side there was a second terrible dragon monument.

Ignoring the magistrate, Jodathyn stared in dumfounded horror at the device he was to be tortured within. The ancients had called them Vadroil's Singing Heads. Jodathyn had read tales in the more obscure texts he found within the palace library. The intended victim was placed within the bronze tomb, the fires lit, and as they screamed, the dragon's nostrils smoked and the wails of the victim rang out in a macabre symphony. It was said Vadroil had used these on his enemies for entertainment. Many believed that they had never truly existed, but here they were.

Even though he had promised himself that he would be brave to the very end, Jodathyn screamed and struggled. The lawmen held him tight. The sympathetic one was mumbling prayers fervently under his breath. Jodathyn could feel the man's hand travelling over his back in soothing circles.

"Please!" Jodathyn cried out over the crowd. "Behead me and be done with it!"

The people of Kudah were staring at him in bewildered fascination. Jodathyn turned to them, hoping to at least have one friendly villager who might speak up for him, or alternatively kill him quickly. No one moved.

"Lay him in and stoke the fires," the magistrate snapped. "I can't wait to hear his song."

Jodathyn breathed in great gasping sobs. His legs refused to hold his weight and crumbled beneath him.

"You self-righteous ... He's just a boy. Let him go!" someone shouted from the crowd. A few jeers followed.

"Enough! Anyone who defies me on this matter will suffer the same fate."

A frightened hush fell over the people as Jodathyn was dragged forward. He turned his head and bit the stoic lawman on the hand.

The man roared but did not strike him. "I know you're afraid, boy. Let's get this over with for both our sakes."

"Otherworlds! You're a mad man!"

Jodathyn's head shot up, looking over at the crowd. Curran Norrys was barrelling through the villagers and was heading towards the magistrate. He shouldered past a man who looked like he was a blacksmith and another who looked like the farrier.

"He's a frightened boy," Curran growled. "Let him go."

"He's a criminal." The magistrate crossed his arms against his chest.

"He's a lad that dreamt of seeing justice done." Curran spat in the magistrate's face. Murmurs ran through the crowd as spittle ran down the magistrate's cheeks. "He has enough courage to help those you've tormented with your twisted laws."

There was a smattering of applause at Curran's defiance. One frown from the magistrate, however, and the crowd stilled.

"You keep the oath you made as a young man," the magistrate said. "I will be merciful. I honour a man who keeps his word."

"My stand against you has nothing to do with the oath I made as a King's Guard!" Curran roared. He stepped forward, raised his hand, and struck the magistrate across the face. "Too long have you been a plague in Kudah. Too long you have ruled unchecked."

The magistrate reeled and fell to the ground. Stunned, he glared towards Jodathyn. He stood to his feet, brushing off his robes. With a flourish, he grabbed a weapon off the nearest lawman.

"Finish him!" Magistrate Swyft snarled, brandishing his sword.

Jodathyn was bundled into the bronze dragon. Keen to see his duty done, the cranky lawman pushed Jodathyn's head down. Jodathyn fought, throwing his torso through the opening, stopping the door from being shut. Curran growled and made a running leap for the bronze dragon.

"Enough!" the magistrate cried. He followed Curran and in one swift motion impaled the barkeep with his weapon.

"Curran!" Jodathyn screamed as the big man fell to his knees, a stunned expression on his face.

Jodathyn was forced back into the bronze head. The fires were lit, and the lid was closed. He screamed, feeling the prickling burn of the fire beneath him. He tried to reach out to Tornyth … but the herbs still dampened his connection with the dragon.

"Retribution is coming to Kudah!" Jodathyn hollered. "You will be displayed naked and ashamed …"

Nausea rolled over Jodathyn as the air became hot and sticky. He had hoped the caress of fire might awaken Tornyth, but he felt no stirring beneath his skin. He was blistering and sweating. The pain was unbearable.

Thrusting his head back, Jodathyn bellowed an insult that would have made Nym proud. "Let me out, you maggot-ridden carcass!"

CHAPTER SIXTEEN

Illeanah

The Citadel of Pallaryn

In stark contrast to grime of the local surrounds, Madam Nurlah's chambers were decorated with colourful satins. Illeanah sat in an overstuffed chair, glaring at the gaudy décor of the madam's rooms. The woman seemed to favour red and oranges. It was enough to make Illeanah's head throb.

Opposite her, the queen sat with her hands in her lap. Anyone who didn't known the queen would be forgiven for thinking she was a docile creature. But a well-bred woman could plot, all the while pretending nothing of worth was happening inside her head. Queen Odelle wasn't a woman to underestimate.

"My father would gladly shelter us in Arah. But I think it is unwise to flee to my family," the queen said. She stood and glided towards the window to look down at the bustling streets of the citadel. "It's not safe here."

Will stood in the shadows, nursing a goblet of wine. "I've also thought about that, Della. South is Kamoore and Solan's domains, but it has the advantage of Whitoak's household. West ... well, I'm not looked upon too favourably there."

Illeanah lifted her head in surprise. Really, she shouldn't be shocked that Will had put some thought into their plans. If he was the king's spy, then there must be some spark of intelligence in his head. Especially if he was as close to the king as he said.

"My father's household is loyal to him," Illeanah said. "But Androssah is very close to our enemies' territories. Wouldn't they expect me to run where I have loyal people?"

"Yes," Will murmured. "Wine, Nia? You look like you could settle some of your nerves."

"No, thank you," Illeanah replied crisply. "I'm just afraid for my father."

"I know," Will said, his dark eyes glinting. He lifted his goblet to drink. "You had a good relationship with him. He'd do anything for you."

"What's that supposed to mean?" Illeanah snapped. She was in no mood for courtier mind games.

"Jodathyn was a threat to you marrying well," Will said with a shrug. He stared at her from over the rim of his goblet, as if waiting for her to reach some conclusion.

"Jodathyn is my friend," Illeanah replied. "Father knew that."

"Did he?" Will challenged, lifting an eyebrow. "Yet he asked the king to murder him."

"Liar!" Illeanah cried.

"Enough, Will," the queen commanded. "It does not do to cause rifts between us."

"My heartfelt apologies, Nia," Will said. He placed his wine goblet down with a definite clink. "I'll go ahead and scout for opportunities." Will stepped from the room and Illeanah watched him, feeling annoyed and fascinated by him at the same time. Her confusion when it came to Will Hartcurt was an irritant.

"He's a nice boy," the queen said. "Sometimes he lets his jealousy cloud his judgements."

"*Jealousy*?"

"You have a father," the queen replied. "Kieryn has commanded that Will does not have communication with his."

"That's terrible."

"Yes," the queen said. "Will asked Kieryn to show his family mercy for their crimes, and in return, Kieryn has commanded him to not reach out to them. Will's father sold him for gold. He cannot be trusted to do so again. Not that Will agrees with my husband."

Illeanah was shocked to hear about Will's father. The law was clear on the punishments for the illegal trading of human souls. If convicted, Will could have asked for his father to be put to death. She wasn't sure if Will's forgiveness was praiseworthy or a mark of ill-conceived mercy. "Does Will often argue with your husband?"

"Will doesn't argue with Kieryn, dear." The queen's face briefly lit up at the mention of her husband, and her hand brushed over her belly. If Illeanah looked closely, she could see the beginning of a bulge. She would not be able to keep the child a secret for much longer. "Will feels at liberty to discuss issues candidly with my husband. He has a way of making his feelings known."

"I see. Della ..."

Illeanah was interrupted by the madam of the house flouncing in with a tray of food. Thankfully, the unwholesome woman was wearing something a little less revealing, even if it was a low-cut dress of bright yellow. She settled the food down on a table, her curls falling about her face.

"I thought you might be hungry, my dears. I've sent some of my girls out to garner any gossip that might be of use."

"Thank you, that is most kind," the queen murmured. "Might I bother you for some herbal teas?"

Madam Nurlah looked up with a smile. Illeanah noticed that she had washed her face of her alluring paints. "Of course, my love. Is the babe giving you grief?"

The queen's eyes widened.

"Not much gets past me, dearie. I was a midwife before my life took an unexpected turn."

"I am quite well, thank you," the queen stammered.

"Come, eat. It'll do you a world of good."

Madam Nurlah left with a swish of her yellow skirts, leaving Illeanah to stare in wide-eyed bemusement at the queen. "We've both been fortunate in life," the queen said. "Not all women have the same opportunities you and I were given."

Illeanah was unsure how she should answer the queen's observation. Instead, she changed the subject. "If none of us can go to our families, where do you expect we should go?"

The queen stood and regarded the tray of food. She plucked up a piece of dried fruit and nibbled thoughtfully. "I dare say Will is seeking out his contacts. We will know more soon."

"It will need to be somewhere unexpected."

The queen seemed to consider this. "I'll do whatever it takes."

"Do you think Sion—"

Will came crashing through the door. He was panting as beads of sweat ran down his forehead.

"Will! What's going on?"

Will seemed to come back to himself. He glanced over at Illeanah but refused to make eye contact. She was of little doubt he had bad news and it had something to do with her. Checking that no one was in the hall, Will shut the door behind him with a thud.

"Some of the girls have already returned with news. I ..." He stared at Illeanah, his voice dropping away. "The council has made the first arrests."

The queen gasped and brought her hand to her chest. "Who?"

"Two guards that failed to report a man claiming to have seen Jodathyn."

Illeanah clutched on to the armrests of her chair. Her knuckles went white. She could already feel her lips trembling.

Will nodded. "From what I have gathered, they are working to discredit His Majesty. The King's Guard will be next ..."

"We don't know that ..." Illeanah said. As soon as the words were out of her mouth, she heard her own uncertainty. She stood to approach Will, shaking her head. He was a spy. Merely paranoid.

"Illeanah ..."

"It's Nia now."

"I'm so sorry." Will's eyes closed slowly, and he angled his body so that Illeanah couldn't see his face. "Your father is dead."

"No!" Illeanah cried. Her knees buckled, and she dropped to the floor. "No, no, no ... He was going to find the king." She felt like a vulnerable child and not the strong, confident woman her father had taught her to be. "He's not dead."

Will knelt beside her, taking her trembling hands in his. "I'm sorry." His voice was soft and tender. He looked at her as if he was expecting her to fall apart in his arms. But she was Whitoak. She didn't have the luxury of wailing and moping.

"I killed him!" Illeanah gasped. "I killed my own father."

"Shh ..." Will soothed, trying to take her in his arms. "You didn't ... you don't bear any responsibility."

"*Ri Rshon Hanoch*!" Illeanah screamed, using the curse words that she had heard Jodathyn use in the garden. She pushed Will away. She didn't need a comforting embrace from a stranger. She needed her papa. "It's my fault … He was arrested because of me."

Will looked up. She knew he was looking over her head at the queen. She could almost see his deep eyes begging the queen to take over.

"Will, dear, why don't you see about getting a calming tea for everyone."

Illeanah bit her tongue. This wasn't time for tea! It was time to plan and plot revenge. Will stood, gave her hand one last squeeze, and without a backwards glance, scurried from the room.

"Come," said the queen. Illeanah took her hand and stood. She stumbled over to a cheap chair, inlaid with fake gold paint.

"I'm sorry," Illeanah said, weeping. She choked back her tears. Her father had a certain disdain for the dramatics at court. He wouldn't like to know she had been hysterically crying. Whitoak would expect his daughter to find a way out of the situation. Brushing her hands over her eyes, Illeanah dried her tears and stared straight ahead. Her eyes felt like they were burning. "I know this isn't the time for mourning."

"It is perfectly natural to weep, child." Queen Odelle patted her hands.

Illeanah retrieved her hand from the queen's grasp. "We need to think."

Queen Odelle seemed to be at a loss.

"We cannot stay in the citadel for long."

Will returned into the room, looking contrite and drawn. In his hands, he carried a tray of teas. Glancing at Illeanah, he seemed afraid of what her reaction might be. Illeanah met his gaze coolly. She was not a fragile little girl. She was a Whitoak. Strong and unyielding.

Will placed the teas between Illeanah and the queen. He raked his hand through his dark hair, his handsome face twisted into a frown.

"I feel numb," Illeanah confessed. "And angry."

"I know," Will said softly.

Will indeed did know. Blasted mind reader. "You're reading my mind again."

"Illeanah, it's not something I can control."

"Then you are not trying hard enough. You should learn."

"Do you not think I have tried?" Will replied.

"We were saying we need a safe place away from the citadel. Lord Will, do you have any suggestions?" Queen Odelle asked, trying to change the subject. "I was thinking Habron."

"*Habron*? What's in Habron?" Illeanah asked. Habron was a small town. There was nothing of worth in Habron.

"Well, as we discussed, we need somewhere unexpected. Habron is a small village. North of the village is a little-known trading route that heads north to the Stonethaw Ranges; from there we can enter Sion."

"It'll be a hard journey," Will cautioned.

"I'm prepared to do whatever it takes, Master Will," the queen said.

"We're never going to survive," Illeanah groaned. "Have Madam Nurlah find us some men's clothing to change into."

Holding her breath as she stepped out into the streets of Pallaryn in her men's clothing, Illeanah stole a tentative look at the queen.

"Chin down," Will muttered into her ear. "Hunch a little, and for the love of the Otherworld, don't look anyone directly in the face."

"Who made you leader?" Illeanah hissed. She resisted the urge to hit his smug face.

Laying a conciliatory hand on Illeanah's arm, Queen Odelle nodded gravely. There was a part of Illeanah that had hoped that she could discard her inappropriate man's attire as soon as they left the gates of Pallaryn. But Will had scoffed at her, telling her that Solan's men were looking for women and they wouldn't stop the search within the citadel. It was best to remain hidden in the guise of a man. So Illeanah had left her gown behind for some fortunate whore to inherit.

"Dusk is approaching," Will murmured. "It will help conceal us."

"Lead the way, Will," the queen said. "I suspect you know the best ways to get out of the citadel unseen."

"And hopefully unscathed," Illeanah added.

Sighing, Will took the crook of her elbow and marched forward. "Now, none of this gliding nonsense. Walk like a man."

Illeanah sent him a withering glare.

Will chuckled. "Think upon it as just a game."

"I don't play childish games," Illeanah protested. Her eyes went back in the direction of the palace.

"Come now," Queen Odelle replied. "My brother-in-law told me all sorts of stories about the make-believe games you used to play when he was a ward under your father's roof."

Illeanah wiped away a stray tear. "Well, he's gone now. They both are."

"Think of yourself as an actress," said the queen. "This is just a costume you're wearing, and you're pretending to be something you are not. It's not much different than being at court."

Will snorted. "Trust me. Everyone's pretending to be something they're not at court."

Without further comment, Will turned upon his heel and waltzed into the streets as if he didn't have a care in the world. Illeanah followed with the queen about five paces behind. They turned a corner, finding themselves in the busy cobblestone street, which was lined with different types of trades. Blacksmiths, armourers, tanners, stone masons ... Illeanah looked upon the workshops in fascination.

Even in the early evening, the workshops were busy. She spotted muscled men still working with molten metals, and stone masons were still chipping away with their chisels. She had never explored the trade sections of the citadel before. Her father would never allow it.

Up ahead, Will continued to lead them.

As he made his way past a particularly loud silversmith's workshop, Will paused and glanced briefly over his shoulder. He made eye contact with Illeanah and then stepped into a narrow laneway.

They followed him into the dark space.

Will was waiting for them. He leaned against the wall, looking too relaxed for Illeanah's liking. "Through here is the food market for the less affluent. The madams in this part of the citadel don't like me. I want to move through this part of Pallaryn quickly."

"Don't like you? What did you do to them?" Illeanah asked.

Will smiled tightly. There was the same sad light gleaming in his eyes as there was earlier. "This is my brother Tomas' territory."

"Tells us nothing," Illeanah muttered.

Will rounded on her and hissed, "I rescued whores from Tomas' clutches."

Taken aback by Will's sudden change in demeanour, Illeanah nodded mutely. Will huffed, turned and continued stalking through the alleyway.

"I hurt his feelings, didn't I?" Illeanah asked, turning towards the queen.

"Perhaps you should suspend judgement when it comes to Will. He's a good man who has overcome many challenges."

They stepped out into another cobblestone street, which Will had told them would be full of food vendors. Breathing heavily, the queen paused. The colour of her skin took an almost green hue.

"Oh!" the queen cried as she brought her hand to her mouth. "Oh! Not now ..."

Will's head snapped up, and his eyes bored into the queen's.

"Oh, Otherworlds, Beale. Can't you hold yer drink, man!" Will called out. He took a few steps back and came to the queen's side so that he could support her more fully. "Move on over, Ikayle … I help yer with 'im."

Will's reply to the queen's sudden bout of nausea was so perfect that no one shared them a second glance. Everyone around them assumed that she was a stark raving drunk. They had no idea of what her real problem was.

The queen sucked in a deep breath, and she hung her head. Will and Illeanah half dragged her through the food markets and towards the city gates. They reached the great city walls and stepped through the gates unhindered. Illeanah waited for the guards to bark an order for them to be stopped and interrogated. But within the throng of lowborns, they were hidden. The guards looked bored and inattentive.

The crowd of the common people soon thinned, and they were left standing on the side of the dusty road. The queen, who still looked deathly pale, ushered Will towards a cart driver to see if they might have a ride. After a bit of haggling, the cart driver agreed to take them as far as the King's Orchards. Will paid the man handsomely.

After the Autumn Festival, the orchards would be quiet. They would be able to rest the night in relative safety. What Will would do once the sun rose and the pickers came, she didn't know.

It felt like Illeanah had only just closed her eyes when she was awoken by yelling. She shot up from where she lay on the soft grass.

"On your knees!"

Illeanah shook her head. The voice was familiar. Her stomach plummeted, recognising it belonging to Will's eldest brother, Tomas. She had only met him on a handful of occasions, none of them pleasant.

"Did you finally father a child on a whore, Willyrd?"

"Let me go, Tomas!" Will's voice cried.

Illeanah scrambled to her feet, the movement catching Tomas' eye. He was holding Will against his broad chest, a sword under his chin. Will looked weary, like he would welcome the sword to slice his throat.

Tomas' keen eyes pierced Illeanah, then the queen, and a cruel smile twisted on his thin lips.

"My, my, my, what trouble have you got into, brother? Taking your little group to the place where you betrayed your family to Kieryn Pallarus."

Will struggled against his brother's grip. Tomas was a decade older and stockier. Illeanah had heard tales of Tomas' quick temper and brawling. The rumours of his brutality were well known at court. She shivered, wondering if Will had suffered his brother's love of violence.

"If you recall, Tomas," Will gasped, his hands fluttering by his sides, betraying how nervous he was. "You never paid for your crimes. I pleaded for mercy on your behalf, and is this how you would repay me, brother?"

"Ha! You should have got your revenge while you had a chance," Tomas barked. He leered down at Will, his eyes alight with his victory. "Shame you didn't maim yourself the way you intended that day."

Will gave a strangled cry and reared back, loosening his brother's hold. He punched his nose. Snarling, Tomas reached out for Will, picked him up, and slammed him into the ground. Illeanah could hear the distinct sound of a winded grunt as Will's body lay limp.

"You're pathetic."

"Leave him!" Queen Odelle cried, unable to contain her outrage.

In comparison to Will's talents, Illeanah's powers were paltry. They were almost worthless. She buried down her deep-rooted fear of her talents and tried to call the power forward. What could her power of rejuvenating plants do?

Pressing the point of his sword into the back of Will's neck, Tomas forced his younger brother to lie prostrated on the ground. He leered up at the queen. "I know who you are … You're going to die a terrible death, Odelle Pallarus. Perhaps we should wait until we have your precious prince and let you watch as we tear the little imp into pieces."

Will tried to get up, but Tomas kicked him in the side.

"Roots …" Will grunted as he lay panting on the ground. He might be a perplexing puzzle, but he had gotten them out of the citadel alive. Will didn't deserve to die by his brother's sword. "Illeanah … please."

Will's suggestion had merit. Once more, Illeanah reached forward to the little power that she possessed. She swallowed, concentrating her efforts on the root systems below their feet. In her veins, she felt the old familiar warming in her insides. Her father always warned her that powers and gifting always corrupted, polluting the human soul. She had always found the allure of her power a pleasant temptation. She gave herself over to her gifting, and power sung in her blood. It was stronger, wilder than she had ever felt. The ground beneath her feet quaked, and she relished the look of shock on Tomas' face.

With an inarticulate cry, her fingers twitched. Roots burst through the ground, wrapping themselves around Tomas' feet. Tomas yelled and twisted about, slashing the winding roots with his sword. Slowly they slithered up his muscled thighs until they wrapped around his mid-section. No matter how much Tomas slashed and fought, the roots kept climbing, encasing his body.

Free, Will crawled out from underneath his brother's boots. He stayed crouched on the ground, his face tilting up to regard his brother's panicked expression.

"Please …"

The roots constricted. Tomas' mumbled pleas melted into inhuman screams. Illeanah watched in detached horror as they hugged the unfortunate man until he lay limp, broken and silent.

In the hush that followed, Will stumbled to his feet. He approached her, reaching out with a shaking hand. He wrapped his own arms around her, and this time she didn't push him away. His hand came to her hair, and he patted her back. That was when Illeanah realised that she was sobbing.

"Hush now." Illeanah heard Will's calm voice speak in her ear. The timbre of his tone was deep and pleasant. "He wasn't going to let any of us walk away. You did what you needed to. It's over. He's gone."

Illeanah sniffled and backed away, searching Will's face. Releasing the power, the roots slithered away from Tomas' body, which hit the ground with a thud. "You knew?" she unnecessarily asked. "How long?"

Will smiled. "For as long as I have known you."

"You never said anything ..."

"Wasn't my secret to share." Will shrugged. The smile on his face melted away as he turned to look at his brother.

"We need to get rid of the body," said the queen. She had stepped up to Tomas' still form and toed him. "He's a big man."

Illeanah dabbed at her tears with the edge of the horrible man's shirt she was wearing. "His size is not a problem." She was pleasantly surprised at how steady her voice sounded.

Taking a deep breath, Illeanah gestured to a piece of earth. Before their eyes, the earth dug itself out, large enough for a grave. She turned towards Will, whose legs had collapsed under him. He sat staring at his brother's corpse, his handsome face blank.

"Do you want to say your farewells?" Illeanah asked. Tomas was family, after all.

Will shook his head. "I dreamt of this day. What type of man does that make me?"

Shrugging, Illeanah gestured, and tree roots unceremoniously rolled Tomas' lifeless body into the unmarked grave. Everyone watched, fascinated, as the roots pushed the dirt to fill the hole.

"It's obvious the grave is fresh," Will murmured. He seemed to be going into shock.

Illeanah quirked a watery smile. With a flick of her wrist, grass and weeds took over the mound until it looked the same as the grass around them. If one didn't know there was a grave, they would not see it. Tomas Hartcurt would simply disappear.

CHAPTER SEVENTEEN

Jodathyn

The Village of Kudah

The screams of the villagers joined Jodathyn's wails of agony in a symphony of terror. Jodathyn's cramped world of heat and suffocation tilted wildly on its axis. He tumbled in the dark, his body lurching from side to side. His skull struck the side of Vadroil's blasted singing head, and he saw stars.

The bronze groaned under the pressure and then split. And finally, he was able to suck in a lungful of air. Even through the haze of pain, he used his burnt fingers to drag himself to where he could see a sliver of light through the smoke. He was aware that he was slipping into a shocked state of mind. Hysteria was quickly taking over his body, which was shaking uncontrollably.

Long grey claws tore into Jodathyn's instrument of torture, and it peeled away. A gentle dragon hand pulled him from his heated prison, and a black snout sniffed at him. His head lolled to the side.

Not far from them, Curran lay. The barman's glassy eyes watched the dragon in awe. Jodathyn parted his lips; an agonised cry ripped from his throat. "Curran!"

Pulling himself to his elbows, Jodathyn tried to crawl his way over. The black dragon's claw returned, picking him up and then placing him carefully at Curran's side. Lifting one hand, Curran reached out to touch Jodathyn.

"You live ..." he gasped. Halfway through his movement, his hand slumped, and he let out a long sigh. Draped over the barkeep's body, Jodathyn sobbed.

"Sidrah! We have to get him out of here!"

Lifting his head, Jodathyn looked for the familiar voice. Seated behind Sidrah's great crowned head was Nym, her silver hair glinting in the morning light. There was a fierce frown adorning her face. In her hands she had one of the swords from the tournament.

Jodathyn took time to glance back at Sidrah through his tears. Sidrah's amber eyes dimmed. She plucked Nym from her back and set her on her feet. "Find me the weasel of a magistrate, Nym Blade-Tongue."

Nym looked like she wanted to reach out to Jodathyn and offer some sort of comfort. She considered Jodathyn's slumped form, then stalked through what remained of the crowd. Jodathyn could hear her demanding that the people hand over the magistrate.

"You are in a world of trouble, hatchling," Sidrah said.

Jodathyn clutched onto Curran's jerkin. "Please, *sudunah*, is there nothing you can do!?"

Sidrah's brow furrowed. "I'm sorry, *sudunyn*, he was at the door of the Otherworld, and now he has passed through where I cannot follow. I didn't have the power to help him ..."

The sound of metal compressing and groaning interrupted Sidrah. A loud thump and clatter halted Jodathyn from his mourning of Curran. He lifted his head to see another dragon had landed upon the second bronze dragon head. His russet scales glinted in the glow of the remaining fire, which he reached over and blew out in one breath. Swaying his head about, he regarded the bronze statues, then he took them between his claws and squeezed them into an unusable mass. The grin on his face was one of savage enjoyment.

"What are you doing here, Deovyn?"

"Currently? Extracting revenge." Deovyn, the russet dragon, continued to crush the bronze dragons. When he finished with his fun, he stepped away and came over to peer down at Jodathyn.

Jodathyn stared back. Although the russet dragon was larger than Tornyth, Jodathyn noticed he was smaller than Sidrah.

"I'm here to help and to see the *vehyl*. It's been many years since I have seen one," Deovyn said. He cocked his head to the side. Something within the action gave Jodathyn a clue that Deovyn was a much younger dragon than the stern Sidrah. "Aren't you going to heal him? He looks dreadful."

Sidrah huffed and turned her long neck to stare down at Jodathyn again. Jodathyn had never felt so foolish, lying beaten and blistering on the hard cobblestones. Sidrah's face tightened in distinct displeasure, and he steeled himself for a sound berating. The tongue-lashing didn't come.

Instead, she breathed her healing power over him. He felt the tightening sensation of skin and muscle stitching back together. His flesh tingled until it was soft and tender. As his body healed under the guidance of Sidrah's power, the pain diminished, and Jodathyn became aware of warm stickiness of his back and shoulders.

Lowering his head so that he might study Jodathyn, the russet dragon pressed his snout cautiously against Jodathyn's side. Ignoring the terrified cries of the onlookers, Jodathyn lifted his hand to touch the warm scales of the young male dragon. The russet dragon crouched, his hind legs shuffling forwards, his stare intense. The orbs of his eyes were tawny rather than the bright amber of Sidrah or Mandros. "I am Deovyn the Small and Mighty. Greetings, *sudunyn*."

"Greetings," Jodathyn murmured. He turned towards Sidrah. "I can't manifest. I'm drugged."

Deovyn's nostrils flared. He inhaled deeply, his head whipping up in distaste. The villagers shrieked at the abrupt movement. "I can smell it on you."

Jodathyn tentatively sniffed at his clothing. "I smell like smoke more than anything."

"Smoke doesn't bother me in the slightest," Deovyn grumbled. "Those herbs tend to cling to their victims."

Jodathyn sighed, scrambling to his feet. As he stumbled, Sidrah righted him with her foreleg. He mumbled his thanks and looked down at Curran's lifeless body. The terror he had felt during his botched execution left him feeling light-headed.

"We can take him into the mountains and bury him as dragon-friend if there is no family to honour him here." The cheeriness of Deovyn's face fell as he regarded Curran's corpse. "*Vehyl* can be strangely cruel."

"Well, *vehyl*," Sidrah said, eyeing the cowering humans that had crowded about them, "does he have family?"

"None that I can speak for." Dithering towards them, with the hesitant steps of the very old and frail, was Kya. In her hands, she held a small bundle. She shuffled her way directly towards Jodathyn and pressed it into his hands. Cupping Jodathyn's tear-stained cheeks, she brought his face down closer to her own so that their foreheads touched.

"I'm dirty ..." Jodathyn mumbled, feeling all of a sudden teary again.

"That doesn't bother an old woman in the slightest," Kya said, hushing him. "Here, sweet boy, some food and a comb. Your handsome Pallarus curls could do with a brush."

"Thank you," Jodathyn whispered, looking down at the bundle. "I would not take food from your table."

Kya kissed his cheek and released him. "Please take my gift. It would make me happy to think I have served one of such noble blood."

Jodathyn nodded. "I've nothing to give you in return."

"You freed my husband and have shown the poor of Kudah kindness."

"Come, Jodathyn," Sidrah said. "Say goodbye to the old one. It's time to go."

Leaning up against Sidrah's leg so that he might not fall over, Jodathyn looked up into her amber eyes. "There's another human they are holding hostage ... please ..."

"Not another word," Deovyn interrupted, thrusting out his chest. "I'll go and get the *vehyl*. Where?"

"There's a brick building out the back. She'll be afraid."

Deovyn laughed. "*Vehyl* women love me ... They think I'm adorable."

Before Jodathyn could say anything to the contrary, Deovyn took off. Biting his lip, he watched his newfound brother fly to the other side of the house. Hopefully he wouldn't frighten Et-hir too badly.

"Deo and I will take you somewhere safe to rest," Sidrah said, taking up Curran's limp body. He couldn't help it. Jodathyn stared at Curran, willing to see any sign of movement or life. There was none. Jodathyn swallowed a lump and blinked back fresh tears.

"He died for me."

"A noble end," Sidrah replied.

"Sidrah ..." Jodathyn said, licking his lips. For the first time, he let his gaze roam over the gathering villagers. He lowered his voice before continuing. "Last night ... I saw Galgothmeg. I think he is looking for me."

"Which was why you were commanded by your *pallu* and *aluel* to stay safe on the island, away from Galgothmeg." The black dragon rounded on him, her lip curling in anger. "And look, here comes Nym Sharp-Tongue."

Sidrah was indeed correct. Blade in hand, Nym had Magistrate Swyft in her strong grip. With a ferocious growl, she forced him to stumble forward as he took notice of the black dragon and panicked. Nym dumped him at Jodathyn's feet.

"Stop snivelling, you over-ripe, worm-eating maggot," Nym growled. "Be a man ... and face the consequences of your actions."

Sidrah unfurled her wings and loomed over the cowering man. Jodathyn immediately recognised it as an act of intimidation. He tried to garner some sympathy for the magistrate; he failed.

What a terrible way to die. Presiding over the dark shadow that was the dragon of Nobility and Honour.

"Dragon blood has been spilled in your town," Sidrah said gravely. "Vengeance doesn't belong to me. One who is greater has that duty and honour."

Jodathyn felt his heart sink. "You're not going to do anything?"

Sidrah pinned him with a serious look and shook her head. Ignoring Jodathyn's outrage, she turned back to the quivering magistrate. "Tell me, did you know who he is? Did you know he is a scaled prince?"

"I swear, all I knew was that he was a thief and liar." Magistrate Swyft tried to inch away, but Nym kicked him.

"You're the liar!" Kya called from the crowd. "Come here, and I'll teach you a lesson. I tell you this truly, dragon. He paraded the boy ... degraded him, humiliated him. Aye, he knew his bloodline. He knew very well. He boasted to the village of the victory he had over house Pallarus and the dragon he bore inside of him."

"Who's to argue over a testimony like that?" Deovyn returned with Et-hir clinging to his neck. He turned to Jodathyn, grinning. "See, women love me!"

With a horrified cry, Et-hir slipped from Deovyn's neck and ran towards Curran's body. She spoke in Sionian, her words so rapid that they bubbled over one another. She reached up to grasp Curran's cold hand, and she wept.

"I'm sorry. It's all my fault." Jodathyn went over to comfort her.

"No!" Et-hir cried. She whirled on her heel and stormed over to Magistrate Swyft, who watched her mourn Curran, a haughty gleam in his eyes. She drew back her hand and slapped him across the face. The resounding crack was enough to make Jodathyn wince and step back.

"No! He is the monster of Kudah. He took my brother from me! He treats the people poorly! He's the one who hurt you and killed Curran. Why, I ought to ..." Et-hir stepped forward and struck the magistrate again.

"Someone stop the mad Sionian!"

No one moved. Et-hir slapped him for the third time. "I need a bad word to say in Ramian!"

"*Rshon mahthyt*!" Jodathyn supplied.

Et-hir proceeded to repeat the word and started yelling again in Sionian. Amused, Jodathyn stood to the side. Nym approached him and leaned over to whisper, "Can you translate?"

Jodathyn quirked an eyebrow. "Of course. The polite translation would be she's cursed the children he might sire. And calls him the by-product of a dog and a snapdragon. Her expressive language rivals your own."

"Snapdragon?"

"A reptilian creature, long snout, pointed teeth, and found lurking in waterways. In Sionian culture are known for either shrewdness or bathing in sludge."

"As enlightening as all of this is," Sidrah said, "our young hatchling here has a very, very angry Papa Dragon. I'm sure our king would love to have words with you."

"I wanted to hear more about snapdragons," Deovyn muttered. He quieted at Sidrah's unimpressed look.

"Very well, dragon," Et-hir said. She wiped her tears away with the back of her hand. She executed a swift bow to Sidrah. "I'm Et-hir, daughter of the Silk Rose and Sionian trader. I'm calm. Let's depart."

"Come now," Deovyn said. He nudged Curran's body gently and took the dead man up in his claws. "It's high time we find somewhere safe to rest."

Sidrah and Deovyn flew them west into the mountains of Paru. There upon the mighty peaks, they laid Curran Norrys, born of Kudah, to rest. Jodathyn lingered by the grave of the man he only met a few short days ago. Did Curran know that his fate was sealed the moment he welcomed him to his tavern?

The chill of the mountains was biting. Being cloistered first in Androssah, Aviah Valley and Pallaryn, he had never seen the magnificence of the mountain ranges of Rama. He was torn between wonderment and a grating sadness.

"In the days of old, it was a great honour of the *vehyl* of the western side of Haven Bay to be buried in the mountain," Sidrah said.

"I wish I could have spared him that honour," Jodathyn murmured.

Deovyn raised his snout. "He is close to the sky and Wind Song forevermore."

Under the watchful eyes of his dragon siblings, Jodathyn returned to the cave, which happened to be an old mine entrance. Et-hir and Nym sat huddled in the shelter, Kya's bundle spread between them.

"What happened in Kudah?" Jodathyn asked. "I mean, how ..."

Nym stood, brushing her hands on her trousers. She glanced down at Et-hir and then to the dragons. "Curran came to me after the last bout—which I won, by the way; he was frantic that you had gone missing."

"I didn't tell him my plans," Jodathyn mumbled.

Nym's lips twisted. "Yes, I know. I had to tell him what you were up to. He wasn't going to take no for an answer. He didn't like your plan ... he was uneasy. There was a spy among the prisoners."

"Then Curran came and hid us in the barrels," Et-hir continued.

"Yes, I hung around to hear what they planned. Curran and I took off into the forest. I had heard from Theo's stories that humans summoned dragons using fire and smoke. We spent the night building a big bonfire. At dawn, Curran raced back to the village to buy us time ..."

"The fires worked," Sidrah continued. "Your ghostly-haired friend got my attention. I was already looking, of course. Your last messages had concerned me greatly, *sudunyn*."

"I never intended for any of this to happen," Jodathyn replied, turning his face away in shame.

"Cheer up," Deovyn said where he was lazing by the entrance of the mine. "At worst you and I have earned a snout-smacking from *Aluel* ... He won't be far away now. He was right riled after he found you missing."

Jodathyn shivered.

CHAPTER EIGHTEEN

Orion

Solan's Summer House, Aviah Valley

Orion paused to gaze at the monolithic turrets of Solan's summer house as they meandered through the garden gates. In the height of Lord Solan's power, the great house would have been alive with activity. Now it lay abandoned, its overbearing shadow covering the sweeping lawns and overgrown gardens. It was a silent witness to the evils that had happened within its boundaries.

Recalling the conversation that he had with Jodathyn in Belrah, Orion glanced up the towers once more. Had this been the place that Jodathyn played with servants and freed them? He had originally puzzled over Jodathyn's use of the word *freed*. He had come to the conclusion that Aviah Valley may have also been a household of slaves. He shuddered in revulsion. He had heard plenty of cautionary tales from his father that slavery still lived in Rama.

"If I had a house like this, I would close the gates behind me and barricade myself in," Theo said. The thief slipped off the back of Voran's warhorse and tilted his head to observe their surroundings. "Could you imagine having food on the table every night, and wine, and a bed?"

"Let's see what we can do about finding a bed for tonight," Orion replied. Even when he had lost his entire inheritance, he never went without food or a comfortable bed. As one of Jodathyn's manservants, he had been looked after well. He should have been more grateful for his good fortune.

Beside Orion, Prince Carvelle huddled closer as he studied the house with a sense of awe. He grasped on to Orion's hand. "When he was a little boy, Uncle Jod played here. Uncle is scared of this house."

"Sometimes places come with bad memories," Voran replied. His voice was gruff. "Your uncle has plenty of those."

Carvelle looked up to the big warrior. "I heard Papa talking to Mumma. Uncle Jod still has nightmares, Sir Voran." Since hearing the barkeep in Halbeth call Voran "sir," Carvelle had taken into his head that the big man was a knight and had been calling him "sir" at any given opportunity.

Voran turned his steely eyes forward, jaw clenched. He said no more.

Orion hid his smile behind his hand.

"Let's get inside," Theo suggested. "If it's abandoned, it should be easy enough."

"I'll go and put the horses in the stables," Orion offered.

"The thief and I will scope out the house to look for anything of value." Voran dropped a heavy hand on Theo's shoulder. Despite him forgiving Voran, Theo was still a little cautious of the giant man. Not that Orion blamed him. Voran had left a sizeable egg on Theo's hard skull.

"Can I help with the horses?"

Orion held out his hand. "Of course, Your Highness."

Carvelle ignored Orion's hand and skipped ahead, singing the first few verses of Theo's original song *The Apple Tree Prince*. Orion grinned back at Theo as he took Voran's reins. "He's going to be singing that for all eternity."

"High praise indeed that a royalborn enjoys my song," Theo answered levelly. "At least some appreciate my skills."

Chuckling, Orion joined Carvelle in his song as he followed the prince to the stables. Carvelle ran ahead as he continued on to the second verse.

The king is dead, the king is dead.
Our dear prince was sent away,
To live in that wretched hall,
One cold and dreary day ...

The song abruptly halted as Carvelle entered the stables. "Doesn't look like much in here!" he shouted.

"That's okay, we can still settle the horses somewhere comfortable and safe."

Orion led the two horses into the stables. It looked like the place hadn't seen an animal in a long time. As he expected, each stall was empty, their gates swinging on their hinges. Orion hated the sight of an abandoned stable.

Sighing, he removed the horses' tacks and saddles. Carvelle disappeared. Orion thought the youngster had become bored and wandered off, but the prince proved this assumption to be incorrect when he returned with a rickety little stool and a brush for the horses.

"It looks a little broken, but it might be okay to brush the horses."

Orion took the brush with a smile of thanks.

"I found one for me too!" Carvelle pulled out another brush. "You brush Zoryn, and I'll brush Zyan."

Orion watched with amusement as the young prince set his stool into position to brush Voran's horse. They worked in companionable silence until Carvelle jumped off his stool to hand Orion his brush. "I'm too short. You can finish Zyan, you're taller. I'll go and see if I can find a trough or a well … The horses need a drink." Off Carvelle scampered. "They might like some oats too! Grass must be getting boring!"

"I don't like your chances of finding oats!" Orion called after the prince, shaking his head.

Orion brushed down Voran's horse, patting his nose. The horse snuffled at him and pawed the ground. "We'll have a few days of rest here, my impatient friend."

Carvelle returned to the stables, soaking wet and dragging a bucket.

Orion put his hands on his hips. "What happened to you?"

"I found a bucket."

"I see that."

"I also found a pond."

"Well done."

"I fell in the pond."

Orion snorted, trying to contain his mirth. Carvelle glared up at him, clearly not amused.

"Let's give the horses a drink, and then we can go inside and dry you off."

Prince Carvelle clambered upon the rails. Out of the corner of his eye, Orion watched. He had heard all the tales from Valt about Master Jodathyn's love of climbing. He had also been warned that while Jodathyn might look like a quiet, bookish type of lad, he was a difficult one to get a hold of if he set his mind to it. Orion believed these observations; Valt had been tremendously angry the night Jodathyn had slipped his guard and escaped into the citadel.

"Orion, do you have a family? I think you would make a good big brother."

Orion started at the sudden sharp pang in his chest as the prince asked the unexpected question. It had been years since he thought about his siblings and dreamt of what life might have been like. Unlike his brother and sister, he had not succumbed to the sweating sickness. The memory of his mother's distress when she had found him playing in his brother's room was something he would never forget. He could still hear her screaming for his father to come quickly. His father had dashed up from the stables, taking two stairs at a time. Confused by his mother's cries, Orion had stood in the middle of his brother's room wide-eyed and frightened.

"Do not let anyone know the little one was in the sickroom," his father had said to his mother gruffly. Angry, his father had scooped him up and escorted him out to the stables. Perplexed, Orion had been made to sleep with the horses. His father slept beside him, and his mother had been banned from coming too near. Two days later, just before dawn, his mother had come stumbling towards the stables. He was curled underneath his father's chin, half asleep.

"Phill, they're gone," was all his mother could say before desperate sobs had overtaken her.

His father had made a half-strangled grunt as he tucked his coat around Orion's shoulders. "This ailment takes the children and leaves the parents, Marrie. There was naught we could do."

"They're my children!" his mother wailed. "Shall we lose Orion? He's only five summers!"

"Did you tell anyone that we found Orion in the sickroom?"

"No, of course not, husband," his mother had whispered.

His father had grunted again and pressed his lips to Orion's forehead. "As long as no one knows he was in the sickroom, he will be safe. He's well, Marrie; there's no sign of sickness. His strange beast magic has made him strong against this ailment."

Orion's mother had never quite been the same after her devastating loss. His father had become overbearing in his attempt to protect Orion from the world. For all their faults, Orion had dearly loved his parents.

"Papa says when someone goes silent like that, it means they don't want to talk about it. I am sorry, Orion."

Jolted back into reality, Orion forced a smile. "Your father is a wise man."

Carvelle blinked slowly. "Papa is the High King of Rama. Of course he is wise! Are you remembering bad memories, like Sir Voran said?"

"You do know Voran isn't a knight," Orion said quickly, changing the subject.

"Yes, but calling him Sir Voran annoys him. He tries not to let it show."

"That's very cheeky, my prince."

"Did I make you sad?"

Orion blinked. "I lost my family. I am alone."

Carvelle took Orion's hand in his and smiled up at him. "I can be your family. You can be the big brother!"

By the time Orion and Carvelle entered the house, Theo and Voran had put together a simple meal. The four of them ate in what at one time must have been the guards' communal dining hall. Once everyone was finished, Orion gathered their plates and left through the adjoining door to explore the kitchens.

"I think I made him sad," he heard Carvelle tell the other two. "He doesn't have any family left."

He wandered into the room. He placed the plates down and put his head in his hands.

"Orion. Are you well?" Theo stood by the door, watching him with his dark eyes.

"I'll be alright," Orion replied.

Theo entered the room and closed the door behind him. "If you need someone to talk to …"

"Thank you, but I'm well." Orion knew his tone was a little clipped. He was much like his father in that respect.

"I know we come from different worlds. You've grown up with the whole honour code, and I'm a thief. But I've lost most of my family too, so I can listen."

"Technically, I stole a horse," Orion pointed out with a wry grin. "I also stole weapons off a dead man. I guess that makes us more alike than we first thought."

"That's true. Though if you're being reasonable, the dead man didn't need his weapons."

"All I ever wanted was to make my father proud."

"Orion," Theo said. "You're loyal to your master, and you are protecting the Crown Prince of Rama! And not to mention the guy you shot between the eyes! I think your father, wherever he is, would be proud."

"Is Carvelle still telling that story of how I shot that arrogant toe-rag?"

"He's telling 'Sir Voran' about it right now."

Orion snickered.

"I'm betting two coppers that if the king turns up, one of the first stories Carvelle tells his papa is about you shooting Pasch the Putrid," Theo said.

"*Pasch the Putrid*?"

"The name Carvelle has given to the villain of the story."

Orion sighed heavily. "Two coppers? I didn't know you had coin."

"Stole them."

"When?"

"Yanyima. On our way out. They deserved it."

Orion shook his head and gave a bark of laughter. "You are incorrigible, Theo."

The house had some useful provisions even though it had been abandoned. Voran found a cache of weapons. He selected an extra axe for himself before stomping his way through the house.

Orion was quite content to meticulously sort through their findings. He inspected each arrow carefully and chose for Theo a pair of daggers to slip into his boots. As much as he hated the idea of the prince running about the halls with a weapon, Orion added a small dagger to his hip in case they needed to arm the boy.

He didn't want to dwell on what the High King might say about his son being armed.

Among the weapons, they had also found odds and ends of leather armour. Orion spent a good part of the afternoon sizing Theo and Carvelle with different pieces. To say Carvelle was pleased to be getting his first armour was an understatement. He sat by Orion's side, watching as Orion dismantled the smallest leather pieces to adjust the sizing.

Theo kept them company. The thief spent most of the time biting his lip as he watched the door.

"Theo is concerned about Voran," Carvelle said. "He makes the thief nervous."

Theo blushed and looked away.

"He makes me nervous too," Orion admitted. "A good leader knows when to ask for help."

"Sir Voran doesn't bother me," Carvelle declared. "He hasn't forgiven himself for what happened to uncle. It makes him cranky."

"Let's get you onto a chair and see how this fits, hmm?" Orion held up his handiwork.

The prince eagerly grabbed a chair, dragging it to the centre of the room. He climbed up on the chair, pushing out his little chest. "I'm ready."

Theo grinned at the proud look plastered on the prince's face. They worked together to fit the young boy in Orion's makeshift armour.

"There you go. All fitted," Orion said and stepped back and admired his work. Considering the lack of tools at his disposal, he was proud of the results.

"A true work of art," Theo said. He had moved away to closely inspect the bows. He ran his fingers along the strings, mimicking the way he would caress the strings on his lute.

"I think I may look a little bit silly," Prince Carvelle told him, wrinkling his nose.

"Well, the main thing is leather armour should slow down any arrows or knives. You don't wear armour to look pretty," Orion replied, adjusting the prince's shirt.

"Sometimes the best art has purpose and function, my prince." Theo had turned away from the bows and had picked up an arrow. He held it up and inspected it curiously.

"I saw some horsemen from Silverdyne once. The leatherwork on the saddles and armour were all very nice."

Orion smiled indulgently at Carvelle. He remembered having arguments with his own father about wanting to use his decorative armour to train in. He had been stubborn about it when he was young. "That would have been dress armour. We have sensible armour too."

"Did you have fancy saddles and armour once?"

"Yes," Orion answered. "I had a very good saddle once upon a time. My very gifted Sionian mother had made it. It had my name, my father's name, his father's name, and his father's name embossed into the leather."

"One day I'll make sure Papa gets you an excellent one," Carvelle declared. "Do you suppose when I am big, I could have a nice saddle too? I want dragons embossed on mine."

"I think one day you will have your own saddle and as many steeds as you like."

"I think two horses is a sensible number. I don't need a whole cavalry. Did you know Uncle Jod only has one horse? He's very fond of his animals."

Orion turned his attention away from the prince to Theo, who seemed to be trying to work out how to notch an arrow. "Would you like me to show you?"

Theo looked up with a guilty expression on his face. He put the bow down, looking embarrassed at being caught touching it. "I've never been much good with anything other than art. If trouble comes, I'm going to be a liability in a fight."

"You can't expect to be as good as Orion," Prince Carvelle said. "He's been training his entire life."

Theo looked down at the bow and then Orion. "What if I'm no good?"

"That's why we train," Orion replied, leaning forward. "Nothing worth doing is easy. I can certainly show you how to shoot a bow well."

"Maybe you'll have better luck hunting if you can shoot something," Carvelle added, nodding sagely.

Theo looked blankly down at Carvelle, a large grin splitting his face. "Very well, show me how to pluck these strings."

Over dinner, Voran grumbled that the three boys had disappeared, leaving him to strip the beds and wash sheets alone. The big man had even found blankets and taken them out for a thorough beating for them to sleep on while they waited for sheets to dry.

It came as no surprise to Orion that Theo found the cellar and produced a collection of wine and ale to mollify Voran. By the time dinner was over, Voran was quite merry and told them stories of his time in Pallaryn.

That night, Theo chose to bunk with him and Carvelle instead of taking his own space. "Night, horse boy," the thief grunted in the dark, dragging behind him his pilfered bedding.

Orion smiled secretly into his dusty blanket as the prince hummed in his sleep.

Perhaps, with Theo, I'm not so alone after all.

CHAPTER NINETEEN

Jodathyn

The Mountains of Paru - The Old Kudah Mines

Jodathyn was trapped in the dark. But he wasn't alone; he could sense other human bodies pressing against him. Peering through the blackness, he could see the white of their terrified eyes staring back at him. His hands were bound with a thick rope.

"Where am I?" he cried.

"We're Lord Thylyssa's now. He owns the Kudah Mines and the Stronghold."

Something in the back of Jodathyn's mind echoed the name. It seemed so familiar, and yet he did not know the man.

"Where is the Stronghold?"

"It's an ancient place; a land of blood and battles. We're in the belly of the mountains. Here our bones will lie."

Jodathyn's hands shot out and were met with a solid burning wall. The skin on his back, arms, and legs was blistering. He screamed, thrashing. Turning his head, he came face-to-face with Curran. The barman's eyes stared beyond him; a red stain blossomed over his shirt.

"I'm sorry," Jodathyn croaked, taking in the sight of Curran's wound. Even the skin in his throat was cooking. "I didn't mean for you to die for me."

Curran's sightless eyes blinked, still looking at the beyond. His lips barely moved as he spoke. "And yet I am buried upon the mountain ... and you fly free."

Jodathyn grasped on to Curran's jerkin. "I wanted you to live!"

"We don't get everything we want in this world, Prince. Look around you; the world is on fire. Soon there will be nothing but ash."

Jodathyn was tumbling onto cobblestones. The coldness of them burned. Curran was right; the world about them was on fire. Lifting his face, Jodathyn realised that he was home in Pallaryn. The streets of the great citadel ran red with blood. The oppressive sound of screaming and wailing was so terrible that he longed to cover his ears.

Everywhere he looked, Jodathyn found death. Bodies lay like broken dolls, discarded where they had fallen, forgotten by the citizens that were trying to flee. Beside him, a flower seller lay dead; a crimson stream of blood flowed from his skull. A delicate yellow flower, spattered with blood, was still in his outstretched hand.

Pallaryn, the shining citadel of Rama, had fallen.

Above him Grey Shadows flew, hunting human prey from up above.

Scrambling to his feet, Jodathyn attempted to grab a hold of a fleeing citizen. His hand grasped hold of a woman. His cry of delight at seeing Illeanah died in his throat. She looked past him, her fair face twisting into a frightened scowl. He felt her power thrumming through her, which left him feeling confused.

"Illeanah!"

She didn't recognise him. Her body dissolved like the morning mist.

A mighty roar to Jodathyn's left made his stomach lurch. Sword raised, Kieryn swung his weapon, and Jodathyn screamed, feeling a searing pain in his jaw and gut. He stumbled backwards and fell beneath tumultuous waves. He was drifting down into the deep. Clawing at the water surrounding him, Jodathyn fought to return to the surface. It remained out of reach.

Blood pounding in his ears, Jodathyn gave up and let himself slip further into the watery grave. As he felt his consciousness succumb, a great claw tore through the water. It grasped around his middle, and he was hoisted into the air. Running his hands along scaly ridges, Jodathyn realised with a jolt the dragon carrying him was blue of scale. Not green as he expected.

Jodathyn's vision swam as the blue dragon landed by a gentle stream with a thump. The giant claw released him, and he lay sprawled on the pebbles. He stayed there on his hands and knees, coughing water from his lungs and retching. The blue dragon glanced down at him and then ambled away, apparently unimpressed.

"Who are you?"

For a long moment, the dragon observed him with eyes that gleamed with ancient wisdom. Then he spoke, his voice rumbling. "Come here, hatchling."

"I am over a thousand years old," another voice that seemed painfully familiar answered. "I think I am beyond being called hatchling."

Jodathyn started and turned to find a dark-haired man leaning up against a tree. He wore simple hunting leathers, which were in stark contrast to the crown upon his head. The sleeves of his shirt were rolled up, and Jodathyn caught sight of the large dragon tattoo gleaming on his bronzed forearm. Squinting, he realised the tattoo was of an impaled dark dragon. A strange and bloody tattoo.

"Yet here you are in your vehyl *flesh, Arturyn."*

"Sometimes it feels good to walk on two feet again, Aluel."

"Indeed, and not perhaps a hope that your newest mynrell *may glimpse at your* vehyl *form ... and trust you more."*

"You are dead and gone, Aluel ... and yet you still visit my visions."

"I will never truly be gone from this land, mynrell. *The land, the sea, the sky, they run in my blood. We are one."*

As Arturyn, the human form of Mandros, couldn't seem to see him, Jodathyn approached him boldly. Curiosity got the better of him, and he stared him full in the face.

"Your mynrell *is much like you, Arturyn," the blue dragon said. His golden orbs slid to where Jodathyn was standing. "He has endured much, and yet he has flourished. He needs a wise teacher, one that can accept he has much to learn."*

Arturyn raked his hands through his hair. "I am angry with him … He tried to break the bond. Sidrah and Deovyn …"

"I am very angry with him too," the blue dragon replied drily. "But he called for help, and Sidrah answered the young one's call."

"He should have called for me!" Arturyn snarled, thumping his fist to his chest. "He is my son! My mynrell. *Not Sidrah's."*

"I recall a young green dragon doing the same, many years ago now. He mewled for General Roane like a lost little hatchling. Got himself in a right scrape, he did."

"Yes, I remember. Shall you ever allow me to forget it?" Arturyn closed his eyes. "What do you suggest I do, Aluel?"

"Our enemies are tightening their nets. Ground him somewhere safe until both of your fiery blood has cooled."

"Tornyth isn't exactly obedient."

The blue dragon raised his head and pierced Jodathyn with a stern stare. "He'll do as he is told."

Arturyn's head shot up, his inability to see Jodathyn lifted. Jodathyn froze like a child who had been caught with his fingers in the cook's pie. For a long moment, they stared at one another.

A vein in Arturyn's forehead ticked. His lips twitched into a displeased frown. "Where are you?"

"Galgothmeg is coming…" was all Jodathyn could think to mumble. With the clear anger on Arturyn's face, he felt as if his mind had stopped working. "Kudah … west—the mountains somewhere."

"Stay there. I'm coming."

It was a great rumbling sound that pulled Jodathyn back into awareness. His head was resting upon Deovyn's right claw. The smaller russet dragon's head lolled to the side, the warm breath from his ajar maw indicating he was asleep. He didn't remember entering the cave or laying his head down.

Jodathyn lay where he was, staring at this dragon brother's slumbering form. Every few moments, Deovyn's face twitched, his nostrils flaring as he emitted a low growl.

Feet shuffling and loud laughter drew Jodathyn's attention away from Deovyn. Sitting up, he looked for Sidrah and found her missing.

"Come on, hit me harder!" Nym's voice cried.

There was an *oof* and raucous laughter.

Curious, Jodathyn stumbled to the cave's mouth and peered out. A few paces away, Nym and Et-hir were sparring. He watched as Et-hir tried to copy Nym's stance. Nym counted down, and the girls scuffled again. In moments, Nym had Et-hir pinned to the ground.

"You're improving," Nym said. "I've been fighting my whole life."

Et-hir grumbled.

"If Nym was a man, I would suggest grabbing dangling parts," Jodathyn commented, crossing his arms against his chest and leaning against the rock of the cave. "I found it most effective."

It took them a little while to understand what he said, but when they did, Nym raised her eyebrow and Et-hir giggled.

"Care to demonstrate?" Nym asked, a smirk upon her lips.

"He might need that at a later date to sire heirs," Et-hir chimed in. "I hear men are generally fond of those parts."

"I have two brothers. I can vouch for male vanity," Nym replied.

"I will forego the demonstration," Jodathyn said. He glanced back at the cave. "Where's Sidrah?"

Et-hir rolled to her feet, her hand flying to her dark hair, which she had neatly braided into a tight crown upon her head. Her eyes darted towards Nym and then back to Jodathyn, a slight blush to her cheeks. "She's worried."

"She's on the lookout for Galgothmeg, the red blot on a cow's behind."

"This is all my fault."

Nym opened her mouth to speak. But Et-hir's smile became strained. She chanced a look at Jodathyn and then her eyes darted away. A strangled noise left her throat. "Please, excuse me ..." She dashed past Jodathyn, her fingers trying to pat down her hair.

Confused, Jodathyn watched her go, his brow furrowing. "What was that about?"

Nym smirked at him and winked. "I'm sure you can work it out, handsome."

"She blames me?" Jodathyn's shoulders slumped.

"She blames herself." Nym shook her head and rolled her eyes. "You're a dim-witted puss berry, aren't you? You make her—"

Whatever Nym was about to say was interrupted by Deovyn lumbering out of the cave. The russet dragon took one look at Jodathyn before sweeping him off his feet, dangling him upside down. Crying out in surprise, Jodathyn could only squirm as the ground swam before his eyes.

"Now that you have rested, *sudunyn*, time to play!"

"Don't you dare drop me!" Jodathyn cried. Using all his upper body strength, he tried to reach up to loose Deovyn's grip on him. The dragon shook his head back and forth, making Jodathyn flop side to side.

"Put me down, Deovyn!" Jodathyn growled.

"The girls have had their spar ... my turn."

Jodathyn was sure he was going green. With a delighted roar, Deovyn dropped him to the ground. The russet dragon took a few steps backwards and nudged Jodathyn with his snout. Warm air blew across Jodathyn's face as he looked up at the dragon.

"You're not like Mandros or Sidrah at all."

"Thank goodness for that," Deovyn said. "We can't all be stern and serious. I'll leave that to the old wise ones. Sidrah will return soon ... Time to wrestle."

"You want me to wrestle you?" Jodathyn looked Deovyn up and down, his eyebrow raised.

Deovyn, for his part, danced from side to side.

"Manifest, you silly, snake-skinned beast!" Nym shouted from the side. "Show the impertinent wrath-lizard what a man from house Pallarus is made of!"

Deovyn's suspicious sounding laugh turned into a cough. Jodathyn sent him a withering glare. He hadn't as yet confided in Nym exactly who Mandros was.

"Let's see exactly what Arturyn's spawn is capable of," Deovyn replied, flashing his fangs.

Clambering to his feet, Jodathyn rolled his shoulders. He quirked a smirk in Nym's direction before manifesting into his dragon form. Even in their most potent state, Jodathyn had noticed that the suppression herbs didn't last longer than a night. Sleep also helped the effects to wear off.

"Oh, you're adorable!" Deovyn crowed. "You're smaller than me!"

Tornyth lashed out with his fangs to nip Deovyn on his side and swished his tail around to try and unbalance his dragon brother.

Deovyn laughed and nimbly stepped out of the way. "Come for me, *sudunyn*!"

Tornyth lunged again, attempting to leap upon the russet dragon's back. Deovyn had other ideas, however, and rolled so that Tornyth found his snout hitting the ground. His larger brother had no mercy on him. He grappled with Tornyth, pressing him down with his weight and grasping on to his horns.

For a long moment, Tornyth lay winded, then Deovyn gave his head a gentle shake. "See that, Tor?" Deovyn said as he released him. He stepped away and cocked his head to the side. "Once an enemy dragon has a hold of your horns, he can control you like a pony."

If Tornyth thought that Deovyn was now inclined to show him mercy, he was wrong. Lowering his horns, Deovyn charged at him. Tornyth darted to the side and rammed his shoulder against Deovyn's.

"More force," Deovyn cried. "Don't worry about hurting me."

Using Deovyn's lax attitude, Tornyth took his brother's wing into his mouth. He felt Deovyn's involuntarily shiver and did not clamp his teeth down on his brother's wing.

"Very good," Deovyn said. Tornyth moved away. The russet dragon rewarded him by tipping him over with a flick of his horns. "The bones and membranes of our wings are fragile. A downed dragon is a dead dragon. Always been on your guard—I'm playing with you, *sudunyn*."

Growling, Tornyth flipped himself over and latched on to Deovyn's ankle and pulled. Deovyn fell to the ground with a hoot of laughter. Tornyth kept dragging his leg, using all his weight to move Deovyn.

There was a part of Tornyth that knew Deovyn was humouring him. He was aware that he was a seasoned battle dragon, and truly he didn't stand much of a chance with him anyway.

Curling his neck about, Deovyn bit the sensitive flesh where Tornyth's jawbone met at his neck. Surprised by the pain, Tornyth pulled back, releasing the russet dragon.

Deovyn lazily shook his neck; his expression was sombre. "I'll never forget the first time *Aluel* nipped me there. Battle dragons call that the death bite. It's been the undoing of many a dragon. Always protect your neck and belly."

"I'm not good at fighting."

Deovyn opened his mouth to reply but was interrupted by a roar. Tornyth raised his eyes to the sky. Sidrah was bearing down on them. Fast. Even in the distance, he could tell something was awfully wrong. His eyes slid over to Deovyn. His brother's expression shuttered. The relaxed demeanour he was becoming accustomed to had hardened.

"What's wrong?" Et-hir came rushing from the side.

Even with how his belly constricted with discomfort at his brother's sudden change, Tornyth was pleased by the cool touch of Et-hir's hands upon his scales. He stamped down the rumble of pleasure as she ran her fingertips down his side absently. This little woman, who had never seen his dragon form, was unafraid of him.

Deovyn's eyes were glassy. Tornyth could tell that he was reaching out to someone else.

"Galgothmeg is here!" Deovyn hissed. "We're going into battle. Stay down."

"*Battle*?" Nym took one glance at Deovyn and the approaching Sidrah and dashed towards the cave. As she passed Et-hir, she grasped the other girl's hand, tugging her along. "Move!"

In the distance, Tornyth could now see the outlines of dragons, their coloured scales glinting in the midday sun. His lips parted in wonderment. His wings fluttered, longing to join them. Deovyn sent him a pained look and nudged him to turn around. Tornyth's joy turned to fear. Dozens of Grey Shadows were approaching. The air about them thrummed with warning rumbles and promises of violence.

"Galgothmeg won't be far away," Deovyn warned. "He likes to appear out of thin air moments after the first clash. Get to that cave!" He leapt into the air to join Sidrah.

Not wanting to cause any further problems, Tornyth obeyed. He sat by the entrance, trying to spot Mandros in the myriad of dragons approaching. Surely the *vehyl* of Rama had now noticed dragonkind had returned.

Nym laid her hand upon his shoulder.

Creeping forward, almost on her knees, Et-hir joined them. Tornyth could feel her shivering in fright as she stared up at the two groups of dragons. He sidled alongside her as gently as he dared. Nym smirked, and he glared back as she rolled her eyes.

A deafening roar ripped through the skies. Tornyth could now clearly see Mandros leading his battle dragons. Sidrah and Deovyn had neatly tucked themselves into formation into the lines of dozens of battle dragons. He could only watch while dread curled in the pit of his stomach alongside a fluttering of fascination.

The anticipated clash of dragon upon dragon was terrible. The roars of pain and shrill shrieks of the Grey Shadows echoed through the mountain range. Even Nym pressed herself closer to his warm side.

When a familiar red silhouette plummeted onto Mandros' back, all of Tornyth's anger and resentment towards the green dragon was forgotten.

"Stay here," Tornyth roared.

"Wouldn't dream of moving," Nym muttered, shaking her head.

Tornyth ignored Nym's displeasure and let the fury bubbling within his blood loose. He repressed the roar that was lodged in his throat. It wouldn't do to warn Galgothmeg of his advance.

CHAPTER TWENTY

Tornyth

The Mountains of Paru - The Old Kudah Mines

Tornyth shot into the sky. The wind caressed his scales, a whisper of blood and vengeance in its song. A soundless leer spread across his face as he came upon Galgothmeg and Mandros. The two great dragons were snarling and snapping at each other's throats, too busy to notice the rapidly approaching Tornyth.

Grabbing the red dragon's tail in his mouth, Tornyth heard the outraged roar of confusion. He growled in victory, darting under Galgothmeg's belly, pulling the red dragon off course. Mandros was free to manoeuvre out of the red dragon's range.

Galgothmeg's roar of frustration mingled with Mandros' deep throated rumble of fury. The sky around them was swarming with dozens of Grey Shadows, their ghostly, tattered forms creating a shroud of oppression. Opposing them were dozens of dragons with Mandros. Tornyth's dragon instincts whispered to him that many were ancient, some even older than

Mandros. They were experienced battle dragons, each one of them, those who had seen Vadroil's strife firsthand.

Tornyth dropped Galgothmeg's tail, turned himself upwards, and speared his way through two approaching enemy dragons. The mad, wraithlike dragons' unnatural eyes were focused upon him.

Mandros whipped round, forelegs extended and teeth gnashing. The Grey Shadows, so intent on capturing Tornyth, flew straight into his lethal embrace. Mandros immediately discarded them, and they plummeted to the ground below. The mountain range quaked with the sound of their demise.

Tornyth tucked his wings close to his body and fell into a tight dive. On his way down, he grabbed a Grey Shadow's tail.

"Land!" an olive dragon growled at him, intercepting two Grey Shadows who thought to take Tornyth unaware. Tornyth recognised him from the vision at the dragon council, Roane, who had said he was good friends with Mandros. Banking to avoid the claws of a Grey Shadow, Tornyth glanced around to see that he did not have an opportunity to land. Roane snapped down on a grey dragon's neck, almost taking the head clean off.

"Off with you!" Roane rumbled.

Together, Tornyth and his prisoner careened towards the ground. Shrieking, the Grey Shadow attempted to fight himself free, but Tornyth held him fast. Moments from hitting the ground, he stretched out his wings to hover. He released the Grey Shadow's tail, and the grey landed with a resounding thud. He didn't rise.

Tornyth spared no time to celebrate his small victory. While Mandros and Roane were keeping Galgothmeg at bay, three Grey Shadows had regrouped to attack him.

Tornyth banked to the side, his attempt to shoot back into the sky thwarted by yet another two Grey Shadows. He climbed alongside the sheer mountain face, his belly raking the cliff face. Grasping on to the side, he tore chunks from the mountain, letting them cascade down upon his pursuers.

Tornyth turned his head to the side. His trick with the rock had bought him precious time. Deovyn was speeding towards him with a ferocious intensity. Behind him was a snarling golden dragon that Tornyth vaguely recognised from his visions.

Facing forwards just in time, Tornyth dodged a Grey Shadow coming head on. The Grey Shadow flipped over, grabbing his underbelly with his sharp claws. Growling, Tornyth wrenched himself free of the Grey Shadow.

An enraged purple dragon came alongside Tornyth, plucking a Grey Shadow from the sky. Tornyth tore past her.

The golden dragon came up on his right-hand side with an astonishing speed. He rumbled as he warded off yet more Grey Shadows. "Up with Deovyn!"

Tornyth was perplexed until the russet dragon shot past him. "Get 'em, Zapyr. This way!"

Obediently, Tornyth followed as the gold dragon, Zapyr, rammed headlong into a pair of Grey Shadows.

Tornyth shuddered at the horrendous sound of bellowing and bones breaking. Still, Deovyn led him higher until they were hovering a few miles above the battle.

Bewildered, Tornyth looked at the ground below. Dozens of Grey Shadow bodies lay crumpled on the ground. Victory was theirs.

"Should we not help?" Tornyth asked.

"Oh, no, *sudunyn*, don't you even think about it. *Aluel* is furious. And Zapyr gave me charge over you." To accentuate his point, the russet dragon nudged him a little higher with his snout.

Tornyth regarded the gold dragon below, who moved with ease as he dispatched Grey Shadow after Grey Shadow. Seeing his curiosity, Deovyn lazily wheeled around. "Zapyr the Splendid. Our brother. The original King's Guardsman. *Aluel's* favoured war advisor."

"I don't think I'll ever get over the fact you are all legendary *vehyl* from long ago."

Tornyth idled around and winced when Galgothmeg grabbed Mandros by his hind leg. Snarling, he went to dive only to find Deovyn blocking his way.

"You've helped quite enough for one day," Deovyn said. A moment later, the russet dragon was swearing in an archaic language. "Averyn!"

Whipping his head around, Tornyth could only watch as a large orange dragon was overwhelmed with Grey Shadows. He opened his mouth in a wordless cry of horror as wings were ripped from the back of the orange dragon.

Bellowing in rage, the orange dragon desperately tried to fight off the half a dozen Grey Shadows that had attacked him. His descent was slowed by the attack, but his outraged roar was cut off as he hit the ground with a thump. Tornyth could see that his head bounced, and his keen hearing heard the crunch of bones. Beside him, Deovyn was screaming. The words were unknown to him, but their sound could only be interpreted as pain.

Rumbling in fury, Tornyth's path to the Grey Shadows was blocked by Deovyn. "Our place is to stay put ... Zapyr will be with Averyn."

"Who was he?"

Overcome with emotion, Deovyn shook his head sadly. He growled as the Grey Shadows squabbled over the tattered and torn wings. Every few seconds, he nudged Tornyth a little higher. All the while, one of his tawny eyes was on the still form of Averyn.

Below, Tornyth watched as Zapyr moved to attack the Grey Shadows, scattering them like birds. Three other large male dragons joined him to pick off the enemy. None of them turned their crowned heads to look at the orange dragon.

While he circled above with Deovyn, Tornyth could hear their low rumblings of mourning of a fallen brethren in battle.

"This is death in battle, Tor," Deovyn murmured. Tornyth wished he had words to comfort Deovyn. "There was nothing you could do for Averyn. He's gone."

Mandros had freed himself from Galgothmeg and landed by the orange dragon's side. Tornyth could see the emerald dragon nudge him with his snout. Averyn did not respond, and Mandros' lips curled back as he studied the dragons flying above.

Tornyth knew the moment Mandros had spotted him; he felt Mandros' fury.

"He's gone," Deovyn whispered. "He's truly gone ..."

"*Aluel* is fuming ... I would land and face his wrath." Sidrah joined them, a stern frown on her face. Around them, Tornyth saw that a few female battle dragons had also approached and were hovering at the outskirts to get a better look at the stranger in their midst.

"Deo should land with him. Our great *pallu*, our king, is quite unhappy," a speckled brown dragon muttered. She glanced down at Mandros, who was barking orders below at two large males. Of Galgothmeg, there was no sign.

"Looks like we ran Galgothmeg off, his tail between his legs no doubt." Deovyn laughed. It sounded forced. Almost hysterical.

Sidrah gave him an almost pitying look.

"I suppose I should ask if you are hurt." Sidrah exhaled and looked Tornyth over.

"A few scratches on my belly," Tornyth replied, trying to get a good look at a silver female who was flying lazy laps around him. A purple dragon eyed him wearily at a distance. "It's only surface damage ... only stings."

"I highly suggest you get your claws on the ground," Sidrah said. She nodded to the silver and purple dragons. "You two. Take my brothers down and guard them. Kudah and I will check the skies for any stragglers."

Deovyn gave Tornyth a gentle nudge with his wing. "Down we go, *sudunyn*. Time to face *Aluel's* displeasure. Catch me!" Tucking in his wings, Deovyn dived. The female dragons Sidrah had insisted land with them watched him with expectant expressions. There was little choice but to follow Deovyn to the ground.

"Males …" he heard Sidrah grumble.

Zapyr was already waiting for them. As Tornyth's claws touched the loose rocks of the ground, the gold dragon glared around at Deovyn. "The white dragon was to stay hidden, Deovyn."

Deovyn frowned and snapped his teeth at the gold dragon. "I would like to see you command him, Zapyr! If *Aluel* can't control him …"

"Indeed," Zapyr snarled. He rounded on Tornyth, pinning him with strange azure gaze. The gold dragon let Tornyth stare and approached. The muscles of his powerful hind legs rippled as he moved. "I don't know whence you came, *sudunyn*, but you need to learn to behave yourself."

Tornyth felt anger boiling in his belly. He was tired of his position and blood forcing him into situations he didn't want to be in. He glanced rebelliously in Mandros' direction; the green dragon was flanked by two more dragons, one of them Roane. Their gaits were taut; they were ready to plunge back into battle. They all wore stony expressions; their glowing eyes were focused on Tornyth. Feeling his lip curling, Tornyth growled and turned a heated gaze on to Zapyr, who infuriatingly looked unimpressed.

"I'm not a plaything," Tornyth snarled. He glanced around to Deovyn but found the russet dragon lying down next to Averyn's still form. "I won't be moulded and used by dragonkind. I won't!"

Mandros continued forward as if he had not heard Tornyth's outburst. The other dragons, strangers to Tornyth, looked on. Some exchanged bemused glances, while other swayed side to side. Mandros didn't pay his companions any attention. His focus was solely upon Tornyth.

The moment he was in lunging distance, Mandros lurched forward, his jaws coming around Tornyth's horns. In the next instant, Tornyth was flipped over into an undignified position. Mandros released his horns and then clouted Tornyth's snout. Shaking his head in shock, Tornyth's vision blurred with tears. Mandros smacked his snout again.

"You are my *mynrell*. My son," Mandros rumbled. "I gave you very clear instructions, Tornyth, Winter's Dragon. Never in my long years have I witnessed such profound disobedience."

"Never, Mandros?" Roane asked. He flicked his eyes to Deovyn, who glared back in indignation. Roane rumbled. At Mandros' withering glare, the olive dragon grinned, showing his sharp teeth.

"Roane, find Sidrah. She and I need to have words."

The expression on Roane's face fell. "Your *mynrell* called for help," he said, keeping his voice low. "She answered. You would do the same for any of us."

"He's my son."

"I'm no one's son," Tornyth snapped.

Mandros' whacked Tornyth's snout again. "Quiet, hatchling."

Tornyth shrunk before Mandros, whose tail was flicking side to side in clear agitation. Tornyth lifted his foreleg to rub at the unpleasant sting.

Roane frowned and took off without further argument.

"Leave him alone!"

Much to Tornyth's exasperation, Et-hir burst into the scene. She stumbled between the assembled dragons, pebbles falling beneath her boots as she made her way to Tornyth's side. High above her head, she held a tree branch. Tornyth wondered where she had found a tree to source such a weapon. Rushing forward, she gave Mandros' tail a mighty whack, much to the astonishment of the dragons about her.

Nym followed close behind, a playful smirk on her lips. Tornyth was eternally thankful she, at least, didn't have a weapon.

Mandros growled in annoyance, and Et-hir whacked his tail a second time. "Down, beast!"

He lazily flicked his tail out of the way and regarded Nym with a cool expression. The assembled dragons murmured and rumbled at the audacity of a small *vehyl* attacking their *pallu*. Zapyr even lowered his body closer the ground, ready to pounce.

Tornyth didn't give the dragons more time to react. He leapt past Mandros and stood over the two humans, blocking them from the dragons about them. He crouched lower to the ground, making the girls squeal and flatten themselves along the ground. To get to the humans, the other dragons would have to move him out of the way.

"You slimy-scaled, half-wit lizard. If you lower any more, I'm going to give you a belly scratch you're likely never going to forget!" Nym screamed. Tornyth tried to ignore the shifting of the others as Nym sputtered curses from underneath him.

"That's no way to talk. He's trying to be helpful," Et-hir returned calmly. "Oh, look, his belly is already scratched up. Poor dear."

"You're one to talk. You whacked Papa dragon's tail, you ill-timed excuse of a bar wench."

"We can't see anything, Tornyth. Do you mind getting off?"

Tornyth eyed the other dragons warily. He felt small and cornered. Mandros must have brought with him two dozen dragons, and now all their avid attention was on him.

"It's okay, Tornyth, we promise not to eat your foul-mouthed, fleshy bone sacks," Deovyn said with a toothy smile. With one last nudge at Averyn's side, he stood and stepped away from the fallen warrior. His smile seemed forced.

"Contrary to popular belief, humans do not taste good," a red dragon, whose colour was so dark he looked black, replied. "They give me terrible indigestion."

"Enough, Deovyn, Edisyn. What do you have to say for yourself, Tornyth?" Mandros looked thunderous.

"It was an impressive stunt, really," the purple dragon offered. "I never thought of grabbing Galgothmeg's tail before."

"Quiet, Salvea."

"Can you please get off?" Et-hir said. Tornyth cold feel her tiny *vehyl* fingers prodding at his body. "It's getting hard to breathe."

"And it's hot," Nym rejoined. Her pokes weren't so gentle.

Abashed, Tornyth stood and let the humans crawl out from beneath his belly.

"This would be the lady Nym. Careful, she has a tongue so sharp that she can cut through any dragon hide," Deovyn said. "Tornyth also rescued another human. This is Et-hir."

"I need no palace brat to rescue me!" Nym said.

"Technically, I did rescue you, Nym," Tornyth grumbled. "I broke you out of a prison cart, and we hid up a tree. Or did you conveniently forget?"

"I stood beside you when you decided to take Galgothmeg on in your human form!" Nym yelled back.

Tornyth winced at the look of fury that crossed Mandros' face. "I didn't ask you to! You're the deranged one who actually came back!"

"You're deranged."

"You took on Galgothmeg as a *vehyl*!" Zapyr raised his regal neck; his stern blue gaze swept over Mandros. "Send him home to *Lullah*. We can't have a liability like him on the battlefield."

"I don't need mothering!" Tornyth snapped, annoyed by the suggestion that he did. "I'm not yours to command."

"You have much to learn, hatchling," Zapyr replied before Mandros could respond. "Didn't your *vehyl* father teach you any regard for your elders?"

"He didn't want me. He wanted me and *elt vehyl* dead."

"You had a father-by-heart," Mandros whispered. "An old man who loved you with such fierce devotion. Did he not teach you how to behave?"

"He tried ..." The mention of Donatein killed the fire in his blood that wanted to fight.

A dragon of teal scales leaned forward. "Dragon young can be notoriously difficult to raise. Seems to me you have an heir who is more like you than you think."

Mandros shifted, his gaze drifting over to his battle dragons.

"He'll learn how to be a free dragon in time," the teal dragon continued. "They all do. In time, he will appreciate the kind of miracle he is to dragonkind."

Mandros sighed. "Very well. Tornyth, you will fly to Aviah Valley. You will stay grounded there. No manifesting to your dragon."

"I don't wish to go to Aviah Valley."

Mandros frowned. "It's time to return. Stay hidden. We have both spoken heated words ... dragon blood runs hot. When you are ready to properly submit and apologise, call for me."

"Mandros—"

"Your nephew, whom you love so well that you would enrage your *aluel*, is there. Go. Be safe, *mynrell*."

"Mandros, please—"

"Zapyr will accompany you to ensure you do as you are told."

"Mandros—"

"*Aluel*," Mandros said. "You say your *vehyl aluel* abandoned you and meant to murder you ... Well, I might be angry, but I am your *aluel*. I don't think it will be long before you see exactly how foolish you have been. Perhaps then you can tell me what this little tantrum was all about."

Mandros whirled about. He sprung into the air without a backward glance. Several of the dragons followed him. Some glanced back at him, peering at him with querying gazes. Soon all that was left was the teal dragon, Deovyn and Zapyr.

The teal dragon gave him a playful nudge. "We've all been on the receiving end of our *aluel's* anger. Even Zapyr ... I seem to remember an incident with several lengths of wood, paint, and a hammer."

"Just heal his belly and be on your way, Curarfur."

The smirk didn't leave the teal's face, even as he healed Tornyth's cut-up belly. As with Sidrah's power, the ripped skin knitted together.

"Come, Deovyn," Curarfur said. "Best not to keep your *aluel* waiting."

Deovyn nodded and stepped closer to Tornyth. "Farewell for now, *sudunyn*. Remember: belly, neck and horns ... protect at all costs."

Zapyr growled.

"It's sound advice," Deovyn said, lifting his head to regard the larger gold dragon. "I just hope he never needs it. Tornyth might fly well but I don't think he has the battle fire within him."

"Stay out of trouble, Deo," Zapyr replied. "Until we meet again, peace fly with you."

Together, they watched as Curarfur and Deovyn spread their wings to take flight to follow Mandros and his league of dragons.

Tornyth took the time to study the golden dragon's face as he, too, watched the skies. "May the sun kiss your scales, the stars bless and guide you. May the rainstorm help you grow, and the moon give you her light in your darkest hour." Zapyr's deep rumble sent shivers up Tornyth's spine.

In his human existence, he was Kyran, the first of the King's Guard. A man who was honoured to have fought and won many battles against Vadroil. Tornyth couldn't help but wonder what he might have been like when he still possessed a human half.

"What are those words?"

Zapyr exhaled, blinked, and stared down at Tornyth. "The Dragon's Prayer." He shook his great head, his luminous eyes shining with an expression Tornyth couldn't identify. "Now I have two young *sudunyn* to watch over ... Otherworlds, preserve me."

CHAPTER TWENTY-ONE

Jodathyn

Solan's Summer House, Aviah Valley

Below them, Solan's summer house looked no more than a child's plaything. Tornyth's insides twisted as he studied the place of his childhood torment. Even now he could feel the soft blades of grass as he wrestled with Ruevyn after a long day's work. His stomach cramped, remembering the relentless hunger. In his mind, he could summon the hollow eyes of the other servants and feel something warm and sticky running down his back and belly. Shuddering, he pulled himself from his waking nightmare. It had been a long time since he had one of those.

He flitted an uneasy glance towards his magnificent golden brother.

While they had been soaring together in the air, Zapyr had been stoically silent. Now the golden dragon raised an eyebrow. "What is it, *sudunyn*?"

"It's nothing," Tornyth replied. He felt Nym running her hands down the scales on his back. "I have no desire to return to this place."

"You must," Zapyr rumbled.

"I wasn't arguing with you," Tornyth replied.

Every part of his being was desperate to reunite with his nephew. He longed to wrap his arms around the little boy and never, ever let him go. However, the thought of returning to Aviah Valley filled him with dread and left him feeling ill. Never, not even in his worst nightmares, had he thought he would return to the place that left him damaged and weak.

But he was Pallarus. It was expected that he would face his past with dignity and grace. Tornyth wasn't sure this was something he could do. From the very moment Lord Whitoak had whisked him away from Aviah Valley, he had run from his past. Some secrets were too horrible, too terrible, to tell.

Et-hir leaned forward so that her cheek was flush against his scales.

"Are you ready to land, *sudunyn*?"

Tornyth nodded glumly. He followed Zapyr's path to land upon the green of the lawns. Zapyr turned to study him with his keen blue eyes so that Tornyth felt that all his secrets were laid bare.

"This place makes you uneasy?"

"I'm tired," Tornyth said, the lie coming unbidden to his lips. He could tell by the way Zapyr tilted his head to the side that the gold dragon did not believe him.

"Uncle!"

Tornyth raised his head. Along the grass, Carvelle ran towards them, his limbs flailing in excitement. The young prince tripped, sprung back up, and hurtled towards him. Tornyth eyed Carvelle, and he was thankful to see that his nephew looked safe and healthy.

Tornyth greeted Carvelle with a bellow of delight. His wings flapped with involuntary joy. The prince stood before him panting, looking up at him. He bounced one foot to the other.

With his incredible dragon eyesight, he took in each of the freckles that lined Carvelle's button nose and the flecks of browns, golds, and oranges that made his lively eyes.

Carvelle reached him and stretched up on his tippy toes to touch Tornyth's snout. "Uncle, you are magnificent."

"Get away from him!"

Tornyth glanced up to find that Orion was rushing at him, his sword lifted to attack. He took a few clumsy steps backwards, trying not to trip over Nym and Et-hir, who were halfway dismounting from his back. Zapyr lifted his head, flashing his fangs.

"No! Zapyr!" Tornyth cried. Before he could growl an order for Orion to stand down, his servant struck him on the nose with the flat of his sword.

"Back!"

"Hitting dragons on the snout hurts!" Et-hir cried, trying to get the sword from Orion's grasp. Reeling back, Orion looked at the newcomer in confusion. The sword was poised just above his head to give Tornyth another thwack. His eyes darted towards Zapyr, who was growling.

"Put that sword down, foolish *vehyl*," Zapyr commanded.

Tornyth had to admire Orion's resolute stance. There was a slight shift as his servant held his ground.

"I appreciate the enthusiasm ... but ouch!" Jodathyn mumbled, standing where Tornyth had been only moments before. He rubbed his nose, looking at Orion indignantly. "That's going to bruise."

Orion's sword dropped to the ground with a clatter as he continued to stare at him in befuddlement. His face twisted in horror at his own actions. "Master?"

"Orion Maysden has been looking after me," Carvelle said.

"I can see that," Jodathyn replied. "Zapyr, this is Orion, my manservant. He means no harm."

"Never known a manservant to belt his master," Zapyr commented. He lowered his head to glare at Orion. Wide dragon nostrils flared as he sniffed at him. "A Silverdyne boy. A military lad ... and servant."

Orion shuffled. "It's a long tale, my lord dragon."

"Indeed, perhaps another day you might regale me in your story," Zapyr continued. "I am pleased the ancient practice of the horseman's lock continues through the generations. It was ancient even in my day, and it was those in Silverdyne that reclaimed the practice during the Dragon Wars."

"Silverdyne is a proud city," Orion said, "with a long and noble history. I am a son of a long line of Silverdyne warriors. I wear my horseman's lock with pride."

"Yes, I know," Zapyr replied. He pressed his snout to Orion's midsection. "I like the smell of your blood."

Astounded, Orion stepped back. He darted a concerned gaze towards Jodathyn, who shrugged.

"We dragons can sense certain ... bloodlines. Yours is an ancient line of warriors and great *vehyl*."

Orion sniffed. When he spoke, his voice took on a bitter tone, and Jodathyn felt a pang of sadness for him. "And look at me now!"

Withdrawing, the dragon pulled back. "You're not dead yet, Orion one-who-whispers, and your time has not come yet."

Orion opened his mouth to ask more, but the gold dragon whipped around to glare at Jodathyn. "No manifesting, and stay here and hidden. Do you understand?"

"Yes," Jodathyn answered. Even now, he could feel his hackles rise at being spoken to like this.

Zapyr turned to stare again at Orion until the horseman bent to pick up his fallen sword to avoid his intense gaze. With a grunt, the golden dragon unfurled his wings and lunged into the sky. Orion straightened, his keen eyes tracking the dragon until he disappeared.

"Uncle, I must tell you all about my adventures!" Carvelle gabbled, grabbing Jodathyn's hand and dragging him towards the house. "We are staying here."

"Storytelling is all very well and good, but we're all starving," Nym complained. "Is there food here?"

"And wine?" Jodathyn grumbled.

"There's plenty of wine," Orion assured him. He was still staring into the clouds. "Anyone mind telling me what that was all about?"

"Who is your pretty new friend, Uncle?"

Jodathyn ushered Et-hir towards his nephew. "This is Et-hir."

"You should marry her. She's pretty, and she likes you," Carvelle stated. "I don't care what Lord Whitoak says to Papa, you should marry and make babies."

Feeling heat rush to his cheeks, Jodathyn spluttered as he ran his hand through his hair. He flitted his grey eyes over to Et-hir to see how she took the cheeky prince's comments. Thankfully, Et-hir seemed neither alarmed nor offended. Indeed, she was trying to stifle her laugh as Carvelle turned his attention to her.

"Uncle Jodathyn would make a wonderful husband, miss. He is kind and fun."

"Jodathyn would have to pass my tests first, Your Highness."

Carvelle seemed to consider this new information seriously. "Perhaps you can tell me what he needs to do to impress you. You like my uncle, no? He doesn't snore too badly."

"I like your uncle well enough." Et-hir sent Jodathyn a bemused sort of grin. There was a soft pink blush to her cheeks.

"Carvelle, please stop," Jodathyn groaned.

Carvelle looked at him with innocent eyes and a sly smile. "I missed you, Uncle."

"I missed you too."

"I knew you would come back ... Orion was afraid you wouldn't."

Orion grunted. He was still staring unblinkingly to the horizon.

"Uncle, you remember Fydellah, the forest lady?" Carvelle paused his trek and leaned into Jodathyn's side. "You told her that when I am king, you would gladly bow down."

Jodathyn ran his hand through Carvelle's hair. "Yes, that's true."

"When I am king, Uncle, you will bow to no one. No one will treat you poorly ever again. That's my solemn vow." Carvelle looked up into Jodathyn's face, his expression earnest. "You're forever my hero."

Uneasy, Jodathyn took his nephew's hand and let the boy take him inside.

"Theo and Voran should have some food ready." Orion tore his gaze from the sky and started to move towards Solan's summer house.

"Theo's here?" Nym asked. She had been quiet for the most part.

"Where else would I be, sister?" Theo had emerged from the back door. He was grinning ear to ear, his eyes on his sister. "You're safe."

Nym gave an uncharacteristic cry of delight and ran to greet her brother. The small party watched the siblings embrace until Theo punched Nym in the arm. "You're crazy going off to challenge an angry dragon. Where have you been?"

"Here and there," Nym said, punching Theo back. "Where have you been?"

"There and here," Theo replied. His grin faded slowly, and he turned to Jodathyn. "You should have a quiet word with Voran once you have eaten."

"*Voran*?"

"I believe you are known to each other," Orion said. "It was good fortune we met him on the road."

Theo rubbed the back of his skull and scoffed. Chuckling, Orion shook his head and turned away from the thief to face Jodathyn fully. "Come, Master, you look tired. I'll get you some food, and then you can rest."

Jodathyn followed after the young horseman, who led them into a smaller room where they had set up a miniature armoury. He caught sight of leather armours, bows, arrows, daggers and all sorts of weaponry.

"Look, Uncle, Orion made me a little suit of armour!" Carvelle cried as he held up a small leather breastplate.

Orion smiled sadly. "I thought it would be best to be prepared."

"Come, sit," Carvelle said, easing Jodathyn into a chair.

Jodathyn closed his eyes and suppressed a shudder of horror at being inside the house of Aviah Valley.

Carvelle trotted off into another room and returned with a bowl of steaming stew. He made his way to his uncle and set the food before him.

"I have been helping!" Carvelle told him, puffing up his chest. "Orion is getting Nym and the new girl something too!"

"I am sure your papa will be pleased," Jodathyn replied, closing his eyes against the fatigue.

"We have been most appreciative," Orion said. He had two more bowls in his hands, one for each of the girls. He gestured for them to find somewhere to sit, and Nym flopped herself down on the floor, stretching out her legs. Et-hir hoisted herself to sit upon a side table. She flicked a concerned gaze towards Jodathyn.

"Are we safe here?"

"Mandros seems to think so," Nym answered, nodding gratefully as Orion handed her a bowl. "Thank goodness for food. Dragons seem to forget we mere humans need to eat."

Jodathyn agreed with a grunt and ate, barely taking time to chew and savour the thick, rich texture of the stew. He was ravenous.

"Where did you get meat?" Nym asked.

"Hmm, this is good," Et-hir said between mouthfuls.

"Voran made some friends in the nearby village," Theo said. He watched Nym eat, as if he was afraid that she might disappear again.

"He's the only one that's allowed to go," Carvelle said, pouting.

"We don't want to be recognised or draw attention to ourselves," Orion replied. "We all have to do our part."

Jodathyn felt his eyes droop and his bowl start to slip from his fingers. Orion rushed to his side to grab the bowl before it could clutter to the ground. He felt his vision blur, and the room about him became hazy.

The most prominent image was his brother's stern countenance looking down at him, the royal banners snapping in the breeze behind him. Guardsman Jael's earnest gaze had never left his face as a horrendous illness churned in his belly. He had cringed at the sound of his brother unsheathing his sword, and he could hear his own desperate sobs. Then came the pain.

Jodathyn came back to himself, lying on the floor. He could feel the insistent tapping of Carvelle's small palms against his cheeks. A firm grip on his shoulder kept him grounded instead of falling back into a waking vision. For a long moment, he lay still, not moving as a burning nausea washed over him.

Slowly, Jodathyn blinked. Theo and Orion stood by the walls, observing the situation. Et-hir came running back into the room with a cloth and a basin of water. She hurried to his side, falling upon her knees before him.

"It's been miserable for Jod, Master Axtin," Nym murmured to the side. She lifted an uncertain hand to her hair. "It's stress … That's what the healers said happened to my hair."

Et-hir dabbed the wet cloth against Jodathyn's forehead. Her gaze met his, all soft and gentle, so that the fluttering in Jodathyn's stomach had nothing to do with feeling ill. She tore her gaze away from him, and her eyes flicked down upon Carvelle.

Pulling himself to his elbows, Jodathyn cursed. His stomach lurched as he struggled to his feet. The large hand upon his shoulder came around to support his weight.

"*Ri rshon hanoch* … Can't these cursed visions leave me alone?" Jodathyn muttered. He turned his head to glance at the person holding him up. He hadn't seen Voran Axtin since his ex-personal guard had to flee Pallaryn for his life. If he had never decided to try and poison Lord Solan, he wouldn't have lured Voran away from his duty. If it wasn't for him, Voran Axtin would still have a position at the palace. The creases along the giant man's face had deepened with age and worry.

"Oh, Voran, forgive me," Jodathyn muttered. "I never thought to see you again. Donatein told me you had to flee ... It was all my fault."

"What's this nonsense, Master Jodathyn?" Voran replied gruffly. "You almost died because I neglected my duty."

"I was so foolish," Jodathyn said, shaking his head. His eyes darted towards Nym, who was biting her lips. He couldn't quite find the words to confess his crime.

Voran didn't seem to see his agitation. "Bah, look at you. Grown into almost a man. I knew Valt would look after you."

It was strange. Jodathyn had known Voran from the time he was a boy. He had spent many hours with him. But now when he looked at him, all he could see was Valt's face staring at him. Jodathyn forced himself to look away and to swallow his guilt. Valt was dead. The dead did not walk among the living.

"There's rumours that a royal party is very close," Voran said in a low voice. "That and also two great winged beasts ... horrible demon lizards."

Jodathyn couldn't help it. After all the tension from the last few days and the stress of his visions, he tilted his head back and laughed. "Voran. I was one of those terrible demon lizards."

Voran's face stilled into a blank stare. He rested his large hands on his hips.

"I'm a dragon," Jodathyn said.

"I can't believe I missed it," Theo grumbled.

"Perhaps I can give you a flight once Mandros lifts my ban," Jodathyn said, turning his eyes upon the thief.

Voran nodded slowly. "Master, you should never speak of these things."

"Voran, there's no escaping the fact I'm a large scaly reptile. I don't intend to hide my nature anymore," Jodathyn said. "We should prepare ourselves to meet Kieryn ..."

Voran turned towards Orion. "Orion can ensure the stables are ready. Theo and I'll make room for our guests to bunk down in."

Orion stood still, looking pale and wretched. His eyes flicked towards Jodathyn and then Carvelle. His fluttering hand came to rest upon his neck.

"You faced a fierce dragon in my defence just this afternoon!" Carvelle said. "Surely you aren't scared of my papa. I have plenty to tell him about you!"

CHAPTER TWENTY-TWO

Illeanah

West of Pallaryn

The dust from the road coated Illeanah's tongue, and her backside throbbed from being in the saddle all day. She didn't know how the queen took their current predicament with the grace that she did. Travelling on horseback, in borrowed men's clothing, was a sweaty, dirty endeavour.

Not long after they had hastily buried Tomas, a man arrived in the King's Orchard with three horses. It seemed that Illeanah had severely miscalculated Will's influence within the citadel.

When the man had left without saying a word or expecting to be paid, Illeanah was confused. Will had taken the reins of the horses and smiled in his disconcerting way. "I owe the man nothing, Nia. He's paying a debt. Don't worry your pretty little head over it."

"I'm not worried!" Illeanah snapped.

Will grinned at her roguishly, flashing his perfect white teeth. She tore her eyes off his handsome form, determined not to admire his strong shoulders or the easy confidence of a man who knew he was in control. Away from Pallaryn, he seemed to be a different man entirely. And it infuriated her.

So here she was, on the back of a stranger's horse, running away and puzzling over Will Hartcurt. What type of debt would a common man have with Will? After all, he was a young man who was alienated from his family and had little prospect in life. What she had seen of his private rooms indicated that he didn't have much to his name. It had seemed a pitiful existence for a lord living under the king's roof.

"I'm quite content with life," Will said to her right. She could see evidence of a smile tugging on his lips.

Illeanah turned her head to look at him, where he sat on his mount in his self-assured manner. "Don't. Read. My. Mind."

"I cannot help that your thoughts are so loud. You may continue to admire me from a distance. I'm quite used to it, I assure you," Will replied, and his grin widened. "You aren't the first woman to admire my strong shoulders or my—"

"That's where you get your inflated ego from," Illeanah concluded. "Listening to people's private thoughts."

"In truth, it's a headache of living with courtiers, who have very little happening between their ears. Nothing relieves the pain."

Illeanah considered what he said. "It hurts then," she reasoned, "your gift?"

"There's nothing more peaceful than my dark and quiet chambers at the end of the day," Will replied with a grimace. He rubbed his temple with his fingers.

"It is a difficult burden," the queen said, sighing. "I'm sorry that there isn't more Guardsman Jael can do for you."

"It must be borne." A smile lit Will's handsome features as he glanced over at Illeanah. "How about a game to pass the time?"

"A game?"

"Do you not pride yourself in your mental dexterity?" Will teased. "A game to distract us is what we need."

"How do we play, Will dear?" the queen asked. She rubbed her belly absently. "I could do with a distraction."

"I shall tell you someone's private thoughts, and you guess who they belong to."

"Very well," Illeanah conceded, deciding to ignore her judgement that the game was intruding upon other people's privacy. It wasn't exactly ethical, but she always loved a riddle. "I don't mind a challenge."

Will leaned back in the saddle, closing his eyes and lifting his chin to the sky as he pondered. Illeanah had to wonder how many thoughts he needed to sort through to come up with something suitable for the game. The thought made her uneasy. Who knew how many of her secrets Will had come by.

"This person was wondering about the merits of letting Jodathyn go where he should not ... and what the reaction of the gruff Captain Tiernan might be."

"Has to be a guardsman," Illeanah said. "Can't say I know too many of them."

"Young," the queen deduced. "The older ones know better than to cross Captain Tiernan."

Illeanah racked her brain as Will nodded.

"There's only one guardsman that routinely vexes the captain, and that's his own son, Carew."

"Well reasoned, Your Majesty. The younger guardsmen had bets on how and when Jodathyn was going to get himself in trouble." Will chuckled, but his mirth quickly faded away. He frowned. "It's not funny anymore."

"No," said the queen. "I worry about Jodathyn as I fear for my son."

"Jodathyn is stronger than he knows," Will said. To Illeanah, it looked like the young lord wanted to reach over and pat the queen's shaking hands. Indeed, she looked paler than usual this morning.

"This one was considering the merits of filing down his large, squirrel-like teeth after he got turned down quite painfully by a lovely maiden's father after he asked for her hand in marriage."

Illeanah scoffed. "Simple. Frayn. Pompous toe-rag. I heard father likening him to a squirrel."

"Poor Frayn." The queen sighed.

Illeanah raised her eyebrow. "He's horrible."

"He signed Jodathyn's old manservant's death warrant under the king's nose. He's a slug," Will gritted out.

"Self-conceited, full of his own self-importance, and spoiled," the queen replied. "Perhaps Frayn isn't as confident and strong as he would like us to think. He's a young man who has found very little joy in life."

Illeanah contemplated what the queen had said about Frayn. It was true. Frayn's father, who had been highly favoured by the two previous kings, had been a harsh man. Sometimes cruel. Under his father's thumb, Frayn spent his time tripping over himself trying to please him. Her father said that was what made him weak. She had even heard it said that Frayn had failed to earn his father's respect or admiration.

"Very well, a harder one this time," Will continued. "And they coupled upon the hill until the dawn ..."

Illeanah blinked, feeling heat rise to her cheeks.

"Will, you scoundrel!" the queen gasped. Illeanah could tell she didn't mean it by the teasing light in her eyes. She lifted a delicate hand to hide her smile.

"Got to be an old lord," Illeanah said with derision.

"I'm afraid not," Will replied.

"The library master," the queen hazarded. "He's an interesting sort."

"Again, no."

"A guardsman in his cups?"

"No."

"That old lady who has a fascination with gambling. Lady Damaris—"

"Nothing wrong with a good gamble," Will muttered.

"I bet you are good at gambling," Illeanah commented. "But I guess that would be bordering on cheating ..."

Will flushed and looked away. "It is not Lady Damaris or any that frequent her card table."

"A stable boy ..."

Illeanah shook her head. "A laundry maid ..."

"Do you give up?"

Illeanah wearily nodded her head. "I fear you have won this round, Will Hartcurt."

"Jodathyn."

"*Jodathyn*?" Illeanah couldn't believe what she was hearing. Jodathyn was a gentleman.

Will laughed at Illeanah's flabbergasted expression. "I came upon him trying to translate a drinking song into the ancient tongue to upset that devoted manservant of his."

The queen burst into uncharacteristic fits of giggles. Her hand flew to her mouth. "Oh my dear, Jodathyn is like any healthy young man!"

"The difference is Jodathyn is wise enough to know when to keep his mouth shut," Will added. "Who knows, maybe one day he'll pluck up the courage to finally kiss you. He's thought about it, you know."

"I don't love Jodathyn," Illeanah whispered, looking down at her hands. "Not like that."

"I know," Will said, his smile fading. "Your feelings are perfectly valid. Jodathyn will—"

The queen gasped, raising her pale hand to point in the distance. At first, Illeanah thought she was ill. But Will was at the queen's side, gripping her elbows to stop her from falling off the horse. The whites of her eyes were wide as she stared behind them at the dusty road. That was when Illeanah heard the sound of horses' hooves thundering on the road.

Illeanah twisted in the saddle, catching her first glimpses of heavily armed soldiers. Their leader raised his drawn sword over his head and gave a triumphant yell. A plume of dust rose behind them. How had they not heard their approach? For the briefest moment, Illeanah prayed they were King's Guardsmen coming to escort them to safety.

But then Will screamed, "Not King's Guard! They're Solan's men."

"Give me a dagger, Will, so that I might defend myself and my child to the end." The queen held out her hand for a weapon. Her face seemed impassive as she observed the quickly approaching men.

"No!" Illeanah cried, ignoring the flutter of worry in her gut. "It's not going to end like this. Flee, Will. Protect the queen! I'll be right behind you!"

Illeanah saw the moment that Will's dark eyes clouded over with understanding. She knew he had gleaned from her thoughts what she was going to do. His long, elegant fingers wrapped around the handle of his sword.

"No!" Illeanah screamed. "I don't need a weapon like you do."

Will's expression shuttered; he nodded in Illeanah's direction. As his eyes drifted back to her face, Illeanah saw respect.

"May peace ride with you," Will murmured, kicking the sides of his horse, urging the queen to do the same.

Wheeling her mare around, Illeanah didn't watch Will and the queen's retreat. She could not bear to see the queen's soft eyes pleading with her to flee also. Illeanah couldn't trust herself not to be tempted by the idea of safety. No. She had to trust that Will, being more worldly than her, might be able to protect and defend the queen.

All her life, she had hated her power. It was one secret that she had kept to herself. Neither her father nor Jodathyn knew of her true nature. It was ironic that they were both gone and she was about to reveal herself to strangers.

Killing Tomas Hartcurt in the King's Orchard had given her no joy or peace. It horrified her that something so ancient and wrong grew within her. Now it was time to see what she was capable of. She couldn't allow her power to lie dormant if it meant the queen's demise. Above all else, house Pallarus must survive.

Behind her, along the side of the road, were large oak trees. They had thick, wide trunks and deep roots. Breathing in, she called upon her dark and mysterious powers. She grappled with the trees' root systems, loosening the soil about them so that they were unbalanced. They fell with a deafening thud. Three ancient trees now lay between Solan's men and the queen.

If Solan's men wished to pursue the queen, they would be an obstacle. It would take them time to move around. But Illeanah had no intention of allowing them to reach the oak trees alive. They had to get through her first.

They were close now. She could see their jeering faces. Lifting her hand, she urged other trees to listen to her command.

Roots snaked from the ground, slithering onto the road. Strong tendrils caught the horses' hooves and tightened. The first four animals crashed down to the road, with whinnying screams of pain and confusion. Their riders toppled from the saddle to either be crushed by their mounts or pounded into the road by their companions behind them. Illeanah knew that she would remember the terrible nose until her dying day.

More riders came; she bid the branches to swing low and unsaddle them. She closed her eyes, sweat beading on her forehead as she commanded the nature around her to destroy her enemies.

This proved to be her undoing.

A bowstring twanged. A flare of pain in Illeanah's thigh broke her concentration. She fell upon the road, writhing and screaming. Through her tears, she counted four men still standing. She gritted her teeth, and her leg spasmed as she fought to get to her feet.

Her arms were grabbed in tight fists, and she was brought to her knees in the dirt. "Stupid girl!" one of the men barked. He backhanded her with his gloved fist. Illeanah's ears rang in protest. "You killed most of our company."

Illeanah looked up at the remaining men who had crowded around her, then to the still bodies on the road. She swayed where she was on the road before glaring at the man who had spoken. She licked the warm blood off her split lip and laughed. "Truth be told, I would do it all again. Imagine strong men like yourselves being taken down by one scrawny woman."

Illeanah had expected to be dragged to the dungeons for questioning. Instead, her captors escorted her to the king's audience chamber. Behind enclaves and doors, she thought she could see terrified eyes peering out at her. The people were being ruled by their fear of Solan.

As Illeanah and her captors passed a familiar King's Guardsman, she cried out. She stomped on feet and struggled. She cared not for the flaring pain in her leg. Somehow, she had to get Tryst to understand what had happened.

"Tryst!" Illeanah screamed. "They're going after her! They'll kill her!"

The guardsman recognised her; she could see it in his steely gaze. While her captors saw a mildly curious guardsman, she had seen the minute flinch and the hand hovering over the pummel of his sword.

"She's crazed," the man on her left grunted. Illeanah took the opportunity to shake her head. She could not afford to have Tryst attempting to rescue her. He needed to rouse the King's Guard and get to the queen. Otherwise, her sacrifice would be in vain.

"She should see a healer," the guardsman replied. "Poor thing. What's she going on about?"

"Babbling on about magical trees." The man on the left chuckled. "She's a right feisty one."

"There's a healer in the barracks on duty. He can take care of her." Tryst looked pleased with himself.

"We're not taking this one to no healer … She's too violent for that. Step aside."

Illeanah watched as Tryst's face fell. Her guards pushed him aside and marched her forwards. She looked over her shoulder at him in sheer desperation. Somehow, she needed to tell him where Will had planned to take the queen.

"I so wanted to meet your wife!" Illeanah cried, and she could see understanding dawning on Tryst's expression. He turned neatly upon his heel and stalked away. Illeanah watched him go with an air of helplessness. "Now I shan't."

Illeanah was dragged right before the audience chamber and pushed through the doors. For all its fame, she had never stepped inside. The audience chamber was reserved for those who had been summoned. She sucked in a deep breath, trying her best not to show any weakness or fear as she hung like a limp doll between her brutish escorts.

Unable to hold her own weight with her wound, Illeanah's feet were dragged along the ground. She was stunned by the daunting size of the chamber, so much so that she could only marvel in open-mouth amazement at the craftsmanship.

She beheld the High King's golden throne, astonished that Lord Solan was already sitting in the king's place. It was a deliberate act of treason. None save the crowned king could sit upon the throne. Not even the king's heir would do such a thing.

Illeanah was thrown forward, and she landed with a soft thud, face down onto the hard stone floor. Her bound hands shot out to break her fall, and she felt a sharp pain in her shoulder.

Fearfully, Illeanah looked up. To Solan's right hand side stood Lord Kamoore. She already knew it was useless to hope he would show her any sympathy. He was not a man to be trusted; he notoriously sided with Solan on every matter. The proud man was parading himself in vibrant colours and gaudy jewels like a whimsical peacock. She had no doubt that while Kamoore was busy preening, Solan was planning his downfall as well.

She turned her attention to the third lord in the room, Thylyssa. He was a tall man, with plain facial features that seemed to be permanently frozen. There was little expression to give any clue what he was thinking. If whatever she heard about him was true, Thylyssa was a dangerous man.

For the most part, the king put up with the antics of the great lords. Her father always said that sometimes it paid to have one's enemies close. Especially if you had a spy that could read minds. King Kieryn must have found Thylyssa detestable to have him exiled.

Illeanah pushed herself to her knees, ignoring the sharp bite of her wound. She idly wondered if her father had been humbled on this very spot. Had they humiliated him before they killed him? She felt tears of rage prick at her eyes as she glared up at Solan.

"The king's council seems diminished, Lord Solan. I thought you would want to have many on your side, even the squirrelly little nitwit, Frayn."

"Illeanah Whitoak, born of Androssah, daughter of the traitor Hallidyn Whitoak, you are charged with high treason." Kamoore's voice echoed through the chamber as he glanced towards Solan with his little beady eyes. He ran his thumb over a particularly ugly red jewel on his bony finger while he bared his teeth at her.

Illeanah eyed him with a raised eyebrow. She tilted her nose upwards and answered curtly. "Treason to help house Pallarus, you say?"

"I'm not the one filthy in my own squalor, helpless and bound," Kamoore snarled.

"Yet I have more pride than you," Illeanah responded. "I haven't betrayed the realm for my own selfish gain."

"You're a proud slip of a girl, aren't you?" Thylyssa murmured. It almost seemed his lips did not move. "If you can lead me to Will Hartcurt, perhaps you'll find I can be merciful."

Before she replied, Illeanah made a show of looking the lord up and down. "I think you have underestimated me, my lord."

"A shame."

"Enough of this foolish vendetta against the Hartcurt boy," Solan said, rapping his fingers against the golden throne.

"He's more valuable than you realise. I want him alive."

Solan rolled his eyes as if he was bored with the whole conversation. Upon the floor, Illeanah shivered, thinking about what Will's power might do for a lord who wanted to misuse it. She remembered Will had said, that he had been responsible for Lord Thylyssa's disgrace and exile. Did Thylyssa know what Will was capable of?

"Patience," Kamoore said as he twisted his ring around on his finger. His eyes darted over to Solan, who was ignoring them. He frowned and looked back to Thylyssa, a sly smile stretching his pointed face. "Our benefactor has promised much reward."

Thylyssa studied his nails. "A benefactor I introduced you to … I know exactly what he can offer us."

"You two can be tedious," Solan said. "Back to the matter at hand. Kieryn and Odelle Pallarus have been charged with treason." His dark eyes held no pity for Illeanah. Within their depths, she saw her own doom. He was enjoying her fear, she knew. Men like Solan liked to savour their power over those they perceived as weak. But she was not weak. She was a Whitoak. She would be strong, unyielding and upright, no matter her fate.

"Foolish wretch of a girl," Kamoore hissed. He snatched up a thick piece of parchment and waved it about. Solan leaned back in the throne, content to let his contemporary make a fool out of himself. "Kieryn Pallarus wrote a letter to the Sionians, begging them to help him in his treachery to conceal the betrayer of Rama."

Illeanah sniffed.

"Jodathyn Pallarus holds a severe sickness," Kamoore continued to shriek. "The dragon is taking over his body and his soul. We are now to go to war."

"Jodathyn is alive then?" For the first time in the last few hours, Illeanah felt a stirring of hope.

"You will publicly denounce your allegiance to house Pallarus upon the castle walls tomorrow morning," Solan told her.

"I am not a plaything for you to tease, Lord Solan." Illeanah raised her chin. "I decline your offer."

"It wasn't an offer, girl!" Kamoore snarled.

"You should accept my answer with more dignity, Lord Kamoore," Illeanah replied. She let a soft smile touch her lips. She had made her choice.

"You will do well to know you are speaking to the three kings of Rama."

"You would do well to remember whose daughter I am." Illeanah laughed, and she tilted her head to observe the tick developing in Kamoore's cheek. She schooled her features to take on a pitying look that she knew would vex him greatly. "Do you really think Solan will share power with you, Lord Kamoore? I am afraid I can't vouch for Lord Thylyssa's generosity."

Lord Solan seemed to be considering Illeanah's words. "I may not have Odelle Pallarus in my grasp, but I have you, my dear. If you want a stage, then a stage you shall have. Take her away."

CHAPTER TWENTY-THREE

Jodathyn

Solan's Summer House, Aviah Valley

As a child, Jodathyn had spent many hours playing with the lowborn children in the surrounding gardens of Solan's summer house. While the knights were busy training, they had been relatively safe from the bad-tempered soldiers of the house.

Thankful that everyone was so busy with their own thoughts that they didn't notice him slip away, Jodathyn walked the garden paths alone. He came upon an old garden seat and paused his exploration. Perching precariously on the edge of the chair, he let his gaze sweep over the lawns. Solan's house was cursed. Even here, sitting with only birdsong for company, his heart thrummed with grief.

"I wish we never came back," Tornyth grumbled. *"We should take Carvelle and fly away."*

"Aluel will be angry. And the Grey Shadows ... they might be close," Jodathyn murmured, fiddling with the frayed hem of his tunic. He tried to imagine that he was somewhere else. His fingers itched for a goblet of wine.

The soft fuzz of drunkenness might chase away the ghost of the past, or at the very least, dull the memories. He hated Aviah Valley and the feelings that were welling up inside of him.

"Master, might I have a word?"

Jodathyn started. Orion, his manservant, stood a few feet away, his hands clasped tightly in front of his body. His eyes remained averted as he shifted from foot to foot.

"Be my guest." Jodathyn patted the empty space beside him on the garden seat. For a long moment, Orion openly stared at him. Then, with a purposeful frown, he sat down next to him.

"Master, I wanted to talk to you about the Sionian woman."

"What is it with all this master nonsense, Orion? I thought we established that we were friends."

Orion's smile didn't quite touch his lips. "We need to talk about your woman."

Jodathyn fought to hide the surprise on his face. "What is it?" he asked, his tone clipped. The dragon within stretched and raised its head. Tornyth had become fond of Et-hir.

Orion inhaled and looked at his hands in his lap. "My father was a Ramian man, my mother a Sionian woman. While in Silverdyne their marriage was accepted and celebrated, among those of the eastern and northern regions, in particular the highborns, it was not so."

Jodathyn blinked. "Her name is Et-hir."

Instead of looking abashed, Orion flicked his gaze up to look into Jodathyn's face. "It's plain to see that Et-hir means a great deal to you and you to her. But you may face opposition. I thought it only right I should warn you."

"I am not an eastern Ramian. I was born in Pallaryn."

"You're a royalborn. She's not."

Jodathyn slumped. "I know. And the last few days have been challenging—"

"I heard Nym and Et-hir discussing ... what happened in Kudah ..." Orion stalled. He turned his eyes away in the direction of the small village of Aviah Valley. Jodathyn knew very well what Orion had heard the girls discussing. He clenched his fists by his side. "Voran wants to send for a healer in the village to see you, but he's afraid you'll be betrayed."

"The dragons had a healer," Jodathyn muttered, feeling his cheeks burn.

"Nym has been searching the house for clothing for you and some soap." Orion snorted back a laugh. "She said she knew how important soap was to *her* palace brat."

Jodathyn's lips twitched. It seemed Nym knew him well. He was itching for some good quality soap. "Any luck?"

"No," Orion replied. "Nym has convinced Voran to go into the village tomorrow to get you soap and clothes. She's absolutely adamant that you'll feel better when you've had a chance to clean up."

"I don't see what is so bad about not wanting to smell of sweat and other—"

"We'll all wash up tomorrow," Orion said. He patted Jodathyn's knee. Jodathyn looked down at his servant's hand with a raised eyebrow. But Orion was looking towards the horizon again.

"Lady Illeanah," Jodathyn muttered. "You said that she told you she loved me."

Orion inclined his head.

"What if I'm unsure if I feel the same way?" Jodathyn closed his eyes. "What if I thought she was my only chance at love and convinced myself I may have had feelings that weren't there? Before, she was my friend. Now ..." Jodathyn spread his hands in helplessness.

"I'm afraid I'm not the best person to ask about that," Orion replied. "That's something we all have to work out for ourselves, from the highborn to the lowborn."

"Et-hir is different. With her, she lightens up the darkness in my world and chases away the shadows. Would it be ridiculous to say I feel safe with her to be who I am? It seems wrong that I should suffocate her glow because of my own selfish greed."

"To want love is never selfish," Orion said. He looked up into Jodathyn's face and waggled his eyebrows. "And I'll support you if you wish to court her. She would look good on your arm. I just want you to be prepared for opposition."

"I cannot have her," Jodathyn replied. "It's impossible."

"Because she's Sionian or because she's lowborn?" Orion shook his head and sighed heavily.

"Because I am the Son of the Crown."

Orion leaned forward as if he was in deep contemplation. "You might stand a chance in Sion."

For a long moment, they sat side by side in companionable silence until they heard Carvelle calling out for them. The little prince rounded the bend with Et-hir close behind him. A smile curled upon Orion's lips as he turned towards Jodathyn.

"I'll distract the prince," Orion said. "If you truly don't think you have a future with a woman at your side, then take now to play pretend."

Before Jodathyn could protest, Orion leapt to his feet and intercepted Carvelle. He was pleased with the ease with which his nephew took the manservant's hand. The prince dragged Orion away, chattering away happily. Over his shoulder, Orion sent Jodathyn a smug look.

Et-hir tilted her head to the side, her brow furrowed as she turned to Jodathyn, who stood to greet her. "What was that about?"

Raking his hand through his curls, Jodathyn couldn't help but frown. His fingers snagged in knots.

Et-hir reached up and touched his hair. "You should have taken time to brush your hair with the old woman's comb."

"I know," Jodathyn muttered. "But I hazard you haven't come out to the gardens to talk about my hair."

A shy smile lit Et-hir's face. She dropped her hands to her side. "You do have beautiful Pallarus curls. But no, I ... That night in the cell ..."

Jodathyn felt his back stiffen. His palms felt sweaty as he clenched his fists to his side. He tried in vain to hide all his confusion and doubt. Whatever did Et-hir think of him, seeing him like that, naked, bloodied and in the most frightening moment of his life? He felt a hot flush burning at the skin of his cheeks as he remembered their stolen kisses.

Reaching out, Et-hir grabbed his hand in her own. Her eyes slid to stare at the green grass at their feet. Tentatively, she took a step closer. "That night changed everything. You're royalty. Unattainable ... But I want you more than any man I have ever met. You have so much compassion and kindness within you. I'm in love with you, Jodathyn."

"A man like me doesn't know what love is." Jodathyn wanted to pull his hand away but found he could not.

Et-hir's soft palm was on his cheek. "Nonsense. You live it, Jodathyn. The love you have for your family and the less fortunate ..."

Jodathyn took Et-hir's hands in his own. "I am not destined to know a woman's love."

"Jodathyn, I don't understand," Et-hir said. She tilted her head to the side. Jodathyn wished he could comb his hand through her hair. She had brushed it loose today. Instead, he squeezed his fingers into a tight fist. "Is this a Ramian practice?"

Shaking his head, Jodathyn moved away so that he was not looking at her as he spoke. "My brother, my king. It was told to me that he promised that I would not have a wife or have children."

"Why ever not?"

"My affliction."

"*Affliction*?"

"The dragon. They believed I am cursed."

Jodathyn heard Et-hir moving behind him. Her small hands touched his waist as she pressed herself along his back, her cheek resting just below his shoulder blades. "Have you spoken to your brother?"

"No," Jodathyn admitted, and his shoulders slumped. "There wasn't time. But the way he refused to look at me ..."

"There are potions to ensure a woman is barren—"

"Et-hir, I couldn't possibly ask you to give up an opportunity to have your own family. Especially for a man like me."

"I would fight for the man I love," Et-hir murmured. "I'd do it for you."

Jodathyn swallowed past the horrible lump in his throat. He turned to face her. The unfairness of his station in life left him feeling vulnerable. "I am looked upon with scorn in my brother's court."

"Then let me look upon you with favour," Et-hir replied. She took his hand and led him towards the garden seat. Confused, Jodathyn watched as she clambered to stand upon it. Looking down at him from that height, she bent at the waist and then pressed her lips firmly to his.

Jodathyn could feel his insides melting. His mind, usually so sharp and astute, seemed incapable of coherent thought. When his knees almost buckled from underneath him, Et-hir chuckled, breaking the kiss.

"I'll need to get a step stool made. I have never cursed my short stature so."

Lifting his hand to his lips, Jodathyn could only think to say one thing. "We'll find a way."

The smile that brightened Et-hir's face was like the sun after a rain shower. She said nothing but leapt into Jodathyn's arms, forcing him to hold her against his chest, her legs dangling.

"Really, Et-hir, I am filthy!" Jodathyn protested.

"Sionian storytelling is different to Ramian. Our stories speak of all the grit, grime, and blood on heroes ... It's what makes them heroic."

When Jodathyn and Et-hir returned to the house, they were met with a disgruntled Theo. The thief scowled at them and folded his arms against his chest.

"Looks like the pair you of you enjoyed an afternoon of leisure while the rest of us have been kept busy. Orion can be so—" Theo paused, his eyes narrowing as he observed Et-hir's blushing cheeks. "I see."

Jodathyn was tempted to open his mouth and apologise when Et-hir spoke up. "Why don't you wash up for dinner? Jodathyn and I will take on the meal prep."

Et-hir looked at him with her expressive brown eyes, and Jodathyn nodded in agreement. His stomach fluttered like he had swallowed a little honey bird.

"Perfect," Theo snickered and clapped Jodathyn on the back as he sauntered past.

Jodathyn let Et-hir take his hand and tug him towards the kitchens. "Do you think he knows?"

Et-hir winked at him. "He has eyes, Jodathyn."

As the entered the kitchens, Jodathyn stared around in awe. He didn't have a reason to imagine that the room for meal preparations would be so large. When he lived here, only paid servants were allowed in the kitchens. Solan and his knights were afraid that the slaves might smuggle knives out and start a rebellion.

"What would you have me do?" Jodathyn asked.

Et-hir nodded towards a basket of vegetables. "Start chopping."

A smile tugged on Jodathyn's lips as he selected some vegetables. Ignoring him, Et-hir bustled around the kitchens, humming and singing a Sionian trader's song under her breath. Listening carefully, Jodathyn memorised the words of the songs, translating them as he went. When she reached a chorus, Jodathyn joined her.

Et-hir's voice abruptly halted.

Pausing his task, Jodathyn looked up to see what was wrong.

"I'm singing in the Sionian trader's dialect. You understand this dialect too?"

"I had hoped to be an emissary for my brother. I studied Sionian and her dialects in depth." Jodathyn tilted his head to the side. "I wanted to impress your king."

"Did you impress him?"

Jodathyn winked. "He insisted that I be seated with him, and we enjoyed teasing the great lords in Sionian during some of the feasts."

Et-hir grinned and stepped up to him. She stood on her very tippy toes, wrapping her arms about his neck and pressing her lips firmly against his own.

Kissing Et-hir made Jodathyn feel light-headed, and yet he didn't want the moment to end.

"I'll have you know I taught him. Gave him his first real kiss, I did."

Caught unaware, Jodathyn stepped back from Et-hir, noticing his hands were around her waist. He faced the intruder and frowned at Nym's amused expression.

"Seems he is a quick study," Et-hir replied with a laugh.

"Always knew he was a clever one," Nym said with a wink. "Is food ready?"

"Not long. We'll be out in a few minutes."

"Do I need to steal Jodathyn back so that you're not distracted?" Nym asked. She nodded to Jodathyn. "Voran wants a word."

Nodding, Jodathyn leaned forward and pecked Et-hir on the cheek, much to the delight of Nym. He stepped from the room and barrelled straight into Voran's chest. Jodathyn looked up into the hard gaze of his ex-personal guard

"Master Jodathyn," Voran grunted. "Might I have a word?"

"Nym said you wanted to talk," Jodathyn replied, crossing his arms against his chest.

Voran's eyes slid to the kitchen and then back to Jodathyn's expectant face. "In private."

Jodathyn sighed. "What is it, Voran? I don't keep secrets."

Frowning, Voran shook his head. "We both know that is a lie."

Jodathyn stared back.

"Very well," Voran muttered. "I need to know what you said to the king and his guards about me."

"Nothing," Jodathyn said. "I said nothing."

Voran peered down at him. "Are you sure?"

"Voran, I am told that I begged for your life," Jodathyn replied. "You weren't arrested. As far as I'm aware, Kieryn never sent men to look for you after you left Pallaryn. They believed the poison was for the queen ..."

"Other than the poisoning incident, did you say anything else?" Voran was too busy worrying about his own situation; he missed Jodathyn's wince. Jodathyn was the only one that knew of his lie to the King's Guard. The queen hadn't been the target. Intent on killing Solan, Jodathyn had mixed the poison himself. It was Solan's spies that had forced the poison down his throat, broken his arm, and left him for dead.

Jodathyn felt a spike of anger at the unfairness of Voran's line of questioning. Who was Voran to question him like this?

"I suppose your word will just have to do then," Voran muttered. He turned on his heels and stalked away.

"You've changed, Voran Axtin," Jodathyn muttered to himself, watching the big man's back as he stalked away. "And I don't like it."

Although he had been quite happy during dinner preparations, Jodathyn felt his mood plummet as their group met to eat the evening meal together. The few happy hours in the garden pretending that he might earn the love of a woman seemed tarnished in the wake of Voran's interrogation.

Jodathyn barely ate during dinner. He looked up through his lashes at Et-hir and Nym, who sat together enjoying each other's company. They talked about their impressions of the dragons and the fighting bouts that Nym had won. Anytime Et-hir caught him staring, her lips parted into a sly smile.

Theo, Orion and Carvelle sat apart from Voran, who seemed to be in an agitated state of mind. He could feel the bowl cooling against his fingertips, and still he did not eat.

Yawning, Carvelle pressed his small body against him. "Uncle, I'm tired … Can you tuck me into bed tonight?"

Jodathyn smiled down at his nephew and drew him close. Pressing his lips against his brow, he was about to reply that of course he would, when Et-hir interrupted him.

"Prince Carvelle, why don't I take you upstairs?" she said, standing and holding out her hand. "I can tell you all sorts of wonderful Sionian stories, and your uncle can finish his dinner."

Carvelle considered Et-hir's proposal. "Two stories. Do you know any pirate or trader tales?"

"I can tell you the tale of the pirate king, Zazzir, and the snapdragons."

"What's a snapdragon?" Carvelle asked.

Et-hir smiled and held out her hand again. "Come, and I will tell you."

Standing up on his tiptoes, Carvelle kissed Jodathyn's cheek. "Goodnight, Uncle Jod."

"Good night, my prince."

Carvelle took Et-hir's hand in his own. But at the door, he stopped and turned around. "Uncle, I'm glad you are back. When you are near, I'm not so afraid."

Jodathyn smiled, swallowing past the lump in his throat, and blinked back unexpected tears.

"I appreciate everything that you did," Carvelle continued. "No one would tell me what happened … but I know you were very brave. And you found me again."

Jodathyn nodded his head and stared awkwardly into his bowl of stew. He observed the floating lumps of meat, not daring to look up at the sea of staring faces.

"Say something …" Tornyth growled.

"I thought you should know, Uncle." Carvelle's voice sounded small. He had disappointed him.

Jodathyn cleared his throat and forced his eyes away from his dinner. "Thank you, Carvelle. Goodnight, dear one."

Et-hir tugged the little prince's hand and led him from the room. Jodathyn watched them go, feeling torn and anxious. He had intended to try and eat something more substantial, however, his stomach had cramped into knots. The group had been cheery throughout dinner, hopeful that the king was nearby. That maybe their ordeal was nearly over. He didn't want to ruin the atmosphere.

"I'm leaving in the morning," Voran said.

Feeling his stomach drop, Jodathyn's head shot up. He found himself staring into Voran's fathomless eyes.

"I can't risk being here when the king shows up," Voran continued.

Jodathyn watched Theo and Orion exchange weary glances to one another. Orion, who had been sitting cross-legged, made an attempt to stand.

"So you're abandoning me again." Jodathyn sighed.

"While you may say you've not—"

Jodathyn held up his hand. "Stop. Do as you wish, Voran. I'll not hold you here against your will."

"Jod, are you well?" Nym asked. She stood and made her way over to him. She placed her hand gently on his shoulder.

Jodathyn took the opportunity to push his bowl into her hands. He stood and stepped out of her reach. "Don't tell my nephew of anything that has happened."

"We wouldn't," Nym assured him. Even her voice had taken on a gentle tone. It grated on Jodathyn's nerves. She should be treating him like a normal man. Where were her insults and name-calling?

"I'm not a scared animal. I don't need your coddling."

"I could do with a hug. Maybe we should follow Et-hir upstairs," Tornyth whispered.

"Take yourself outside for a walk," Voran grunted, not even looking up from his own food. "You won't want to see your pretty lassie seeing you like this."

Embarrassed, Jodathyn looked around at his misfit band of friends. Nym rolled her eyes at him, pressed her palms against his shoulder blades, and pushed him into the kitchens.

Standing alone in the kitchen, he heard the titters of laughter from the group as Nym rejoined them. Not liking the thought that he was a point of mockery, he glanced around and spotted two bottles of wine. Stalking forward, he snatched them up.

The kitchen had a back door leading into the gardens, so without further thought, Jodathyn stepped from the doorway and into the dark. At the end of the path, he uncorked a bottle and took a big swig as he started to wander aimlessly.

The gardens were cool and quiet. Jodathyn shivered, as if he could feel the ghosts of the past brushing him with their fingers. He took another swig, and another.

By the time he found his feet taking him to one of his childhood hiding places, he was already feeling tipsy. He stood at the edge of the stream, listening to the gurgle of the water. He cocked his head to the side. Did he just hear children laughing?

"Rue!" Jodathyn cried, before he remembered that Rue was now like him, all grown up. "Merciless Otherworlds," Jodathyn choked, taking another drink. "I'm going mad."

"We should stop drinking," Tornyth said.

Thinking it was best to leave the stream, Jodathyn turned away. There was an ironic twist of justice if his story was to draw to a close at Aviah Valley. Would it be here that Kieryn would draw his sword upon him and cut him down?

He was about to open the second bottle when he found himself in the place he had been avoiding since arriving. Sinking to his knees, he looked up into the gnarled branches of the apple tree. She was still standing. He gasped at the sight of her. This tree held memories of both great joy and pain.

To dull the throbbing of his heart, Jodathyn skulled the bottle of wine until he could drink no more. Drunkenly, he caressed the grass beneath his hand. In his mind, he could still see the blood coating the green in a gruesome painting of crimson.

"Please, no!" Jodathyn wailed as he brought the bottle to his lips. It was useless. Drunkenness would not take away the pain. No level of intoxication could bury his torment.

Bringing his hands to his face, Jodathyn wept until he had no more tears. In disgust, he picked up the now empty bottles and threw them away from him.

"Too late now," Tornyth said. *"We're going to be sick come morning."*

"Master!"

Lurching himself to his feet, Jodathyn peered into the darkness. "Here!"

Gasping, Jodathyn wasn't prepared for the vision clouding his sight. He saw his brother's face again, twisted in fury. Behind him, Jodathyn could see the flash of the King's Guard banners. The king and his men were battling their terrified mounts. He felt the whoosh of wind … and a terrible, ear-piercing shriek. Looking up at the night sky, he counted three Grey Shadows. Kieryn bellowed an order; the sound of his words was drowned out by the shouts of the men around him.

The Grey Shadow landed before Kieryn. And within the beast's eyes, he saw his brother's death.

"Let it be," whispered a traitorous voice. *"Let the Grey Shadow kill the king. Together, we can kill Galgothmeg and rule."*

"Who are you?" Tornyth demanded. *"How did you get into our mind?"*

"Didn't precious Mandros tell you? There are many dragon powers."

Jodathyn turned to see the Grey Shadow strike Kieryn down. He saw his brother's body lying broken on the road, surrounded by his men. Jodathyn fell to his knees beside Kieryn's body and looked into his vacant eyes.

"I'll even let you keep the little prince. Let your brother die this night. You'll never have to know the bite of his sword."

"Leave me!"

"I can show you how to kill Galgothmeg, how to save Rama. It's something Mandros would never allow. He wants all your glory, all your fame, all your power to himself, my heir."

"Jodathyn!" Rough hands grasped Jodathyn's shoulders and jolted him out of his waking nightmare. He blinked and looked around. Orion's concerned face was peering into his own.

"Otherworlds!" his servant exclaimed. "How much did you have to drink?"

Jodathyn swayed on the spot and swallowed past the vomit. "Two bottles, good sir."

Orion frowned, closing his eyes, and mumbled under his breath. He offered Jodathyn his hand and pulled him to his feet. "It's very late. Come inside."

"No."

Even though Jodathyn's head throbbed with pain, he was certain of one thing. Grey Shadows were hunting Kieryn. If he didn't intervene, the king would perish tonight. If he was going to act, he had to do so swiftly.

"Master?"

"We have a problem."

"Your drunkenness …"

Jodathyn sniffed. "We're about to be attacked. Run to the house. Tell Et-hir to find Carvelle and hide … everyone else, meet me by the stables. We're at war."

CHAPTER TWENTY-FOUR

Kieryn

The Village of Avah Valley

Curious of the infamous Aviah Valley, Kieryn studied the quaint cottages and the cobblestone streets of the village. From the safety of his saddle, he watched as his King's Guard dismounted. Tiernan alone stayed by his side, watching as his men split into groups to scout for supplies and replenish their stock.

"We'll rest here for the night," Kieryn said, turning his horse's head around so that he could face Tiernan. His captain frowned. "Did you not say that Aviah Valley is a safe village?"

"Indeed, Sire," Tiernan replied. "Solan is strongly disliked here. Our sources say he hasn't been in these parts for quite a few summers."

Sweeping his gaze over the men, Kieryn felt an ache in his chest he couldn't explain. "The men are tired. We need provisions. And I'm concerned about camping out in the open so far into Solan's territory."

"You'll make a stir, Your Majesty."

"I trust you'll keep me safe," Kieryn murmured, shifting his weight in the saddle. "I'll make a stir whether I stay or go."

Tiernan grunted in agreement.

"Your Majesty, can I tempt you with something to eat?"

Surprised at being addressed by another, Kieryn glanced over his shoulder. Ruevyn smiled at him, as if he were speaking to an acquaintance and not the High King. Kieryn considered him in silence, and the farmer continued to stare back. The pleasant smile on Ruevyn's face never wavered. There was a confidence in the young farmer that Kieryn did not encounter often.

"I have never had someone look at me quite so boldly, Master Kelvie."

Ruevyn further surprised Kieryn by chuckling. "You're an ordinary man, Your Majesty. And ordinary men have needs. Good food, for example. You've not eaten in the last day. A right proper country meal will make the world seem less painful."

"I am not at all hungry," Kieryn replied. He lifted his gaze, expecting Fydellah to tell him he spoke a lie. From his observation, the need to tell people whether or not they were speaking the truth was a reflex to her. Kieryn hid a grin and shook his head. He had become accustomed to having a truth discerner in his ranks. "I thank you for your concern."

Ruevyn Kelvie didn't need the aid of a truth discerner to hear his lie. "Liar," he scoffed, rolling his eyes.

"You are entirely too bold, Master Kelvie," Tiernan growled at Kieryn's side.

Ruevyn threw his head back and laughed. "Tell me, Sire, when was the last time a man was brutally honest with you without fear of reprisal?"

"Too long." Kieryn sighed.

Ruevyn winked. "At least you know I'll be blunt. I'm not the type of man to speak in flowery prose. I say what I mean."

"You're a wise man, Ruevyn." Kieryn chuckled and glanced over his shoulder. "Where's your companion, Fydellah?"

Ruevyn pointed across the street, and Kieryn spotted Fydellah among wooden cages that held several colourful birds. A small blue parrot cocked his head to the side and shuffled towards her as she crouched down to croon at him. Keen to make a sale, the shop keeper made his way over to her to start a conversation. Frowning, Fydellah shook her head at him and made a hasty retreat.

"She's from Myryn," Ruevyn said as if it explained his companion's fascination with the birds. And perhaps it did. Myryn was famous for being a natural sanctuary to thousands of birds. It would not be unreasonable to assume she was missing home.

"I'll find something to tempt you into eating," Ruevyn continued. Before Kieryn could argue the point, the farmer had dismounted and disappeared.

Aghast, he faced Captain Tiernan, who had been a silent presence at his side. His captain shook his head and drawled in a deadpan voice, "Oh, the audacity."

"No doubt Jael will approve of the impertinence," Kieryn said.

Tiernan laughed and turned towards Carew, who was loitering around the horses. From what Kieryn could see, he was checking the supplies. "Go and find His Majesty a fine local ale."

Carew's youthful face lit up with a grin as he tapped the side of his nose with his finger. "At once, Captain Papa. I have a nose for sourcing a good ale."

"Yes, I'm aware," Tiernan grunted as his son scampered off. Carew paused by Fydellah, and with his usual Candyde flair, offered his hand and tugged her off into the village. Fydellah looked back at the birds with an expression full of longing.

Kieryn raised his eyebrows.

"If Master Kelvie is going to get you some country fare, you'll need a local ale to wash it down, Sire."

*

Carew returned alone with news that he had sourced a local tavern that would be delighted to serve His Majesty. Indeed, the innkeeper had eagerly cleared out his grumbling patrons so that the king might enjoy his meal in peace.

Since the proprietor had already vacated his customers, Kieryn felt he had very little choice but to accept the offered hospitality. It seemed rude not to.

That was how he, Kieryn Pallarus, the High King of Rama, found himself setting foot into a warm country tavern. Ever faithful, Tiernan remained close by his side as he studied his surroundings.

"Is this like the establishment my brother thought to visit?" Kieryn wondered aloud.

"This one is more reputable, my king," Tiernan replied. "I'm not surprised that Jodathyn declared beer to be poison after visiting a certain alehouse."

The owner, a short man with bulging arms full of tattoos, bustled out of the back room to welcome them. He spread his arms wide, grinning as he bowed. "Greetings, Your Majesty. Welcome to my humble establishment, the Prince's Pride Inn."

"It was not my intention at all to scare off your customers," Kieryn told the man. "If my men were insistent—"

"Bah, Sire," the owner said with a shrug of his shoulders. "That lot will be back by lunchtime tomorrow, keen to hear all about Your Majesty's visit. Just you wait and see. They ain't going nowhere … I've got a fine pork with roasted apples. How does that sound?"

"Your hospitality is greatly appreciated."

"Take a seat then, gents. I'll get me girls to serve you!"

Tiernan indicated towards a large table, and Kieryn obediently allowed himself to be ushered over to a seat. Guardsman Carew sat opposite him, ignoring his father's frown, a cocky grin spread over his face. Kieryn wasn't fooled by Tiernan's gruff demeanour; he saw the slight twitch of the captain's lips. Tiernan had once upon a time been as carefree as Carew. His captain was fiercely proud of each of his three sons.

Used to his father's stern bearing, Carew banged his fists on the table. "Now, Your Majesty, you'll eat like a true Ramian man!"

"By all means, please join me, Guardsman Carew," Kieryn replied.

"I think I will, Sire."

Among his courtiers, Kieryn was placed upon a pedestal. He could never shake the feeling that the great lords were waiting patiently for him to misstep and fall to his doom. He lived with the constant worry that he would fail his country. Perhaps he already had.

It was different with his guardsmen. With them, they saw something else other than the gold and power. They didn't worship the ground he stood upon, but they saw the man behind the crown, and still they served him diligently. Dare he hope that they saw him for all his faults and failings and still respected him? That some might even like who he was as a man?

"Captain," Kieryn said. His gaze landed upon the other guardsmen who stood against the wall. "It has been hard upon us all. Your men can sit and relax tonight."

"Majesty, I do not think ..."

"Who will dare attack me with your fearsome silhouette by my side? Never fear, I wouldn't dream of asking *you* to relax."

Carew's suspicious snigger turned into a cough at the dour look his father sent in his direction. The younger man tilted his chair and addressed his comrades. "Sit, eat and be lazy," Carew bellowed across the tavern. "It's His Majesty's orders."

Not needing to be told twice, the men cheered and crowded around the tables. The barman wandered out of the kitchen; his eyes lit up as he took in the sight of the famous King's Guard sitting.

"Let's get the food out while it's hot, girlies."

Two adolescent girls followed the barkeep from the kitchens, each carrying four steaming plates expertly along their arms.

Meanwhile, the barkeep set his plate in front of Kieryn with a flourish. "Nothing like a hearty meal to take away one's sorrows."

Kieryn inclined his head. But the barkeep wrung his hands. "I didn't mean … I mean to say … terrible business about your lad. Such a young fella, the little prince."

"Have you heard anything?"

"Oh, no, Your Majesty." The barkeep shook his head. "I wouldn't keep something like that to myself. Nasty business it is. Horrible to think about. About the same age as Prince Jod when he was here."

Kieryn's head shot up. "You've met Jodathyn as a boy?"

"Not me. I was off adventuring in my youth." The barkeep leaned forward, whispering. His eyes darted towards the king's men to see if they were listening in. "But local lore said Prince Jodathyn was mighty fond of going missing. They say he got himself and other little ones out of trouble that way."

"Oh, Jod."

"According to the baker, every now and then Jodathyn would send one of his little friends to buy the burnt bread. Never had enough coin, but the baker gave it to the scrawny little mouse. She was tiny, she was."

Not particularly surprised that Jodathyn had another friend he didn't know about, Kieryn turned his face away. What he wouldn't give to turn back time, to set things right.

"Perhaps a more pleasant tone of conversation," Kieryn murmured, well aware of Tiernan's appraising gaze on his face and Carew's hands tapping his thighs under the table. "You said you were an adventurer?"

"Oh yes," the barkeep replied. His eyes glinted as he glanced to check on the two young servers. "Came back here to look after my brother's daughters."

"They're your nieces?"

"And fine girls too! They do me proud. Did not mind coming home to be with them."

"Where have you been?" Carew's eyes lit up.

"Everywhere … but I spent the most time in Sion. Near the Silk Palace you can find all sorts of wonderful trades. It's where I got my skin painted, see? The artisans in Sion will decorate anything. They're the best in the known world."

"No Ramian designs?" Kieryn asked lightly.

"No offense to my countrymen, but Ramian tattooist are for criminals … Sionians are artists and far superior. They say even the Sionian king has his own court tattooist."

"Indeed," Kieryn murmured. He schooled his face to look politely interested. This was not something that the Sionian king had ever told him about. Although, previously he wouldn't have been the slightest bit interested. As the barkeep said, tattoos were for those marked as criminals.

"I spent a great deal of time on the sea too!" The barkeep slapped Carew on the back. "So many fascinating creatures a man can find when he's out at sea."

The door to the tavern opened, letting in a cold gust of wind. Fydellah entered, her eyebrows arched at the cheerful guardsmen. She gazed about the tavern until she spotted Kieryn. Ignoring any greetings from the King's Guard, she moved through the tavern. Kieryn frowned. He had become used to the girl's unflappable demeanour. She was walking with purpose as she strode up to Kieryn's table. In her wake, Ruevyn followed.

Fydellah paused, looking the barkeep up and down. The barkeep stared back. Unmoved, she cleared her throat, crossed her arms against her chest, and tapped her foot.

"A moment, if you please," Kieryn said.

The barkeep bowed and stared back at Fydellah before turning on his heel. "I'll get you something to eat, miss."

Fydellah tracked the barkeep's progress through the tavern until he paused by Ruevyn and stopped to talk to him. She turned back and spoke the words that Kieryn longed to hear. "The prince is close."

For a long moment Kieryn stared up at her dumbfounded. He stopped himself from looking at Tiernan to check if his captain had heard the same words. He dared not believe his ears. "Where?" he choked.

"We don't know for sure, Fy," Ruevyn's words were reserved. "The butcher was unsure."

Looking over her shoulder, Fydellah raised her eyebrows at him. "The message seems clear enough: 'dog whip house has answers.'"

Ruevyn scoffed. "They're not Jodathyn's words. He would never refer to Aviah Valley so flippantly. It could be a trap."

Beside Kieryn, Tiernan shifted. "Can you tell us more, Kelvie?"

"The butcher approached us and said he had a message for the king."

"And that's it?"

"That's all he knew," Fydellah confirmed. "I asked him if he had seen any royalborns. He said no, just a red giant with the message 'dog whip house has answers.' He was speaking the truth. I questioned him thoroughly."

"A *giant*?" Tiernan leaned back at his chair. Kieryn knew his fingers were itching for his sword.

Kieryn went to stand, but Tiernan, breaking normal protocol, touched his arm. "Ruevyn is right. It doesn't sound like Jodathyn …"

"My son …"

"If we approach the house in the dark, we may surprise anything ill waiting to ambush us."

Kieryn fought the urge to pout. He ground his teeth together. "If this was one of your sons?"

"Your Majesty, I would hope my friends would care enough to advise caution," Tiernan replied. He flicked his eyes over to Carew, who looked away. "I can only imagine your pain."

"Very well, Captain. I'll await your orders."

Tiernan wasn't amused.

Kieryn shifted in the saddle, earning himself a sideways glance from Tiernan. The progress towards Solan's summer house was tedious. His captain had demanded that he ride shoulder to shoulder with him. The two non-combatants, Ruevyn and Fydellah, rode behind him while the rest of the King's Guard encircled them.

The men had sensed his mood. No one spoke. Only the sound of horse's hooves on the road broke the silence of the night. On they travelled, and Kieryn huddled himself in his cloak. The nights were turning colder as low winter approached.

Since Fydellah had broken the news that his son might be near, Tiernan's presence had become overbearing. Would his captain grab his reins if he urged his stallion into a gallop? He longed to break away and scatter his guardsmen's formation. Surely his King's Guard would move out of his way if he forced them to. Kieryn tightened his grip on his reins and studied the captain in the corner of his eye.

Tiernan shook his head, and his nostrils flared. He reached over to pat the neck of Kieryn's stallion, and his eyes glanced up at him. The message was clear. *I will stop you, even if it costs me my rank.*

"It's not far," Tiernan murmured.

Fydellah's soft gasp behind him tore Kieryn's attention away from his captain. He turned to look at her. Her chin was tilted to the side.

For an eerie heartbeat, there was complete stillness. Not the stillness that came with peace, but the calm before a raging storm.

"Don't you hear that?" Fydellah hissed. "Hooves ..."

Kieryn was surprised he hadn't heard the sound of horsemen approaching. It was unmistakable. The speed they were travelling at this time of night could only be described as reckless.

"Captain!" a voice cried out. "Have your men aim for the wings! The wings!"

Two men holding torches aloft tore into view. The younger of the two, a boy Kieryn recognised, charged his horse toward the nearest of his guard. He thrust his lit torch at the flabbergasted man as he wheeled his horse about and steadied it. "Hold it high so I can see!" the boy said.

"Jodathyn's man!" Ruevyn unnecessarily said with a breath.

Jodathyn's young manservant ignored the King's Guardsmen that surrounded him. His bow was in his hand, notched, and he was aiming for the sky. "*Ri Rshon Hanoch*! Hold the light still!"

"How do you like your chances of taking out a dragon with that?" the second horseman, a large giant of a man, grunted. "What's the plan, Maysden?"

"If you want to take the opportunity to run, then by all means, do so," Jodathyn's servant said. "I'm staying."

"Orion? What—" Tiernan made to break ranks.

"Tighten the ranks, Captain!" Orion hissed. "You're being hunted by dragons."

"A truth ..." groaned Fydellah.

A deafening shriek tore through the air, and a thundering roar answered. For the briefest moment, Kieryn's mind seemed to freeze. Then the King's Guard tightened their positions around him.

Wheeling his horse around, Kieryn caught sight of a dreadful creature, which was larger than a lowborn's cottage. Its widespread wings were torn and tattered. Against the dark of the night, it was a terrible, pale shadow.

A breath caught in his throat. The sight was both terrifying and curious.

"Carew, stay by the king's side!" Tiernan bellowed.

The usual cheer was absent from Carew's face; he was already pressing closer to Kieryn's side.

The ground trembled under the resounding roar. Kieryn dared not let his eyes leave the sight of the monster in the sky to glance over his shoulder. Perhaps if he didn't look, he wouldn't feel the mind-numbing fear washing over him.

As Kieryn thought the creature readied itself to dive, its ugly head raised. It let out a cry that Kieryn could only describe as one of surprise.

There was a streak of light as fire burst across the sky. The shouts and screams of horses left him paralysed in fear. Blinded by the fierce light, he sensed Guardsman Carew grabbing his horse's reins. He felt the warmth of the flames against his skin. Above his head he heard a terrible thud and squeezed his knees to keep himself safe in the saddle.

Behind him, Fydellah wasn't so lucky. She hit the road with a scream.

"Get her up, Carew!" Kieryn yelled over the din. He snatched his reins back.

Carew shook his head, his fingers still clutching his reins. Another guardsman had dropped to the ground to assist Fydellah. She looked stunned by her fall as the guard insisted she mount his horse.

"DRAGON!" Fydellah's scream made the blood in Kieryn's veins freeze.

There upon the road was indeed a marvellous beast of gleaming white scales. It turned its large, slitted orbs of silver towards them. Kieryn felt a thrill of terror as a shrieking grey dragon landed almost on top of the white dragon.

Flaring his nostrils, the white dragon brought its jaws around the underside of the tattered dragon. Thick, black blood dripped from the wound. The white dragon continued to hold on to its quarry while lowering itself onto the road. A dark-haired boy with a silver earring slipped down first, followed by a woman with hair that was almost white. In her hand, she brandished a sword.

"If you won't fight, move!" Orion cried out. In one swift movement, his bow was tucked away and he dismounted. The next instant, his sword was unsheathed and he was running towards the dragons. There was no hesitation as the young man swung his sword with a yell and brought it down on the exposed neck of the grey dragon. He ignored the dark splatter of dragon blood over his face and hands and brought his sword down again and again.

"Get in the air, you lazy lizard!" the silver-haired woman was screaming at the white dragon. "You're vulnerable on the ground."

The white dragon opened his jaws, releasing the still body of his foe. Inclining his head, he flared his nostrils and regarded Kieryn. The beast took a tentative step forward and as one, the guardsmen all lifted their weapons. Kieryn could feel his heart thumping in his chest. Silver eyes blinked, and the dragon paused and took two swift steps backwards.

"Go!" screamed the silver-haired woman.

Another shriek.

"Oh goodie!" Carew cried. "It's brought friends!"

Kieryn looked round, desperately trying to catch sight of the other dragons. He didn't see them in the sky. That didn't mean they weren't there, lurking in the darkness.

"Give me a spear. I'll go with you, dragon!" Carew dismounted and pushed his way through the ranks. He grabbed a spear from a much older guardsman.

Growling, the silver-haired woman intercepted Carew with her blade drawn. Surprised by the hostility, Carew threw down the spear and unsheathed his own sword. Their blades met with a clash. Teeth clenched, the woman snarled something into Carew's face. Carew paled, looked back inquiringly at his father, and then back to the woman.

The dragon huffed, shaking his head. He reached out with a clawed hand and grasped Carew around his middle. Beside him, Kieryn heard Tiernan's soft groan of horror. "Enough, Nym," the dragon said. "I know this one. He's a good sort."

Nym leered up at Carew while the white dragon placed him onto his back. She took up his abandoned spear and thrust it up at him. "You hurt him, you answer to me, soldier boy."

"Use my armoured spikes for shielding," the dragon said, spreading his wings. "Aim for belly and throat."

"Two more incoming!" Orion shouted. He had vaulted back into the saddle, sending a contemptuous glance to his older counterpart. "Challenge one. I'll do what I can from here."

With Carew astride his back, the white dragon crouched and leapt into the air. Feeling helpless, Kieryn turned his disbelieving eyes towards Tiernan, whose face was uncharacteristically slack. He watched as his captain drew in a deep breath, dismounted, and drew his sword.

"Stay back," Tiernan snarled. From the tense muscles of his shoulders, his captain was ready to fight to the death if necessary. Kieryn sighed. His job was to stay put and survive at all costs. Sometimes Kieryn hated being king.

Above them, a resounding shriek caught Kieryn's attention. There was time to lift his chin and watch as the white dragon collided with the grey monstrosity, his talons outstretched. Kieryn took in Carew's spear puncturing the foul beast's side before his eyes tracked the approach of the last creature.

It landed with a heavy thud on the dirt road. The creature roared, scattering the King's Guard. While the older men retreated to find a more defensible position, Orion, no more than sixteen summers, held his ground.

Very slowly, Orion loosened one hand from the guard of his sword. The creature snarled and snapped at him. The beast eyeballed the servant and then swayed his head to glare at him. In the dark, soulless eyes, Kieryn saw his death.

"*No!*" Orion stood in the way of the creature. There was power in the boy's words. Kieryn could feel the tingle of magic brush over his skin. He wondered if his men felt it too. "*Stay!*"

Another step closer.

"Surrender ... don't kill!" Orion said.

The grey dragon's terrible, empty eyes turned to observe Orion. Kieryn could see the tremors in the young man's hands. He seemed to pale with whatever he was feeling under the weight of the dragon's stare.

Growling, Tiernan strode forward. He grasped Orion's upper arm, intent on pulling him away from danger. "Get away from there!"

"No!" Orion cried. "Let me help her ..."

Orion slapped the captain's hands off him, and then he was running towards the fallen grey dragon. As his palms touched the scaled hide of the beast, he tilted his head back and screamed. The boy with the silver earring shot forward as Orion's knees buckled from underneath him.

"Leave!" Orion cried. "I command you to leave!"

The grey dragon shuddered beneath the weight of Orion's words. Then one by one, the grey scales peeled away from her quivering body. Underneath, she was a glittering mauve. At one time, she would have been a beautiful creature. The dragon huffed and lay her head down. She blinked her eyes, and Kieryn could see the return of a gold tint to her orbs. They shone with an untold pain as she regarded first Orion, then the guardsmen.

"I'm sorry!" Orion gasped as the dragon closed her eyes. "I'm so sorry. Don't die ..."

"Free," the dragon murmured. She inhaled a deep breath, exhaled, and then was still. "Free."

"She's dead, Orion," the boy with the silver earring said. "Whatever you did, you ended her torment."

Tiernan sheathed his sword and strode over to the two boys. He clapped the unknown lad on the shoulder and glared at the older man in their midst. Defiant hazel eyes stared back at the captain as the red-haired giant spat on the road. Kieryn watched the boy pale and dart a concerned glance between the two older men. Tiernan's grip tightened on his shoulder as he pushed him into another guardsman's hands. "Get back." Turning towards the boldly staring woman with silver hair, Tiernan snapped, "You too!"

The silver-haired woman snarled at him, but at Tiernan's deepening frown, she stepped towards the younger boy and pulled him from the guardsman and further away from Orion and the dead dragon.

Satisfied that the strangers were obeying him, Tiernan leaned down and grasped Orion's elbow. "Jael, he's burning!" Tiernan cried over his shoulder.

"Yes," came Jael's voice from somewhere to Kieryn's left. There was a rustle of his cloak as he, too, dismounted to join Tiernan and Orion on the ground. "Power almost always manifests heat."

"What did we miss?"

Kieryn jumped at the sound of Carew's voice. He turned slowly, coming face-to-face with the large silver eyes of the white dragon. The dragon was covered in thick blood, so that his scales looked black.

"Gentlemen, this is Tornyth," Carew said, hiking his leg over the dragon and sliding from his back. "That was an impressive landing … didn't think a dragon could be so stealthy."

"Neither did I." The dragon shuffled backwards, dipping his head and executing a clumsy bow. It was an unmistakable human gesture. "My king."

Carew reached up to pat the dragon's side, murmuring something in a low voice. The dragon rumbled as he lay down in the dust of the road, which stuck to the blood on his side.

"*Jodathyn?*" Kieryn dismounted, despite Tiernan holding out his hand to stop him. The dragon didn't move as he made his approach. "Are you in the dragon?"

"I am Jodathyn." The white dragon nodded. He exhaled, which upset the dust on the road and made the company's horses prance back in fear.

"Who is this ragtag bunch?" Carew said, wafting his hand the small group of strangers.

"They are my friends," the dragon muttered. He tilted his head to look in Kieryn's direction. "Please, don't hurt them. I promised them no harm …"

"Where is my son?" Kieryn demanded. His voice came out sharper than he would have liked. The reasonable part of him knew that Jodathyn would never have allowed Carvelle near a skirmish. But the sheer desperation to see his son outweighed his common sense.

Groaning, Orion dragged himself to his feet. Jael was at his side to assist. "Your Majesty, he is hidden back at the house, which is just over the rise. Have two of your men escort me back; he'll come out of hiding at the sound of my voice."

"Majesty, I don't think—" a guardsman muttered at his side.

Orion shuffled uneasily. "Sire, I commanded Prince Carvelle to remain hidden unless he heard Jod's or my voice."

"Commanded, did you?" Kieryn felt a flicker of amusement. "Jod, is it?"

Swallowing, Orion stumbled to his feet. "Yes, Your Majesty. I commanded the prince."

"And my son listens to you, boy?"

Orion nodded. "Yes, Your Majesty. Whether he obeys is an entirely different matter."

Kieryn chuckled, shaking his head. "Then go to my son. We'll be at the house shortly."

Orion bowed unsteadily, Jael grasping his arm. He vaulted into the saddle of a very familiar grey stallion. Whitoak had told him the boy had stolen from his stables, but his favourite failed to mention it was his horse that had been taken.

Perhaps it was unwarranted, but Kieryn felt a stab of justice with the thought. Whitoak was immensely proud of his fine animals, and the grey was his most prized stallion. It would have stung that a servant had the courage to steal from him.

The King's Guard awaited their orders. Tiernan nodded at two of his men to mount up and follow Orion back to the house. Kieryn watched them disappear into the dark. This time at a more sedate pace.

He turned towards the large frame of the white dragon, who continued to observe him with large silver eyes. As he moved closer to stand before the dragon, it shrunk back from his presence. It lowered his belly to rest flat upon the ground and tucked his tail around himself. "My king, my sovereign lord, I bow in submission of your judgement."

Kieryn felt his brows furrow upon hearing the dragon utter the traditional words. He longed to reach out and touch the snout of the creature. But he stayed his hand. He had little knowledge of how much control the beast had. It would not do to lose his hand because of a foolish fancy.

"I would like to speak to you in your human form, if you please."

"I would rather not, my king" the dragon said. His eyes darted towards the King's Guard. "Carvelle is most eager to see you."

"As I am to see him," Kieryn replied.

The dragon took a shuddering breath. He swallowed, glancing around at the guardsmen again.

"Dragon, are you crying?" Kieryn asked. This time he did raise his hand, and then thinking better of it, dropped it limply by his side.

"I'm afraid," the dragon admitted. "And I know you'll be terribly angry with me, Your Majesty."

"What have you done that you believe would anger me?"

Before him, the dragon melted away, and Kieryn could not contain the cry of dismay.

Chapter Twenty-Five

Jodathyn

Solan's Summer House, Aviah Valley

Jodathyn glanced up at Kieryn, whose face had drained of all colour upon seeing him manifest back into his human self. The king's surprise was immediately masked with a stern countenance, but Jodathyn could still see the confusion.

Under the gaze of both his brother and his guardsmen, Jodathyn was painfully aware that he was covered in blood. His clothing was little better than a beggar's, and the effort of changing back to human brought the drunkenness back with a vengeance. With a pitiful groan, he grasped his belly and tried to swallow back a mouthful of vomit.

He had found that when he manifested into Tornyth, the alcohol had not affected him so much. Voran had grunted it was something to do with his much larger body size. Now, back in his human flesh, he felt worse than ever.

Perhaps he should have called for Mandros before going into battle with the Grey Shadows, but he had been still angry. Not to mention, he was worried what the green dragon might have thought, seeing him in an inebriated state.

"Jodathyn?" Kieryn's voice pierced through the night. "Are you *drunk?*"

"I am afraid so, my king." Jodathyn bowed his head to allow his curls to hide the expression on his face. He drew his knees underneath him. Over the last few weeks, he had seen this very moment: Kieryn's furious face, the sickness, the sound of the sword, and the pain as he lay dying.

"Blessed Otherworlds, how much did you drink?"

Jodathyn shuddered, his eyes darting to Carew Candyde, who was still holding the bloody spear. His eyes were drawn to the point, which still had a sliver of flesh dangling.

"Two bottles of old wine," Jodathyn muttered.

"Of very old, good wine," Theo muttered. Nym nudged her brother hard in the ribs. "Mine. I believe."

Jodathyn hazarded a look into Kieryn's face and drew a deep breath. "If you must put me to death, I will not fight you. But please let those who have helped me—"

Kieryn held up a hand imperiously. "Jodathyn, stop."

"Let them go, my king, I beg you. And Carvelle … don't let him see … not this."

"Jodathyn, I'm not here to hurt you."

"I *saw* this moment." Jodathyn wasn't listening. He shook his head from side to side. "What a sense of justice that I should die in the same place … Can't you hear them? The ghosts?"

Jodathyn began weeping again, taking in great, gulping breaths to the point his lungs were burning. He didn't care who saw his final moments of cowardice. Otherworlds, his head was spinning.

A King's Guardsman stepped away from the group. It wasn't until Jodathyn could see the black, shiny boots that he realised the man had stopped before him. He recoiled, remembering a moment when he was much younger, staring at another man's boots. It was a moment of pain and blood.

The guardsman murmured something to his brother before sinking to his knees. Firm fingers tilted his chin up, and through his blurred vision, he looked into the dark pools of Jael's eyes.

"Are you not well?"

Jodathyn shook his head. He was so inebriated that the healer's words made very little sense to him.

"Breathe. You are tired and emotional."

"Can't you hear them?"

"Shhh." Jael reached out and grasped Jodathyn's shoulders. "You've got yourself in a right state, haven't you?"

"He needs help," came Nym's voice from far away. "We met an ex-guard who told me I had to get him help at the palace. A mind healer … or some such business."

Jodathyn had enough awareness to understand that Nym was talking about Curran Norrys. He choked back another sob. "My fault."

"It's the man who ran him through with a sword's fault," Nym replied.

"Your Majesty, this place wouldn't be helping," came another voice. "Really doesn't surprise me that Aviah Valley has resulted in Joddie drinking himself silly."

"Indeed, Master Kelvie." Kieryn drew his sword, and Jodathyn's head shot up in horror. But a strange, small smile tugged on Kieryn's lips as he turned and handed his weapon to Captain Tiernan. Deliberately, Kieryn took each of his rings from his fingers, his eyes never straying from Jodathyn's. The king gestured, and Jodathyn was dumbfounded to see Ruevyn by his brother's side. He blinked in confusion as Kieryn placed his rings, many significant to his role as High King, in the farmer's cupped hands. Could it be that his two lives were colliding into one reality? Unclasping his cloak, Kieryn held it out to Jael. The healer stood and stepped aside.

"Now, Jodathyn, I stand before you not as a king to be obeyed and adored, but as your older brother. I'm here as your kin, your flesh and blood. Please, brother, help me understand."

"He'll kill you," Jodathyn muttered. "He said he would kill you! I mustn't speak of it ..."

"Jod, what did Solan do to you?"

Jodathyn's eyes flicked up.

"Little brother, your words reveal more than what you say."

"Otherworlds." Jodathyn remembered that Kieryn always seemed to hear the meaning of his words by what he had omitted. The drink had made him clumsy. "He can get to you. He's proven it."

"Tell me, little brother. I won't be mad, I promise." Kieryn knelt upon the road, taking Jodathyn's face in his firm hands.

"It's my fault ..."

A silhouette of a woman walked forwards. Jodathyn stared at her in shock as she, too, knelt on the ground. "Fy ..."

"That's a lie. It's not your fault."

"Meena's angry."

"That's another lie."

"I can't talk about it ..."

"A lie. Take a deep breath, then release it, and then let the words come. It's always better to speak the truth, trust me."

"I know this is hard, Jod," Kieryn murmured. "But please, brother, it's time. Is it about how they hurt you ... with the dog whip?"

"It wasn't a dog!" Jodathyn cried, his voice cracking under the weight of a secret he had held on to for so many years. "She wasn't a *dog*!"

Jodathyn heard Kieryn's sharp intake of breath, and then his brother's strong arms were wrapped around his shoulders, tugging him close. The dam had been broken, and Jodathyn heard himself muttering over and over, "She wasn't a dog ... I couldn't save her! I couldn't. I wasn't strong enough."

Kieryn's shoulders shook as he held Jodathyn. Jodathyn could feel his brother's fingers in his curls as he cried against his shoulder.

"Her name was Meena." Jodathyn heard Ruevyn's footsteps come closer. He felt Ruevyn's hand on his shoulder, squeezing it as if to give him strength. But Jodathyn felt weak.

"They were killing her … I couldn't stop them!"

"Meena was another child slave in the household," Ruevyn continued. "Jodathyn covered her body with his own. He was stubborn then as he is now … They had to pry a screaming, spitting Jod off her body."

Kieryn's arms tightened around him. Jodathyn could feel his body shaking as he wept uncontrollably now that his horrible secret had been revealed. All he could do was listen to the sound of his tortured voice, which did not sound like him at all.

Eventually, Jodathyn fell silent, and Kieryn helped him to his feet. "Let's get you to the house, brother. Your friends have gone up ahead to get a bath drawn for you."

Jodathyn looked up to see that indeed, only Jael and Tiernan remained behind. How everyone and the horses had all left with him being unaware he did not know.

"I'm sorry … I know you are keen to see Carvelle." Jodathyn scrubbed at his eyes with his fists.

"I'm also keen to ensure you are well, Jod," Kieryn answered. "I want to make sure both my boys are safe and well."

"I'm covered in blood and so are you," Jodathyn muttered, wiping his hands frantically on his trousers. "I don't think Carvelle should see this."

Tucking his cloak about him, Kieryn hid the stains. Jael removed his cloak and placed it about Jodathyn's shoulders. Jodathyn teared up at the small kindness.

"Papa! Papa!" Carvelle leapt out of the front door in nothing but his shirt and bare feet. Jodathyn couldn't help but look into Kieryn's face as his brother laid eyes on his son. Even in the gloom, it was easy to see the relief in the king's expression as Carvelle jumped down the stairs two at a time to greet them.

Kneeling as the prince collided into him, Kieryn took his son in his arms. He pressed a bearded kiss to his son's cheeks, and Carvelle squirmed happily.

"'Tis a dream," Kieryn muttered. "A dream that my child should be returned to me safe and well."

"You should order Uncle Jod to eat something," Carvelle told his father. "He's not eating."

Jodathyn snorted inelegantly.

"Papa, wait until I tell you about our adventures!" Carvelle started babbling. "Uncle Jod saved me! We hid in the trees and we won the game and we stole a horse and he got into a big fight. We climbed a big hill and down a muddy river ... and Orion!"

Carvelle took a deep breath, his head tilting to the side as if remembering something important. He held up his hand, then turned pertly on his heel to dash up the stairs again.

Orion, along with Theo and pair of guardsmen, had stopped at the top of the stairs to observe the reunion. When Carvelle reached Orion, he grasped the horse boy's hand and dragged him down the stairs again.

Even as exhausted as he was, Jodathyn couldn't help but giggle drunkenly at the way Orion's eyes widened at the prince's awkward presentation of him to his father.

"Orion shot someone in the head … He saved my life. You should have seen it!" Carvelle lifted a little finger to his forehead to mimic the arrow. He went cross-eyed and pretended to fall over dead. "Orion didn't let the bad man slice my throat open. Nope! He was completely dead. Then Uncle Jod got taken away by a bad dragon, and Orion looked after me the whole time, along with Theo." Carvelle pointed up the stairs to Theo. "He and his sister, Nym, are thieves, and we broke them out of jail. They're the best thieves in Rama!"

Theo's face blanched as he eyed the two guards on either side of him.

"Now, back to Orion. He disagrees with me, but you have to command him to change his horseman's lock! It's on the wrong side now. So go on, Papa, command him."

"It seems Master Maysden and I are overdue for a discussion," Kieryn murmured, his eyes raking over Orion's face. "His horse seems awfully familiar."

"Illeanah Whitoak gave him the horse, but Uncle Jod said that's still stealing," Carvelle said.

Reaching down, Kieryn smoothed his hand through his son's hair in a silent gesture to quiet him.

Orion flinched as if he had been struck.

"Brother, I would ask you for clemency for those who helped me." Jodathyn stepped forward to try and intervene, but Kieryn didn't seem to be interested in anything he had to say.

"Is there any other crime you wish to confess, Orion Maysden, born of Silverdyne?"

Orion's eyes darted to where Jodathyn was standing. There was a slight tremble in his clasped hands as he licked his lips. He belatedly sunk to his knees before the king. "Your Majesty, I was employed to Jodathyn's service to spy on him."

Jodathyn's sharp intake of breath was painful. He parted his lips to speak, but Jael nudged him to be still.

Carvelle had no such compunctions. "You're a spy! That's naughty, Orion!"

"Yes," Kieryn said. "The spy who said enough to stay in service but never divulged his master's secrets. Lord Whitoak thought to be rid of you, but I commanded him to leave you alone. Did he not tell you that you were released of his employment?"

Orion shook his head.

"It was a clever ploy, Master Maysden, to tell Whitoak all about Jodathyn's reading habits as if they were somehow meaningful." Kieryn shook his head. There was a hint of laughter in his voice. "You had him flummoxed for weeks. Now go, gather your merry band. I fear my brother is in no shape to speak of all that's happened."

Orion shifted, his teeth biting down on his lower lip. He nodded curtly and rose to stand. He spun on his heels to do as the king had commanded him. At the doorway, he nudged Theo inside.

At Kieryn's nod, Jael escorted Jodathyn up the stairs. Warm air washed over them as they stepped through the threshold. From across the entryway, Et-hir dashed to meet them.

"Jodathyn!" she cried before dissolving into a litany of Sionian. Jodathyn was so drunk that her words cascaded over him, leaving him confused. He blinked when she paused. She stared up at him, awaiting an answer. He blinked again and looked over his shoulder, seeing that his brother and the rest of his party had followed him inside.

"Jodathyn!" Et-hir growled, stomping over to him, ignoring the presence of the king and his men. "What is going on? And are you drunk?"

"I'm afraid so," Jodathyn murmured.

"You little Ramian fool!" Et-hir cried, slapping his shoulder. "What were you thinking? Drunk. And not a word from anyone on what's going on. First Orion comes bursting into my room late at night, telling me to wake the prince and hide. Next, he turns up with armed men ... then more men and more!"

"Oh," Jodathyn murmured.

"Oh, indeed," Et-hir mimicked.

"Er, not to worry," Jodathyn said, hoping to soothe her. "There was a little scuffle ..."

"Papa!" Carvelle tugged on the king's sleeve until Kieryn looked down upon him. "May I present Et-hir. Orion says Uncle Jod is smitten with her. She's lovely, don't you think?"

"You are the Ramian king?" Et-hir's eyes widened. The copper of her cheeks darkened with embarrassment.

"Yes, I am."

With little thought to her actions, Et-hir slapped Jodathyn's shoulder again. Her widened eyes never left Kieryn's face.

"Nym taught Uncle Jodathyn how to kiss," Carvelle continued. "She says he's more enthusiastic kissing Et-hir though."

It was Jodathyn's turn to almost swoon with embarrassment as Kieryn's dark, piercing eyes sought his own. Kieryn tilted his head to the side and stage whispered into Jodathyn's ear, "Now why didn't you tell me about your pretty Sionian lady earlier?"

Et-hir blushed profusely as she stared up at Kieryn. She glanced to Captain Tiernan, who dwarfed her.

"Jodathyn didn't tell me how much older you were," she said. "I mean, Your Majesty ..."

"Yes, Jodathyn is very much my baby brother," Kieryn replied. "Perhaps one day soon he'll be able to grow a decent beard."

"He's just fine without one," Et-hir murmured, still staring, clearly overwhelmed by Kieryn's presence.

"Is that right?" Kieryn goaded. He placed his hand on Jodathyn's shoulder and murmured into his ear, "I'll leave you with Jael now. I'll come and see you later."

Jodathyn glanced up at him, his eyes feeling gritty and sore. He nodded clumsily. "Yes, Carvelle needs you."

Carvelle stumbled forward, wrapping his arms around Jodathyn's legs. He pressed his cheek against his uncle's side. "I meant what I said earlier. You're my favourite, Uncle Jod. And no one is going to ever hurt you again, or I'll have Papa chop off their heads!"

"Goodnight, nephew," Jodathyn replied.

Kieryn smiled sadly and turned to Jael. "Look after him."

"Of course, Your Majesty." Jael gently took Jodathyn's elbow, coaxing him forward. Another guardsman waited at the bottom of the stairs to escort them to a private room.

It was then the realisation came upon Jodathyn. He had done it. He and his friends had reunited father and son.

The nightmare was over.

CHAPTER TWENTY-SIX

Illeanah

The Citadel of Pallaryn

It was futile. Illeanah sat huddled in her cell in an attempt to keep warm. The men's clothes she was wearing did little to keep out the coldness seeping into her bones. Her body ached from the pain and the frigid, damp air. Hissing, she pressed her fingers to her wound. A soft cry passed her lips as she inspected the makeshift bandage in the dark.

The indecipherable howling of the other prisoners was enough for her to fear she might go mad. She squeezed her eyes shut and breathed the stale air in deeply, trying to hold back her tormenting thoughts.

Deep in the stone-cold dungeons, her powers were useless. Her experiments with her gifting hadn't gone beyond growing wildflowers or revitalising dead plants. She had been too afraid of being discovered to do much more. What had happened with Tomas and later the men on the road had been wild, uncontrollable desperation. But this she did know: as frightening as her gifting was, it was useless without first the spark of something green and growing.

Hers was a power of partnership. It worked alongside the wonder that was plant life and gave it new purpose.

When she had been escorted back to Pallaryn, she had tried to call on her powers. She suspected that she also required deep concentration.

Drawing her knees closer to her chest, Illeanah whispered the words to her favourite poem over and over. She let the soothing words surround her, pretending she was back home in Androssah. Her father had thought poetry a frivolous pastime, but when she was eight summers old, she had found an old book of poems which had belonged to her mother. Her mother's poems had given her a sense of connection with the woman who had birthed her. Since then, she kept a small collection of poems hidden among the skirts of her best court dresses.

Illeanah lay her cheek on her knees, forcing back frightened tears. She was a Whitoak; her father would expect her to stay strong. Resilience and control were the hallmark of a successful courtier.

Unclasping her hair, Illeanah used her fingers to brush out the knots and then slowly, using only her memory, braided intricate designs into her hair. She let herself get lost in the complicated patterns. This way, she could keep her mind off her terror.

Gradually the air in the cell began to cool. Illeanah could only assume this coupled with the other prisoners quietening down meant that it was night. She knew that she should sleep. Her growing anxiety would not let her rest, however.

"Lady Illeanah."

Her reverie was broken by a hooded man who came to the door of her cell.

Illeanah scrambled back.

A torch sputtered and flared in the dark, lighting up a young man's face.

"Don't be afraid," he whispered, "I bought you something to eat."

"Frayn! Does Solan or Thylyssa know you are here?"

Frayn shook his head, stepping closer. He bent to place his torch to the ground. From the inside of his thick, dark cloak he took out a hunk of bread.

"Here." Illeanah watched, feeling strangely detached as he slipped his hands through the bars. "I doubt they'll feed you."

"You would feed a traitor, Lord Frayn?"

"It's our actions that condemn us," Frayn replied. Since she had last seen him, he seemed to have aged a decade. She could see the dark circles of sleepless nights framed his small, beady eyes. His narrow face seemed shrunken, and his long fingers came up to grasp the bars. Something had changed. While he had always been a wispy man, he seemed like a shadow of his former self. "I'm not sorry for mine. I'm only sorry that there isn't more I can do for you."

Dragging her injured leg, she took the offered food. "It's very kind of you to bring me something to eat."

"You must know ..." Frayn's voice trailed off. He pursed his lips, considering his next words. "That I have always admired you."

Speechless, Illeanah looked up at him.

"You're hurt."

"Just a scratch."

Frayn rubbed his crooked nose with his long, spindly fingers. "I'll bring you something for the pain."

"Don't be foolish!" Illeanah cried. "You'll get caught."

"You are your father's daughter. Strong and unyielding. Yet there is something kinder, more noble in you than him."

"My lord, your words are too generous."

"I dare say, I'll be joining you soon," Frayn said. "If my courage holds ..."

Lord Frayn turned to go; his shoulders slumped in defeat. He stopped again and looked back at her; his eyes were glistening.

"Farewell, Lord Frayn."

Frayn turned away. He didn't look back at her as he stalked away. Illeanah listened until his footsteps died away and she was left alone in the dark.

She had known that Frayn had been interested in a few of the young notable women at court. Most unmarried lords were. But she hadn't known that he had held her in high regard. She had assumed he had asked for her hand in marriage because her father had the ear of the king. Never had she imagined that he asked because he admired her. It was a flattering thought.

Her father had likened Lord Frayn to a drowning fly. He was a floundering lordling trying to emulate his late father. In retrospect, she could sympathise. Wasn't that what she had always tried to do? She worked and studied diligently so that her father could boast of her accomplishments. And yet, she had never told him about her budding power or her love of poetry. She had kept secrets from him, afraid that he might reject her. And it hurt to realise that she would never have the opportunity to show him her true self.

Alone in the dark, she clutched her simple meal and wept.

The clipped sounds of the jailer's boots sent shivers up Illeanah's spine. Wincing at the pain in her leg, she pressed her body against the wall and waited.

Two burly wardens stepped through the gloom and stopped by her cell. Between them, they held a moaning prisoner. They produced a rusty key, and Illeanah listened to the scraping sound of the lock as the guard fumbled to open the cell.

Their prisoner was pushed, and he fell forwards, groaning where he lay.

"Nothin' smart left to say?" one of the guards guffawed.

"Oh, I have a lot to say," the prisoner replied. His educated tone was laced with pain. In the dark, Illeanah identified Lord Frayn's voice. "But you don't have the intelligence to understand any of my insults."

The second guard kicked him, and Illeanah heard the whoosh of air as it left his lungs with the impact. Most of the fight had been beaten out of Frayn, and seeing that he was no longer fun to torment, the guards left without another word.

Waiting until they were out of sight, Illeanah dragged herself forward and grasped Frayn's arms to help him to a more comfortable position. For a skinny man, he was still quite heavy.

Frayn's head lolled to the side as he regarded her. "Solan's men have taken the castle. Soon he'll have complete control of Pallaryn."

"They mean to dispose the king," Illeanah told him. "I helped the queen escape."

Frayn swallowed, his face twisting in pain. "I know. I was there when they arrested your father trying to get word to the king."

"Why didn't you do anything?"

"I did," Frayn replied, his voice oddly flat. "I wrote letters."

"*Letters*?"

"Outlining Solan and Thylyssa's plans. I sent them out ... it seems my own manservant betrayed me."

"Jodathyn always said that being kind to your servants was a good idea."

"The little fool may have been right."

"I think this proves his point," Illeanah told him darkly.

Frayn chuckled, winced, and held his side. He took a small packet from his pockets. "I brought you a gift."

Illeanah took it, her hands trembling as she inspected the small packet.

"For the pain," Frayn said.

She glanced up at him, touched by his thoughtfulness. "We should share, my lord."

Frayn shook his head and gestured for her to take it. "I apologise, I didn't have time to purchase anything more effective … It's weak. But take it. The only gift I can give, my lady."

Illeanah frowned and Frayn gestured again. "Please. Let me do one good work before …"

There was no choice. Illeanah tore the packet and took the pain killers. Frayn was right. They were weak. It did very little to dull the throbbing of her festering wound.

"What's happened to the King's Guard? Do you know?"

"Some have been arrested. Some are barricaded in the guardhouse, and some are throughout the city killing off as many of Solan and Thylyssa's men as they can."

"Perhaps they should leave the citadel."

"They can't. They're King's Guard. They will never leave their posts." Frayn looked at her, and he shook his head. The frown on his face said it all. "Besides, Lord Thylyssa has closed the citadel gates. His men are manning the walls. Anyone who tries to leave is killed whether man, woman, or child. There's no getting in or out."

"It's hopeless then. Pallaryn is lost."

Frayn turned his face away from her. "Our fate approaches."

"What do you think they mean to do with us?"

"I think you already know, my lady." Shivering, Frayn slid his hand down the length of his trousers and slipped his fingers into his boots. In the dim light, Illeanah could see that he had hidden a small velvet pouch. He stared down at it, and she could see his self-loathing evident on his face. "I have failed."

"How so?"

"The house Frayn dies with me ... and I have not the courage to face what must be unassisted."

"We've made a stand for our king and the values that uphold this kingdom. We can only hope history will remember us kindly."

"History is written by the victors." Frayn sighed and opened the pouch. He closed his eyes. "I wish I was still a young boy in Pyth, watching the sailboats from the shore with my father. They were my happiest memories."

"I don't see how you can say you have failed."

"I'm a nervous son riddled with anxiety ... reduced to using herbal mixtures to be able to function," Frayn snarled.

"I am certain your lord father will welcome you to the Otherworld with open arms and you will see the boats again."

"Lord Solan found two of my letters ..." Frayn revealed with a strained smile. "I sent four ..."

"How can you be sure they don't have all your letters?"

"Kamoore, the daft fool, believes I only sent two letters. His taunts of triumph confirmed they believe they have all my correspondence. I didn't disabuse him on that notion."

"Frayn, you're absolutely marvellous!"

Frayn smiled wryly and shook his head. "My father would have been able to stop Solan taking complete control."

"Don't be so harsh," Illeanah said. "My own father failed and lost his head."

"We're in good company then."

Illeanah chuckled darkly, which turned into peals of nervous laughter. She clamped her lips shut and glanced over to Frayn, who was watching her with large, sad eyes.

"Sorry, that was inappropriate. Do you think he was brave?"

"Who?"

"My father, upon the scaffold," Illeanah whispered. "Since I heard the news, it's all I can think about."

"I hear he was steadfast till the very end," Frayn said.

"Do you suppose he suffered?"

Leaning his head back, Frayn studied Illeanah. He ran his tongue along his split lip and slowly stretched out his legs. "My herbs will help."

He dipped his finger into the pouch and when he withdrew it, Illeanah could see it was coated with a fine powder. Turning away from Illeanah, he put his finger into his mouth. "It'll help. I used to take them before every council meeting so that I would not dissolve into a bundle of nerves."

Illeanah raised her eyebrows. "Is your anxiety truly that bad, Lord Frayn?"

Frayn's eyes narrowed as he turned his face away. "You have no idea what it is like to live under the shadow of a great man. Even Solan was afraid of my father."

"Well." Illeanah sighed. "You are a lord. You will be given a chance to make one last address to the people of Rama. Make it count."

"I plan to." Frayn handed her the pouch. "I composed my dying speech when I wrote those letters."

Illeanah accepted it cautiously. Fiddling with the twisted cord, she laid the pouch in her lap. "These will calm my nerves?"

Frayn ran his hand through his hair. "They'll do more than that, if you will let them. They can give you peace while you wait."

Closing his eyes, Frayn lay down on the dirty straw that their jailers had so graciously provided them with. It seemed impossible, but moments later, his breathing evened out and he was asleep. Illeanah glanced down at the pouch. Peace before she must meet her fate was all she could hope for.

She opened the pouch, dipped her finger in, and sucked at the herbs. It was bitter on her tongue, but almost immediately she felt her heart rate steady. The tremor in her hands, which she had been hiding from Frayn, ceased.

The nervous energy fled her body. Lying down on the dirty floor, she closed her eyes. She would rest, just for a moment.

CHAPTER TWENTY-SEVEN

Orion

Solan's Summer House, Aviah Valley

Orion studied his companions as they awaited the arrival of the king. Theo paced up and down the small sitting room. Every few steps he paused, shooting Orion a frightened look. From the moment Carvelle had revealed to the king he was a thief, Theo had been jittery.

Nym crossed her arms against her chest and tapped her foot. "Stop that incessant pacing!"

"I'm nervous," Theo muttered. The thief turned towards Orion as if expecting him to tell him what he needed to do. "Orion said the king wanted to *speak* with us. What do you think that means?"

"Exactly that," Voran grunted.

"At least you didn't steal from the king's stable," Orion said. He glanced at the empty doorway. He expected to see the king or one of his guards standing there, ready to drag him away, possibly to string him up on a tree.

Frowning, Nym looked up at the ceiling. "What do we tell the king about our Jod, the drunken little dewberry?"

"The truth," Orion replied. "You don't want to be caught in a lie by the High King."

Voran grunted. "The King's Guardsmen are a crafty lot. They'll smell an untruth the second you utter it."

Orion stiffened.

"Yes, we all know how much you hero worship them," Theo said. He resumed pacing.

"The truth is our only option," Orion replied. "Jodathyn's body bears the marks of what has happened."

"Not all of it," Nym grunted. "The flying she-wolf healed him."

"That King's Guardsman that is with Jodathyn is a well-known healer. You can safely bet that he'll have ways to get Jod to talk," Orion replied.

"Jael Aryk. Yes, he's a particularly wily one," Voran growled. "Surly too."

Orion shifted. He didn't know where Voran got that idea about Jael Aryk. From his experience, the troop medic was perfectly amiable. When he still had the hope that he might join the King's Guard, Orion had been careful to observe them all closely. He dutifully learned their ranks and specialties. The night after Jodathyn's misadventure to the Whytehorse Alehouse, Orion had watched the troop medic examine his master. Jael had been patient with a mortified and reticent Jodathyn. When his master had been embarrassed by his scarring, Jael had removed his own shirt so the scars on his dark skin were visible. The troop medic had effortlessly won trust from Jodathyn and had eased his master into conversation.

"Speaking of bets," Theo said, grinning wolfishly at Orion. "Pay up, Maysden. You lost our bet."

"Bet? What bet?"

Waggling his eyebrows, Theo licked his lips. "Oh yes, I hadn't forgotten. Two coppers that one of the first stories Prince Carvelle tells the king is about you shooting a man in the head."

Orion scoffed. "Carvelle first spoke of Jodathyn."

"It's all in the wording, you hay-tossed barn boy," Nym growled. "Don't you go cheating my brother, now."

"I'm not cheating anyone!" Orion cried.

"What is happening in here?" Captain Tiernan stood shadowed in the doorway, his face looking dour.

Orion wished the ground would split open and swallow him whole. He wasn't sure how much embarrassment he could handle in one night. The captain stepped into the room, allowing Et-hir to enter. Orion looked her over. She was biting her lower lip and glancing over her shoulder.

"What are you doing here, Axtin?" Captain Tiernan growled, piercing Voran with a glare Orion could only describe as venomous.

Lifting his chin, Voran growled, "Making myself useful."

Tiernan scoffed, his keen eyes sweeping over Nym and Theo. "Thieves, I hear."

Theo's skin flushed bright scarlet, and he shifted under the weight of the captain's gaze. Nym, however, glared haughtily back. "I prefer the term gatherer."

"Don't you ever draw a blade on one of my men again, miss."

Nym snarled. "I'll challenge anyone that threatens my palace brat, Captain. I don't care what colour of cloth he wears."

Captain Tiernan's lips twitched with amusement, and he turned away from Nym. "No one has answered my question. What is happening in here?"

"Maysden is trying to get out of paying a bet," Theo said triumphantly. "*Thief.*"

"We'll talk about this later, Theo," Orion hissed as Captain Tiernan's stare swivelled to pin him where he stood.

Theo might think he was only playing, but Orion didn't want the captain to learn more about his poor decisions. There was still a small part of him that hoped to impress the man. What would the captain think of him, witnessing him losing his coin to a frivolous gamble?

"Care to enlighten me about this bet, Master Maysden?"

Feeling sick to his stomach, Orion sunk to his knees as the king entered. Prince Carvelle wrapped himself around his father's neck. Upon spotting a chair, the king lowered himself down with a soft groan.

"You are getting heavy, my child," the king murmured.

Carvelle rearranged himself in his father's lap with a contented sigh.

Out of the corner of his eye, Orion watched as the others knelt.

"Master Maysden?"

Orion was sure he had never been so humiliated. His cheeks had never flushed a more crimson shade of red than tonight. He sent a cross look to the unrepentant Theo. He didn't want to explain himself and the silly bet to the king. "It is a simple matter, Majesty. Theo bet me that his royal highness, Prince Carvelle, would tell you about me shooting a man in the face the first opportunity he got."

"Actually, Sire," Theo interrupted. "The wording was 'would be one of the first stories.' It's all in the phrasing, Orion Maysden."

The king pursed his lips, shaking his head and chuckling. "Orion, lad, that was truly an unwise bet. Did you not get to know my son in the time you have been with him?"

"We got to know each other really well," Carvelle said, burrowing further into his father's robes. "Orion and Theo taught me to cook and build fires ..."

Pressing a kiss to his son's brow, the king replied, "Time for you to get to bed. Once I am done, I'll come and tuck you in. I want to see you asleep, little prince of Rama."

Carvelle pouted as his father waved to Captain Tiernan and handed his son over. The king's eyes never left his son as Tiernan took the child from the room. Orion could understand his reluctance.

"I am afraid, Master Maysden, I'll have to rule against you. You lost the bet."

"There you have it. A royal decree that I win," Theo crowed triumphantly. Orion cursed his ill luck that Theo seemed to have found his courage.

"Stand, all of you," the king commanded. "I have heard stories from Fydellah and Ruevyn of their encounter with my brother. Who is it that joined Jodathyn next?"

Standing straight, Orion inclined his head. "That would be me, Your Majesty."

"Please enlighten me."

It wasn't a question. So Orion told the king of Donatein's discovery, of overhearing of his arrest warrant and his escape.

When Captain Tiernan returned to the room, he had reached the part in the tale where he had shot the stable hand in the head. Keeping his eyes off the captain, Orion faithfully told the king about the moment he killed the man threatening the prince.

The king held up his hand to pause the story. "Was this your first kill, boy?"

There was no use in fibbing. Orion said simply, "Yes, Your Majesty. I'm sorry that Prince Carvelle was witness to it. I was afraid the fiend might hurt him if I delayed. And I made the decision to take him out."

The king tilted his head to look up at his captain, who stared back with his serious blue eyes. The captain nodded curtly, and the king returned his gaze to Orion. Shifting, Orion could only wonder what that was about.

The others in the group seemed quite content to let him do the talking, so Orion continued to tell the king about Jodathyn's efforts to break Nym and Theo out of the prison carts. He skimmed over the drinking game. When it came time to talk about the dragon Galgothmeg, he paused.

"There's another dragon, Majesty," Theo cut in.

"I heard of the green dragon."

"Yet another," Nym muttered. "He's not friendly."

"Galgothmeg," Theo added. "He took Nym and Jodathyn, leaving us behind."

While Nym rather succinctly described their ordeal of being taken prisoner, Orion tuned out the words Nym spoke of the prison ship. He didn't want to concentrate on the king's face as he was told about Jodathyn's tattoo or the beatings. While Nym spoke, he noticed another two guardsmen take their posts outside the doorway. He repressed a shudder, knowing they were awaiting the king's next command.

If the king decreed that he was to be arrested, he would of course not offer up a struggle. He would surrender. The code of honour he had been taught from boyhood demanded it to be so.

He was aware of Theo explaining the situation in Yanyima and meeting Voran. Et-hir spoke softly about finding Jodathyn, and when she couldn't continue to talk about the attempted execution in Kudah and the death of Curran Norrys, Nym laid a gentle hand on the other girl's arm and continued the story for her.

"Curran Norrys?" the king murmured. "Yes, I do believe I have some memory of him. He was set to become a captain, no?"

"Yes," Tiernan gruffly replied. At the mention of Curran's name, Tiernan's eyes had lowered, and his shoulders slumped ever so slightly. Orion had to wonder how well the captain had known Curran Norrys. "He did not agree with some of your father's decisions, so an injury became an excuse to dismiss him."

"And the dragons, Miss Nym?"

"Mandros, the green one, seems to be their leader. He is fond of Jodathyn," Nym replied. She cocked her head to the side. "He's brought with him a squadron of dragons in order to take Galgothmeg down."

"That gold one sniffed me like I was his next meal," Orion muttered.

Theo smirked, sending him a sidelong glance. "He liked you. Bossy, stern older male type that likes to bark commands ... right up your alley for a mentor, don't you think?"

Orion's cheeks burned as Tiernan's lips quirked into a smile.

"The dragons with Mandros mean us no harm, Sire," Et-hir said. "Sidrah was very sweet, and Deovyn is quite the charmer."

Nym shot Et-hir an incredulous look. "I wouldn't call Sidrah sweet by any stretch of the imagination."

The king held up his hand to stall the conversation. "Friends, it is getting late, and we have matters to attend to. Orion Maysden, come here."

Orion stepped forward to approach the king. He bowed deeply at his feet and hoped that he might find some mercy in the hands of Kieryn Pallarus. "Your Majesty."

"Something I have learned in recent times is that right and wrong is not always easy to discern. When you stole Whitoak's horse and fled the citadel, I stopped the King's Guard and lawmen from pursuing you. I had prayed for you, Master Maysden. I had prayed that you, lad, were smart enough to run to the coast so that you might live. Yet, here I find you, by your master's side. Not only have you saved the life of my son, but you never abandoned him. And tonight, you saved the lives of myself and my men.

You have strength, Orion Maysden. My son is correct; your horseman's lock is on the wrong temple. Now turn, so I can assist you in fixing it."

Numb, Orion felt the king's fingers tugging on his braid. It was rare for the High King to personally change a horseman's lock. Such news usually came via message, and the Spearmaster in Silverdyne had that honour. A horseman's lock being changed had certainly not been done by the ruling king's hand in at least three hundred years. This was a high honour, indeed.

"The night we first met, I thought your appointment as a servant was an intriguing mystery. I told you I would investigate what happened to your parents, did I not?" the king continued as he gently nudged Orion to turn his body so that he might begin to braid.

Orion nodded.

"Be still, Orion. You might be skilled at braiding on the move, but I am certainly not. Your father served with distinction. Now there is a man in

Silverdyne, Spearmaster Natayn, he has taken ownership of your property while you cannot. Captain Tiernan has a letter for the magistrate with my seal upon it. I would have you ride out to Silverdyne with two of your comrades, gather as much weaponry, men, horses, and equipment as you can and return to my side. My correspondence with Spearmaster Natayn certainly sounds like he is keen to see you return so he might assist you in honouring your parents as a good son should be able to do."

"My lands? My cousin?"

"The land is your inheritance," the king said. "Your cousin will not pose a problem."

"Comrades, Majesty?"

The king smiled. "I'm offering you a place among the ranks of the King's Guard. Mind that you are young still, younger than your captain likes. His job is to ensure you have the best chance of survival to grow into your role as one of my men."

"We're at war. Death happens."

"Yet it is still my job to limit our casualties if possible," Captain Tiernan said. "Rise, Guardsman Maysden. Take a few hours of sleep, and then ride with all haste to Silverdyne as your king has bidden you to."

Orion was quite surprised when he was able to stand on his legs without them shaking under him. Saluting the king first, then his captain, he stood to attention.

"And Master Maysden," the king said, a smile upon his lips. "Whitoak's horse. He suits you well. Look after him, he's yours now. Goodnight. I shall see you on your return."

Knowing he had been dismissed, Orion turned upon his heel. He kept his gaze off Theo, who looked to be begging him to stay with his eyes. He could not. He had been dismissed. The two guardsmen in the doorway nodded to him as he came level with them.

Pausing, Orion could only stare unblinking ahead. This morning he had woken up as a criminal in charge of keeping the king's son alive.

Tomorrow he would rise as one of the King's Guardsmen. It should have been impossible. He had admitted his crimes to the High King. It was not permitted for anyone who had committed a crime, no matter how small, to be recruited into the ranks of the King's Guard. He pinched the skin on the inside of his arm, testing to see whether or not he was in the middle of an elaborate dream.

"We're going with you. I'm Edd Ryfern, born of Tannryn." One of the guardsmen landed a heavy hand upon his shoulder, effectively breaking his daydream. Orion blinked and smiled thinly, hoping to hide his unease. "This way. We've found a room where we can take rest and rise in the early morning."

Orion could only nod in assent as the two guardsmen led him away. He glanced up at the guardsman who hadn't spoken. Hazarding that he was older than Edd, he thought the man cut a striking form. He was tall, with closely cropped hair and shrewd eyes that were watching him. Like Jael, he had a darker complexion common to the western regions. A memory flickered before his eyes. He had watched this man spar and consequently learned his name. Quick on his feet, Lyntton Pressun, born of Farholm, was the guardsman who routinely tested the skills of the green recruits.

Swallowing, Orion snuck another glance. He would be the greenest of the green recruits, and he wondered how long it would be before Lyntton decided to test him.

"We ride hard tomorrow, Guardsman Maysden," Lyntton said, looking down upon him. "I'm Lyntton Pressun, born of Farholm. I know very well you know my name and that I'm in charge of the younger guardsmen. Do not disappoint me."

"I won't," Orion was quick to assure him.

"Give the boy a break, Lyn," Edd grumbled. "You don't want to frighten him off."

Lyntton scoffed. "I think you'll find it'll take a lot more than my efforts to scare the lad off."

"I won't disappoint," Orion asserted.

"There you have it," Edd declared. "Now leave him alone. Interrogate him on the road if you must. But I want to get to bed."

Orion sighed and looked back in the direction he had left Theo with the king. He could only hope that his friend would be safe in the hands of their sovereign.

The hard lines on Lyntton's face softened. "The king is a generous man, prone to mercy," he said. "Your friend will come to no harm."

Trust. That was what it came down to. His life was now pledged to the High King, and in turn he had to trust in the king's decisions. Upon his return, he'd see Theo again.

CHAPTER TWENTY-EIGHT

Kieryn

Solan's Summer House, Aviah Valley

Kieryn leaned back in the chair and regarded Orion's stiff form as he left the room. He turned to regard Tiernan's raised eyebrows. "He's a good lad. Keep an eye on him."

"Always do, Majesty," Tiernan grunted. "Still young."

Kieryn waved his hand to dismiss Tiernan's concern. "You and I both know that he's a soldier at heart. If we are going to war, a boy like Orion Maysden will find himself on the battlefield with or without our help."

Tiernan sighed. "Very well, Your Majesty, I'll make sure that Jael speaks with him and assesses him. First kills can be difficult to navigate."

"Get some rest, Tiernan. Make sure Guardsman Maysden gets that letter to take with him."

Tiernan nodded. His blue eyes skimmed over the two thieves and landed on the older guardsman that had joined Jodathyn's crew. His eyes hardened. Kieryn could see by the clenching of his fists that his captain had recognised the red-haired giant. Tiernan Candyde was too disciplined to speak his mind in front of his sovereign. Come morning, he suspected a few of his guardsmen might have a quiet word with one Voran Axtin.

In response to Tiernan's hostility, Voran Axtin's eyes narrowed, his lips curling. Upon his dismissal, Kieryn had closely questioned his guardsmen about the incident. Voran Axtin had not left Pallaryn without a fight. He wondered if the red-haired man knew that the only reason he hadn't been taken into custody was that a delirious Jodathyn had begged for his life. If he had been in Pallaryn and had known the depth of Voran's failure, his brother's pleas would not have saved him.

Kieryn dreaded talking to the man who he blamed for his brother's near death. He was still angry that he had taken him under his employ to watch his brother, only to find out that Voran wasn't diligent in his duty to protect Jodathyn.

To take his mind off Voran Axtin, he turned towards the cringing thieves. "Upon the morning, Nym and Theo Torkelle, born of Korkalie, you will have a royal pardon for your crimes of thievery. In the matter of farmlands, I would like to consider the matter fully."

"Majesty," the siblings said in unison.

"But I do have a question for you both. Do you both want to farm the land or is there something else?"

It was Theo who answered first. "I was an apprentice stonemason, Your Majesty, but when we lost our home, my master threw me out. I was doing well … I would like to finish the trade."

"Very well, Master Torkelle, I will find you a gifted master and a house for you to rebuild your life. And Miss Nym?"

Nym fiddled with the hem of her shirt. She looked away, uneasy. "I never thought I would be good at anything."

"Well, my dear," Kieryn said. "You have time to consider what you would like. I'll do for you as I have done for your brother."

Kieryn turned towards Et-hir, who was watching him with a concerned expression. He could see from the firm press of her clasped hands, she was attempting not to tremble in his presence. He repressed a sigh. As High King, he had gotten used to people's natural fear of him.

"Et-hir, I do not think it is wise for you to return to Kudah," Kieryn said. "What is it that you would ask of me?"

"All I want is to find out what happened to my brother," Et-hir whispered, her eyes downcast. "The magistrate in Kudah took him to the mines. He hasn't returned."

"I will send men to investigate those claims, of course. Ask of me something else."

"Jodathyn," Et-hir whispered. "I ask your permission and blessing to court your brother."

"That is an unusual request, my dear." Kieryn felt his lips twitch. He had seen the look of admiration in his brother's face as he beheld her. From his first impressions, she would make a good match for Jodathyn.

"Ramians have unusual customs, King Kieryn," Et-hir replied. She lifted her chin, and Kieryn could see determination to take her chance to speak plainly. Here was a woman he had offered anything to, and she was asking for his brother. The outcast. "A woman in Rama can keep her family name and rule on the throne. Why cannot a woman ask to court the man she loves?"

"Your arguments are persuasive, Et-hir of Sion," Kieryn replied. "If this is what both you and Jodathyn want, you have my blessing. However, Jodathyn is not yet a man, and I wish him to be well recovered from this ordeal and ready to be a good husband before I will bless a marriage. Do you understand, my dear?"

Bowing her head, Et-hir murmured, "It is more than I dared hope for, King Kieryn."

Kieryn turned from her and let his gaze fall upon Jodathyn's ex-guard. He kept his silence for a long moment, watching as the big man almost shrunk into himself. "I can say I'm honestly surprised to see you, Voran Axtin. When I sent my men to question you further concerning the incident of Jodathyn's near death, you had disappeared. I cannot say I can forgive you. I give you your life and some land wherever you like. But don't dare attach yourself to my brother or my son."

"Most gracious, Your Majesty," Voran murmured, bowing his head. The giant kept his eyes on the floor, but Kieryn could see the tightening around his jaw.

Kieryn ignored the bitterness that wound through Voran's tone. He cared very little if he had made an enemy. "Now if you excuse me, I'll see my brother before I retire for the night."

Standing, Kieryn felt the muscles in his body protesting. He longed to lay down his head and close his eyes. But he had promised to see Jodathyn, and he wanted to assure himself that his brother was now faring well. After all the shocks he had learned, he wanted to see his brother to make sure he was real and not imagined.

At the bottom of the stairs, he met Carew. The young guardsman was dithering on the spot, looking furtively at the upper landing.

"Guardsman Carew, I was not aware you were on watch tonight."

Carew jumped, turned, and bowed in one swift motion. "Your Majesty. Jodathyn's clothes might be beyond salvaging. I thought—I am one of the few guardsmen that packs two spare uniforms, courtesy of being the captain's son. I know Jodathyn isn't a guardsman, but we're a similar build. And nor do I want to interrupt Jael with Jodathyn being so ... fragile."

"That's very thoughtful, guardsman," Kieryn said, interrupting the unusually jittery Carew.

Carew offered Kieryn his uniform with a bow.

"Go get some rest."

Carew glanced once more up the stairs, biting his lip. "If you need me to go hunting for anyone ..."

"Carew, I believe you gave your poor father enough of a fright jumping on the back of a dragon like that."

"He was a friendly one," Carew said, his characteristic grin returning. He winked. "I might have to get in the habit of pestering him for a flight now and then, Your Majesty."

"Goodnight, Guardsman Carew."

Carew bowed, and Kieryn turned towards the stairs. He followed his instincts to the room where Jael had taken Jodathyn. He leaned against the closed door, listening to the murmured voice of Jael. Occasionally Jodathyn answered. For the first time in years, he lifted his fist and knocked on the door. It felt foolish and wrong. But Jodathyn deserved his privacy.

"Yes."

"It's me, Jael," Kieryn replied. He cleared his throat. "Can I come in?"

"Come in, Majesty," came Jodathyn's voice. It sounded flat and defeated.

Kieryn prayed that he wouldn't see his brother broken and bleeding. He felt awful for his feelings of dread.

Strong, you must stay strong for Jodathyn's sake. Then he swiftly opened the door and stepped into the room.

Jodathyn was perched naked on the bed, a towel draped over his lap to preserve his dignity. He sat with his back to the door so that Kieryn could see the long spidery scars littered across his back. Kieryn winced, imagining the welts and burns that his brother suffered.

A quick glance around the room revealed the pile of clothes Jodathyn wore, now stained with dragon blood. The bathwater and a wash bowl on the side table was likewise polluted.

"Oh, Jod, are you in any pain?" Kieryn asked.

Jodathyn shook his head. "Dragon blood is stubborn ... It's not mine."

Stepping further into the room, Kieryn placed Carew's uniform on a window seat. Jodathyn watched him with weary eyes.

"Guardsman Carew thought fresh clothes would help."

Jodathyn's fingernails scratched at the skin of his arms. His movements were frantic.

"Stop that!" Jael slapped Jodathyn's hands gently. "We don't want you opening up a festering wound."

"Show me, brother."

Jodathyn stared up at him. The emotions in his grey eyes were easy to read. Kieryn saw worry, shame, and fear.

"Don't be embarrassed, Jod. Your companions have told me much of what has happened. I don't think any less of you." Kieryn came closer so that he sat in front of Jodathyn. Taking his brother's arms, he turned them over. From the moment Nym had described Jodathyn's tattoos, he had been wishing and hoping it wasn't so. Marking Jodathyn's skin were rune tattoos which denounced Jodathyn's dragon nature. Above that was the now all-too-familiar eye and spear.

"They're hideous," Jodathyn whispered, licking his lips. Kieryn could only stare in horror at the small beads of blood around the tattoos. His brother's skin looked raw from all his scratching. Shivering, Jodathyn refused to look up at him. "I know I can't come home …"

"Of course you're coming home with me!" Kieryn exclaimed, grabbing Jodathyn's chin so that he could force his brother to look at him. "This degradation to your body isn't your shame to bear."

Jodathyn rubbed his arms again. Jael responded by slapping him and running his fingers over the runes. The skin around them healed, but the ink remained. Jodathyn stared down at them, looking forlorn. Healing magic could only do so much. This Kieryn knew from experience.

"The king's council …"

Kieryn brought his brother's forehead to his own. "Hang my council. The lot of them. You're coming home with me. I don't care about the tattoos or the dragon or anything else."

Jodathyn sighed and jerked his head out of Kieryn's grasp.

"Our first king was Arturyn the Unifier. He was an escaped slave born in our ancient times; he would have been similarly tattooed."

Jodathyn blinked, as if he hadn't thought of that.

"Do you know what the escaped slaves, like Arturyn, did about their tattoos?"

"They tattooed patterns over the top," Jodathyn murmured. "Arturyn had a dark dragon impaled on his right arm."

Surprised, Kieryn opened his mouth to ask how Jodathyn knew this fact, but he decided it was a conversation for another time. "We can change these runes into something more suitable for the king's brother."

"A burning ship?" There was a brief glimmer in Jodathyn's eyes as he looked up into Kieryn's shocked face. "We could ink in some burning human torches jumping overboard."

"Maybe something with less violence would suit you better, brother." Jodathyn looked down into his lap. His shoulders slumped further.

Kieryn smiled. "I can arrange it, Jod, if that's what you want."

Jodathyn nodded wearily. "Argh ... I really don't feel well."

"That's the amount of alcohol you've drunk, young man," Jael said.

Jodathyn groaned.

Standing, Kieryn grabbed an empty basin, holding it underneath Jodathyn as he emptied his stomach. He leaned over and pushed Jodathyn's waves away from his face.

"Has he been terribly sick?" Kieryn asked. He knew that Jael liked his patients to learn from the natural consequences of their actions. "He feels hot."

"It's the dragon," Jodathyn said. "He's warm ... he's close to my skin now."

Jael's lips quirked. "I've eased the way a little for him."

"I cannot begin to imagine how disappointed in me you are," Jodathyn rasped.

"Disappointed? No. I think it's a rite of passage of every young man to drink himself silly once or twice before he learns." Kieryn held back Jodathyn's hair as he lurched forward and vomited again.

"Not you?" Jodathyn asked with a gasp.

"Yes, even me," Kieryn replied. "I have never, never been so proud of you."

"What's there to be proud of?" Jodathyn scoffed.

"Deep breaths, Jod." Kieryn removed the basin from under his brother's nose. Under his palms, he could feel the muscles of his brother's taut body begin to relax.

Jael quietly pressed a goblet of fresh water to Jodathyn's hand and bid him to drink and rinse. Kieryn watched his brother demurely follow the healer's instructions before speaking again.

"You found a way to keep Carvelle safe, often sacrificing yourself. You faced a dragon to save my son, and you survived a prison ship. You faced execution with grace in Kudah. When you thought facing me would end your life, you thought not of yourself but my son and the others. Otherworlds, Jodathyn, you have shown such courage. Why would I not be proud?"

Jodathyn smiled, his eyes taking on a glassy sheen. With a raised eyebrow, Kieryn glanced to Jael, who stared back unapologetically. He had experience with healers sneaking calming mixtures in his goblets before. From Jodathyn's sagging shoulders and the fluttering of his eyelids, it appeared the mixture was beginning to work its magic.

Kieryn glanced up to Jael and shook his head. He pointedly looked down at Jodathyn, who was half-smiling sleepily.

"Jodathyn, I want you to answer me honestly," Kieryn said, turning towards his brother. A sly, teasing smile tugged his lips as Jodathyn looked up at him with wide-eyed seriousness. "Tell me, do you intend on wooing the lovely Sionian?"

"Think I kinda ... maybe already did. I'll ask my brother for tips. He's married." Jodathyn's lips quirked. He leaned forward and giggled. "My brother won't let me have a wife or breed ... so nothing there for me. She's better off without the loathsome toad that I am."

Kieryn turned towards Jael, his eyebrow raised.

"He's no longer aware of his surroundings or of what he speaks, Your Majesty. You'll have to forgive his loose tongue."

"Otherworlds, Jod, I thought to tease you," Kieryn muttered to himself.

Jodathyn's hand sought Kieryn's. There was a lopsided grin on his face that told him Jael spoke truly and Jodathyn wasn't aware of what was happening. "Mandros, the dragon of Flame and Fury, says I have three daughters."

"I hope that one day you'll know that joy," Kieryn said, helping Jodathyn to wiggle down onto the bed. "I think you need to get to sleep."

"Oh, I forgot, I'm not Vadroil's heir ... I'm Arturyn's ..." A gleam sparkled in Jodathyn's eyes. For a split second, Kieryn saw the silver slits of the dragon within Jodathyn emerge. This time, he was not afraid. "Arturyn chose me."

"Sleep, brother," Kieryn said, standing up from the edge of the bed. "It's safe to rest."

Jodathyn's eyes fluttered closed. His breathing evened out.

"Was that the—" Jael stepped forward, look uncertain of what he had been witness to.

"Dragon looking back at us? Yes," Kieryn replied.

At the door, Kieryn glanced over his shoulder. Drawing in a breath, he tried to dismiss from his mind everything he had learned. Sleep would elude him tonight. "We need to talk about Jodathyn. Otherworlds, Jael, it's awful."

"Do you have any orders in regards to your brother's recovery, Your Majesty?"

Kieryn shook his head and felt his eyes welling with tears. He scrubbed his hands across his face. "All I want is for him to be well. And for that I release my brother into your care. I know I can trust you'll do what is best for him."

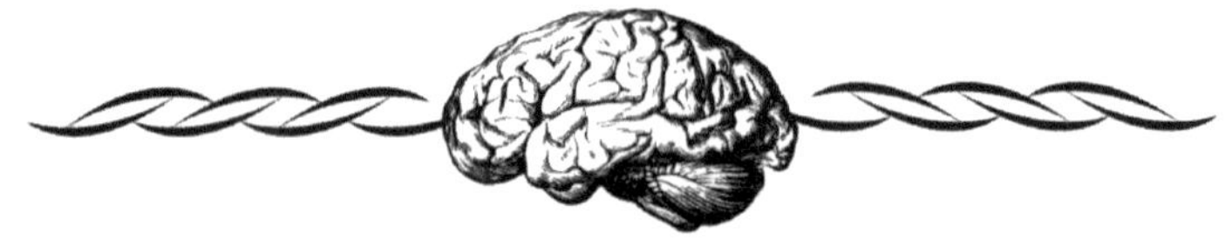

CHAPTER TWENTY-NINE

Will

The Village of Arimac

Illeanah's mind had been frantic at the time of their discovery by Solan's men. From the wisps of her thoughts, Will had deciphered she had been prepared to lay down her life. He had known of her courage, hidden beneath her mask of intelligent indifference. Her grit and determination as he escaped with the queen left him with a curious mixture of guilt and admiration. The last thought he deciphered from her was that he was the one that had the necessary skills to get the queen to safety.

He should have been the one to lay down his life and give up his freedom. Since the day Kieryn Pallarus had found him in the orchard and chosen him as a spy, he had felt his time for freedom was limited.

Will had never asked what the king had said to Lord Thylyssa when he had expelled him from Pallaryn. With his gifting, he didn't have to. Although the king was naturally more guarded than other men, Will could easily discern his deepest thoughts. The king had been disturbed by Will's story, and from his mind Will had been able to ascertain that Thylyssa hadn't been grateful for the king's clemency.

In retrospect, Will should have been prepared for his old master's return to Pallaryn. A man like Thylyssa was crafty and waited in the shadows. He wasn't a fool to challenge the king openly and risk his life. The revelation that Thylyssa had been in communication with both Solan and Kamoore shouldn't have been a shock.

Sighing, Will ran his hand through his hair and glanced at the queen. They had been travelling hard and fast since Solan's pursuit. But sensing her growing discomfort and illness, Will had stopped their horses. The queen had frowned at him as he offered her his hand. She dismounted and slumped on a nearby log. He felt what she didn't want him to know. Although she was exhausted and dizzy, she didn't want her physical condition to slow their progress.

"There's a small village nearby," Will said. "Arimac."

Queen Odelle looked up, her frown deepening. "The risks …"

"It's small," Will continued.

Brushing her hands against her trousers, Odelle continued to stare up at Will. "We should change the horses. They are fine animals. Perhaps we should sell them in exchange for something more modest. And other supplies …"

Will joined the Queen on the log and observed the dark circles under her eyes. He could feel her next request before she spoke. Unsheathing his long hunting dagger, he handed it to her, hilt first.

"Do you know how to use it, Your Majesty?"

The queen raised her eyebrows at him. "Don't be a fool. I'm the only daughter of a Northern lord, married to the High King of Rama. I imagine sticking a man with a blade isn't much different to poking one's husband with an embroidery needle."

Will's confusion at her sarcasm must have shown on his face.

"I can use a blade, Will dear, just as well as my husband. I just choose not to."

"The queens of Rama …"

"All queens are taught to use a blade to kill a man. It's an old tradition from our ancient times of war," Odelle replied. She smiled up at Will, her eyes glinting. "It is not often I surprise you."

Will chuckled. "Indeed, not much gets by me."

"Well, Will dear, it's Della, and I'm relying on you getting us to the nearby village."

It was dark by the time they reached the sleepy village of Arimac, which suited Will. He escorted Della into the tavern and left her at a table, which was tucked into a corner. From here he could keep an eye on both the occupants and the door. The tavern was half-full of farmers, who were content with murmured conversations of livestock, family and drink.

Their thoughts did not stray from the mundane and boring. But after the last few days Will had experienced, he was relieved to be away from the plotting and scheming.

He made his way to the bar and was greeted by a middle-aged woman with long frizzy hair who seemed to be the barkeep. She studied him as he approached, and her eyes glinted at his clothing. Her mind was already on ways she could convince him to stay and spend his coin.

Slipping his fingers into his purse, Will pulled out four gold coins he had tucked away for emergencies. He let the barkeep catch sight of the coins and then leaned on the bar.

"Good evening. A home-cooked, hearty meal would be most welcome for myself and my companion."

"Of course, sir," the barkeep readily agreed.

"I hear you have a terrible memory for faces." Will tapped his fingers on the coins.

The barkeep's eyes didn't move from the gold. "Absolutely miserable memory, good sir."

"My companion is unwell. Perhaps a discreet midwife would not be in the realms of impossibility."

"The village midwife is most dedicated." A sly smile tugged on the barkeep's face; she was thinking Will had got his lady friend in trouble. Della would be mortified if she knew what Will was doing, but the king was relying on him to keep his wife and child safe.

"A room for the night."

"Yes, of course."

Will pulled out another gold coin and placed it on top of the others. "You have been most accommodating."

"I'll call for the midwife while you have your supper."

"It's much appreciated."

Della's eyes narrowed when the barkeep came to their table to whisper that the midwife had arrived. The queen stood stiff-backed when the barkeep urged her to come upstairs to their room.

"One room?" Della hissed. She looked affronted. "Will, we cannot. My husband ..."

The barkeep looked between them with a frown of confusion. She brought her hand to her chest. "Oh, my dears," she gasped, dropping her voice to a whisper. "Are you in danger?"

The queen glared at Will. Her expression clearly said his actions had been inappropriate and unwelcome.

Will stared back defiantly and raised his eyebrows. "It'll serve the illusion that we are a couple. I promised him I would look after you and the babe if anything were to happen."

Della's nostrils flared, which Will found unusual. In all of the years he had served the Pallarus family, he had never seen the queen angry or frustrated. Where the king seemed to struggle with powerful emotions, his wife seemed to be always in control. King Kieryn had often relied on the calm reflection and advice from his queen on matters that required a delicate hand.

Will frowned and looked carefully up at her. He could not fault her for her feelings. She was just as afraid as he was. She was pregnant and ill. And then there was the ever-constant worry she would lose her unborn princess. After all, she had already lost two daughters. Then the loss of her eldest surviving child had left her grief-stricken. The ordeal had been a harrowing one for her.

"Fine," Della gritted out, startling Will out of his daydream. She leaned against the table, drawing her face close to his. "Sell the horses and exchange them to something less suspicious. You'll have to change your clothes too. Get me some leathers, something that makes it obvious I am a woman and oh, get me a nice, good sword."

Blinking, Will stared at her as if he had never seen her before. A *sword*?

Della smiled sweetly. "They'll be looking for a woman trying to disguise herself as a man ... it's time to change disguises. And if anyone comes for me—I want the satisfaction of a sword in my hand. Don't come up to the room."

Will felt at a loss as Della climbed the stairs as the barkeep led her to their shared room. He could see her speaking rapidly with the barkeep, but he was too far away to listen in to their thoughts.

He knew he had been given a command. So he finished off his own meal to go and find someone willing to buy and sell this time of night.

The queen's requests had been a little unreasonable for the hour, but he had his own mind reading gifting to guide him. He had been able to sell the horses to a delighted farmer. With the coin, he had searched the village of Arimac until he found an old lawman who had gambled away much of his earnings. He had been most appreciative to find a buyer for his two shaggy horses and one of his swords. Will had been unsure of where he was going to find leathers that would fit the queen. He had resorted to knocking on the door of the tailors and paying double for what they were worth.

At last, his errands were done, and he could return to the tavern. As he entered, the barkeep beckoned him over with her crooked finger. She was grinning from ear to ear.

Puzzled, Will approached her. He could tell from her excited thoughts that he would like the changes in his companion. His curiosity piqued he climbed the stairs with her and let her show him their room for the night.

"Your friend asked that you leave through the back door so no one might spy her."

Will nodded. It was a wise precaution and one that also made their story credible.

The barkeep lifted her fist to the door and knocked. From inside, Will heard Della granting them access. He opened the door and nearly fell back in surprise.

"Did you bring me leathers to wear?" Della asked. "Do you think it will go well with the disguise?"

"You look absolutely fabulous, dear," the barkeep announced.

Della nodded, effectively dismissing her. As the barkeep left, chuckling at Will's reaction, he studied the queen, who stared back at him. "What do you think?"

"I don't think anyone would recognise you."

The queen lifted a delicate hand to her hair, which was now cropped short and black. Her eyes were almost a dark brown, which left Will feeling confused. Odelle Pallarus was famous for her long blonde hair and big blue eyes.

"I asked the barkeep to bury my hair," Della said when Will was not forthcoming with any comments. "I fear she might think I'm a little silly."

"How?" Will gestured uselessly.

Della laughed. "Sionian magic. Their queen left me a vial that would change my hair colour, which really isn't magic at all. Just dye. The second vial changes the eye colour of a person. Unfortunately, that one is magic and permanent."

"No one is looking for a dark-haired, dark-eyed woman," Will said with an exhale. "It's perfect. Does anyone else know you had these?"

Della shook her head. "My ladies thought it vain. They do not know I kept the vials just in case."

Not knowing what to say, Will turned away. He slid with his back against the door while the queen blew out all the candles.

"Goodnight, Will."

Tired, sore and overwhelmed, Will grunted, thankful he at least had a belly full of food. His eyes closed as he heard the queen take in a deep breath.

"Can I ask you about Lord Whitoak?"

"What about him?" Will felt a spike of annoyance.

"You didn't like him," Della said.

"Many disliked Lord Whitoak and for good reason."

There was a pause. Will heard the rustle of sheets as the queen turned over.

"But what are *your* reasons?"

Leaning his head back against the door, Will peered up at the ceiling. "Did Lord Whitoak ever show me a shred of respect or understanding?"

"He was a hard man," the queen admitted softly. "Kieryn trusted him. Whitoak kept Jodathyn safe in Androssah for a year. Loved him as his own. He brought him home ... healed our family."

Will grunted. "Whitoak was an intelligent man."

"You are speaking in circles, Will."

"Lord Whitoak thrived off the backs of others."

"You have your own network; I saw you at work in Pallaryn."

"People bowed down to Whitoak for the same reason they bow to Solan. Fear. I hope to inspire something more."

"Which is?"

"Loyalty."

"A man's loyalty is a treasure indeed."

"Lord Whitoak used his spies' information for his gain. Not the king's nor Rama, but his own."

"I don't understand."

"You say that Whitoak loved Jodathyn. That's not true. He loved what Jodathyn represented: a way to stay within the king's good graces and keep close to the throne. He never spoke to the king of what he found at Aviah Valley. All these years, and he never spoke on Jodathyn's behalf."

"Will, are you saying there was more to the story?"

"There always is." Will rolled his shoulders, trying to imagine what it might have been like in Solan's summer house as a slave. His father had always said he should be grateful not to have been sold to Aviah Valley. "Whitoak had known the true conditions in which Jodathyn lived. He knew Jodathyn couldn't speak up for himself, and he used your brother-in-law's silence to his advantage. While the king was suspicious of Kamoore and Solan, he portrayed himself as the epitome of loyalty, when in fact ..." Stretching out his legs, Will considered his next words carefully. "I, for my part, am sorry I didn't encourage Jodathyn to speak up. To think he's lived all these years in silence. It was inevitable that he would take a stand against the great lords eventually."

"Do you suppose Jodathyn is still out there somewhere?"

"Trust me, Jodathyn is stronger and more resilient than he knows," Will replied. "It's more than the Pallarus stubbornness in his veins."

CHAPTER THIRTY

Illeanah

The Citadel of Pallaryn

Jodathyn visited Illeanah in her dreams. Seeing him as a child, with his alluring grey eyes and cheeky grin, she knew it was her imagination. The year that he had spent living with her and her father had been a happy one. Once Jodathyn had recovered from his injury, he had become a wonderful playmate. Her father had been selective with who she might be able to befriend, so she hadn't interacted with many children.

Her dreams were full of the heady scent of the High Spring Festival. The fields around the Lake of Mirrors in Androssah were full of wildflowers. Voices of adults spoke with an excited murmur that accompanied the buying and selling of livestock. She stood among the milling adults as Jodathyn ran past and tagged her.

He ran barefoot, with his trousers wet from where he had paddled in the Lake of Mirrors. His cheeks were flushed with excitement. It wouldn't be long before her father stopped him to scold him on the proper, dignified behaviour he should be exhibiting as the Son of the Crown. She knew her father would shake his head at disgust at the wildflowers that she had woven into his curls.

Jodathyn had been such a compliant companion; he had let her do all sorts of things to him when he was young.

As Jodathyn turned to offer her his hand, the pleasant dreams of Androssah and her lake faded from her consciousness. She wanted to cry out and beg for her mind to take her home. To take her to a time she was a girl, paddling on the shore of the lake during the High Spring Festival.

Illeanah opened her eyes to her dark, foreboding cell. Frayn was shaking her shoulder, holding out his pouch. Blinking, she sat up and bit her tongue to stop herself saying something harsh to her fellow prisoner.

For a long moment, she listened to the jeering of the prisoners. Frayn jiggled his pouch full of precious herbs under her nose, and then she heard it. The steady beat of the guard's footsteps. "Quick, my lady. It'll help. Trust me."

She shoved her finger in the pouch and quickly sucked the dry herbs into her mouth. Frayn was right. It was better to be in the beautiful haze of confusion than remain fully aware of the terror.

Inside her ribcage, her heart fluttered like an injured bird. The silence was resounding as the footsteps stopped outside her cell. She licked her dry lips, wishing that she might have a cup of water to soothe her thirst.

Frayn took his pouch, tucking it into his boots.

The herbs were beginning to weave their magic once more. Illeanah, although awake, was transported back to the world of her childhood.

The guards stomped into the cell and grabbed her to stand. Since she had not stood on her injured leg, she cried out in surprise at the pain the guards' treatment caused. Turning her face away, she ignored them as they bound her wrists. Instead, lost in the fog of the herbs, she watched the spectre of Jodathyn making faces at the guards.

They were led from the dungeons in silence. Onwards they marched, until Illeanah felt the pleasant stirring of the cool night air. She raised her head to the sky, staring up at the silver stars as they looked down upon her.

The guards growled at her slowed footsteps and shunted her forwards. Instead of taking her through the palace, they took her on a route she had never taken before. Soon they urged her to begin the ascent to climb the palace walls.

Illeanah paused. The walls of the palace were lit with what looked to be hundreds of torches. The ancient building must look quite a spectacle to anyone wandering about in the citadel. Above their heads, she could see the flags snapping in the wind. The flaming crown and sword that had looked over Pallaryn for centuries was gone. Instead, other house's flags were seen, notably Solan, Thylyssa, and Kamoore. There was another addition she had never seen before. It was tied up higher than the other three. A black background with the snarling head of a dragon.

The spectre of little Jodathyn stood looking up at it, making a rude gesture. He turned to look at her, smiling and waving. Illeanah marvelled at the power of Frayn's herbs. She could even see the boyish dimples on the ghost of her childhood friend.

"Whose flag is that?" Illeanah croaked.

"You won't have to worry about that, my pretty," a guard grunted.

"Nah," his companion replied. "That's our problem now."

"Climb."

Gritting her teeth against the pain in her leg, Illeanah did as she was told. There was little point antagonising the guards. They would take her to her doom one way or another.

"Good evening, my lords," Frayn said from behind as the great lords turned to leer at them.

Solan, Thylyssa, and Kamoore all indeed looked like they were dressed as kings.

"How long do you think it'll take for the first of the new kings to die at the hands of another?" Illeanah asked.

"Not long," Frayn drawled. "Kamoore will be the first to die."

Kamoore's thin face twisted into an ugly sneer.

"Enough," Solan snarled. "You're here to die."

Thylyssa smirked as he looked to Kamoore, who was busy fiddling with his ugly rings upon his fingers.

Illeanah was ushered forward and to her shock and dismay, she noticed a small group of injured King's Guardsmen also bound and looking grim. The great lords had even gone to the effort of removing the royal insignia from their uniforms.

Lifting his chin imperiously, Frayn glared at Solan. "Arresting the King's Guard, that's low even for the likes of you, Solan."

In response, Solan laughed and turned to stride to the edge of the wall. Throwing his arms out wide, he cried, "Good people of Pallaryn. Tonight, the king's council has officially dug out the scourge of house Pallarus, which has been feeding off the helplessness of Rama and her people. Too long has the traitor Kieryn Pallarus protected those who would harm our proud nation. Where is he now? Like a coward, he has fled. And for what has he abandoned you? For his brother, I tell you. Vadroil's Heir has risen. Kieryn Pallarus has sided with him. Any in our kingdom that supports him is guilty of high treason.

This is why after a long and arduous deliberation, the king's council has stripped all powers of the King's Guard. These men will be replaced by my own soldiers until such time we can replenish our numbers. Let it be known that if a King's Guardsman was to lay down his arms and surrender, he will be interviewed and if it is deemed suitable, he will be dismissed from his post.

The king's council would also like to demonstrate to you, the Ramian people, that all are equal in the sight of the law. Here I bring two highborn traitors the council has found guilty of their crimes. The penalty for high treason is severe. Tarryn Frayn and Illeanah Whitoak, it is with a heavy heart the council condemns you to die by the axe."

It was a shock to hear the words spoken, even though Illeanah had been expecting to hear them. She glanced as far as she could at the pale faces of the common folk below. Even through the pleasant haze of Frayn's herbs, she felt a new overwhelming terror. She wrenched back on the guards holding her. She may have screamed … she wasn't too sure.

There was a look of resigned pity on Frayn's face as he looked at her. He was dragged forward and forced to his knees. Before him was a chopping block, which she saw the black-clad executioner gesture to.

Even on his knees, Frayn possessed a strange calmness. Illeanah didn't know if it was the herbs or if he had finally found his courage. She liked to think it was the latter.

"Mark my words … You will pay for your crimes in this world or the next. I demand my right to address the charge you have laid against me. It is my right under Ramian law as a highborn lord of the council."

The executioner glared down at Frayn and then shifted his weight to look back at the great lords for instruction. He obviously hadn't been prepared for the prisoner to make such a request.

Solan, much to Illeanah's glee, was silly enough to nod his head and allow Frayn to speak. Thylyssa looked bored by the proceedings.

Frayn stood, his shoulders back and his chin held high. "Citizens of Pallaryn, fellow Ramians, before I lay down my life, I wish to say what an honour it was to serve you, my countrymen, and my king. In the days that come, I implore you to show fortitude and solidarity."

Frayn paused, and Illeanah could see him shivering.

"Peace be with you, Lord Frayn!" someone below shouted.

Composing himself, Frayn continued his speech. "My father taught me many things. But this one lesson comes to mind. *Araae helphelwyn. Terini gorthorawyn*. It underpins the very fabric of what it is to be a citizen of Rama. Live Valiantly. Die Honourably. I never truly understood how a man might achieve this. Tonight, I know. I can die with the knowledge I have served my country to the best of my abilities. Tonight, I learn the lesson of what it means to die honourably. Think kindly of me. Farewell, sweet Rama. *Araae helphelwyn. Terini gorthorawyn!*"

After he finished speaking, Frayn sank to his knees again. A strange stillness came over the crowd.

And then the chanting started. "*Araae helphelwyn. Terini gorthorawyn!*"

Glancing over his shoulder, Frayn shook his head, smiling in victory in Solan's direction. Ramians were a fiercely proud people. If Solan and his lackeys insisted on taking the citadel via blood, the people would revolt. He had done his part in ensuring Solan's job was difficult.

Solan snarled and gestured sharply at the executioner. Frayn was pushed forward and even though he was unresisting, his head was forced onto the chopping block.

Illeanah could not help but watch in helpless fascination as Frayn's eyes fluttered shut, and she wondered if he was already back home on the beach watching the sailboats out on the ocean. For his sake, she hoped he was.

The crowd's chant became a fever pitch. Their cries became a sound of crashing waves.

The executioner raised the axe, and it came down with a mighty *thwack* and a spatter of blood. The first blow wasn't enough. It took two more swings of the axe to sever Frayn's head from his shoulders.

Leering, the executioner lifted Frayn's head up by the hair for the crowd to see. "Behold the traitor!"

"Behold, a hero of Rama," Illeanah whispered to herself.

Poor Frayn's body was dragged to the side, leaving a crimson smudge over the rampart. Illeanah looked away, disgusted and saddened. Squeezing her eyes shut against the grisly sight, she fought dizziness as she uttered a quiet prayer.

Her knees no longer seemed capable of holding her up. She had the vague realisation that she was keening. A strange, frightened noise escaped her throat. And then she was gasping for breath.

The guards behind her pushed her forward to the chopping block, which was glistening with Frayn's blood. Weakened, she fell to her knees. Crying out, she tried to scuttle away from the sight of her doom. Never mind that she was a Whitoak and Whitoaks were strong. She could feel the stickiness of Frayn's blood seeping through the material of the horrid men's trousers that she had been forced to wear.

Looking up at the executioner, she decided it was worth trying to beg for her life. "Please, no, mercy."

"You have been condemned to die, girl. Lay your head on the block."

With an inarticulate cry, she turned to Solan and his lackeys. Again, she tried begging. "Please ..."

A twisted, cold smile lit Solan's features, and Illeanah gasped back a frightened sob.

"My lords!" one of the bound King's Guard cried. His voice was calm and firm and easily carried so that the people down below heard what he said. "If indeed you are doing this for the law and the law's sake alone, let me go and calm the girl and help her. Show your people you are not such a monster. Cut her free."

Illeanah tilted her head back and observed how Solan's features seemed to have frozen over. She could see a vein throbbing in his neck. The guardsman had given him very little choice; he had to comply with the request or risk the people seeing him in a poor light. Frayn's last moments had damaged Solan in the people's eyes. She doubted the citizens of Pallaryn would forget this night anytime soon.

Thylyssa rolled his eyes and jerked his chin forward. "Get on with it," he growled. "Cut her ropes."

Illeanah's ropes were cut, and all she could do was look at her wrists in wonder. The guardsman stepped forward. Illeanah listened to his sure footsteps. She wanted to scream at him to rescue her, but he was just as trapped as she was.

When he knelt down beside her and took her cold, shaking hands, she recognised him. "Tryst ..."

"Courage, my lady."

Crying out, Illeanah threw herself against his chest.

"Let Lord Frayn's herbs do their work," Guardsman Tryst whispered into her ear. "Try and relax and meditate on something beautiful. Trust me."

Illeanah nodded her head against his shoulders. Little Jodathyn's apparition appeared behind her. She felt the small hands hugging her from behind.

"Come play with me," Jodathyn's ghost whispered. "We'll go play by the lake. Won't that be fun?"

She remembered the beautiful dream of Jodathyn and her playing by the Lake of Mirrors.

"Oh, Jod, forgive me!"

"I will hold your hand until ..." Tryst's voice trailed off.

"The end," Illeanah whispered. "That is most kind of you."

Solan was impatient. On his signal, the executioner grabbed her upper arm. Her eyes darted towards Tryst, and he smiled at her encouragingly. He followed them and knelt with her. His large, calloused hands took hold of her own as she was forced to lay her head down on the bloody block.

He squeezed her hand and smiled once more. "Courage, my lady."

"Thank you," Illeanah gasped as she closed her eyes and surrendered herself to the inner workings of the herbs. She recalled to her mind the smell of the wildflowers and the feel of Jodathyn's curls as she weaved them into his hair. She remembered the sound of Jodathyn's laugh and the feel of the wet pebbles and mud as they played upon the shore.

All thoughts of the blood-soaked block and Lord Solan's jeering face melted away. She did not hear the sound of the axe whooshing through the air or feel the stunning blow to the back of her neck. She did not feel the moment her fingers went lax and let go of the warm, strong hand that held her in her final moments.

Illeanah gasped, as if she had been underwater. She took her very first breath, renewed and dazed. The horror on the walls of Pallaryn lay forgotten behind her. Her life that she lived was no more than a shadow of a dream.

She was lying in a field of flowers, the sun beating down on her face. The trousers stained with blood and tears were gone. She wore a soft cream gown stitched with delicate yellow wildflowers. It was one of her mother's gowns that she had cherished from girlhood.

"No more tears, daughter."

"Papa!"

Strong hands lifted her up, and she found herself once more in her father's arms.

"Illeanah?" A woman stood in the tall grasses. Long auburn hair tied back with lilac ribbons. Soft pink lips smiled, and the woman's face was aglow with joy. She spread her hands in welcome. "You look so beautiful in my dress."

From the precious few likenesses she had found in Androssah, Illeanah knew this was her lady mother. A cry of delight escaped her lips, and then she was running through the field, laughing with glee.

Illeanah was home forevermore among the wildflowers of high spring.

CHAPTER THIRTY-ONE

Jodathyn

Solan's Summer House, Aviah Valley

With a pitiful moan, Jodathyn rolled over, clutching his aching head. Now that he was returning to consciousness, it felt like he had an army of knights trampling through his brain.

Squeezing his eyes shut, he tried to close his mind off to what he had seen in his visions. He remembered with fondness the beginning of his dream, before his visions took over.

He had been in Androssah, wading in the cool waters of the Lake of Mirrors. Illeanah had been walking in the fields, her long coppery hair woven with wildflowers. She wore a simple summer dress of cream. There was a radiant peace to her face as she looked up and smiled at him.

Leaping from the lake, Jodathyn tried to reach her.

"You shouldn't be here, Jodathyn," Illeanah had said. "It's not your time."

Jodathyn shook his head. "What do you mean?"

Cocking her head to the side, Illeanah observed him. "I hope she'll love you the way you deserve."

"Illeanah, you will always be my friend."

"Yes, you will be dear to me forever."

"I don't understand."

"Brother of my heart. I am no longer among the living. It's time for you to go."

Jodathyn opened his mouth to protest, but Illeanah leaned over and tucked a yellow wildflower into his hair. He went to reach out to her, but she stepped away, an odd, serene smile on her face.

The warmth of the sun dimmed and instead of standing in the middle of a field of flowers, he was standing on the outer wall of the palace. He watched in disbelief as the royal banners were torn from the wall.

"What are you doing?" Jodathyn had cried.

But no one paid him any attention. In the place of the banners, they raised pikes, each adorned with the head of a King's Guardsman. Gasping in horror, Jodathyn walked among the forest of heads. At the very end of the row was the head of Lord Frayn and Illeanah.

Jodathyn screamed and rushed forward to clutch at the sleeves of the men who were erecting the pikes. Again, they paid him no attention.

Numb with grief and shock, Jodathyn looked down. From here he could see the guards' gate. A cart full of headless bodies rumbled along the cobblestones. He could see most were guardsmen, still in tattered uniforms. On the top was a woman's body, clothed in men's trousers.

"It is you who is responsible for the fall of Pallaryn."

Turning upon his heel, Jodathyn came face-to-face with a red dragon. "Galgothmeg." Jodathyn inhaled. "Would it be terribly disappointing for me to tell you that you no longer frighten me?"

"I don't desire your fear," the red dragon replied. "Only your death."

"I will fight you until my dying day."

An ugly leer had split Galgothmeg's face. Above him was a squadron of Grey Shadows converging onto Pallaryn. Far behind them were coloured dots of a legion of dragons.

"I'll see you on the battlefield," was the last thing Jodathyn said before he had woken up.

His head felt like a battlefield now.

"I am never drinking again …" Tornyth murmured.

"If you ever get so poorly drunk on my watch again, Jodathyn Pallarus, I assure you I will not be giving you a hangover cure."

A plaintive moan escaped Jodathyn's lips as he realised that he had not been alone in the room. There was a movement to his right, and Jael appeared at his side. Jodathyn blinked up at the guardsman.

"There's a cure for this malady?" he murmured. He thrust his hand out and waggled his fingers. "Give, and where's the king?"

"Be nice. He can help my aching head."

Jael stared down at him and raised his eyebrows. Unnerved by the older man's close scrutiny, Jodathyn whispered, "Please, mercy, Jael. You have no idea what I saw last night."

Jael gripped Jodathyn's shoulders and helped him to sit. "You will need to get dressed in Carew's spare uniform and eat something before you see the king."

"Uniform?"

Jael smirked at him as he stepped towards a side table and picked up a pewter mug. "We can't have you wandering around naked. Carew Candyde offered a spare uniform last night—don't you remember?"

Jodathyn blushed crimson at the memory of last night.

"And what do you mean by *your watch*?"

Jael's expression softened. "You are aware that Donatein Manideep and Valt Axtin are no longer in service?"

"Yes," Jodathyn said. "I'm aware they have died."

"Someone needs to ensure certain needs of yours are met."

"My *needs*?" Jodathyn blinked slowly. The pain in his head was unbearable. He couldn't think straight. "Pardon? I don't understand."

Pressing the mug into Jodathyn's hands, Jael gestured for him to drink up. Jodathyn gave the goblet a tentative sniff. His eyes watered as he started to gag. Never in all his life had he smelled something so foul.

"Is this a twisted punishment?"

Jael's lips pinched into a straight line.

With a mock salute, Jodathyn downed the goblet in one swallow. The unpleasant mixture felt thick on his tongue.

"It's definitely a punishment," Jodathyn gasped, trying to keep Jael's concoction down. "Why would you bother with me? I hardly think it would be an enviable position."

"I'm the highest-ranking troop medic within the King's Guard," Jael said. He looked somewhat bemused. "I'm well versed in more than just dealing with physical injuries, Jodathyn."

Jodathyn felt himself paling. "You're a mind healer?"

"There's no reason to be alarmed." Jael plucked the empty goblet from Jodathyn's hand and set it down on the table. "My powers are not able to touch your mind. But think on this: if I'm assigned to you, then I may see you discretely, without blathering highborns being aware. I'm sure you don't want to be the centre of court gossip."

"It's completely unnecessary."

"Well, thank goodness the king disagrees with you."

Jodathyn shook his head. "Tell Kieryn I'm fine."

"It's not up for debate, young man," Jael replied sternly. "I've seen many of the King's Guard during their career. There's nothing you can do or say that will shock me."

Jodathyn's lips twisted into a leer. "What if I was to tell you I'm a murderer?"

"I know about the man in the forest, Jodathyn," Jael said.

"What about the first mate, whose throat we sliced open, or the lord I planned to poison when I was a boy?"

Jael shook his head. "These tactics don't work on me. Get dressed. I'll send some food up."

Jodathyn bit down on the insides of his cheek, cursing his indiscreet words. Jael may not have risen to the bait, but he saw the gleam of victory in the medic's eyes. He would have to be careful when dealing with Jael Aryk.

When Jael left the room, Jodathyn tumbled out of bed, knowing that he ought to take the opportunity to dress while he was alone. He grasped at Carew's uniform and fumbled with the pants and the shirt.

While he dressed, he noticed that somehow the basins of dragon blood and his old clothing had been removed without him being aware. He had to wonder how many were in his room as he slept off his drunkenness. Surely Jael hadn't done all of it alone.

The basin was now filled with fresh water, a clean cloth, and soap. Jodathyn couldn't help but flush with embarrassment, remembering Jael had assisted in cleaning him up last night. Dragon blood was stubborn.

Tornyth had practically purred within him as the medic insisted on brushing out his hair.

He stumbled over to the basin and scrubbed at his skin until he felt raw. There he stood, leaning over the side table, letting the water drip from his cheeks and nose.

"Jodathyn! Open the door!"

It was an insistent knocking that snapped him out of his reverie. Jolting back into awareness, he tripped over his own feet to get to the door. Jael had locked it behind him.

"What are you doing in there?"

"Opening a door," Jodathyn grunted, swinging it open to reveal a grinning Ruevyn who had a steaming bowl of stew.

"Good morning, sleepy head," Ruevyn said, inviting himself in. "Jael sent me up to bring you something to eat and company."

Jodathyn grimaced as Ruevyn strode through the room and placed the bowl down. "How are you this fine morning? I've been instructed to distract you with pleasant conversation and make sure you eat something."

Jodathyn snorted. "Jael thinks it's his job to look after me. I guess after last night's performance ..."

"Don't be too embarrassed," Ruevyn said. "I daresay the guards have all been drunk in their lifetime."

"Yes, because I can see Tiernan Candyde crying uncontrollably in his cups, being comforted by Jael Aryk."

"Well, your self-deprecating humour is still intact. Could you please sit and eat something? I don't want to explain to anyone downstairs what a stubborn little princeling you can be."

"I'm not stubborn." Relenting, Jodathyn sat. He picked up the spoon and placed it back down. "I never thought I would come back here. I hate this place."

Ruevyn glanced towards the door. "I almost expect to see that old knight stalking around with that awful sneer of his."

Tearing a crust off the bread and dipping it into the stew, Jodathyn considered his next words carefully. He glanced up at Ruevyn; deep lines of worry were etched into his face. "This place is full of ghosts for the both of us."

"I wished I never left you," Ruevyn whispered.

"You were a child."

Ruevyn snorted. "Finish your meal. You're looking scrawny. After, we should get you out in the sunshine."

Jodathyn shovelled food into his mouth to still Tornyth, who was grumbling about not being fed. "How can I face anyone after last night?"

"You're safe. That's all that matters."

Jodathyn quickly finished the stew and stood, allowing for Ruevyn to lead him from the room. They descended the stairs and met with an irate Nym. In her hands, she had a piece of parchment, and Jodathyn saw the royal seal.

"What's that?"

"A royal bloody pardon," Nym snapped as she stormed past them on the stairs. "About time you got out of bed, you lounging lizard."

"I worked in Kudah while you scampered off," Jodathyn retorted.

"Poor little pampered palace brat was asked to wipe some tables."

Jodathyn growled. "I'm not lazy."

Nym scoffed and stomped the rest of the way up the stairs. Jodathyn watched her go, chuckling with dark amusement.

A few of the King's Guardsmen, who were nearby having what seemed to be a deep discussion, paused their debate to watch the disagreement.

"She's a bit prickly," Jodathyn explained. He continued his descent without worrying about Nym's progress. "If she calls you a 'mangled, clay-brained codpiece,' you're in trouble."

"Shut your trap, you fancy, highborn flap-dragon!"

One of the guardsmen turned their attention to him rather than Nym, who was no doubt staring down upon them with a furious glare.

"Carew got called a snivelling, cess-pool swine," a guardsman Jodathyn didn't immediately recognise said. "Where's that on the scale?"

Jodathyn laughed as Carew turned a beautiful shade of pink. "She also called me a cheat."

"She's mad," Jodathyn replied. "What did you do?"

"*Nothing*!" Carew cried. "We were sparring and ..."

"That cheatin' swine changed hands."

Carew leaned over to glare at Nym. "I can fight with both hands. It's a skill. I won the spar with honour."

"He also ate the last of the stew."

"I was hungry!"

"Never mind," Jodathyn said. "She's always angry."

"She's just vexed because her brother ran off with the other young fella and Lyntton."

Carew raised his eyebrows. "Who?"

"The young horseman who shot a man in the face."

The other guardsman mimicked Carvelle's action of an arrow hitting him in the forehead. He went cross-eyed and fell over, his tongue poking out of his mouth.

"Orion Maysden," Jodathyn supplied. "Can I safely surmise since Orion has left with one of your number that the king has taken him into his service?"

"And changed his lock," Carew said. "Father said His Majesty changed and rebraided it with his own hands."

"Well," Jodathyn said. "That'll please Carvelle ..."

"You do look much better," Carew replied to fill the awkward silence.

"Sleep and the hangover cure worked miracles."

"He looks good in uniform too, I must say," another guardsman said with a wink.

Jodathyn flushed. "Yes, thank you, Carew."

Smiling, Carew waved Jodathyn's thanks away. He tilted his head. "What's that in your hair?"

He stepped forward and reached out and untangled something that was stuck in his curls. Carew's brow furrowed at the yellow flower. He glanced up in confusion. "These don't bloom in the autumn ... how?"

Jodathyn heard a roaring in his head. His knees buckled so that Ruevyn had to jump forward to catch him. The next moment, he was screaming. Lately his visions had confused him, but what he had seen last night had been real. He had visited Illeanah, and it had been a goodbye. A final goodbye.

"What have you done to him?" Nym raced down the stairs. Jodathyn could hear her hurried footsteps. She reached his side and glared up at the startled King's Guardsmen. "Get away from him! I swear, if you hurt him …"

Captain Tiernan came running, and his men scattered before him. But Jodathyn could only look in horror at the flower in Carew's hand.

"It was real!" Jodathyn cried. He didn't care that no one seemed to understand what he was saying. "It wasn't a dream. It *wasn't* a dream!"

Chapter Thirty-Two

Orion

Solan's Summer House, Aviah Valley

Orion's father had believed in horsemen being ready for action at any given moment. A part of his training as a boy was being awoken at odd hours to complete mundane chores. He hated it, but his father said it built resilience. He had always been told that one day he would be grateful for his father's discipline, especially if he was ever called to serve his country.

When the other two King's Guardsmen stirred, Orion rose with them, alert and ready. Neither man spoke as they pulled on their boots. Orion lifted his hand to his right temple. Today was his first official day as one of the king's men.

It wasn't lost on him that he was the youngster among the group. Carew Candyde, at twenty-one summers, was considered unusually young for a King's Guard. And here was he, sixteen and fresh.

Orion felt his stomach clamp as he studied the uniforms of the two guardsmen that would be going with him to Silverdyne. Both Lyntton and Edd were decorated soldiers, veterans of the King's Guard.

"Excited to go back home, Orion?" Edd's heavy hand landed on his shoulder.

"Otherworlds," Orion muttered. "I left after getting arrested because I punched my long-lost cousin in the face."

"Trouble-maker, eh?" Lyntton huffed, gesturing to the door with a nod of his head. "We'll have to keep a close eye on you."

The house was still as they left their rooms. All was quiet except for Captain Tiernan, who stood guard at the bottom of the stairs.

The captain nodded to the older guardsmen. "A moment, if you please, Maysden."

Orion listened to the other guardsmen's footsteps as they left, wishing he could leave with them. He forced himself to look up into the captain's serious face.

"You have forgotten something, Guardsman Orion."

Puzzled, Orion shifted, trying to discern Captain Tiernan's expression. "What would that be, Captain?"

Tiernan stepped closer and settled a black cloak around Orion's shoulders. Orion hadn't even realised the older man had been holding it. "We can't have you going home looking like a common gutter urchin from the streets of Pallaryn, can we?"

"I guess not, sir," Orion murmured. He longed to let his fingers travel up the black material of the King's Guard cloak. He resisted the urge.

"Donning the King's Guard's cloak, guardsman, is considered the same as uttering the oath at your king's feet."

"Yessir." Indeed, Orion did know. Sometimes in times of war and conflict, there wasn't always time or opportunity to make the oath. By rights, he should have made his vow last night at the king's feet. His cheeks burned. He should have remembered. It was not the captain's nor the king's duty to remind him to take the oath. "Apologies, sir."

The left side of Tiernan's lip lifted, which Orion had learned meant he was amused. When Tiernan had been assigned to Jodathyn, he had watched him very closely. "We're all exhausted, Orion. You handled yourself well."

"Thank you, sir."

"Is there anything else you would like to report that you may have forgotten last night?"

The captain was giving him an opportunity to get anything off his chest. "Yanyima was particularly hostile, did we mention that? And Solan's men massacred in the woods. I can't shake it from my mind. Am I missing something?"

"It's a puzzle indeed." Tiernan lifted his hands to smooth Orion's cloak. "You are young, Guardsman Orion."

"Yessir."

"Lyntton and Edd are two fine veterans of the King's Guard. They can teach you much."

"I understand, sir."

"For you, from His Majesty." Tiernan handed Orion a letter.

Orion took the cream parchment; it was thick and expensive. He ran his fingers over the king's wax seal. It occurred to him that the king had written this letter in his defence before he knew all that had happened.

"Thank you, Captain."

"Go in peace, Guardsman Orion."

It was a dismissal. Orion saluted and stepped past the captain. He halted a few paces away. "Captain," Orion asked, turning around. "If you don't mind, how is Jodathyn?"

"Better. He's asleep. Jael, our medic, is with him."

"Look after him."

Captain Tiernan nodded at the comment that could have easily been interpreted as presumptuous. "I shall. You should go, Maysden. Welcome to my ranks."

"Thank you, sir."

Orion hurried from the house. He stepped into the pre-dawn air and jogged towards the stables. Lyntton and Edd were already mounted; they had readied "his" horse too. The grey stallion lifted his head and snorted.

"Good morning, Zoryn," Orion murmured, running his hand down the stallion's nose.

"Zoryn?"

Edd looked down at him with a bemused expression.

"His highness, Prince Carvelle, named him," Orion said, swinging into the saddle. "It seems disrespectful to rename him now."

"Carvelle would never forgive you."

Orion turned to the other silhouette coming out of the stables leading a horse. "Theo. What are you doing?"

"I'm coming too."

"That will anger Nym," Orion replied shortly. He glanced at his two companions to see their reaction. Neither of the older men's faces gave too much away.

"Good," Theo said. He scrambled into the saddle. Orion winced. He looked uncoordinated and clumsy. "We're friends, are we not? You and I? The road is dangerous, and you could use an extra sword."

"As long as you tell Nym it wasn't my idea."

"You're scared of her," Theo teased as he fiddled with the reins.

"What fool isn't?"

"I guess we have another sword for the road." Edd sighed, glancing over to Lyntton.

"You do," Theo replied, lifting his chin in an act of defiance.

Lyntton's thin lips twitched. "I'm no nursemaid, boy. We'll be riding hard and fast."

"I'm no milksop."

Edd laughed at Theo's audacity. "What's your trade, boy?"

"I'm sure you heard the prince's statement last night," Theo replied tightly. He raised his chin higher, his eyes flashing as if daring either man to make a disparaging remark. He was obviously expecting it. "Everyone in the house knows I'm the thief."

Lyntton took pity on him. "What my comrade meant to ask was what were you before life beat you down?"

"A stonemason."

"Ah, an interesting trade," Edd replied with a nod. "And your name?"

"Theo. Theo Torkelle, born of Korkalie."

"An honest enough name, I suppose. Come, lads, let's not delay."

From Aviah Valley, they had ridden hard and brought the horses to a slower walk so they could break their fast while still in the saddle. Theo hadn't been amused. When he shifted in his saddle yet again, Orion fought to hide his smirk and failed. The thief glared at him but said nothing in the presence of the two older men.

Lyntton rode further ahead. The king's banner was upon a long spear to announce they were on the king's business.

"I thought you weren't a milksop," Orion teased as Theo shifted again. "Is your bottom sore, dear friend?"

Theo scowled as the King's Guardsmen laughed at his misery. "Generally, I'm not," he replied. The smile on his face was forced.

Orion's fingers touched the edging of his new cloak. "Are we still friends? Or is this going to come between us? I know how you feel about lawmen."

Theo's head shot up. "Course we're still friends. Don't throw innocent people in cages and off their lands."

"Not all lawmen are bad," Edd commented from ahead. He pulled on his reins to bring his horse level with Orion and Theo.

"Korkalie doesn't exactly boast of too many honest lawmen," Theo grunted, and then he shivered. "And Kudah ... Otherworlds, that bronze dragon head. Can't begin to imagine the horror."

Orion swatted Theo with his hand. "Jodathyn made it quite clear he did not want Kudah gossiped about," he hissed. "Why do you think he drank so much?"

"Think Jodathyn has plenty of reasons to drink himself into a stupor," Theo muttered. "Did you see the look on his face when Voran said he was leaving?"

"I saw it," Orion said, his fist clenching around the reins.

"Those two have a secret."

"I think that's enough, Theo."

Theo had the grace to look abashed, but now they had both of the older guardsmen's curious gazes pinning them. Shifting in the saddle uneasily, Orion wished he could ignore the stares.

"Relax, Guardsman Orion," Lyntton barked. "We guarded the door last night; we heard it all."

"The magistrate in Kudah has a lot to answer for," Orion murmured.

There was a vicious gleam in Theo's eyes. "Who is going to get to him first? The High King or the giant emerald dragon that's apparently fond of Jodathyn? I would like to see the outcome."

"You're right bloodthirsty and vicious, you are, Theo Torkelle," Orion replied with a grin. "My preference would be to set Captain Tiernan amongst the lawmen in Kudah. None would be standing after he finished with them."

"You remembering that barman in Pallaryn, Orion?" Edd laughed. "Yes, that was a poetic piece of justice indeed."

"If I remember rightly," Lyntton added, "Jodathyn didn't enjoy the spectacle."

"Oh, he did," Orion said with a bark of laughter. "His backside was probably still stinging."

Orion laughed along with the older guardsmen, so they spent the next half an hour explaining to Theo in great detail what Captain Tiernan did to the barman. Theo listened in disbelief. He leaned forward in the saddle. "Your captain did all that for Jodathyn?"

"He inflicted the same injuries the patrons did to Jodathyn," Lyntton said. "Our captain has a gentleman's sense of justice."

They continued on the road, enjoying each other's company. Even Theo began to relax and contribute more to the general conversation. Orion was aware that the older guardsmen were drawing him into revealing more about himself, but he didn't mind so much. They were learning about him, just as he was observing them.

It wasn't until Zoryn halted on the road and refused to go forward that Orion had an inkling that danger was approaching. The grey stallion's eyes rolled back as he danced to the side. Moments later, his bow was in his hands, and he looked towards his companions.

Lyntton had drawn his sword, and Edd copied him moments later. Beside him, Theo struggled to bring his horse under control.

Stretching out, Orion touched the neck of Theo's quivering mare. He was aware of the other guardsmen watching him. He dismissed the thought from his mind. They were a brotherhood. The more they knew of him, the better they could work together as a unit. *"Peace; still for your rider."*

A terrible screech above them signalled the arrival of Grey Shadows. The moment the grey stallion had misbehaved, Orion had been waiting for the sound.

Not waiting for Lyntton's command, Orion notched his bow, pointing his deadly arrowhead to the sky. If indeed they were being hunted by a Grey Shadow, his bow would not be of much use. Better to be armed and ready to fight rather than remain passive.

"Do you think you can do what you did last night?" Theo yelled over the screaming whinnies of their horses.

"I don't know!" Orion cried. "Go. Take cover."

Theo opened his mouth, looking like he wished to argue. However, the thief clinked his jaw shut as a Grey Shadow flew above them. Whatever he was going to say was lost to him. He could only stare into the open sky at the sight of the gangly, ghostlike dragon.

"Take cover!" Edd was yelling. "Swords are useless."

Orion took aim and fired. The creature veered to the left, and the arrow missed its mark.

"Conserve your arrows for a clean shot!" Lyntton barked.

Orion nodded, notching another arrow. The eyes. He needed to aim for the eyes.

"We need to get the beasties on the ground," Edd shouted over the din. "Orion did his magic trick while touching the damnable things."

"*Ri Rhson Hanoch*!" Orion gritted out. Edd was right. He was only able to command the Grey Shadow when his palms had touched her scaly hide. The moment he touched her, he had felt another foreign presence that had her tightly bound and under control. He didn't like this revelation one bit. Getting close to a Grey Shadow would leave him vulnerable to its teeth and claws. But there was no other choice.

"Have you got what it takes, Maysden?" Lyntton yelled.

Orion nodded, urging Zoryn to Lyntton's side to calm his prancing stallion. He felt the beast tremble under his ministrations. However, he stilled and was calm, able to listen to his rider's commands.

"Keep it busy so I can get close."

Tilting his head back, Edd laughed. "That's the spirit, boy."

Getting the creature to land on the road wasn't a problem. Before Orion could reach out and touch Edd's horse, a Grey Shadow landed on the road with a heavy thump. The ghastly creature stretched out its long, sinewy neck and screeched.

The sound reverberated around them, deafening and terrible. The horses screamed in panic. Orion held Zoryn fast, running his hand along the stallion's neck. He soothed the creature with a gentle caress. "*Still,*" his touch commanded. Zoryn lifted his head in protest, his eyes wild, but was unable to disobey his rider's command.

Theo's mount screamed, throwing the thief from the saddle. The thief landed winded on the road as his mount thundered past him. A horrible realisation came upon Orion then. He could only hold so many beasts with his magic at one time. If he attempted to stop the Grey Shadow, he in all likelihood would lose control of the horses. And if there was more than one Grey Shadow ...

"Throw me your spear, Lyntton! Let's get our man to the beast!" Edd cried. Bellowing, Edd kicked the sides of his stallion in a gallop. Lyntton tossed the spear, and Edd grasped it from the air. The wraithlike dragon snarled at the approaching guardsman.

Taking aim, Orion loosed an arrow. This time, the arrow found its mark. The creature roared in rage as the arrow lodged firmly in his left eye. The dragon reared as Edd rammed a spear into his chest. The spear sheared off. Enraged, the Grey Shadow grabbed Edd in his dangerous claws, squeezing him until his bones shattered.

Theo was shouting. But he couldn't make out the words.

"Orion, hold!" Lyntton yelled as he, too, dashed forward. "Wait for the right time!"

Orion knew he couldn't allow himself to be distracted. He notched a third arrow, pausing and hoping for a clean shot. Hearing Edd's cries of agony as he was being crushed to death, Orion let his impatience rule him, and he fired his arrow in an attempt to bury within the dragon's wrist.

The sounds of Edd's bones crunching were horrifying. Orion tried to put it from his mind. After notching another arrow, Orion shot the creature through his open mouth.

The Grey Shadow dropped Edd on the road, swiped at Edd's horse, and stepped a few paces back. Orion dismounted, leaving his horse behind. He did not want the steed anywhere near the dragon.

Lyntton tormented the dragon on his other side, and Orion saw his opening. He sprinted forward while the dragon was busy. He ran headlong into the dragon's haunches, pressing his hands against its sides.

"Collapse," he told it, even as his hands burned. The hold on his Grey Shadow was stronger than what he had left on the mauve female he had released only last night. *"Don't move. Don't hurt anymore."*

Orion was sickened by the strange blackness that was in the creature's mind. He tore himself away from the animal. When he was certain the Grey Shadow would not attack, he rushed to Edd's side. Lyntton was already there.

"Edd, can you hear me?" Lyntton tapped Edd's cheeks.

Edd didn't respond. His breath rattled softly in his chest. "Lyntton?"

Lyntton bowed his head. "Get to the horses. We need to move to a more defensible position ..."

"We can't just leave him!" Theo cried.

Another horrible screech tore through the skies. "It's not over!" Orion yelled, lifting his eyes to the sky.

"We have to get him off the road." Theo was running forward to see if he could render any assistance to Edd. Lyntton's face was set in a grim line. And Orion knew that if by some miracle Edd was still alive, he wouldn't linger in the realm of the mortal world for much longer.

Raising his head to the sky, Orion noticed two shadows circling. They had been spotted. "Theo, get to the tree line! It's our only hope."

Theo dithered, clearly torn between helping Edd and saving his own skin.

Orion grabbed Edd's left arm while Lytton grabbed his other side. "Go, Theo!" Orion screamed. Together, Orion and Lyntton dragged Edd's heavy body off the road and into a ditch.

"You're feverish," Lytton gasped, falling down beside him.

"I can only hold so many strands it seems," Orion murmured. He lifted his palms, which were red and blistered. "It's burned my hands too!"

"The horses are gone," Theo panted.

Lyntton looked over Orion's raw hands. "Can you hold your sword?"

"Till my dying breath," Orion muttered.

"They'll land soon," Theo murmured, looking up into the sky. "They're playing with us."

"When they land, we fight," Orion said. "We try again ... Let me get to their sides."

Edd's eyes fluttered open briefly. Stunned, he looked at the two youngsters beside him, then Lyntton. He opened his mouth to speak as blood bubbled on his lips. His eyes closed once more before he forced them back open. He weakly grasped the edge of Orion's cloak.

"You make a mighty fine King's Guard ... your pa would be proud ..."

He coughed, and his eyes fluttered closed. His rasping breaths stilled.

Edd had fought his last battle.

CHAPTER THIRTY-THREE

Jodathyn

Solan's Summer House, Aviah Valley

Large, calloused hands cupped Jodathyn's cheek, anchoring him back to reality. He gasped in a desperate breath of air, stunned that he was struggling to breathe.

"Master Jodathyn, tell me what's wrong." Captain Tiernan's face swam before him.

"I'm sorry, Captain," Jodathyn murmured, blinking and coming back to himself. Ruevyn lowered him down so that he sat slumped on the bottom stair.

"What's wrong, palace brat?" Nym's voice didn't hold its regular bite. Crouched beside him, she grasped his knee. Her hazel eyes glimmered with concern.

Jodathyn covered her hand with his. "A vision. I thought it was a dream ... Illeanah ..." He looked at Carew, who was still holding the mysterious flower. It should be impossible that it found his way into his hair. Flicking his eyes towards the guardsmen, Jodathyn tried to convey he wanted them to be dismissed. "I had hoped it wasn't real."

"Everyone, leave," Kieryn said.

Jodathyn wished he could melt into a puddle on the floor. His panicked screams had got the attention of his brother. Worse, Jael was by the king's elbow.

Nym glared up at the king, daring him to say something. When she didn't stand to follow the guardsmen from the room, Jodathyn squeezed her hand. "It's alright."

She stared at him doubtfully so that Ruevyn took her upper arm and dragged her from the room. Captain Tiernan stayed by Jodathyn's side, and Carew stood unmoving, staring down at the flower in his hand.

"Guardsman Carew ..." Tiernan growled in warning.

Carew's brow furrowed. "Something's not right ... It's cold ..."

As Carew spoke, the flower wilted, its colour fading before turning to dust. Kieryn strode forward, grasping Carew's hand as if he could make the flower reappear.

"It doesn't belong in this world," Jodathyn muttered.

"What do you mean?" Jael asked.

"It's from the Otherworld."

"Jodathyn," Kieryn said. "You can't have been there ... you're here with us."

"Illeanah gave it to me."

"Where did it come from?" Jael asked, looking towards Captain Tiernan.

"I saw it twined in Jodathyn's hair," Carew replied. "When he saw it, he became inconsolable."

"Impossible. I scrubbed the dragon blood out of his hair," Jael murmured. "There was no flower."

"Illeanah put it in my hair last night," Jodathyn said. He struggled to his feet and looked Kieryn in the face. "She was saying goodbye."

"Was this a vision, brother?"

Jodathyn nodded.

"Are you well enough to share with me?"

Again, Jodathyn nodded. "I was in the fields of Androssah, and Illeanah was there. But when I tried to reach out and touch her, I couldn't. Then I was walking along the outer wall of the palace ..."

Swallowing painfully, Jodathyn averted his gaze from Captain Tiernan. "The royal banners were gone ... I walked among a forest of pikes, upon which were the heads of the King's Guard. Illeanah and Lord Frayn's heads were there. I saw their headless bodies being carted away from the citadel."

Tiernan swore.

Jodathyn flinched, and the captain brought his hand to rest on his shoulder. "Did you recognise any men?"

"The faces of your men were familiar."

"I'm sorry to ask, master. Can you give me numbers?" Tiernan's warm hands squeezed his shoulder.

"Two dozen ... maybe three ... it's hard to tell, Captain. Sometimes details are hazy or symbolic."

Carew closed his outstretched fist. "Jod, the day a King's Guardsman dons the royal colours, he swears an oath to protect house Pallarus and the realm. We all swore to die at our posts if necessary."

"They were not easy deaths, Carew." Jodathyn scrubbed at his face with his hand. "And there's more."

"Tell me, brother," Kieryn said. "Take a deep breath and tell me."

"There was a red dragon. His name is Galgothmeg, the dragon of Death and Despair. I think he is in Pallaryn, and he has declared war."

Kieryn paled. "Merciful Otherworlds, help us."

"I know what I need to do, brother ... only ... I made Mandros angry at me."

"Mandros, he is the green dragon I have heard of?"

"Yes."

Kieryn's lips quirked in amusement despite the seriousness of the situation. "Jodathyn, you're constantly vexing me, and I don't love you any less."

Jodathyn shifted. "Are you ready to meet with the king of the skies?"

Kieryn blinked, and emotion that Jodathyn couldn't place flittered across his brother's face. The king was at war with himself. "He's a king? A dragon *king*?"

"Dragonkind call him *Pallu*."

"Very well, take me to him."

Jodathyn closed his eyes. "Aluel? *Are you near?*"

"*Nearer than you know, white scales.*"

"*Something bad has happened. I want to talk to you.*"

"*I'm in the garden,* mynrell. *Follow the singing.*"

Jodathyn's eyes snapped open. He glanced up at Kieryn, feeling puzzled. "The great dragon is in the garden. He said to follow the singing."

"Singing? Do dragons sing?" Carew snorted back laughter. There was a hysterical twinge to it.

"Not that I am aware of." Shrugging, Jodathyn made his way towards the garden. He was vaguely aware of Kieryn and Captain Tiernan following close behind him.

Jodathyn raised his face towards the sun as they walked through the garden. The brightness of the day seemed to defy the terrible sense of gravity he felt within his soul. Within him, Tornyth wriggled restlessly, nervous upon seeing Mandros again after their heated exchange.

It wasn't the dragon singing that caught Jodathyn's attention. It was Carvelle's voice.

Friends, have you heard the tale, the tale;
The tale of the Apple Tree Prince?

Heart of gold, our prince found friends,

O' friends of lowly birth.
There was a great apple tree,
Proud it grew from earth.

Kieryn laid a steadying hand on Jodathyn's shoulder as he drew in a deep breath. "Theo Torkelle fancies himself a minstrel. The song is called 'The Apple Tree Prince.'"

"Fancy that," Jodathyn answered, dumbfounded. "My very own song. Carvelle is never going to stop singing it, is he?"

"I've heard it six times already this morning," Tiernan grunted.

"All the better to spread the notoriety of his uncle," Kieryn replied.

Jodathyn tilted his head to continue listening.

Together they made a vow,
The vow of unending loyalty.
That's how a simple man,
Came friends with royalty.

"Meena would have liked that song. She was the songbird of Aviah Valley," Jodathyn said.

Even though Mandros had said he was in the garden and to follow the singing, Jodathyn wasn't quite prepared for the sight of Carvelle clambering all over the emerald dragon. The sharp intake of breath from Kieryn behind him told him his brother wasn't prepared either.

Mandros lay flat, belly on the ground, his snout outstretched to make himself low as possible. The green dragon was rumbling as the small prince ran among the spikes along his spine.

"Oh, he's a big one," Tiernan said under his breath.

"Carvelle, you shouldn't climb on dragons!" Kieryn cried out.

Jodathyn couldn't help it. He laughed and turned towards his brother, who was pale with fright. "That's a happy rumble."

Carvelle ran right to the tip of Mandros's head to swing off his horns. "It's quite alright, Papa! Mandros doesn't mind at all."

"Indeed not, *vehyl* king," Mandros said. "Most dragons don't mind playing with *vehyl* young."

"*Vehyl* means human," Jodathyn whispered.

Mandros turned his head slowly to stare at Jodathyn. "If you don't mind, Little Highness, I would like a quiet word with your uncle and then your papa."

Smiling winsomely, Carvelle slid down Mandros' nose, and the green dragon lowered him to the ground. "I'm going to get Miss Et-hir to tell me more snapdragon stories!"

And off Carvelle scampered. Jodathyn watched him go.

"So you have brought me your brother and a soldier. How delightful." Mandros shifted his great weight, staring at Jodathyn with large, luminous eyes. "Are you ready to tell me about your tantrum yet, white scales?"

"Pallaryn is going to fall."

Large amber eyes blinked. "Yes, which is why I left to bring a squadron of dragons into Rama. Care to explain why you weren't where I had hidden you out of sight?"

Crossing his arms against his chest, Jodathyn jutted his chin forward, ignoring the *tsk* that came from Captain Tiernan's direction. "You knew how I felt about my nephew."

"Yes, I can feel the bond between you. Yet in disobeying me, you helped neither him nor yourself. In fact, you made the situation worse. And what would you have done if you brought calamity upon your nephew's head, petite one?"

Jodathyn opened his mouth to argue. He flicked his eyes towards Kieryn. The king was eyeing the dragon before him with something Jodathyn could only describe as conflicted admiration and hope. Tiernan's large fingers looked like they were itching to grab his sword.

"Do you have any idea what you have done, Tornyth, Winter's Dragon?"

Jodathyn was unmoved. "I saw you at the dragon council."

"The act of claiming an unmanifested dragon is an intimate one. I intervened, stepped into your own inner world of chaos, and plucked you out of your human prison. Do you know how greatly you injured me when you tried to discard our bond?"

"It doesn't negate what you said about using me for your own glory."

"Do you think the worm who calls me his rival has the same strength or power as I?" Lifting his head, Mandros laughed. It was the sound of bitterness. "Did I not already teach you that Sight is easy to manipulate and notoriously difficult to interpret?"

"You did," Jodathyn muttered. He had an uncomfortable feeling that Mandros was going to make a fool out of him.

Mandros, however, glanced over at Kieryn. "Tell me, *vehyl* king, what predictions has your wise council incorrectly divined about your brother?"

Kieryn closed his eyes as if pained. "They've taken the prediction that he is to be bathed thrice with royal blood to mean ..."

"*What*?" Jodathyn turned to glance at his brother. "You never told me ..."

"For good reason," Kieryn replied. His voice was steady, but Jodathyn could tell something was bothering him. His brother turned his eyes towards the dragon. "Please, great dragon, tell me how to thwart it. The prediction is that it is his own blood."

Jodathyn sucked in a breath. He turned his gaze away from Kieryn to Tiernan, whose expression softened.

"I don't have an answer for you, *vehyl* king," Mandros answered. "Twice your brother has been bathed in his own blood. I have not foreseen what is to be. The future is fickle and not fixed. My job as his *aluel* is to ensure that come what may, Jodathyn not only survives but thrives. Now, white scales, do you see the mistake the council and you have made?"

"What mistake would that be?" Jodathyn shifted, concerned by the prediction that his brother had kept hidden from him. A part of him understood why Kieryn had said nothing; a darker part felt anger. He buried his fury.

"Inserting yourself into the prediction is a costly mistake. In worrying about how the prediction only affects them, the king's council discounted your royal status."

"I don't understand."

"That is why I am *Rhson-Aluel*, here to teach you and guide you. If only you would open your ears to listen." Mandros grinned so that his teeth were on display. "You forgot *who* I am and my bloodline. I was insulted one of my rivals dared to suggest I relinquish a son of my own flesh and blood. They would see you destroy Galgothmeg, hiding behind you like a shield. Once you hold no value to them, you'd be discarded."

"You are talking sons and bloodlines ..." Kieryn murmured. "Who are you?"

"I am Mandros the Deliverer, the Father of this Land, dragon of Flame and Fury. When I was a man, I was called Arturyn the Unifier."

Jodathyn watched, bemused, as Kieryn's jaw went slack.

"This is what you need to understand, *vehyl* king. Your brother is the rekindled dream of the return of dragonkind. His bloodline is a blessing for Pallarus and Rama. Through his daughters, dragon blood will rise in strength and power. I assure you, my rivals do not care for this great blessing that is on Jodathyn. They care only that he is destined to be part of Galgothmeg's final fall. He would be the sword they would wield. I would never, never hide behind my own hatchling."

It was Kieryn's turn to looked amused. "*Daughters*?"

"I told you last night, remember?" Jodathyn grumbled.

"You said a number of strange things last night, brother," Kieryn replied.

"Three strong-willed Pallarus women to continue the Pallarus line. Yes, I have foreseen it," Mandros confirmed. "In dragon culture, some believe strong, fiery females keep the bloodline strong and sure. It is why the Ramian *vehyl* have adopted the inheritance rites from their dragon roots."

"Are you saying dragon culture …"

"Influences Rama to this very day. Tell me, Jodathyn's daughter, when she in turn has a child, to which family and bloodline does her child belong?"

"Pallarus, always Pallarus. It is customary that bloodlines run through the most prestigious house."

"Do you know why?"

"To preserve family honour. This is why Pallarus has stood for so many centuries and had many queens."

Mandros laughed. "The dragon word *pallu* means sovereign. There is no word king and queen in the ancient tongues. In ancient times, the bloodlines that held draconic powers were inherently stronger. Whether male or female, a dragon will jealously guard their family lines. Humans have continued the practice. But enough of that. I feel like I am schooling you. *Vehyl* king, we have a war to discuss."

Kieryn dumbly nodded his head.

"Jodathyn, are we quite over our little display of petty behaviour?"

"Yes, *Aluel*, I am sorry."

The hard expression on Mandros' face softened. Above his head, he heard Mandros rumble something that resembled the ancient tongue, but the sounds were slightly off. He could only assume it may have been an ancient dragon saying or prayer.

"While we were parted, I took the liberty of searching for a certain tattooist that considers himself quite the artist. He has paid for his crimes."

"What did you do to him?" Jodathyn murmured.

"I want to snap my jaws down on the man who marked us with Vadroil's symbols." Tornyth lifted his head and hissed at the mention of the man who they called "the artist."

"Nothing for sensitive *vehyl* ears to hear."

Tiernan scoffed back a laugh. "Did you eat him?"

"And give myself indigestion? Ancient One's Talons, no, I am not that kind of dragon."

"My lord dragon," Tiernan said, striding forward. "I want to talk to you about one of my men. Something extraordinary happened to him last night during the monster dragon attacks … I don't think it's normal."

A pleased smile broke across Mandros' face. "Indeed, news of extraordinary things happening to *vehyl* always piques my interest. Often a newly manifested dragon will cause other struggling hatchlings to make themselves known. It's a bizarre and strange phenomenon. One that dragonkind can't explain. Bring him to me."

Kieryn cleared his throat. "*Pallu* dragon, I believe the boy my captain was referring to left at dawn."

"Never mind." The victorious grin did not leave Mandros' face. He lifted his great crowned head and bellowed into the sky. Jodathyn watched in amusement as both Kieryn and Tiernan jumped back in shock and surprise. Behind them, the others had all come out upon the lawn, curious to see the dragon that had landed upon the lawn.

Jodathyn knew the moment that the squadron of dragons became visible. He could see the look of awe on the faces of the guardsmen. Some even dropped their weapons. Carvelle had returned, dragging Et-hir behind him. He jumped up and down in delight, clapping his hands. Laughing, Nym punched Carew's shoulder while the young guardsman stared in open-mouth wonder. Fydellah and Ruevyn stood to the side, both looking wary and uncomfortable.

Kieryn cleared his throat. "You were Arturyn?"

"I still am," Mandros replied.

"You have taken Jodathyn as your heir."

"Yes, *vehyl* king. He is mine."

Lifting his hand to Jodathyn's shoulder, Kieryn shook his head. "I did not take you seriously last night. I thought you referred to yourself as Arturyn's heir as something metaphorical. You meant literally."

"I don't remember that," Jodathyn said, feeling a heat rise to his cheeks.

Kieryn laughed, pulling Jodathyn closer to him in an awkward side hug. The king's beard tickled Jodathyn's cheek as his brother whispered in his ear, "When we take back Pallaryn ... it'll be time to shed this horrible Son of the Crown nonsense. I promise you, you'll have the title of Prince of Rama as you rightly deserve."

"The council ... my mother ..."

"Oh, hang the council, brother," Kieryn cried. "Your mother's inaccurate blathering has caused us enough grief. It's time house Pallarus looks to our future."

Jodathyn raised his eyes to track the progress of the other dragons. He could see his three siblings: Sidrah looking magnificent and noble and Zapyr managing to look distant and regal, while Deovyn flew around him in dizzying circles.

Pushing him forward, Kieryn cried, "Go on, brother. I know you want to. I can feel you trembling with excitement."

Jodathyn glanced behind him at the other humans and then to Mandros, who nodded his great head. With permission granted, he stepped to the side, allowing his brother and Tiernan enough room so that he didn't knock them over. He felt the stirring of his inner dragon and in moments, he was pushing off the ground with his powerful hind legs and in the air.

His dragon ears caught the excited shouts and whoops from down below. The *vehyl* below ... They accepted him as he was, even though within him lurked a beast. They were not afraid or disgusted by him.

Tornyth, Winter's Dragon, didn't need the council's permission or acceptance to exist in Rama. As long as he had a few humans willing to support him, he could be who he was born to be. He could be free to be a dragon; the skies of Rama were his home. It was where he belonged.

Tornyth felt the gentle caress of the Wind Song; the whisper of vengeance and of blood was in the wind. He closed his eyes, and his dragon heart beat in a wordless prayer for those who had fallen in Pallaryn.

Galgothmeg might be in Rama, but come what may, Winter's Dragon had his own rag-tag family. Together, they would face whatever the future might have for them.

His eyes snapped open, and he looked down upon the *vehyl* gathered out on the lawn. Born into the royal house of Pallarus, he had been taught that duty and sacrifice were partners. One could not exist without the other. He wondered who would be still standing once victory was won. Who would step through the veil and into the Otherworld?

An exuberant roar woke Tornyth from his daydream.

Deovyn had darted forward into a dive.

"Catch me, *sudunyn*!"

Tucking his wings in tight, Tornyth spiralled after him. The ground sped up to meet them. Deovyn slowed at the last possible moment, allowing Tornyth to catch him as they tumbled along the grass, all scales, talons, and laughter.

Today, right now, was time for joy and freedom. Soon enough tomorrow would come, and with it the promise of war and bloodshed.

Love it? Hate it? Either way please consider leaving a review on either Goodreads or Amazon. All reviews are helpful.

Psst ... the thrilling conclusion of the Dragon's Heir is not far away!

 amazon.com/author/kjburrage

goodreads.com/author/show/22623993.K_J_Burrage

Character List

Human (Vehyl)

Allard (AL-lard) – A King's Guardsmen

Carew Candyde – (CA – roo CAN – dy – d) – Guardsman of the King's Guard

Carvelle Pallarus – (CA – vell PA – la – rus) – the Crown Prince of Rama, the son of Kieryn and the nephew of Jodathyn

Curran Norrys – (CAR –ran NOR-ris) – the barkeep in Kudah who protects Jodathyn and Nym. An ex-guard.

Edd Ryfern–(ED RIGH – f - urn) – A King's Guardsman

Etirah – (Eh -tear-ah) – A Sionian barmaid in Kudah (her Ramian version of her name)

Et-hir – (ET - her) – A Sionian barmaid in Kudah

Floyde (Lawman) – (FL – oy – d) – A lawman in Kudah

Frayn (Lord) – (FR – ain) – A great lord of the King's council

Fydellah Nahilya – (FI – del –ah NA – hil – ya) – An ex-slave, she was once a free woman

Hallidyn Whitoak (Lord) – (HAL – i – din WIT – oak) – A great lord of the King's council. The King's favourite Lord

Illeanah Whitoak (Lady) – (ILL– len – nah WIT – oak) – Hallidyn Whitoak's daughter and childhood friend of Jodathyn

Jael Aryk (JAY – el AY – rick) – Guardsman of the King's Guard and Troop Medic and Healer

Jodathyn Pallarus - (JOD – ath – en PA – la – rus) – the Son of the Crown, the brother to the High King of Rama

Kamoore (Lord) – (KA – more) – A great lord of the King's council

Kieryn Pallarus – (KEER – ren APA – la – rus) – the High King of Rama

Kya (KI-ah) – An old woman in Kudah

Larelle – (LA - rell) – an orphan found need Habron, believed to be an ex-slave

Locke – (LOCK) – the name Jodathyn uses to hide himself in Kudah

Lyntton Pressun – (LIN-Ton PRESS-sun) – A King's Guardsman

Ninah (Nee - nah) – An old healer in Habron

Nurlah (NUR - lah) – A madam of a brothel in Pallaryn

Nym Torkelle (N-im TOR - kel) – A rescued thief

Odelle Pallarus – (O – Del Pa-la-rus) – the Queen of Rama, Kieryn's wife

Orion Maysden (O – ri -an Mays-den) – Jodathyn's servant, a horseman of Silverdyne

Ripley (Lawman) – (RIP – lee) – A lawman in Kudah

Ruevyn Kelvie (ROO -Ven Kel-vee) – A childhood friend of Jodathyn

Solan (Lord) – (SO-Lan) – A great lord of the King's council

Swyft (Magistrate) – (SW - ift) – The magistrate of Kudah

Theo Torkelle (TH -e-o Tok-kel) – A rescued thief

Thylyssa (THIGH – lis - sah) – A great lord who had been banished from court

Tiernan Candyde (TIER-nan Can-dy-d) – Captian of the King's Guard

Tomas Hartcurt (TO-mas HART-curt) – Will's elder brother

Tryst (TR -ist) – A King's Guardsmen

Voran Axtin (VOR-an AX – tin) – Jodathyn's ex-personal guard

Lord Will (Willyrd) Hartcurt (WIL – lard HART –curt) – A young lord at court with a bad reputation

Dragon (Rshon)

Averyn (AV – er – in) – The orange battle dragon killed in action, believed to be a close friend of Mandros and second father to Sidrah, Zapyr and Deovyn

Curarfur (CUR – ah – fur) – A blue battle dragon under Mandros' command with healing power

Deovyn (DEE- o -vin) – a russet dragon called the Small and Mighty, the son of Mandros. His human name was Jodathyn (JOD-ath-en)

Galgothmeg – (GAL – goth – meg) – A red dragon known as Death and Despair

Mashikah (MA - shis - car) – A sightless dragon, Mandros mate and mother to Sidrah, Zapyr and Deovyn

Mandros (MAND - roz) – An emerald dragon with many titles, including Flame and Fury, Deliverer, Father of this Land, the Green

Roane (ROW - n) – an olive green dragon, known to be a trusted general and friend to Mandros

Salvea (SAL - vay) – a purple female battle dragon, her name is mentioned within the story

Sidrah (SID - rah) – a black dragon called Noble and Honourable, the daughter of Mandros. Her human name was Arturah (AR-tor-ah)

Tornyth (TOR- n -eth) – Winter's Dragon

Zapyr (ZAP - ear) – a gold dragon called Splendid, the son of Mandros. His human name was Kyran (KI-ran)

Deceased Characters and Historical Figures

Ammerie – (AM – ma – ree) – Jodathyn's late mother

Arturah (AR – tor - ah) – The human name of Sidrah, daughter of Arturyn

Arturyn Pallarus – (AH – tur – en PA – la – rus) – The first King of Rama

Bear – (B – air) – Jodathyn's dog

Donatein Manideep – (DON – a – teen MAND – i – deep) – Jodathyn's oldest manservant

Elyssa – (E – lis - sah) – Ruevyn's bethrothed

Hadryn Pallarus – (HAD – ren PA – la – rus) – the late King of Rama. The father of Kieryn and Jodathyn

Jodathyn (JOD – ath – en) – The human name of Deovyn, son of Arturyn

Kyran (KI - ran) – The human name of Zapyr, the son of Arturyn

Parrie (Par - re) – Jodathyn's dog

Soren Monster-Blade (SOR – en) – A human counterpart to Vadroil

Tyr (TEAR) – The brother of Et-hir believed to be deceased

Vadroil (VAD – roy – el) – a dragon of myth and legend who

Valt Axtin (V – al – t AX – tin) – Jodathyn's personal guard

Support Animals

Zarine (ZA – reen) – A stolen mare

Zoryn (ZOR-en) – the grey stallion Orion had stolen. Named by Prince Carvelle

Zyan (ZI-an) – Voran Axtins red stallion named by Prince Carvelle.

Language Guide

Aluel - (AY-l-ool) – Father

Araae helphelwyn. Terini gorthorawyn - (AH-ay HEL-fel-win TE-ree-ne GOR-thor- A-win) – Famous words of the King's Guard. Live Valiantly. Die Honourably.

Brigyn – (BRIG-n) - Winter

Elt – (EL-t) – My

Kairn – (K-AIR-n) – Two meanings – a) bastard/ illegitimate or b) mongrel

Pallu – (PAL – loo) – Two meanings a) sovereign can be king or queen b) wind – out of interests Pallarus means a)Sovereign over seas or b) Sea Wind.

Mynrell – (MIN-rell) – has many meanings son, daughter, heir, fosterling, adopted. All the same and all equal. Dragon use only.

Ri Rshon hanoch - (RI R-ish-on HAN-ock) – Considered coarse language – Old Dragon's Genitals

Rokun – (ROO-k-un) – Word for a human not worthy of dragon respect. Also used for a wicked person.

Rshon Aluel –(R-ish-on AY-l-ool) – Dragon Father. The title given to an older male dragon who adopts a vulnerable dragon. Note dragon adoption does not supersede human parentage. A dragon would refer to their acquired heir's father as Vehyl-Aluel (human father) or Vehyl-Lullah (human mother)

Rshon mahthyt – (R-ish-on MA-th-at) – Dragon Dung

Sudunah – (SUE-dun-ah) - Sister

Sudunyn – (SUE-dun-en) - Brother

Terini – (TE-ree-ne) - Die

Vehyl (V-hay-el) – Word for a human that is worthy of dragon respect. Often used affectionately.

Wirahli Sais-levly – (WER-ah-lee S-ace - LEV-lee) Enslaved Flying Lizard. This is what is tattooed upon Jodathyn's skin and what Mandros' will not speak.

Extra words and dragon concepts

Aluel veh desn – (AY – l -ool V-ay DES -n) – An honourable dragon term meaning father-by-heart. This term is for a man or dragon who has chosen to care for a younger, vulnerable person or dragon. In the case of Donatein he could not foster or adopt Jodathyn but he choose with his heart to love and care for Jodathyn as if he was his own.

Ayraelth (AIR - ay - leth) - Dragon Friend. Word only used to describe a close human/dragon friendship

E vydel el taldyn – (EH VI-del EL TAL-din) – I love you fiercely

Elt rshon desn tollah hy el (ELT R-ish-on DEZ-n TOL-ah HI EL) – My dragon heart beats for you

Ketur – (KET – er) – Beloved (used for life mate only)

Location Guide

Arimac (Arimac)

Astyan (AST-yan)

Adavan Fields (AD-a-van)

Androssah (AN-dr-os-a)

Arah (AH-rah)

Arelle Forest (AH-el)

Arimac (A-ri-mac)

Artroth (ART-r-oth)

Aviah Valley (AY-vee-ah)

Belrah (BEL-rah)

Corlyn (COR-lin)

Farholm (FAH-hol-m)

Habron (HA-bron)

Halbeth (HAL-beth)

Haven Bay (HAY-ven)

Kudah (KOO-dah)

Korkalie (KOR-ka-lee)

Malara Gorge (MA-la-rah)

Myryn (MY-rin)

Paldera (PAL-deer-ah)

Pallaryn (PA-la-ren)

Paru (PA-roo)

Pyth (Pith)

Rama (RAH-ma)

Sant Burgundy (S-an-t BUR-gun-dee)

Silverdyne (SIL-va di-n)

Sion (SI-on)

Stonethaw (STONE-thaw)

Tannryn (TAN-rin)

Thrangul (THR-an-gool)

Torryn (TOR-ren)

Torqui (TOR-key)

Yanyima (YAN-yim-ah)

Acknowledgments

The biggest thank you to the readers of my work. Without you the journey would not continue. Thank you for taking a chance on an indie author. It means the world to me.

Thank you to my mother-in-law, who is always the first to purchase and test my website. Who has even gone the extra mile to pick up the kids to take them to school so I can have my meetings with my editor in peace.

To my parents, who have proudly read and shared my work with everyone they know at the retirement village, convincing people the book is perfect for the grandkids.

To my children who have been very patient with mummy when she writes. They desperately want their own books signed. You're much to young darlings. Your copy is waiting for you.

A huge thank you to my editor Katie Wolfe, for all her coaching, support and answering all my questions. I'm excited to work with her on book three! (We're booked in before this goes to publish)!

To the team at Miblart who have created beautiful covers for my book baby.

About KJ Burrage

KJ Burrage currently calls tropical North Queensland, Australia, home. She has been developing her craft since she was ten years old. Alas, the original floppy discs from 1995 have disappeared!

She lives with her three young daughters, an exuberant pug-cross and a cheeky blue parrot.

Growing up she had grand visions of becoming CS Lewis. When she grew up a little more, she decided she was going to be JRR Tolkien. Now, she's learnt to be proud of her own voice and the pen name KJ Burrage is perfect for her.

She has a Bachelor Degree in Primary Education with a major in literacy and worked as a primary school teacher. She has also been a co-owner of a laser engraving business.

Life can be unpredictable (and unfair). After the sudden and tragic death of her husband, she returned to her passion of the written word.

You can read more at www.kjburrage.com.

facebook.com/profile.php?id=100071328683512

instagram.com/kjburrage_author/

tiktok.com/@kjburrage_writes

goodreads.com/author/show/22623993.K_J_Burrage

amazon.com/author/kjburrage

https://twitter.com/KJBurrage

Discover more about some of
your favourite side characters in
this collection of short stories.
Learn more about the tragic
circumstances that Fydellah,
Orion and Will face and how
they find themselves in the
Citadel of Pallaryn.